Before We Met

Before We Met

Lucie Whitehouse

W F HOWES LTD

This large print edition published in 2014 by
W F Howes Ltd
Unit 4, Rearsby Business Park, Gaddesby Lane,
Rearsby, Leicester LE7 4YH

1 3 5 7 9 10 8 6 4 2

First published in the United Kingdom in 2014
by Bloomsbury Publishing

A CIP catalogue record for this book is available
from the British Library

ISBN 978 1 47125 682 0

Typeset by Palimpsest Book Production Limited,
Falkirk, Stirlingshire
Printed and bound by
CPI Group (UK) Ltd, Croydon, CR0 4YY

MIX
Paper from
responsible sources
FSC
www.fsc.org   FSC® C013604

For Joe, with my love

CHAPTER 1

The rain was beating down, and out here, where the carriageway was exposed, the wind buffeted Hannah's old VW as if it were trying to push it off the road. Usually on a Heathrow run she watched the planes dip down into the airport one after another, barely a minute between them, but tonight the rhythm was broken and it was two minutes, now three, before a new set of lights struggled through the roiling cloud. She tightened her grip again, checked the mirror and pulled out into the fast lane.

The Holiday Inn loomed up on the left, an ugly concrete tooth in silhouette against the sky, the light from its green neon sign leaching into the wet air. She took the exit for Terminal Three, the buzz in her stomach intensifying. Though they were married now, the trip to the airport was still exciting. She didn't need to come and meet him; in fact, it would probably be quicker if Mark caught a cab into town, especially on a night like this, but the drive, arrivals, the crush at the barrier – it all reminded them of the time before they got married, when JFK and Heathrow were the

1

poles around which so many of their weekends revolved.

As usual, the first two levels of the car park were full. Reluctantly, she took the ramp up to level three and found a spot by the lobby with the ticket machines. After a quick look in the mirror, she got out of the car and headed for the lifts.

The arrivals hall was busy, even for a Friday night. Beneath the low suspended ceiling, their faces bleached by the harsh strip lighting, hundreds of people were waiting. Three or four deep at the barrier, they clustered around the centre of the hall and outside the row of small concessions: the usual collection of drivers with name cards, a group of backpackers in shorts and T-shirts they would curse the moment they stepped outside, and an entire extended family, twenty-five or thirty people, all wearing traditional African dress, a blaze of colour and pattern.

She wove a path to the overhead monitors where she saw that Mark's plane had just landed. It would be fifteen or twenty minutes before he came through the doors so she bought a sandwich from the little Marks and Spencer and sat on one of the benches on the other side of the hall. Earlier in the day, she'd been to the delicatessen and bought some French bread and a piece of really good Roquefort, which, with a glass of wine, was all Mark ever wanted after an evening flight, but she was too hungry to wait until then. She'd had nothing to eat since lunchtime: the interview with

AVT this afternoon had run on much later than she'd expected, and it had been past seven o'clock by the time she'd got off the Tube at Parsons Green.

From the bench she watched the mechanised doors emit an irregular dribble of people. On the monitor there was a long list of flights with substantial delays. The passengers coming through now were on the plane that had come in from Freetown, she guessed, two before Mark's; they were an hour and a half late. She watched a lanky, deeply suntanned man in jeans and a khaki shirt emerge and start scanning the crowd. From behind the barrier opposite, a young woman pushed her way forward, her face a picture of joy, and ran into his arms, giving him a kiss that drew a snort of disapproval from an elderly man further along the bench. Hannah felt another buzz in the pit of her stomach. *Come on, Mark.*

She remembered waiting for him on the other side of the Atlantic, before she moved back to London. Terminal Seven at JFK, the one American Airlines used, was stark; no cafés or shops to kill time in, just a newsstand, a coffee concession and a few rows of hard plastic chairs. She'd always used to take her laptop in case he was late but it had been impossible to work when her head snapped up every time someone came round the barrier. She'd never wanted to miss the moment when Mark first caught sight of her and the smile spread across his face. The first few times, the smile had given way to an exaggerated comic grin, as if he was trying to cover his embarrassment at having revealed himself, but that soon stopped and the regular sequence of events was established: he'd squeeze her until she was afraid he'd crack her ribs then they'd get a cab and go straight to her apartment and bed. Afterwards, they'd get dressed again and walk round to Westville on 10th Street for hotdogs.

The doors were opening more regularly now, releasing a steadier stream of people. A number of the voices had American accents, which suggested they'd been on Mark's flight; the ones before and after his had come from Egypt and Morocco. She stood up and went to look. A few men in suits with lightweight cases; two couples; a family struggling with a precarious tower of luggage on a trolley whose front wheels wouldn't cooperate. Spotting his father before his mother did, a toddler slipped out of her grasp and made a fat-legged beeline for him under the barrier, sending a ripple of laughter through the crowd.

After twenty-five minutes, she knew there must be some sort of hold-up. Mark was almost always among the first wave of passengers off a flight, and he'd only taken his small leather bag this time so he would have bypassed baggage reclaim. Perhaps he'd left something on the plane and gone back for it or perhaps he'd been stopped for a random customs check. She pushed back her sleeve and looked at her watch, the Rotary her mother had given her when she'd started university. Five past ten. She brought up Mark's number on her BlackBerry then changed her mind: ringing him would spoil it. She'd wait another ten minutes and then call, if she had to.

By quarter past, however, the American accents had petered out and most of the people coming through the doors were talking to each other in rapid-fire Spanish. The only other person who'd been waiting as long as she had was a man in his fifties wearing a navy blazer and chinos, and now even his daughter appeared. Hannah wondered whether she'd got her wires crossed, but no, she was sure Mark had said Friday, the usual time.

She dialled his number. The call went straight to voicemail and she hung up without leaving a message. It wasn't like him to miss a flight but maybe that was what had happened. Maybe he'd missed it and managed to get on a later one instead. He'd done that once before, coming back to New York from Toronto.

She consulted the monitors again. His flight wasn't even shown any more. Scanning down, however, she saw two more flights from New York; one had just landed, the other was imminent. Perhaps he'd be on one of those. If he were, he'd call or send a text the moment he could turn his phone on.

The crowd was thinner now and this time she got the place at the barrier right opposite the doors – 'the golden spot', Mark called it. Checking

5

her phone every couple of minutes, she waited until ten past eleven, almost another full hour. When the last of the second batch of Americans came through the doors, she phoned him and got voicemail again.

Hannah began to feel alarmed. If he was on a different flight, why hadn't he called her? What if something had happened to his plane? She rang him one more time then gave up her place at the barrier and made her way towards the fire exit. The airlines' information desks were in the departures hall, and crossing the courtyard between the two buildings was far quicker than schlepping through the network of tunnels and escalators.

Wind was swirling around the courtyard, driving the rain in bursts like shoals of tiny fish, lifting it for a moment then dashing it against the ground. The heavy door was snatched from her hand and slammed shut behind her. Overhead, another plane struggled through the cloud, its engines filling the air with harrowing thunder. Hannah put her head down and ran.

The dash took thirty seconds at most but she was pushing wet hair off her face as she came inside. Compared to the arrivals hall, departures at Terminal Three was the picture of well-lit, high-ceilinged modernity, but when she found the desk for American, the airline he usually used, the woman behind it was putting her jacket on.

'I've already turned off the computer,' she said, without looking up.

'I just want to know if my husband was on a flight this evening.'

'Oh.' Now the woman looked up, her face brightening. 'Well, I couldn't have told you that anyway. Data protection, isn't it?'

Hannah felt her usual surge of irritation at petty bureaucracy. 'Seriously?' she said. 'He's my husband.'

'Sorry.' The woman shrugged, looking pleased at the opportunity to wield her power, and Hannah's irritation refocused itself on her. Working in close proximity to the duty-free shops was no excuse for wearing so much bloody make-up. How old was she anyway, under that death mask of foundation?

'Look,' said Hannah, laying her hands on the counter, 'all I really need to know is that my husband's safe. Can you at least tell me whether there have been any problems with the New York flights tonight?'

The woman sighed. 'Nothing like that,' she said. 'Delays because of the wind, but that's it.'

'Thank God.'

Hannah was halfway back across the hall before she thought about where she was going. She tried Mark again. Still nothing. This time she left a message. 'Hi, it's me. I'm at Heathrow – where are you? I came to meet you but I don't think you're here. If you are, ring me.' She hesitated. 'I hope everything's all right. Call me as soon as you get this – I'm worried about you.' She laughed a

7

bit, to tell him she knew she was being ridiculous: Mark was the last person to get into a mess, so if the planes were safe, he was.

Hanging up, she thought about whom she could call. Neesha, his assistant? No: it was almost half past eleven. And if Neesha knew there was a problem, she would have been in touch. The same went for David, his business partner. Mark had gone to America on his own this time so there was no one to cross-check with. If she didn't hear from him tonight, she'd have to wait until the morning before she could start calling around.

Upstairs in the short-stay car park she narrowly mastered an urge to kick the ticket machine. 'Twelve pounds for two crappy hours?' Her voice echoed off the walls of the empty ticket-lobby.

The M4 back into London had gone quiet, too, and the streetlamps cast isolated pools of light on the carriageway ahead of her. On the raised section of road above Brentford she looked into offices vacated until Monday, seeing the ghostly shapes of desks and chairs and computers, and she had the sudden alarming idea that she was looking at a vision of her own career – distant, fading and locked away behind glass through which she could see it but no longer reach.

As she came down Quarrendon Street, the last of her hope disappeared. If Mark was ever home before her, she arrived to find lights blazing from every window but tonight the house was as dark as she'd left it.

Lynda, his cleaner – *their cleaner* – had been and the air smelled strongly of furniture polish. In the kitchen Hannah took a bottle of wine from the rack, poured a glass, then sat down with her laptop and checked her email. Occasionally her BlackBerry went through spells where no new messages would arrive for hours and then a glut would come all at once. That wasn't happening now: the last email on both the phone and the computer was the one from her brother asking how her interview had gone.

She opened a blank message and addressed it to Mark.

Hello Heathrow no-show, she typed. *I'm guessing you're either still on a plane or something's going on with your phone so I'm trying email instead. Let me know what's happening. Missing you here at Quarrendon Street. House – and bed – empty without you . . .*

She took a sip of wine – delicious: his idea of everyday wine came in a different price bracket from hers – then stood up and carried the glass across to the French windows that opened on to the small paved yard behind the house. When she shielded her eyes to block the light from inside, she could see the stone flags and then, towards the back, the shrubs and ornamental cherry tree. The wind had wreaked havoc. One of the wooden chairs had blown across the yard and lay on top

9

of the stone trough where she had grown tomatoes over the summer, and the paving was strewn with leaves and twigs. It was a mess; if the rain stopped, she'd get out there tomorrow and clear it up.

Overhead, a plane tracked in towards Heathrow, now visible through a break in the clouds, now hidden again. Mark was probably still in the air, she told herself, and she'd wake up in a couple of hours to find him getting into bed next to her, and have a heart attack thinking he was a burglar.

She turned back to face the room and stopped. Occasionally she still had moments like this, when the sheer scale of the house struck her all over again. She'd been stunned when Mark told her he'd bought it in his late twenties; both the houses on the street that had sold since she moved in had gone for over two million. 'But that's now,' he'd said. 'I've had it twelve years, since well before the big boom, and it was a wreck when I got it. I bought it from this old couple who hadn't done anything to it since the sixties and I had to do a total gut-job – new wiring, new plumbing, the works.'

'Still . . .'

He'd shrugged. 'I was lucky – the business was doing well and the price was right. It was a good investment.'

The idea that this was her kitchen now had taken some getting used to. She'd loved the one in her New York apartment with its original exposed-brick walls and industrial units, but viewed in the cold light of reality it had been a seven-foot length of

10

corridor. In order to cook, she'd had to play a game like one of those squares with the moveable tiles that you rearrange to make a picture, continually finding new spots for plates and knives and chopping boards on the patch of counter space, the stove-top, the stool. This room was about ten times the size. In the unlikely event that she would ever want to cook for thirty, she could do it here without ever running out of elbow room.

Everything was big – *everything*; if it hadn't been done so stylishly, it would have looked ostentatious. The original kitchen wall had been knocked out to extend the room into the side return, adding an extra six feet of width, and it had been twenty feet wide to begin with. The ceiling was high, the near part of it roofed with huge panes of glass for extra light, and the floor was covered in slabs of Welsh slate with heating underneath for the winter. There were steel-topped counters, a restaurant-sized cooker and, at the back, next to the door to the sitting room, an American-style double fridge.

'I just couldn't go back to a poxy little one,' Mark had said. 'The fridge I had in my apartment in Tribeca was like a wardrobe – it ruined me for anything smaller.'

'You're such a spoiled brat.'

'Can't deny it.' He'd grinned at her, the skin at the corners of his eyes crinkling.

Feeling a burst of longing for him, she went back to her laptop and searched again for any news relating to flights from New York, not just JFK now

11

but Newark and La Guardia, too. Nothing. She was being neurotic, she told herself, worrying for no reason at all. There was a simple explanation and he'd be home tomorrow. Everything was fine.

CHAPTER 2

When Hannah woke up, light was edging round the curtains. The other side of the bed was empty but she quite often woke up alone when Mark was travelling so it was a moment before she remembered that today she wasn't supposed to. She propped herself on her elbow and reached for her BlackBerry. No new messages.

She lay back down for a minute, thinking, then threw off the sheets and got out. Mark's favourite grey cashmere jumper was on the back of the chair and she put it on over her pyjamas. Downstairs the post was on the doormat: just an electricity bill, a statement from Coutts for Mark and yet another mail-shot letter from Savills fishing to see if they had any plans to sell the house. She left the bill and the statement on the hall table with the previous days' post and went through to the kitchen.

While she waited for the kettle to boil she checked her email on her laptop, just in case, but the only messages were junk. Still nothing from Penrose Price either, she thought, and the interview there had been over a week ago now. That job was the one she really wanted, too; AVT yesterday wasn't in the same league. If they were going to let her know by email, though, it wouldn't be on a Saturday, and they would send a proper letter; they were that kind of company. Anyway, it was only a matter of time before the rejection arrived, in whatever form; if it were good news, she would have heard it by now.

She drank her coffee and thought about what to do. Perhaps Mark had caught a red-eye and was just getting into Heathrow now. She picked up her phone and pressed redial. Voicemail again. This time she didn't leave a message; she'd left one last night and emailed as well, and he would know she was wondering what was going on. She felt a stab of annoyance with him for being so inconsiderate – how hard could it be to call and leave a twenty-second message? – but it was quickly followed by a wave of anxiety. Something was wrong. This was so unlike him – he'd never not come home when he said he would without getting in touch.

It was five to nine, still a bit early for a Saturday, but Neesha had a three-year-old, she'd probably been up for hours already. Hannah scrolled through her contacts list until she found her mobile number.

Mark's assistant was a beautiful half-French, half-Indian woman who'd been brought up in South Africa but educated at the London School of Economics, where she'd met and married her husband, Steven. She was twenty-seven and Mark had recently started letting her manage her own small projects, afraid that she would leave unless she was promoted quickly. Pierre, her son, had arrived about ten years earlier than she'd planned to have him, she'd told Hannah at DataPro's summer drinks party, but she was as ambitious as she'd always been. Mark had said that if she was as efficient a project manager as she was an assistant, he expected her to be one of the most senior on the team within five years.

The phone rang. After six or seven rings, however, the answering service clicked in and Neesha's voice asked the caller to leave a message.

Hannah coughed, her throat suddenly dry. 'Hi, Neesha,' she said. 'It's Hannah Reilly. I'm sorry to call you at the weekend but I wonder if you could give me a ring when you get this?'

After a couple of slices of toast and a skim of the news online, she went upstairs and put on her running kit. She didn't particularly like running – *Oh, be honest, Hannah*, said her internal voice, *you hate it* – but over the past three or four months, she had made it part of what she thought of privately as her sanity routine. She had a frightening awareness of how easy it would be to become depressed about her situation without a structure to her days that involved some form of discipline and physical exercise. Not her life with Mark, obviously – when she'd talked to him about it, he'd asked if she was unhappy with him and she'd looked at him as if he was nuts – but work, or her lack of it.

Though they'd been married for nearly eight months now, she'd stayed on in New York for three months after their wedding. Mark had increased the amount of time he spent working in DataPro's American office and they'd talked about him making it his base full-time, flying over to visit the London office instead. His new partner, David, would take over from him there. After a month or so, however, talk of the move had become less and less frequent, and then Mark arrived one Friday evening looking guilty. He'd made her one of his custom martinis – vodka, with cranberry bitters – and told her that the consultants they'd hired to advise them on streamlining overheads during the turndown had strongly recommended closing the US office. He'd gone over the figures again and again, Mark said, and he knew it made sense.

'Are you sure?' she'd asked, feeling her heart plummet.

'It was their number one recommendation – the only one that would make any real difference to our operating costs, actually. I hate it, too – having a New York office was always a goal of mine, as you know – but really, we can handle the US business from London. We don't need a physical presence here. I'm so sorry, Han.'

His salary was bigger than hers by a factor of about five, and she was just an employee, not the owner of a company like he was. There was also the question of visas – they were both British so living in London was by far the easiest option – and while her apartment in the West Village had been rented, he'd already owned this house. She knew before he said it that if they were going to live together, everything argued that she should make the move. So, after some fruitless efforts to convince Leon, her old boss, that she should open a London office for him, Hannah resigned from her job and, five months ago, had packed up her apartment and shipped her belongings back here, her seven years of living and working in New York finished. Until she'd met Mark, she'd thought she'd live there for the rest of her life.

Quite apart from how much she wanted to be with him, though, she was surprised by how much she was enjoying being back in London. Even before she'd met Mark, she'd come back quite frequently to see her brother and her parents and to keep in touch with friends, but after two or three years she'd begun to feel like a tourist, someone who saw all the nice things – restaurants, galleries, the new bars her friends took her to – but had no real connection to the place, no day-to-day relationship with it.

That feeling had nearly evaporated now, and it was lovely to regain some of the British traditions she'd used to miss. Last week, she and Mark had walked over to Bishops Park to watch the fireworks on Bonfire Night. Impressive as the Macy's 4 July fireworks were, for her they didn't have the same emotional resonance, the layered memories of all the local fireworks she'd gone to with her parents when she and Tom were children, with toffee apples and the lighting of the huge bonfire that they'd watched burgeon with garden waste and broken pallets and lengths of rotten fencing in the weeks beforehand until it reached fifteen or twenty feet high. Bishops Park wasn't the same, of course – no bonfire, for one thing, because of city fire regulations – but damp November grass smelled the same here as in Worcestershire, and she'd loved watching the Thames at the park's edge as it slipped silently past them in the dark, its surface catching glints of blue and green and red from the explosions overhead.

Down in the hall again, she sat at the bottom of the stairs to put her trainers on then let herself out of the house, zipping the door key into her jacket pocket. The low hedge behind the front wall was wet with the rain that had fallen overnight and a perfect cobweb on the gatepost was strung with drops like glass beads. She opened the gate carefully so as not to disturb it.

She walked up Quarrendon Street, taking long strides to stretch her legs. She was getting to know some of the neighbours now, at least by sight, and nodded to the man from number twenty-three who was coming down the pavement with the *Telegraph* and a bag of what she guessed were croissants from the delicatessen tucked under his arm. With his quizzical expression and the grey hair that touched the velvet collar of his three-quarter-length camel

18

coat, he reminded her of Bill Nighy. He was typical of the residents here: either wealthy families, who walked their children, in immaculate uniforms and straw boaters, to the nearby private preparatory school each morning, or well-preserved empty-nesters. It was an unusual place for a bachelor in his twenties to have bought a house – there were far hipper areas than Fulham – and while it was very expensive, it wasn't flash at all. Mark could have chosen some vast renovated loft in Docklands or the East End, all glass and chrome and huge leather sofas, but instead he'd gone for a traditional Victorian family house. She loved him for it.

She crossed New King's Road and started jogging gently along the pavement. The trees that shielded the wedding-cake Regency houses from the road here were dripping heavily, the water pattering on to the fallen leaves plastered over the ground in a soaked homogenous layer.

Hannah had known it would be difficult to get another job, especially one like the one she'd had in New York, but she'd wildly underestimated how difficult. She'd thought that with her American experience and a reputation for coming up with campaigns that had done well on both sides of the Atlantic, she'd be able to find a new position within three to four months, even with the economic climate as it was. 'People will always hire the best candidates,' Mark had said the first time they'd discussed it. 'It might take a little while for some-thing you *want* to open up, but don't worry about

19

not getting a job. People are going to want to hire you – they'll be fighting to do it.'

Except they weren't. It had been five months, and though she'd had three final-round interviews, she hadn't received a single offer. At first, feeling confident, she'd only applied for jobs on a level with her old one with Leon but, as three months and then four had passed, she'd started to lower her sights. She told herself that it was only logical – the UK was in recession, jobs were scarce, perhaps she'd been arrogant to think she could immediately be hired again into a similar position; after all, she'd worked her way up with Leon over the years – but when she didn't get those jobs either, she'd started to think that *she* was the problem.

'No,' Mark had said last Sunday, while they were out walking in Richmond Park. He'd reached for her hand and tucked it in under his arm, pulling her against the heavy navy wool of his pea coat. She'd pressed closer and watched the two clouds of their breath as they mingled. Though it was only the beginning of November, there had been a heavy frost overnight and the ground was crisp underfoot. The tips of Mark's ears were pink where they stuck out from under his woollen hat.

'It's just the recession,' he said. 'You know you're good, and the right job will come along. It's like everything – you wait and wait until you don't think you can wait any more and then, just when you think you're going to explode or jump off Beachy Head, it finally happens.'

20

'What would you know about Beachy Head, Mr Tycoon by Twenty-five?' she'd said, prodding him in the side with her elbow, but she knew he was right about the waiting game. She'd been lucky after university – 'Luck had nothing to do with it,' Mark always said – and got one of the few graduate places at J. Walter Thompson, but she'd been stuck in the job she'd had after that, with a smaller agency, for almost a year after she'd decided she had to leave or die of boredom. She couldn't, she'd thought at the time, do another campaign for dog food without going off her nut. The job with Leon had rescued her from that, thank God, but now she was in the same situation again. Worse, actually: at least then she'd had a job, even if it had been peddling horsemeat. Now with every week that passed, she was conscious of the growing distance between her and paid employment, the diminishing relevance of her most recent campaigns. Her currency was devaluing.

Hannah's breath came faster as she approached Eel Brook Common and picked up her pace. She wove around the double barrier that discouraged cyclists from using the park and went on to the grass. The ground was sodden and hard-going but she made herself do two sides of the rectangle before she stopped by the little playground in the top corner. She was getting better but she was never going to be a natural runner, one of those people zipping round now at twice her speed, their breathing barely audible. She was fit but she didn't have the right body shape for it, that was her theory; she was sure that if she were one of these straight-up-and-down types, it would feel much easier. Mark had suggested she join a gym instead, but while she didn't have a job, she didn't feel comfortable paying £80 a month in membership fees. He'd laughed and told her to remember that they were married and what was his was hers, but she still couldn't do it.

She unzipped her pocket and took out her phone to check if she'd missed a call. Nothing. She looked at the time: ten twenty. With the five-hour time difference it would be hours yet before she could reasonably ring any of their friends in New York to ask if they'd heard from him, especially on a Saturday. She'd have to wait until at least one thirty. She put the phone back in her pocket and stretched her arms behind her head, feeling the tension in her neck and shoulder muscles. Six feet away, a chunky black Labrador snuffled contentedly through an abandoned bag of chips until his owner looked up from her conversation and called him sharply away.

Conscious of the cold, she started moving again. In the week, exercise helped her feel like she had a purpose, or at least something to do. She spent hours every day reading the trade press, looking at other people's new campaigns online, emailing her contacts to see if anyone had heard of new vacancies, but if she let her focus slip for longer than a few minutes, she felt the day become a long featureless slope of hours down which she could slide without anything to stop her. The same would happen today if she let it. She was disciplining herself not to job-search at the weekends, to maintain a distinction from the working week, however artificial, but she had to find something to do today to distract herself from the growing sense that something was wrong.

After two arduous laps she headed home, checked her phone and laptop again then went upstairs for a shower. Mark had had the bathroom redone at the same time as the kitchen and while it wasn't huge, it was without a question the most glamorous one she'd ever seen in a private house. All the units – the shower, the bath, the two matching sinks – were sleek and white, the contrast coming from the grey porcelain floor tiles and the dark, almost black, wood whose name he'd told her but she'd forgotten. Was it wenge? She wasn't sure. With its three beautiful tall orchids and the towels that looked fresh from the White Company every time they came out of the tumble dryer, it might have looked like a hotel bathroom, but because Mark had kept the original features – the architraves and the Victorian patterned glass in the window – he'd avoided that and instead the room looked stylish and luxurious.

As she was towel-drying her hair, her phone rang on top of the chest outside the door. Bending to pick it up, she glanced at the clock by the bed. Eleven: probably too early if he was still in New York. It would be Neesha.

'Hannah?'

Mark. She felt a wash of intense relief. 'You're

alive,' she said, breathing out. 'Thank God – I was beginning to wonder if you'd left funeral instructions.' She carried the phone over to the bed and sat down. 'What's going on?'

'I'm so sorry I didn't call last night. God, the whole thing was a disaster – honestly, Han, it was like a farce. First, the guy was stuck in traffic so he was three-quarters of an hour late and I'd pretty much missed the plane before we even started but we'd been trying to set up the meeting for six months so I decided just to suck it up and get on a later flight. In the end, we were at breakfast until almost nine thirty and I got a cab direct to the airport but of course the traffic was terrible and when I finally got there, all the flights were full, totally chocka. I kept trying till nearly three in case any seats came free but then I threw in the towel and came back into the city.'

'Why didn't you ring me?'

'I was going to in the cab but then David called with a problem that took ages to sort out and I thought it'd be better anyway to ring you when I knew what flight I was going to be on. Then, at JFK, I went to get my phone out to call you and I realised I'd left it in the taxi. Didn't notice the number of the taxi, obviously, so there's no chance of getting it back – all my contacts, photos, everything.'

'Bugger.' With a corner of the towel she mopped away a rivulet of water that was running down the back of her neck. Now she felt a burst of annoyance with him. She'd driven out to Heathrow in the middle of a storm, spent over two hours there – last night she'd been picturing transatlantic air disasters, for God's sake. 'Why didn't you ring me from a pay phone?' she said, the annoyance not entirely masked.

'I'm embarrassed to admit it,' he said, sounding sheepish even at a distance of three thousand miles, 'but I don't know your number by heart. Without my phone, I'm stuffed.'

She thought about it. She wasn't sure of his number either, actually, apart from the 675 at the end. Once she'd programmed it in to her BlackBerry, she'd never had any need to memorise it. 'You could have emailed.'

'I was going to, but when I got back to the hotel, the WiFi was down – see what I mean about a farce? Then, I'm ashamed to say, I sat down for a moment and fell asleep in the chair. When I woke up it was already midnight your time and I thought you'd be in bed.' He sighed. 'The WiFi's back up this morning, though – that's how I've got your number now. I remembered you'd put it in that email to Pippa about dinner a few weeks back. God, I'm such an old man. My neck – I was in the chair for about three hours with my head over to one side; I don't think I even moved.'

Hannah felt her irritation start to subside. He'd been working hard lately, even by his own standards. With the recession, business at DataPro was steady rather than bullish, and Mark was making sure of

25

every client by providing the best customer service possible as well as the industry-leading software design that had made the company what it was. And on top of that, there was the issue of the buy-out. A month ago he and David had been approached by an American company, one of their biggest competitors, and though she'd thought that Mark would dismiss out of hand the idea of selling, he'd been at first intrigued and then excited by it.

'The way I see it,' he'd said over breakfast a couple of days after the initial approach, 'it could be a huge opportunity.' He'd paused in the middle of buttering a slice of toast, knife poised in mid-air. 'I've been running DataPro since I was twenty-three – the idea of doing something else is exciting. Actually, it's exhilarating. If we cash out, I could use the money to set up something entirely different. But, you know, I'm forty now, I'm married . . .'

'Really?'

'I am, yes.'

'I had no idea. Lucky woman.'

'Lucky or tolerant – depends who you ask.' He smiled at her. 'But I'd like to spend more time with you, less at the office. And perhaps there'll be other people for me to take into account in the not-too-distant future . . .'

'Other . . .? Oh.' Suddenly there was a serious look in his eyes and she'd glanced away and reached for the coffee pot, taken aback by his intensity. She wanted children, she was pretty sure she did, but she was working up to the idea. She was still getting used to the fact that she was married – sometimes, when she was alone, she'd think about it and feel almost startled. How had it happened? Not much more than a year ago she'd been single.

'So when do you think you'll be back?' she asked now. 'Can you get on a flight today? Have you phoned the airline?'

'Well, actually, that's the thing. The guy I saw yesterday is keen to sign up with us, I think, but he wants me to meet his partner. He – the partner – has been in California this week so he wasn't around yesterday or Thursday, but he'll be in New York on Monday and he's suggested we all meet then.'

'Ah.'

'I know. Yesterday I said I couldn't, but having messed up the weekend anyway it makes sense now just to stay and do it, rather than making another trip, especially if I can get the thing signed there and then. They're talking about Monday afternoon, so if I did that, I could get a red-eye and be home on Tuesday morning. Would you mind?'

'Apart from the crushing disappointment?' She laughed slightly, hoping to distract him from the fact that she really was disappointed. 'No, don't be ridiculous, you fool, of course I don't mind. It makes sense. As you said, it might be a big contract.'

'Significant enough to have a bearing on a potential buy-out offer, I think. If we were seen to have this sort of new business coming in, especially from a US company and especially at the moment . . .'

'Then you've got to do it, haven't you? And it's just a couple of days – I'll survive. Hey, now you're at a loose end in New York for the weekend, you could give Ant and Roisin a ring, see if they're around.'

'Yeah, good idea, I might do that. Could you email me their number?' She heard him take a sip of something and then the rattle of cup on saucer. One of his quirks, a dislike of mugs – she teased him about it. 'Anything from Penrose Price yet?' he asked.

'No, and I'm trying to stop thinking about it. It won't happen now.'

'Keep the faith.'

'No, it's dead in the water. Onwards and upwards.'

'Well, make sure you do something relaxing this weekend, won't you? Don't job-search.'

'I won't.'

'Why don't you go and see that Herzog double-bill at the BFI?'

'No, you wanted to go to that, too; let's try in the week, when you're back. I might ring my brother, though, and see if he's free for dinner.'

'Okay, good idea. First things first here, I'm going to go to the gym and see if I can regain the use of my neck so I'm not walking round like Frankenstein's monster all weekend.' His voice dropped a couple of levels now, became more confidential. 'I'll miss you,' he said. 'Don't make any plans for Tuesday – I'll take the afternoon off if I can. We'll do something fun.'

* * *

28

She dried her hair and put on some clothes then went back down to the kitchen and emailed him Ant and Roisin's numbers. Maybe he could meet up with them for supper tonight or brunch tomorrow over in Cobble Hill; there was that place just round the corner from them that did the amazing eggs with paprika and sourdough toast. And those mimosas – God, she thought, she could drink one now. Booze during the day usually finished her off, but American Sunday brunch culture with its mimosas and bloody Marys was the civilised exception. It was one of the things she really missed about New York.

She thought about Mark sitting across a table from Ant and Roisin, and was jealous. She loved those two, the best friends she'd made while she was over there. She'd met Roisin when the company she worked for, Ecopure, had commissioned the agency to do press ads for a new range of all-natural household detergents. Hannah had taken her out to lunch one day early on and had an experience not dissimilar to falling in love in terms of the strength of the connection they'd discovered. They'd talked about their lives, their parents, where they'd grown up. Roisin said she'd moved to New York from San Francisco on her own at nineteen and worked at three jobs until she'd saved enough money to put herself through a marketing degree at NYU. Hannah had loved that story: the image it conjured up of a determined, self-possessed, nineteen-year-old Roisin. The following week, when they'd gone out for drinks on a non-work footing and staggered out of a place somewhere in the East Village long past midnight, Ro had hugged her and told her, somewhat slurrily, that she hadn't met anyone she liked so much since the day she'd met Ant.

And it had been they who had introduced Hannah to Mark. When Ant scored his big promotion last year, they'd decided that they'd spend the extra money on renting a summer place on Long Island. It was late in the year to start looking but within a couple of weeks they'd found an old, somewhat dilapidated shingle house in Montauk, a few minutes' walk from the beach. Occasionally they went on their own, but most weekends they invited friends out from the city. They always asked Hannah, and she almost always got one of the two tiny sea-smelling back bedrooms that faced on to the long lagoon behind the house. About six weeks after the rental started, she'd arrived in a cab from the station to find a tall, dark-haired man asleep in the Adirondack chair on the veranda, Roisin's panama tipped forward over his eyes, long bare feet resting on the wooden crate they used as an outside drinks table, the last inch of a bottle of Sam Adams going warm in his hand. He was so soundly asleep that he hadn't woken up even when she'd lost her grip on the screen door and it had snapped closed behind her like a jaw.

There'd been a note on the kitchen table to tell her that everyone else had gone to the beach. When she'd got down there and located Ro in the usual spot at the foot of the dunes, Hannah had asked who the man was.

'Mark. A new friend of Ant's,' Roisin had said, leaning forward to retie the straps of her red halter-neck bikini. 'They met at Harry's bachelor party a few weeks back and got on like a house on fire. He's one of yours, actually – a Brit.'

'Really?' Hannah rubbed in some factor 25, feeling the tops of her shoulders burning already. The glare was so intense that even through her sunglasses the beach looked stripped of colour. It was the busiest it had been so far that summer, the wide expanse of white sand fully colonised by other groups of people in their twenties and thirties sunbathing or playing volleyball, couples watching small children tearing around or digging busily in the sand. The occasional older couple sat in deck-chairs reading paperback thrillers. Down in the water she could see Ant and Laura, an old college friend of theirs, trying to stay upright in the breakers. 'You haven't mentioned him before,' she said.

'Really? I thought I had.'

'Oh, like you wouldn't remember.'

Roisin shrugged, making an innocent face.

'I hope you're not scheming.'

'About what? I know you don't do relationships – not decent ones.'

'What's wrong with indecent ones?'

'Nothing at all, in my book. And frankly, if I wasn't married . . .'

'Does he live here?'

'Kind of – or he has done. He's got a software company. They're based in London but they've got an office in Tribeca and he goes back and forth. He used to have an apartment, he was saying last night, but he moves around so much that hotels made better sense.'

'Hmm.' Reluctant to ask more in case she aroused suspicion, Hannah changed tack and asked about the latest management intrigue at Ecopure, a subject guaranteed to bring out the best of Roisin's talent for anecdote.

They'd stayed on the beach all afternoon. At about four thirty, Mark had come down the path through the dunes. He'd changed into a pair of faded blue boardshorts with a dolphin pattern, and Hannah watched from behind her sunglasses as he strode down the beach and waded in. A powerful crawl quickly took him out beyond the rough water near the shore. He swam for twenty minutes or so before coming in and sitting down next to Laura, the water furrowing lines through the hair on his chest and legs as it ran off him. Roisin had introduced Hannah and they'd done the Brits-in-America thing, the usual where-are-you-from, what-do-you-do to establish if they had anything or anyone in common, which they hadn't. His voice was deep and warm, without any trace of regional accent. He told her that he'd grown up in Sussex. 'How about you?' he'd asked.

'Malvern.'

'Are they far apart?' said Roisin.

'Poles.' He'd smiled. 'Light years.'

'About a hundred and fifty miles, probably,' Hannah said. 'Sussex is on the south coast; Malvern's in the middle.'

'I thought Malvern was near Scotland.'

Hannah looked at Mark and rolled her eyes. 'Believe it or not, Roisin and I have been good friends for five years.' He laughed.

They walked back to the house as a group, she, Laura and Ro ahead of the men, and once, turning round to say something to Ant, she'd caught Mark looking at her. The same thing had happened when, after hosing down on the patch of rough sea-grass in front of the house, they'd been in the kitchen getting the stuff ready to take back down to the beach for the evening. She'd glanced up from slicing tomatoes to ask Ro whether she should make a vinaigrette and found herself locked in eye contact with him. She'd looked away first, though these days he claimed it was the other way round.

The temperature had been in the high eighties during the day but it had dropped quickly as soon as the sun started to go down, and a surprisingly sharp on-shore breeze had started blowing. Ant and Justin, another one of his old college friends, had dug a shallow pit in the sand while the rest of them had gone along the tideline collecting driftwood and the remnants of logs brought down to the beach for bonfires on 4 July the weekend before. Mark had returned from the dunes with a branch that was seven or eight feet long, carrying it across his shoulders like a yoke.

They'd used it as a bench, sitting in a line drinking beers from the cool-box while the sun disappeared and the fire got hot enough to cook the sausages. After they'd eaten, he had stretched out on the sand, the glow from the fire catching the planes of his face, and told a long, funny story about a time he'd had his wallet stolen in Rio, gone to the police station to report it and almost ended up being arrested for the crime himself. Eyes hidden by the baseball cap she'd borrowed from Ant, Hannah had watched him, feeling a strange, jumping sensation in her stomach.

Roisin and Ant were tired and went back to the house sometime just after the last colour had faded from the sky behind the dunes, and what Hannah had suspected – that Justin was putting the moves on Laura, whether out of genuine interest or just his reflexive womanising – was confirmed when he asked her to go for a walk along the beach with him. To Hannah's surprise, Laura had got up and dusted the sand off her shorts without hesitating, and she and Mark were left alone. He'd fed the fire another piece of driftwood and settled himself on the sand again. The feeling in her stomach intensified until it felt almost like cramp.

'Ant told me you're responsible for that granola ad I see every time I turn on the TV here,' he said.

'Cereal killers? Yes, guilty, I'm afraid. It's a cheap gag but . . .'

'No, it's great – funny. It seems like it's a big success?'

'Well, the Grain Brothers are pleased – they're shifting twelve times as much Harvest Bite as usual so . . .'

'Twelve times? No bloody wonder they're pleased.' He picked up a stick and stirred the embers. 'Is that what you always wanted to do – advertising?'

'Well, it wasn't a childhood dream but, yes, since university.'

'What about living over here?'

'That *was* a childhood dream.'

'Really? For me, too. I used to sit in my bedroom at home devising ways I could make it happen.'

'Now that's what I call organised,' she'd laughed. 'I just hoped it would.'

They'd stayed out talking for hours, wandering round in the dark for more wood whenever the fire burned down and then returning to their exact same positions. By the time they'd crept back into the house, careful not to let the screen door slam behind them, the fold-down numbers on the seventies stove had said 02.42. They needn't have worried about being quiet: Justin had not been in his designated sleeping spot on the sofa. Down on the beach, they'd talked about everything: serious things – to her surprise, she'd found herself telling him about her parents' divorce – and ridiculous stuff, tales of horsemeat peddling, university stories, the family tortoise she and Tom had once smuggled with them

35

on a family holiday to the South of France. Aside from Roisin, she couldn't remember ever meeting anyone who seemed so interested in the details of her life: the books and music she liked, where she'd grown up and been to school, where she'd lived in London before she moved to the US, even her father's job as an academic at Bristol University.

'I don't want to do a Justin,' he had said in the dark behind her as they were making their way back through the dunes, gorse catching at their jeans, 'but I wondered . . . I'm in New York all next week. Would you like to have dinner one night?'

She hesitated, the muscles in her stomach making a single painful contraction. 'Yes,' she said, her voice carrying back through the darkness. 'That would be good.'

CHAPTER 3

The wind had caused a surprising amount of damage. Though the yard wasn't much more than twenty feet square, clearing it up would take a while. It wasn't just the heaps of fallen leaves and the broken branches on the cherry tree; the wind had carried rubbish into the garden – there were sheets of wet newspaper and a couple of crisp packets, and a white polythene shopping bag was snared in the tree's upper branches, tattered and flapping. Hannah picked up the wooden chair and set it back on its feet then went back inside to get garden-waste bags and the stiff broom.

It was half past eleven now. She'd rung Tom and arranged to meet him at eight at what had become their usual spot since she'd been back, a little place tucked away off the street in Chinatown that did authentic Szechuan. His friend Zhang An had recommended it and Hannah suspected her brother might count as technically addicted to the Bang Bang chicken.

It would be good, she thought, to see him on her own, without the presence of Mark or Tom's wife,

Lydia, who'd taken her mother away for a long weekend in Harrogate. Evenings with the four of them were fun but it wasn't the same. She liked Lydia a lot but Mark and Tom were so different that sometimes the conversation dried up. Nothing was wrong; it was just that, apart from her, they had little common ground. Mark, in particular, made a big effort, talking to Tom about cricket in the summer and now rugby league – once when they were due to have dinner together, she'd caught him on the Harlequins website, reading up beforehand – but they were different types of people. Tom taught English at a school in Highbury and Mark ran DataPro; Tom liked Thomas Pynchon and David Foster Wallace and slim volumes written by anxious young men, and, unless she recommended something to him, Mark read non-fiction – biographies of presidents and business leaders, history and economics – or Penguin Classics.

She rolled up her sleeve and plunged her hand into the little water feature, collecting the freezing mulch of dead leaves that was blocking the drainage hole. The thing always made her laugh. Even the term 'water feature' was hilarious – *infra dig*, her mother would say – but this one was particularly dreadful. Mark's renovation work hadn't extended as far as the garden, in which he'd done the minimum possible while maintaining a space large enough to sit out with a drink in the evening. She'd assumed responsibility for it over the summer, when she'd moved in properly, and in cutting back the Virginia creeper that he'd allowed to run amok, she'd uncovered a small, cross-looking stone face, set into the right-hand corner of the far wall. Investigating further, she realised it still worked, so that when it was turned on at the covered switch next to the French windows, water dribbled out from between the cherub's pouting stone lips into the shallow basin beneath its chin.

'Have you seen this?' Hannah asked, summoning Mark into the garden.

'I have,' he said. 'Hence the creeper.'

'Come on, it's hysterical.'

'It's hideous. It looks like it's at the dentist, spitting into a bowl. Quick, cover it back up before anyone sees it.'

'No way – it's funny. And it works.'

Mark had made a face not dissimilar to the carved one, and put his arms around her waist. 'I like seeing you in the garden,' he said. 'It suits you, English Rose.' He brought his hand up and touched a strand of her hair that had worked its way out of the loose knot she tied it in when she was working. She was naturally blonde, going darker in the winter but quickly brightening up again in the sun, especially around her face. She'd never had her hair highlighted and she knew he liked that, as well as her general *laissez-faire* approach to her appearance, which he chose to interpret as a deliberate aesthetic. One of the first times they'd been to bed together, he'd brought his head close to hers on the pillow and stroked

39

her cheek. 'Are you even wearing any make-up?' he'd asked.

'A little bit. Powder, some eyeliner and mascara. Honestly, though? I'm not very good at it. I see all these immaculately made-up New Yorkers and I wish I could do it but . . .'

'Why?' he asked. 'You're classic-looking, timeless – you don't need to look fashionable.'

Now, flicking her hand inside the rubbish bag until the wet leaves came off it, she thought about how domesticated she would appear to anyone who saw her at work out here and didn't know better. It was amazing that, in a matter of months, she'd gone from being a New Yorker with a string of orchid deaths on her conscience, to a Londoner in charge of a whole garden, however small. When she thought about how easily it might not have happened, too, the change seemed particularly startling.

On the Sunday afternoon of the weekend in Montauk, just before they'd left to go back to the city, Mark had carried her bag downstairs and asked if she was free for dinner on Friday. She had said yes and they'd made a plan to meet at a bar in Chelsea. As the days had passed, back in New York, however, she'd begun to dread it. The stomach ache she'd had that night on the beach came back whenever she thought about it, stronger and stronger as the week went on, and finally she'd acknowledged to herself that it was caused by anxiety. She knew she was physically attracted to Mark – she'd found herself thinking several times about the way the soft material of his old T-shirt had stretched between his shoulder blades as he'd crouched to stir up their beach-fire – but that in itself wasn't alarming: she was in her early thirties in New York, she met men, she wasn't celibate. The problem was that she liked him – really liked him.

In the end, after a night spent tossing in the air-conditioned chill of her bedroom, she'd emailed him first thing on Friday morning and told him that her biggest client had called a last-minute meeting for that evening, followed by dinner with his boss. *I'm so sorry to have to do this,* she'd written. *Perhaps we'll bump into each other again up in Montauk at some point over the summer?* She knew he would get the unwritten message – *don't suggest another day* – and he had. Twenty minutes after she sent her mail, a reply arrived: *Not to worry, I completely understand. See you round the campfire some time.* As she'd read it, what she'd felt was not relief at being off the hook but a powerful sense of loss.

She'd left the office just after seven that evening and, feeling her low mood starting to deepen, she'd cycled down from Midtown to McNally Jackson books in SoHo. She'd discovered the shop when she first moved to New York years earlier and, knowing almost no one then, she'd got into the habit of going there in the evenings, buying a new book and sitting in the café with a glass of wine, sometimes until the shop closed. It was always

41

busy and the clientele was interesting both to watch and to eavesdrop on; she'd seen blind dates that had flopped and one in particular that had gone spectacularly well; people tapping away at screenplays on laptops; parents up in the city to visit children studying at NYU; people discussing business plans for Internet start-ups and holistic therapy centres. She'd also heard some first-rate gossip. Between the books and the busy café, the loneliness she'd sometimes felt at the beginning, uprooted from London, had evaporated.

As she'd chained up her bike outside that evening, the sky above Prince Street had been turning a pale pearly pink. It was mid-July and the city was baking; around her bare ankles she could feel heat rising from the pavement. Inside the shop, she'd spent fifteen minutes choosing a book – the new Alan Hollinghurst, which she'd meant to wait for in paperback, but what the hell? She needed cheering up – and then she ordered a glass of wine at the counter and took it to a window table that was just coming free. The windows were open to the street and she heard snatches of conversation from passers-by and music from cars cruising up to the traffic lights on Lafayette. At the table opposite, a glamorous black woman in her late twenties, Hannah guessed, wearing a silk dress with a red sash, was talking to a member of staff, preparing to go down-stairs and give a reading from her new novel.

The wine was dry and cold, and she was soon absorbed in the Hollinghurst. A light breeze had blown up, cutting the humidity and stirring the short hairs at the base of her neck as she sat with her back to the window. Ripples of applause reached up the stairs from the reading.

She was about halfway down the glass when she looked up from the book. Over towards the shop's main door, browsing the small table of new non-fiction titles, was a man who, from behind at least, looked just like Mark. He was wearing a suit but he'd taken his jacket and tie off. He was the same height as Mark, the same build, and his hair was the same: dark brown, cut short at the back, left longer on the top, where it just started to curl. The man put down the book in his hand and went round the table to the other side, and Hannah's heart thumped against the back of her ribs. It *was* him – it actually *was* Mark. Shit – *shit.* She thought about her email, the blatant lie. *Oh, shit.* It was one thing to make an excuse and bail out on some guy you'd met in a bar, but lying to your friends' friends, especially Ant and Roisin's friends, was not on.

What should she do? She either had to stay put and hope he wouldn't see her or get up and go straight away, before he did. But just as she had a perfect view of him now, the distance between them not more than ten or twelve feet, so he, if he raised his head, would have a perfect view of her. If she stayed put and buried her head in her book, maybe she could get away with it. If she stood up to leave, she'd be more likely to draw his attention.

For two or three minutes she watched him

surreptitiously from over the top of the book, wishing her hair was down so she could let it fall across her face. Evidently he was looking seriously for something to read; he picked up a book, read the back or the inside flap or even, twice, the first page or two before putting it back and reaching for another. It was agonising – when was he going to choose something and just *go*, for Christ's sake? Her stomach was aching again but this time from the sheer fear of discovery.

At last, after perhaps five or six minutes, he chose a book and took it to the counter at the opposite side of the shop. Hannah let out a long silent breath and took a large gulp of wine. The counter was right by the main doors: he'd leave without seeing her; she'd got away with it. Breathing easier but still being careful, she buried her head in the book again, glancing over just one more time to see him pocketing his change and tucking his new purchase under his arm.

A minute later, though, the light to her right was blocked and she was conscious of someone standing by her table. She looked up slowly. Charcoal suit trousers. A crisp white shirt with a fine stripe in the weave, clearly expensive.

'Hello,' he said. 'I thought it was you.'

'God, Mark – wow! Hello. Hi.' Hannah felt the blood rush to her face.

He smiled. 'Great minds.' He nodded at her glass, now nearly empty. 'I'd just come in to do the same thing.'

'Really? Right, yes, it's fantastic here, isn't it? I love this place.'

'Me, too. Any good?' He indicated her book.

'Well, I've only just started but, yes, I think so. He's one of my favourites.'

'I read the one that won the Booker but I'm not much of a fiction reader, I'm ashamed to say. I enjoyed that, though.' He adjusted the position of the bag under his arm, holding it more securely, and glanced over at the counter. 'I'm going to get a glass of wine – can I get you another?'

Hannah hesitated, mortified. He would be within his rights to be severely pissed off with her but, despite the blatancy of her lie, he didn't appear to be bearing any kind of grudge. The least she could do was to return the civility. 'Well, if you're sure?'

'Of course.'

She watched him as he waited. He looked totally relaxed, saying something to the bearded guy behind the counter that made him laugh as he filled their glasses. Mark carried them back to the table and carefully put one of them down.

'Thank you,' she said, 'that's very kind. Look, don't feel . . . I mean, if you've come to get some peace, and read . . . but if you'd like to . . .' She indicated the spare chair.

'Only if you're sure I'm not interrupting *you*?'

'No, not at all.' She shook her head. As he pulled out the chair, she took the opportunity to come out with it. 'Look,' she said, 'I'm so sorry about this evening – it was just a mess, the whole thing. Having demanded that last-minute meeting, the client then called at lunchtime to cancel the whole thing. Apparently, the big boss's wife developed a dental abscess all of a sudden and he wanted to stay with her in Boston.' *God, Hannah, where is this stuff coming from? Dental abscess?*

'Don't worry about it.' Mark waved his hand. 'Stuff like that happens to me all the time. Sometimes I feel like it's impossible to organise any kind of normal social life. A couple of my friends in London get really hacked off with me for being a flake.'

'I know that feeling.'

He took a large sip. 'So you're not going out to Montauk this weekend? You normally do, don't you?'

'Normally – I love the beach – but I've got something on tomorrow night, so I couldn't.' She smiled. 'My assistant's in a band, he's the drummer, and they've got a gig over in Williamsburg. I promised him I'd go, be a groupie for the night.'

He took another sip of wine and she noticed the way his long straight fingers curled round the delicate stem. 'That sounds fun.'

'Well, they've just formed, hence needing the support, but my sources in the office tell me they're pretty good.'

The reading finished downstairs and a new influx of people flooded the café, taking the last few spare seats. The woman who'd been reading stood nearby, besieged by men with tattoos and ironic T-shirts vying to impress her with earnest, reverential questions.

'You know, when we first opened our New York office and I was living here full-time, not just flying back and forth,' Mark said, 'I used to come in here a lot. I enjoyed sitting and having a bite to eat and a glass of wine – it was much better than staying at home alone in my apartment.'

'We probably shared a table,' she said, though she knew she would have remembered if they had. 'I used to do exactly the same. I still do sometimes, if I'm at a loose end unexpectedly. Like tonight.'

'Me, too. Like tonight.'

'Sorry.' She grimaced.

He rolled his eyes. 'Please.' He tipped his head in the direction of the writer and her tattooed acolytes. 'What do you reckon? Any of them in with a chance?'

He was such easy company, the conversation as natural and unforced as it had been on the beach in the dark. Again, he focused almost entirely on her, asking about her job, her family. They finished their wine and Hannah bought another round. Nearing the bottom of the glass again, she began to feel pleasantly buzzed and she realised that she was enjoying herself more than she had with anyone who wasn't a friend or her brother in the past seven years. She diverted her thoughts away quickly from the time before that.

'Do you fancy getting a bite to eat?' Mark had

said as the street outside filled with the peculiar hyper-real Manhattan twilight that made everything seem sharper and brighter. 'I didn't have much lunch and if I have another one of these on an empty stomach, I'm going to start talking complete bollocks.'

Outside, he waited while she undid the chain on her bike – he was impressed, he said, that she cycled in Manhattan – and they walked round the corner to Mulberry Street, the bike ticking an accompaniment alongside. They went to a diner-style Italian place which he'd mentioned had got a great review in *New York* magazine, took the two stools on the short side of the counter near the front and ordered chicken-parm sandwiches approximately twice the size of any sandwich Hannah had ever seen. 'Which,' she told him, 'these days, is saying something.' They discussed the campaign she was working on for a new manufacturer of healthy snacks, and she asked him about how and when he'd set up his company. After that, she couldn't really remember what they talked about beyond a general sense that they'd talked like people who'd known each other for twenty years without ever having heard the other's best stories. The tension came back into her stomach but it wasn't anxiety or embarrassment now but a reaction to being near him, sitting so close on the pedestal stools, their knees almost touching. She'd watched his hands as they held the sandwich or flipped the cap of his beer on the Formica counter-top, and she'd yearned – it was an actual, physical sensation – to reach out and touch him.

The clock behind the bar read half-midnight by the time he turned to her and fixed her with a serious look. 'Tell me,' he said, 'that stuff about the late meeting was a line, wasn't it, to give me the brush-off?'

She'd bitten the inside of her cheek, trying not to laugh, and looked him directly in the eye. 'Yes,' she said.

He shook his head. 'No remorse, even. That bit about the dental abscess was a nice touch, by the way.'

Hannah burst out laughing. 'Perhaps I can make it up to you,' she said, reaching for her glass, 'by inviting you to a gig in Williamsburg tomorrow night? I hear the band is excellent.'

CHAPTER 4

The wind had torn the polythene bag into a hundred tattered pieces, making it look like a leftover Hallowe'en ghoul trapped among the branches of the cherry tree. Hannah was on the top rung of the stepladder cutting it out with the kitchen scissors when she heard her mobile ring on the table inside. She considered leaving it but then thought that it might be Mark again and climbed quickly down to get it.

When she picked up, however, it wasn't Mark but Neesha. 'Hi,' she said. 'How are you? Sorry it's taken me so long to ring back – I've only just checked my phone. We took Pierre swimming this morning and then came straight on to Steven's parents. You must have called while we were at the pool.'

'God, don't worry about it. I'm sorry to have called you at all, especially at the weekend. I was just trying to track Mark down but it's okay, I've heard from him now. He called me from New York about an hour ago.'

'New York?' Neesha sounded puzzled.

'Yes, he missed his flight yesterday and I was

50

worried because he hadn't called, but it turns out he'd just dropped his phone in a cab.'

Neesha said nothing and Hannah felt herself frown. 'Is everything all right?' she asked.

Another pause, momentary but perceptible. 'Fine.'

'Are you sure?'

'Yes. I mean, of course.'

Hannah could almost feel the weight of confusion at the other end of the line. 'What's up?' she said.

'Nothing.'

'No, come on.'

Neesha hesitated again. 'Really, it's nothing,' she said. 'It's just . . . I've got my wires crossed again, that's all. I didn't think he was in New York.'

'Where did you think he was?' Another pause. 'Neesha?'

'Look, I . . . I thought you were going to Rome this weekend.'

'Rome?' Hannah leaned against the kitchen counter. 'You? You mean, Mark and me?'

'I thought he said he was taking you. As a surprise.' Neesha breathed out heavily. 'God, Hannah, I'm sorry. I've totally ballsed up, haven't I? I've got the wrong weekend, obviously, and now I've ruined it all. Shit, Mark's going to kill me.'

'No, Neesh . . .'

'It's my own fault – I've just got so much going on. I love the projects he's given me and I want to do them well – really well – but I can't do that and the PA work, too, not properly, especially when

51

I have to leave early to pick up Pierre. This isn't the first stupid mistake I've made. Look, I feel bad for asking but . . . You couldn't keep this under your hat, could you? I know there's no reason for you to after I've wrecked things for you but if you . . .'

'Don't worry about it, it's fine,' Hannah said. 'It's my fault – I shouldn't have pressed you. Anyway, I hate surprises so you've done me a favour. Our secret.'

Out in the yard Hannah climbed the ladder again but the sense of relaxation she'd had before was gone and in its place was a strange itchy feeling, as if she'd put on a rough wool jumper next to her skin.

What was the matter with her? Everything was fine. Mark was safe, and probably about to sign a new deal that would make a difference to the potential buy-out offer, which itself would mean they'd be able to spend more time together in future. He'd be home on Tuesday and if he could take the afternoon off, they'd do something fun, he'd said. And tonight she was having dinner with Tom, just the two of them, and how long was it since they'd done that? Everything was good – great, actually.

She started pruning small dead branches and ones that had snapped in the wind, dropping them to the ground at the foot of the ladder. Suddenly Neesha's voice replayed in her ear: *I thought you were going to Rome this weekend. I thought he said he was taking you. As a surprise*. Oh, for God's sake, Hannah, she told herself, it was just a mistake – hadn't Neesha said so? Hadn't she said she'd made others since she'd been juggling her new workload? She was like any other working mother, trying to do it all and occasionally getting things wrong under pressure. She, Hannah, would drive herself mad if she started getting hung up about things like this.

But, said a quiet voice, *there's something else, isn't there?* Early last week – had it been Monday or Tuesday? – Mark had been doing an hour's work in his study before supper and she'd taken him a gin and tonic. As she'd come up the stairs she'd heard him talking, but when she'd opened the door he'd turned quickly – *jumped,* said the voice; *he'd jumped* – and hung up the call straight away without saying goodbye, at least as far as she'd been able to hear. When she'd asked him who it had been, he'd said David Harris and she'd been surprised: his partner had only joined DataPro a year ago and, from what she'd seen of it, their relationship was quite formal; she wouldn't have thought they'd just hang up on each other like that.

At the time, she hadn't dwelt on it too much. They could easily just have said goodbye when she turned the handle: the door had been closed and she hadn't been able to make out Mark's words clearly. And he'd jumped because she'd startled him: he hadn't been expecting her to come in. Anyway, what did she really know about how

53

he and David talked on the phone? They talked to each other all the time – things were bound to have relaxed between them.

More to the point, though, she trusted Mark. There was no reason not to – he'd never given her the slightest reason to think he might be interested in anyone else or even registered other women as attractive. In the year and a half since that day on the beach in Montauk, she'd never once seen him do a double take at a pretty woman coming into a restaurant or passing them on the street. Even in Greece over the summer, he'd seemed oblivious to the beautiful tanned Italians and Swedes wandering down to the water in their tiny string bikinis.

She felt absolutely secure with him; it was one of the reasons she'd known their relationship was right – that she'd even allowed herself to get into a relationship with him in the first place. He wasn't perfect, obviously. Who was? There were times when he was tired and uncommunicative, which annoyed her if she'd spent the day on her own and wanted to talk, and a couple of months ago he'd stayed out late drinking with his old college friend Dan Kwiatkowski when she was at home with a stomach bug, which she'd thought was a bit much, but that was all minor stuff, petty. She was absolutely sure he loved her. He did the easy things – complimented her on new clothes, told her she was beautiful – but showed his love most in practical ways. Just before Christmas last year, when there had been a huge snowstorm in New York, she'd arrived home from work to find him on his knees on the sidewalk fitting chains to the wheels of her car. 'Oh-ho,' Roisin said when Hannah told her, 'you've got him. These women who want perfume and designer handbags for Christmas – it's when you're unwrapping anti-freeze and smoke alarms that you know. When a man starts worrying about something happening to you, *that's* when he really loves you.'

How to describe the way Mark treated her? He was just . . . on her side. It was hard to imagine anyone being more supportive of her efforts to get a new job, for example. He'd listened for hours as she'd discussed ideas and opportunities with him and, recently, her worries. 'Keep the faith' – he'd said it again on the phone this morning. She'd started to feel the first sickening waves of depression about it all, but his confidence hadn't wavered.

Hannah shook her head as if that would rid her of the itchy feeling. She was being ridiculous: they loved each other. And what good was a marriage without trust? She felt a surge of something close to anger: she refused – she point-blank refused – to be like her mother, to let insecurity gnaw and gnaw away at her marriage until it collapsed around her ears, completely undermined.

She finished the pruning, came back down the ladder and stuffed the dead wood into a rubbish bag. She collected the crisp packets and soggy sheets of newspaper from the corners of the yard then started sweeping, scratching the broom across the stones to get up the clinging wet leaves.

I thought you were going to Rome this weekend. I thought he said he was taking you. As a surprise.

Now the voice in her head piped up again: *what if, when you went up to his study last week, you caught him making plans to go to Rome? Everything he said this morning – missing the flight, losing his phone, falling asleep – what if it was all lies? There were a lot of convenient reasons, weren't there, why he hadn't been able to contact you?*

Shut up, she told the voice. Shut up with your vile, disloyal insinuations.

Rome, it said again. *A surprise.*

A surprise: despite her resistance, her mind snagged on the word. Had Mark really been planning a surprise weekend away? He often arranged lovely things for them to do – lately he'd got almost as into theatre as she was, and only last week he'd bought them tickets for *La Bohème* at Covent Garden – but he never did it without asking her first. She liked that about him: she'd always thought there was something a bit presumptuous about people who sprang surprises on their partners, expecting them just to drop what they were doing at a moment's notice. And they'd talked about that – he'd agreed with her.

For another ten minutes more she carried on working, trying to distract herself, but the interior voice refused to be quiet. Finally she gave up and went inside to the kitchen. Stalling, she drank a glass of tap water then sat at the table and did a Google search for the number of the W Downtown, the hotel Mark always used when he was in New York. She entered the number into the phone and looked at it for a few seconds. Should she? She couldn't – it would make her as bad as her mother, sneaking round, checking up on things. But she wasn't sneaking round, was she? She was calling her husband at a hotel, where she'd ask to be put through to his room so she could talk to him. She was doing this to silence the nagging voice in her head; that was all. She was doing it to prove what she already knew: she had nothing to worry about.

She pressed the button and heard the number dial. Two or three seconds passed and then it started ringing. After a few seconds of cheesy lounge music, an automated voice told her that an 'associate' would be ready to 'grant her wishes' shortly. More dreadful music, and then the call was answered. She'd come through to the reservations line but explained what she wanted and the associate put her through to the hotel's front desk.

'Mark Reilly?' said the receptionist. 'Please hold.'

Hannah waited, already feeling better. She'd talk to him quickly, tell him she loved him, then get back outside with her mind at rest.

'Hello?'

'Hi, yes.'

'I'm sorry,' said the receptionist, 'but we don't have a guest of that name staying with us currently.'

'Oh.' For a moment, Hannah was completely taken aback.

The silence stretched. 'Is there anything else I can help you with today?'

'I'm sorry,' she said, 'but would you mind just checking again? I was sure my husband was staying with you this weekend – I spoke to him this morning.'

There was another momentary pause, the click of computer keys. 'No, I'm sorry,' the woman said, 'I'm certain we don't have a Mr Reilly here. Perhaps he's at one of our other locations, uptown?'

'Right, yes, of course. I'll try them. Thanks.'

She hit 'End' and put the phone on the table. She could feel her heart thumping. Mark always used the branch downtown because it was closest to Wall Street, where most of DataPro's clients were based, and anyway, there was no way he'd stay in Midtown because he hated it there, all the busyness and the tourists. But what if he'd had to? argued a different part of her brain. What if he'd tried to check back in downtown after he'd missed his flight and they'd been fully booked?

Feeling slightly more positive, she opened her laptop again and found the numbers for the other Ws. There were three of them now, at Union Square, Times Square and on Lexington. One by one, working her way uptown, she called them all, but every receptionist gave her the same response: no current guest of that name.

Mark called the study his eyrie. He'd had it converted from the old loft space, and the roof sloped steeply on both sides, making it feel like a tent or a tree house. The stairs to it were steep, and its windows looked out over a landscape of chimneys and aerials and old satellite dishes to the spire of the church on Studdridge Street and the tower blocks to the south on the other side of the river. He'd kept the furniture simple: a Lloyd Loom wicker chair that he sat in to read, an antique Turkish rug and his beautiful Georgian desk with its original tooled-leather top.

She yanked open the long drawer that ran above the knee-well, trying not to think about what she was doing. Without any idea what she was looking for, she sifted through the contents: staples, pens, half a roll of Extra Strong Mints with the curl of torn wrapper still attached, a paper poppy from Remembrance Sunday, and then, in a Swan Vesta matchbox, the brittle remains of a four-leafed clover she'd found and given to him for good luck. There was his pass from Ladies' Day at Royal Ascot in June, where he'd taken some clients on a corporate jaunt; an old cassette, *Hendrix* written in felt-tip pen on the label; a few Euros in coins, and an anatomically challenged blue dog made in Fimo clay by Dan and Pippa's son Charlie, baked in the oven and given to Mark a few weeks ago by way of godson tribute.

Bending, she went through the rest of the drawers one by one. Three of them were empty, one had a cigar box full of bulldog clips and Bic biros, and another contained back issues of *Prospect* and the *Economist*. She ran her hands round the back of the drawers and into their corners but there was nothing to suggest an illicit affair, no photographs tucked away or handwritten notes, no business cards from hotels she didn't know he'd been to. In fact, there was nothing suspicious or unsavoury at all, not so much as a furtive copy of *Hot Babes*. Relieved, she laughed at the idea. She couldn't imagine Mark buying porn – much too uncouth.

The only thing that surprised her at all was that the drawer on the bottom right was empty. This, she knew, was where he kept the old box-file with his financial paperwork; he'd showed it to her a couple of weeks before they got married, 'in case I ever get hit by a bus'. Thank God, she'd never had to open it, and she kept her own financial paperwork separately, downstairs in the sitting-room bureau, in the accordion file she'd always used.

She looked round the room but the box-file was nowhere to be seen. He must have taken it out to pay bills or move some of his savings, but where would he have put it? She hadn't seen it round the house anywhere but that wasn't surprising: he did all his personal accounting up here at the desk. For a few minutes the voice in her head had been mercifully silent. Now it started whispering again: *Where's the file? Why would he take it out of this room?*

Hannah perched on the chair and rested her head in her hands for a moment, fingers over her ears as if she could block out the voice that way. She was appalled at herself – she was behaving just like her mother in the final weeks before Dad left.

Ringing hotels . . . going through desk drawers. It was so sordid, so – grubby. Hannah had promised herself she'd never become that sort of person.

Where's the file? asked the voice.

All right, she told it, angry now; all right, I'll look for it. I'll look for it, find it, and then the mystery will be over, won't it? Standing, she took a final look around the room and then went downstairs where she checked their bedroom and the two spare rooms. The box-file wasn't there and nor was it in the sitting room, either under the coffee table or in the bureau or on any of the shelves. In the kitchen she went as far as checking the drawers and cupboards, but she didn't find it anywhere.

The clock on the cooker said twenty past one; she should have some lunch now if she was going to be ready to eat supper with Tom later. She wasn't hungry at all, though. Putting her gloves on again, she went back out to the garden and started yanking up weeds and the long strands of grass that were sprouting in the empty tomato trough and round the base of the shrubs next to the wall. After five minutes, however, she stopped.

Where was Mark? In New York, she told herself; the Rome thing was just Neesha's mistake. Obviously he'd stayed somewhere other than the W this time or, having missed his flight, he hadn't been able to get another room there and had checked in elsewhere.

If that was the case, though, argued the voice in her ear, *shouldn't he have said which hotel he was at, especially since he'd lost his mobile and the hotel phone was the only way of talking to him?* And why the hell hadn't she asked him? But then, she reasoned, why would she have? She'd assumed he'd be at the W; she'd had no reason to think otherwise.

She remembered the phone call she'd interrupted, the startled look on his face when she'd opened the study door. And now his missing paperwork. She made herself stand straight, shoulders back, and took several long, slow breaths. The sun had gone behind a cloud and, without it, the air was so cold it seared the inside of her nostrils. She was being ridiculous, as hysterical as her mother at her most outrageous. She loved her husband and she knew he loved her. She trusted him and there was no reason not to.

Nonetheless, with a feeling of inevitability she understood that, having let in the element of doubt, she would now have to find the box-file. Until she could look at his bank statements and be sure that he hadn't hidden them to conceal evidence of money spent on hotels and dinners and presents for someone else – *trips to Rome* – the nagging, insinuating voice in her head was not going to be quiet.

CHAPTER 5

DataPro's offices took up two whole floors of a substantial modern building set back from the river at Hammersmith in the immaculately bland gardens of an upscale business park. He'd started here, Mark had told her, with two rooms: his office and one for his two programmers. Initially he'd leased those on a month-by-month basis but as the business had grown – and grown – the office space had grown with it and he'd added first the suite across the hall, then the one next to it, and the one next to that. The Internet start-up that had moved into the building at the same time and overconfidently signed a ten-year lease on the floor above had gone bust in 2001, and DataPro had taken over their space and now occupied a duplex of more than twelve thousand square feet.

Hannah left her car in Manbre Road and walked round to the entrance to the park. There was no security guard in the booth on Saturdays. She skirted the end of the car-barrier and followed the pavement until she reached the lawn that stretched away from the foot of DataPro's building to the Thames footpath running directly along the river's edge. Someone had raked the lawn already today, she saw: though the wind last night had left the silver birch trees almost naked, there was scarcely a stray leaf in sight.

Cold sunlight reflected off the building's fourteen mirrored glass floors and from the pools of the fountains set either side of the main entrance. Just get it over with, she told herself. Go up there, look, then go home and forget all about it. She took a final galvanising glance at the river then spun in through the revolving doors.

The atrium was a vast marble-floored room from whose distant ceiling hung a sculpture of tangled steel that made her think of space junk, one of those defunct satellites doomed to orbit the earth for ever. The bank of lifts was on the back wall but before them came a line of turnstiles. Without a security pass, there was no way through. Tony, one of the regular doormen, was at the desk, however, his neat grey head bent over the sports pages of the *Mirror* that he'd smoothed out tidily in front of him. She'd met him several times, first when she was visiting from New York and Mark had brought her in to meet DataPro's staff, and then pretty regularly since she'd moved back. Tony was employed by the building, not DataPro, but Mark had introduced them that first time and the doorman always recognised her.

'Mrs Reilly?' He looked up from the paper and smiled at her. There was a chill in the air in the lobby and he was in his cold-weather uniform, a ribbed oiled-wool sweater with the name of the management company embroidered over his heart. 'This is an unexpected pleasure.'

'How are you, Tony?'

'I'm doing all right, thank you, yes, not too bad. Wild weather last night, wasn't it? I walked through Bishops Park on my way in this morning and there were branches down all over the place.'

Hannah made a face. 'Yes, I've just been tidying up at home.'

'Well, we're under control here. The gardeners have been this morning, got the grounds looking spick and span again.' He looked at her as if she should be relieved, as if untidiness outside might pose some sort of threat to Mark's business.

'That's good. Tony, I wondered, could I zip upstairs for a couple of minutes? Mark's away for the weekend but we've got a meeting with the bank manager first thing on Monday and Mark's just told me he's left all the paperwork in his office. Would you mind?'

'Well, it's totally against the rules,' he said. 'Without a pass, no one's allowed past the—'

'I can imagine, and I'm sorry to have to ask – it's just . . .'

'Oh, I'm only pulling your leg.' He gave her a little wink. 'Of course you can go up. Mr Harris is around but he's just popped out to get a bite of lunch. I'll let him know you're here if he gets back before you go.' Tony stood up from behind the desk and walked over to the smoked-glass

65

security gate, which he opened with a card attached to the extending lead on his belt. 'There you go.'

The lift carried Hannah soundlessly to the seventh floor where she stepped out into the lobby. The receptionist's desk was unmanned, of course, and there were no lights on in the row of offices behind the plate-glass wall in front of her. Upstairs, no doubt, at least some of the programmers would be in. Mark paid big bonuses for projects completed early, which meant that they worked round the clock, weeks and weekends. Their floor was a lot more relaxed-looking than this one. It wasn't Silicon Valley but there was a large room with sofas and beanbags, table football and snooker, and a cupboard full of caffeinated, sugar-heavy drinks and lethal snacks. A lot of the programmers were in their twenties and there was a definite university computer-club atmosphere up there.

By contrast, this level was corporate, the face of DataPro that visiting clients saw. Here everything was light. The desks were large and clutter-free, with computers that were replaced every year, and those walls that weren't glass were painted fresh cream. The carpets were sand-coloured, and the entire floor was dotted with lush bamboos and a type of glossy deep-green succulent she'd never seen anywhere else. The place had a beach-like, almost tropical feel.

Mark's office was at the end of the corridor. It was the same one he'd always had, he'd told her, one of the original two rooms. When she'd asked, surprised, if he hadn't been tempted by the much larger corner office with its full-on view of the river, he'd said that this one had sentimental value, and it was big and smart enough to use for client meetings if he didn't want to use the conference room.

Hannah pushed open the heavy glass door and went in. The outside wall was glass, too, and offered a view over the rooftops of Hammersmith. Directly below was the entrance to the building and then a good sweep of the lawn, but if you stood almost in the corner and looked to your left, you could see the river. If she'd had the chance to bag the corner office she would have jumped at it, she thought. The river wasn't especially beautiful here; the opposite bank was scrubby, especially now in November when the old year's growth was dying, and this far west there was none of the architectural glory of the centre of London. In fact, the only real man-made feature of any note was the old Harrods furniture repository which stood on the opposite bank. Nonetheless, this was the Thames, pewter-coloured today in the late-autumn sun, rolling steadily onwards as it had done for centuries, powerful and inscrutable.

She turned to Mark's large blond-wood desk. She had to be quick – the last thing she wanted was to meet David and have to lie about what she was doing here. And if he saw her, he would mention it to Mark for sure. How long would he take to get his lunch? Apart from the business park itself and Charing Cross Hospital on

Fulham Palace Road, this part of Hammersmith was largely residential, and from here it was a ten-minute walk to even an uninspiring corner shop. Tony hadn't said how long ago David had gone out, though.

Her eyes rested for a few seconds on the framed photograph that Mark kept on his desktop, just to the right of his computer. Neither of them had wanted an official photographer – in the context of the rest of their wedding, it would have seemed too fussy and formal – but Ant had insisted they'd want some pictures and had taken on the role himself. Hannah picked up the photo and looked at it. There they were on the steps of Chelsea Town Hall, Mark in his gorgeous navy suit, grinning and squinting into the sharp April sun, one hand curled firmly round the waist of her oyster silk shift dress. She had a hand up too, shielding her eyes from the storm of confetti that Pippa and Roisin had just unleashed over their heads. Mark's smile – being the focus of it was like standing in front of a large plate-glass window and feeling the sun stream through, light and warmth together.

Just after the picture had been taken he'd turned to kiss her, confetti still scattered on the shoulders of his jacket. 'Look at you,' he said. 'You're everything I've ever wanted.'

About a hundred times that day, during the wildly extravagant lunch at Claridge's, the champagne afterwards and the cab ride out to Heathrow for the flight to Capri, she'd looked at him and

68

thought, *My husband*, and had hardly been able to believe it. Now, just eight months later, here she was sneaking about in his office on a Saturday afternoon. She felt a wash of intense revulsion at herself. Come on then, she thought; just look for the file and go.

The drawers opened effortlessly, as if cushioned by air. She went through them one by one, not letting herself be distracted by anything else, just looking for the grey marbled cardboard of the box-file. By the time she reached the last two, she'd convinced herself it wasn't going to be there, but as she opened the lowest of the three drawers on the right-hand side, the spot corresponding to the one the file occupied in his desk at home, she saw it. She lifted it out on to the desktop and pressed the round plastic button at the side to release the lid.

Inside was a pile of paperwork an inch or so thick, a statement from Mark's Coutts current account on the top. She scanned quickly down the list of recent transactions but there was nothing that caught her eye, no large amounts of money going out to Tiffany, the Waldorf-Astoria, or even – as far as she could tell – some high-end florist. She sprang the clip that held the papers in place and took the statement out but, as she was turning to the second page, she saw what was next in the file, a letter from the building society, and her eyes homed in on a number. *£130,000.* She picked the letter up and read the full sentence. '*Following our recent meeting, I am pleased to be able to confirm an*

69

extension to your mortgage of £130,000, as requested.'
She skimmed the rest and then turned to the sheet
attached, a revised schedule of payments. Almost
without thinking, she put out her hand, pulled up
Mark's chair and sat down.

If the schedule was correct, they owed just shy
of £700,000. *'Seven hundred thousand'* – she
murmured the words aloud, shocked. She'd had
no idea their mortgage was so huge – it was an
incredible amount. Even when she'd had a job,
there was no way her salary could ever have
supported a loan of that size. It was in Mark's
name, of course, and any salary she had was
irrelevant, but he'd told her he didn't have much
of a mortgage left at all; that having owned the
house for over a decade, he'd paid off several large
chunks as well as making the regular payments. It
was the main reason she'd agreed, after several
heated discussions, to let him go on paying it as
he always had, without any contribution from her,
until she found a new job.

But extending the mortgage like this, without
talking to her about it, that was something else. How
could he do it? Weren't they married? Weren't they
supposed to talk about things like this, make
decisions together? Perhaps, she thought, Mark
would argue that he hadn't wanted to worry her
about it while she didn't have a job – and her not
having a job was because of him, since she'd had
to resign hers to move back to London – or perhaps,
because he'd owned the house for so many years

70

before they met, he still thought of it as in some way his, or at least his responsibility.

But however he was justifying it to himself – if he even felt he *had* to justify it – Hannah was angry. How could he? *Following our recent meeting*: he'd had an appointment at the building society, been in to discuss this with someone without even mentioning it to her. Which meant he'd come home one day in the not-too-distant past and lied about what he'd been doing. She turned the page back over and glanced at the date. 29 October – less than a fortnight ago. *God.*

She sat back in the chair and the anger became something else. At first she couldn't name the feeling but then she identified it as hurt. She was hurt. Didn't Mark want to involve her in the business of their life? Didn't he think of her as a partner in their relationship, an equal who would want to know what was going on and be involved? Because this did involve them both, even if she wasn't contributing to the mortgage payments at the moment. She would, as soon as she got a job, and anyway, what if something happened to him? She'd be left with a £700,000 mortgage she'd known nothing about.

The hurt had another element. Rationally or not, she felt humiliated that he hadn't told her – belittled. When they'd met, she'd been entirely independent, succeeding at her career, supporting herself financially, renting an apartment in the West Village and living a good life in one of the most

71

expensive cities in the world while managing to save, too. Now look at her: unemployed, living in someone else's house on someone else's money, and not even being kept in the picture about that. She took a deep breath and felt the anger burn in her chest.

And then there was the other big question: why did Mark need to extend the mortgage at all? Clearly there was something going on she didn't know about. Was he in some sort of financial difficulty? She frowned. The idea seemed incredible. Mark wasn't struggling – he couldn't be. He earned a huge salary and lived like he did, albeit in the best of taste.

She thought back over the past few weeks. Had anything changed? Was he behaving any differently, so far as money was concerned? No, she didn't think so. True, he hadn't been talking about anything expensive like updating the car or booking a holiday, but the way he spent money day to day was the same: they went out to dinner just as often and he took black cabs without thinking. He'd bought her one of the huge hand-tied bouquets of flowers from the stall near Aragon House last weekend and, having bought one herself for her mother's birthday, Hannah knew how expensive those were. And he'd come home with two new shirts last week; if he were really under the financial cosh, would he still be shopping on Jermyn Street?

Perhaps it wasn't him who was in trouble but

DataPro. Maybe he was borrowing money on his personal account to pump back into the business. How could she find out? She'd have to ask, and if he was hiding this new mortgage from her, he evidently didn't want her to know. But again, she was confident that DataPro wasn't in trouble. They'd talked a lot about the recession and how it was affecting the business, and he'd told her several times that things had slowed a bit but were steady. Though they weren't huge accounts, they'd signed two new clients since the beginning of last month, and there was the prospect of the one in New York, too. 'Flat but comfortable,' was what Mark had said.

She dropped the papers back into the box and leafed through the next few, seeing letters from Jupiter Asset Management and UBS, Santander and Kent Reliance. *'Dear Mr Reilly,'* read the one from Santander. *'Thank you for your letter dated 24 October. I am pleased to confirm that following your request, your two-year fixed-rate savings account will now be closed and the final balance transferred to your linked bank account.'* She flicked back through the others and they all said the same: his accounts would be closed and their final balances – minus, in two cases, interest penalties for withdrawing the money before the end of fixed terms – would be transferred to his current account. None of the balances were huge by the standards of someone with a salary like his, but in total he would have about £73,000.

Hannah experienced a wave of something close

to nausea. What the hell was going on? What was he doing? Why was he marshalling all this money?

Another woman, said the insidious mental voice, but she dismissed it. Why would he need to gather his money together if he were having an affair? It didn't make sense. *It does if he's planning to leave*, said the voice. *Maybe he's got a mistress and he's going to use the money to buy another house, one where she can live and he can visit her until he's summoned up the balls to leave you.*

Stop it – just stop it! This was insane – she was thinking like some sort of madwoman. Mark wasn't having an affair; he didn't have a mistress. A mistress, for Christ's sake – what sort of concept was that, anyway? This was London in the twenty-first century, not Paris in the nineteenth. And Mark wouldn't bother with a protracted lie like that, another woman, another house. He wasn't that sort of man. If he wanted to be with someone else, he'd just tell Hannah and be done with it.

Pushing the chair back, she stood up and walked to the window. She leaned forward until her forehead rested against the cold glass. She was hot and her heart was beating quickly. She focused on the coldness against her skin and tried to think. If not another woman and not DataPro, then what?

Debt. She stood up straight again, lifting her face away from the glass. What if he was in debt? Yes, that made more sense; that rang much truer than the idea of his having someone else. What if he had debts he was ashamed of, and couldn't bear her to find out?

Mark was someone who took risks; she'd always known that. Look at this place, DataPro: how many other twenty-three-year-olds came out of university, hired two of their contemporaries and offices in London, and started touting their services around the major financial players of the City? She would never have had the nerve to do that. Instead, she'd worked her way up in companies where the financial gambles were taken by other people and she could be sure of being paid at the end of the month. The idea of setting up her own business hadn't even crossed her mind at that age.

Yes, some sort of financial gamble, a risk that he'd taken and regretted – the idea took root. He loved brinksmanship, pushing his luck: she'd seen it even that very first afternoon in Montauk, when he'd swum out beyond the breakers. The current was strong all along the beach there; even very confident swimmers came unstuck against it. Now Mark was forty, he was less of a daredevil physically, he said, but over dinner the other day his friends the Kwiatkowskis had told her about the ski trips they used to go on together, before their sons Charlie and Paddy were born.

'Well, we say we went on holiday together,' Pippa had said, resting her elbow carefully on the table among the glasses and empty cheese plates, 'but really we only saw Mark to speak to after dark. Dan and I would be pottering round on the blue runs, nerving ourselves up to try a red run on day three, and we'd see Mark from the ski lifts, all in black like the man from the Milk Tray ads, hurtling past on his snowboard as if the hounds of hell were after him or something.'

'There was this one afternoon,' said Dan, 'where I was literally thinking about the protocol for repatriating his body – would we have to go through the embassy or would the insurance company sort it out? Pip and I were feeling pretty smug – we'd just done this hairy red run and we were—'

'Hairy!' Mark laughed. 'It was a nursery slope.'

'It was the hardest of the red runs, pal. Anyway, we were getting the lift back up and we saw him coming down this black run. Jesus . . .' Dan shook his head. 'One side of the run was fairly smooth, steep as hell, obviously, but at least it was covered in snow. The other half . . . Basically, it was a rock-face with a bit of snow here and there, where there was actually enough of an angle for it to stick on. Bear in mind this was the first week your husband had ever used a snowboard – we watched him come down that thing and I reckon the board must have made contact with the run only six times. He was bouncing from crag to naked crag – it made me feel sick just to watch.'

Hannah turned her head and looked at the river, her heart beginning to slow down. Debt . . . If that was it, how had he got into it? A bad investment? It couldn't just be something straightforward gone wrong. If he'd put money into a unit trust or something and it had tanked, it wouldn't have left him in debt; he'd just have lost what he'd invested. And it would have been money he'd had to start with: you didn't borrow to make that sort of investment; the returns weren't high enough. You'd have to pay all the fees and then enough to cover the interest on the loan before you even started to think about a profit. And Mark would regard something like a unit trust as a staid, long-term investment, she was sure, steady, not spectacular. No, he definitely wouldn't have borrowed money to do that.

Something higher risk, then, less regulated. Had he been spread betting? That was a quick way to get into serious trouble. You could open these accounts with an online broker, she'd read about them, where you started without depositing any money and just ran your account until they asked you to settle up, betting on things to go up or down half a point – shares, commodities, currencies, whatever was going – betting against yourself so you spread the risk, changing your positions every day, every hour, every few minutes, even. What if he'd got into that? She could imagine it, Mark online at the office, playing the market just for the buzz of it. He could have done that and made a miscalculation, or just have been called away to do something urgent without closing his position, and come back to find himself thousands and thousands in hock.

But it needn't be that, either: once you moved in the kinds of circles he did, there were countless ways to make and lose money. He knew so many entrepreneurs and speculators, and he was always talking about someone or other with a new project in the works who was looking for venture capital. Only a few days ago he'd been talking about a guy who was trying to raise cash to set up a TV production company, and last month there had been someone who was buying mining land in Brazil. What if Mark had decided to remortgage the house, empty his savings and invest in something like that? Well, if he had, shouldn't he perhaps have mentioned it? 'Pass the marmalade, would you, Han? Oh, and by the way, I've decided to put half a mill into a Kazakhstani oil pipeline. I'm having to remortgage the house but no need to worry your pretty little head about it, sweetheart.'

In the quiet of the office she heard herself snort. Maybe that *was* it – the scale on which he operated surprised her less and less these days. Immediately, though, she remembered something else. About once a month in New York, he and a group of four or five friends had had poker evenings. Generally, Mark came home half-cut afterwards and she'd assumed that the poker was really just an excuse for them all to get together and have a few beers. One night, though, he'd got in some time after two and put fifteen hundred dollars on her bedside table and she'd realised that they played seriously. Teddy, who'd lost most of the fifteen hundred, Mark said, had been chilly with both of them until the next poker evening, when the tide had turned somewhat and he'd gone home a thousand richer at Ant's expense, much to Roisin's fury.

What if this was down to gambling? Could something that had started off as a bit of a laugh have escalated into something more serious? Maybe when she thought he was at business dinners he was really at casinos. Maybe he'd had a big win and got addicted. On the other hand, was he really the kind of person to keep beating his head against a brick wall when he was losing? Would he do that, Mark, keep telling himself that the next big win was one more bet away – then one more?

She turned away from the window, went back to the box-file and lifted the pile of paperwork out on to the desk. Nothing in the Coutts statement suggested he was gambling; there were no transactions with anything that sounded like a casino or a bookies or, as far as she could tell, any online gambling site. There were no huge cash withdrawals, either, just the £250 he took out once a week or so for newspapers and drinks and cabs. She set the statement and the mortgage letter aside and flipped quickly through the rest of the papers, looking for anything that related to debt – letters about loans or demands for payment. There was nothing, though. Even his three credit cards weren't maxed out: together, they had a combined balance of just under seven thousand pounds, which, when your finances worked on Mark's sort of level, was nothing at all.

She flicked through the last few papers, Coutts and Mastercard statements from over a year ago, her eyes still skimming the transactions but no longer really expecting to find anything relevant. When she turned over what she thought was the last sheet, however, her hand stopped in mid-air.

In front of her on the desk, the very last piece of paper in the file, was a statement from Birmingham Midshires. Mark didn't bank with Birmingham Midshires, though. She did.

She picked up the paper, noticing a slight tremor in her hand, and looked at the name and address in the top left-hand corner. Her name, not Mark's. She looked at the date. It was the most recent statement, the one she'd been sent at the end of the tax year in April, showing her new balance with the year's interest added: just under £47,000. She remembered opening it, feeling frustrated by how low the interest rates were then filing it away in her accordion file. So why was it here? Why was it in Mark's box?

The tremor in her hand magnified and she slapped the statement down on the desk, the sound startling her. There was no other explanation: the only way the statement could be in his file was if he'd taken it out of hers and put it there.

She glanced at the clock above the door. How

long had she been here? David would be back with his lunch any minute, surely. Well, that was a risk she'd just have to take, wasn't it? If he came in and found her, she'd think of something. She couldn't wait until she got home; she needed to know now.

Pulling the chair up to the desk, Hannah opened Mark's laptop and turned it on. A few seconds passed and then a dialogue box appeared demanding a password. *Shit.* Well, of course it was going to be password-protected, wasn't it? DataPro was one of the most sophisticated corporate software-design companies in Europe. Glancing at the clock again, she tried to think. Numbers, not just letters or a word: she'd got a telling-off about that when he discovered she used MalvernHills as the password for her Hotmail account. Leaning forward, she tapped in his birthday, 110772, and hit return. *The password you have entered is incorrect. Please re-enter your password.* She thought again then tapped in her own birthday. Wrong again. *Shit, shit.* How many chances did she have before the system shut itself down? Would it send out an alert? One more go, she decided: three strikes and you're out. She closed her eyes and focused. Numbers *and* letters, she realised, not one or the other; personally significant but not legal data. She opened her eyes. It was a long shot but – yes, it felt right. She typed in the name and street of their old favourite hotdog restaurant in New York: Westville10. Heart thumping, she hit return. *Bingo.*

The computer was beyond fast and within four or five seconds she had the browser open and was typing in 'Birmingham Midshires'. When the page came up, she reached for her bag, got out her diary and flicked to the back where her codes and passwords were written down. Yes, she knew you weren't supposed to, but how else were you supposed to keep track of them all? She could spend her whole life trying to remember the answers to her 'personalised security questions'. Well, she thought bitterly, maybe she was about to learn her lesson the hard way.

She hit the 'Log in' button and entered the passwords. She had codes for four airlines' frequent-flyer programmes, Amazon, iTunes and numerous other sites for online shopping, but her banking arrangements, at least, were simple: this ISA, her HSBC current account, and then, also managed via HSBC, two thousand shares in a tech company that she'd bought three years ago on a hot tip. She'd paid two pounds each for them but the last time she'd looked, last week, they'd been worth £120 in total.

She hit 'return' and the page with her account details started to open. Suddenly she didn't want to see. She pushed the chair back and stood up. Her heart was thumping behind her sternum. She rested her head against the cold window and closed her eyes. When she opened them again, she saw a man jogging up the steps to the entrance seven storeys below. David.

Quickly, she came back to the computer, took a breath and looked at the screen.

She'd expected it – really, from the moment she'd found her statement she'd known – but that didn't make it any less shocking: her ISA had been cleared out. The balance onscreen now read £29.02. She stared at it until the numbers blurred in front of her eyes. £29.02. She clicked on the link to her recent transactions and there it was, four days earlier: a transfer to M. J. Reilly of £46,800. It was gone – he'd taken it all.

CHAPTER 6

The glass panels shook as the front door slammed behind her. Still in her coat, Hannah sat down at the foot of the stairs and put her head in her hands. A sharp stabbing pain had started behind her left eye and was spreading across her forehead. It was so intense she thought she might throw up.

On the way back from Hammersmith, the shock had been joined by a feeling of intense loss. Her savings, everything she'd managed to put aside in the fifteen years she'd been working, were gone. Before she'd met Mark, her ISA had been her flat-deposit fund, the money she'd planned eventually to use for buying a place of her own. New York prices were mad, of course, and she'd loved her rented apartment and hadn't wanted to move to a different, cheaper area, so she'd put it off and put it off and then she'd met Mark and that had been it. All that work, she thought now, all those months of little transfers, especially at the beginning, just after university, when she was living in London for the first time and had no real money to spare. Determined to be independent, though, and never ask her parents for anything again, she'd opened a savings account and set up a direct debit of £75 a month. She'd watched it slowly accumulate, feeling proud and in control; as soon as she'd got her first small pay-rise, she'd increased the direct debit to £100. Her first-ever bonus, too, £300 – she'd bought a pair of cheap winter boots, then resisted temptation and salted the rest away.

Now came a hot sweep of panic: she was broke – completely broke. She had about £250 in her current account, the near-worthless shares and £29.02: less than £400 in total. And without a job, she had no way of earning any more: there was no salary coming in at the end of the month. She was sweating, she realised, her armpits were wet, and a string of adjectives was running through her head: stuck, screwed, powerless. Fucked.

Needless to say, she hadn't been able to get out of DataPro without being seen by David. She'd called the lift then stood in the lobby and watched the numbers on the overhead panel as it climbed towards the seventh floor, agonisingly slow. At last the doors pinged open and, without looking up, she'd stepped in and almost collided with him as he came out. *Shit.* She'd had a momentary impression of his body warmth and a sharp, lemon-soap scent before he moved away with a short laugh of embarrassment, his hand on her forearm holding her away from him as much as greeting her.

'Hi.' He'd pressed the button to stop the doors

closing and let go of her arm. She'd stepped back out into the lobby and he'd followed her. He was smiling, his expression friendly but curious. 'Hannah – lovely to see you.'

'You, too,' she said. 'How are you? Tony said you were in.'

'Yes, just popped out to get a bite to eat.' He'd lifted the evidence, a brown-paper bag spotted with grease. He was in weekend wear: jeans and a brushed-cotton plaid shirt with a faded T-shirt underneath, a pair of Adidas shell-toes. She couldn't remember ever having seen him out of a suit before. He was thirty-eight, she knew, but today he'd looked about twenty-five.

'Saturday afternoon in the office?' she said.

'I'm doing projections, whipping some figures into shape before we meet Systema. Mark's told you about their approach, obviously?'

'Yes, of course. Interesting times.'

'Could be. I'll be here most of the weekend anyway. How about you, though? I thought you two were going away?'

'To Rome?'

'Yes.'

'Oh, that's still a couple of weeks off yet, unfortunately.'

He'd looked confused for a moment but then his face cleared. 'Oh, I see. Well, if you're here, you can't be there, can you?' He smiled. 'Is Mark with you?'

'Mark? Er – he's at home.'

'Oh. Right.'

Hannah had seen the question in his eyes. 'He's shattered, I think,' she'd said. 'He'll probably be zonked out in front of the TV when I get back.' She patted her bag hammily. 'He left our electricity bill here by mistake last week – got it mixed up with some other papers. I've just been to Westfield for a bit of shopping and said I'd pop in and pick it up on my way back so we can pay it before we get cut off. Usual domestic chaos.' Her laughter had come out sounding a lot more convincing than it had felt.

'Right,' David had said again, but the unasked question had lingered in the air between them: if Mark was in London, why was he at home on the sofa while David was spending all day at the office?

In the kitchen Hannah stood at the sink and downed three Aspirin with a large glass of water. Mixed with the shock and hurt was another feeling now: fear. Yes, she admitted to herself, she was afraid. What the hell was going on? If Mark needed her money so badly, why hadn't he just asked for it? They were married, they loved each other, didn't they? They were supposed to be a team, to support each other. If he'd asked her for it, she would have given it to him straight away. Why just take it like this unless he didn't want to tell her the reason – or couldn't?

What if he was in trouble? Not just money trouble, *real* trouble. What if he'd crossed someone dangerous?

For a moment the idea seemed ludicrous – *someone dangerous? Come on, Hannah, back to the real world* – but then she remembered a story that Paul, a friend of Dan's, had told over dinner the other day. He was in commercial property and the company he worked for, a specialised arm of one of the large estate agencies, had started doing business in Russia, going over and giving presentations to super-wealthy Muscovites to convince them to buy investment property in London. The presentations had been a success and they'd been hired to find properties for several new clients, but afterwards, Paul said, one of the clients had refused to pay their commission. It was a substantial amount, nearly half a million, and Paul's company had chased and chased and eventually instructed their lawyer. Soon after starting work, however, the lawyer had come back and advised them quietly to write the money off. If they didn't, the implication was, the repercussions would be violent.

Could Mark have got himself into something like that? DataPro did a lot of business overseas, and they'd handled a couple of projects for new Eastern European clients earlier in the year. What if one of them had refused to pay, he'd pursued it and they'd come after him? But why not tell her something like that? There would be no reason to hide it. And anyway, in that scenario, they would owe him, not the other way round.

Gambling made more sense. What if Mark was in debt to violent people and they were threatening to mess him up? She exhaled sharply through her nose. It was ridiculous – she was being ridiculous. What next, the Mob?

She stalked the room, successive waves of anger and panic breaking over her. She fended them off by focusing on what she could do. She could call the office and talk to David. If it were something to do with DataPro, he would know. But actually, would he? He'd thought they were both in Rome: Mark had lied to him, too. And what if it were nothing to do with the company? She liked David as far as she knew him, but that was hardly at all – she couldn't stand the idea of him knowing their personal business and thinking there were problems in their marriage. And what if there was a simple explanation for all this – there still could be, couldn't there? – and Mark returned to discover she'd involved his business partner?

She thought about his financial paperwork. She should have brought it back with her and gone through it here, line by line. She'd looked as carefully as she could in the office but she'd been too flustered, too shocked. Unlike her, as far as she knew, Mark wasn't stupid enough to keep a written record of all his banking passwords so she couldn't access his accounts online. She'd have to wait until tonight, somehow make sure David had left the office and then go back there. Unless . . . .

On the hall table was the pile of Mark's post. Hadn't there been a letter for him from Coutts this morning? She ran into the hall, picked up the pile and flicked through it. Yes, here it was. She dropped the rest of the letters and clutched it to her chest. It was just a normal window envelope, plain white paper, not one of the glossy pamphlet things advertising a promotion. It would be a letter about his account or a statement. She hesitated. They never opened one another's post – why would they? And if she opened this now, she'd have to get rid of it afterwards: she wouldn't be able to explain having opened it.

She looked at it a second longer then stuck her finger under the flap and ripped the envelope apart. Inside were three sheets of paper, his monthly statement. Her eyes ran down the transactions but nothing jumped out: no big transfers, no bookmakers, no La Perla or hotels. But if Mark were staying at hotels with another woman, she realised, he'd pay on his DataPro card so there'd be no risk of her seeing. She felt a rising sense of hopelessness. The statements for his business accounts went straight to the office; it would be nearly impossible for her to access them.

Back in the kitchen, she smoothed the statement out on the table and went through it item by item, Biro in hand. There were the new shirts, the gas bill, their supper at Mao Tai last Tuesday, the tickets for *La Bohème*. There was a payment to the delicatessen at the top of the street, and then the butcher's shop next door for the ribs of beef they'd had a couple of weeks ago. Lea & Sandeman, the wine merchants, and the private gym

Mark used in Chelsea; £25 to W. H. Smith at Heathrow Terminal Three, for books, no doubt. She could identify almost everything, and by the time she reached the end there were only two transactions with Biro crosses next to them: a payment on the second page to someone or something called Trowell and then, near the bottom of page three, another to or at 'Woodall'.

Reaching for her laptop, she typed 'Trowell' into Google. The first hit was a link to Wikipedia, the snippet of text underneath telling her that Trowell was a village in Nottinghamshire. She scanned down, seeing links to a garden centre, a definition of 'trowel' in an online dictionary, and then links to social networking sites and people with the surname Trowell. She looked back at the statement. There were no initials, no obvious indication that the payment had been made to a person, though that didn't rule it out.

She typed in 'Woodall'. This time the first hit was a link to a site of motorway service stations. She skimmed down the page. The next was a Wikipedia entry for William Woodall, politician, 1832–1901, and the third another Wikipedia entry, this one for Woodall, 'a small hamlet in the civil parish of Harthill, with Woodall situated in the metropolitan borough of Rotherham, South Yorkshire, UK'.

She went back to the search bar at the top and added 'Trowell'. When she hit return this time, the first thing she saw was a link to a trivia site, and a line of text underneath that read: 'Which motorway has service stations named Woodall, Trowell and Tibshelf?' The answer, which appeared straight after the question, eliminating any fun to be had in guessing, was the M1.

Hannah stood up and went to the pinboard. She unhooked the calendar and brought it back to the table. The payment at Trowell had gone out on 12 October, the one at Woodall on 26 October, both Fridays. In the little squares for both days, Mark's large, confident handwriting read *Germany – Frankfurt*.

CHAPTER 7

Though it was nearly eight o'clock, Knightsbridge was still clogged with traffic, no more than two or three cars at a time making it through the lights. The couple in the seat in front were riding the bus like a bumper-car, leaning against each other, their feet up on the plastic ledge that separated them from the glass expanse of the enormous windshield, his feet encased in grimy trainers, hers bare in a pair of canary, yellow patent-leather heels that Hannah, feeling like an old woman, thought she'd regret within the hour. Thermals from the heater underneath their seat carried back a woody, masculine scent that Hannah recognised as Gillette body-spray: she'd had a boyfriend at college for a week or two who'd worn it.

The boy turned to look out of the window, adjusting his arm beneath the fake-fur trim of his girlfriend's hood. The bus was now inching its way past Harvey Nichols, where the windows were already dressed for Christmas. Against a backdrop of glittering silver cloth, a mannequin in an exquisite gothic lace dress swung on a trapeze with an insouciance suggesting she was already several glasses into the bottle of champagne dangling from her stiff plastic fingers. In the next window along, another sat astride a golden reindeer in nothing but flimsy silk underwear and heels, a male mannequin in full evening dress, shoes and all, pressed indecently close behind her, the sex pest at an absinthe-fuelled office party.

How long was it now until Christmas? Six weeks or thereabouts. God, she'd barely given it a thought. Last year, they – she and Mark – had spent the holidays with her mother in Malvern. As children, she and Tom had alternated between their parents, spending Christmas Eve and the day itself with one, moving to the other's house for Boxing Day and the rest of the long week that stretched towards New Year's Eve, changing the order the following year. Since they'd been adults, however, and especially while she'd been in America, Hannah had felt that she should spend the day itself with her mother. Dad had Maggie, and Chessa and Rachel, her two daughters from her first marriage, who always turned up in what Dad called their 'charabancs' with their own blonde daughters, two apiece, and their husbands, and the collection of semi-wild dogs that Chessa serially adopted from animal-rescue centres.

Though her own plans hadn't been negotiable – it was Tom's turn to spend Christmas with Lydia's family, and her mother would be left alone if she didn't go – Hannah had hesitated to ask Mark to come with her last year. She'd wanted to spend the holiday with him but had struggled to imagine him in the little red-brick railway worker's cottage which her mother had moved into after the divorce and had barely changed since, where even the air seemed trapped, heavy with regret and the sense of a life tentative and half-lived. The previous year, lying on the bed in her old teenage bedroom, the sound of *The Archers* seeping up through the kitchen ceiling, the word moribund had come into Hannah's mind. What would Mark, with all his energy, think of the place? But then, she'd thought, her mother's house was part of her, Hannah's, life, too. It was where she'd spent half her childhood. If they were going to have a future, she had to trust Mark and let him in.

She'd waited until a Friday at the very end of November, when she'd met him at JFK and they were lying in bed in her apartment, catching up on each other's news and ignoring the rumbling in their stomachs that indicated it was time to get up, face the cold and go round the corner for hotdogs at Westville, their habitual post-airport, post-bed spot. She'd broached the subject gingerly but Mark had pulled her on to his chest, tucked her hair behind her ears so that it was out of his face and said simply, 'I'd love to come with you.'

'Really?' she'd said, sounding very surprised.

'Of course. I was beginning to feel offended you hadn't asked.'

'Oh.' That idea hadn't occurred to her.

'I'm joking. But of course I want to spend

95

Christmas with you, and I want to meet your mother. Both your parents.'

Happy – and relieved – she'd kissed him and he'd slipped his hands down her spine and kissed her in return. 'I want to know you,' he'd said.

'You do know me.' She'd sounded indignant, hating the implication that he didn't already, the distance between them that implied.

'*Really* know you: the difficult bits as well as all the fun stuff.' He kissed her again, for longer this time. 'I want to see where you grew up – I want to get to know your mother. And I like the idea of being there. Not just *with* you but – you know what I mean. I know you don't find Christmas easy. If I'm there, maybe I can . . .'

To her shame, Hannah had felt a lump form in her throat. 'It's not that I don't . . . It's just that Mum's always so sad.' Her voice croaked slightly and she coughed to disguise it. 'She tries to hide it but it's worse at Christmas, especially because she knows my dad's mobbed with people and . . .'

Mark had tipped her sideways so she was resting inside his arm, her head on his shoulder. She'd felt his breath in the parting of her hair. They'd lain like that for a couple of minutes, neither of them talking, until it dawned on her how selfishly she'd thought about the whole issue.

'Where do you go?' she'd asked him quietly. 'Normally, I mean?'

She'd felt his chest rise and fall. 'Last year I went to Dan and Pip's,' he said. 'That was fun – Pip's a great cook, as you'll see, and all her clan was there, and their little boy Charlie was playing in the boxes and ignoring his actual presents. You can imagine.'

She pressed further, as gently as she could. 'How about before that?'

'Well,' he said, 'when I was with Laura I spent it with her – once just the two of us in London, once at her parents' in Somerset.' Hannah felt her usual flare of irrational jealousy at his ex's name. 'But last year,' he said, 'I was on my own. I've done three Christmases on my own, actually – I realise that makes me sound like a miserable bastard . . .'

'No.'

'I don't know, it's just a weird time, isn't it? Since my parents died, I haven't really felt like it. It was her thing, you know, my mum – she loved it, looked forward to it from about June on. She used to make so much effort: home-made Christmas puddings and mince pies and a huge *Stollen* and these little decorations that she'd had since we were children, all carefully wrapped up again in tissue on Twelfth Night.' Mark's profile was silhouetted against the glow of the lamp on her bedside table and she could see that the muscle in his jaw had set hard.

'I'm sorry,' she said. 'I didn't mean . . .'

'No, it's fine, it's good. It's nice to remember. Poor Mum.'

Hannah hesitated before she asked, 'What about your brother?'

He'd turned his head sharply, almost dislodging her from his shoulder. 'What about him?'

'I mean, you're not in contact at Christmas? You don't ring each other once a year, just to . . .?'

'No.'

Seconds passed, and through the open door she heard the last bars of the Wilco album playing on her iPod in the sitting room.

'What?' said Mark, and she was surprised by the brusqueness of his tone.

'Nothing. I was just trying to imagine what it would be like not being in touch with Tom, and I can't – he's like this unchangeable fact of my life. In a lot of ways he's my best friend as well as my brother.'

Mark shrugged. 'You're lucky.'

And without Tom, she'd thought but hadn't said, she might not at that moment have been lying in bed with Mark, inviting him to Malvern, letting him into her life in a way she'd never done with anyone before.

Just after Christmas the year previously, before his school term had started up again, Tom had flown back with her to New York for five days. He wanted to see *her* New York this time, he'd said, not the Empire State Building and Grand Central and the Met; he'd done the obligatory-landmark circuit. So they'd spent the days walking for miles in the excoriating cold, stopping for coffee at Joe's and Oren's Daily Roast, hot chocolate at the City

Bakery. She'd taken him to the Strand for used books and then down to McNally Jackson and the Tenement Museum on Orchard Street, which he'd loved. On his last full day, they'd had dumplings for a dollar apiece on Ludlow and then walked on down through Chinatown to join the throng of tourists on Brooklyn Bridge in the afternoon. They'd leaned on the railing beneath the great central arches, the intense winter light over the East River almost burning their eyes as it reflected off the water and the gleaming glass canyons of Lower Manhattan. Beyond, the new World Trade Center was still under construction but already dwarfed them all.

They'd stood shoulder to shoulder for several minutes, watching the Staten Island ferry ply back and forth, a small tanker rounding the tip of Manhattan on its way up the Hudson. Some brave souls were out in a yacht, its sail a sharp white triangle against the prevailing blue. A sudden gust of wind had blown the ends of her scarf into her face and Hannah had straightened up and shoved her hands into her pockets. 'Come on, Thomas, let's get moving. We'll solidify if we stand here much longer.'

Tom, however, had said nothing and stayed put.

'Did you hear me, cloth ears? Let's go.'

He'd shaken his head. 'There's something I need to say.'

'So let's walk and talk.'

'No, let's stay here a minute.'

She'd squeezed in next to him at the railing again and glanced at his face. He'd looked serious, almost grim, and she'd started to feel worried. What was he going to tell her? Was he ill? Was it Dad? Mum? She'd jostled him, needing to leaven the sudden atmosphere. 'Enough of this mystery – say your piece.'

'Han,' he said, turning to her, 'I think you should stop messing around.'

'Messing . . .? What are you talking about?'

'With men. Relationships. You're wasting your time.'

She laughed. 'Have you been talking to Mum? Has she put you up to this?'

Tom's expression stayed utterly serious. 'No. This has got nothing to do with her. This is what I think.'

'Oh, no,' she'd groaned and thrust her hands deeper into her pockets. '*Et tu, Brute?* Just because I'm thirty-three – there's more to life than marriage and babies, you know.'

'I do know. But that doesn't mean those things aren't worth having. You know I'm proud of you, I think your career's amazing, we all do, but . . .'

'But what?' The wind whipped her voice away, made nothing of the steely note she'd put into it.

'It's a waste if you don't have someone to appreciate it with.'

'Oh, come on . . .'

'I mean it. I want you to be happy.'

'I am happy!'

'But you could be happier. You don't need to prove anything to anyone any more, Hannah. You don't need to prove you can do everything on your own. I know it's all to do with Mum, and making sure you're never in her position, but—'

'It's got nothing to do with her,' Hannah had replied, her voice suddenly savage. '*Nothing*. I'd never be like she is.'

'Reacting against her is still a response to her – it's still . . .'

'I'm not *reacting against her*,' she cut him off. 'I'm not trying to prove anything – anything at all. This is about me. *Me*. This is my choice. This is how *I* want to live.'

'Bullshit,' her brother said, and the expression in his eyes was hard. 'It's about her, and you're being a coward.'

She'd felt fury bubble up inside her. 'My God, I don't believe this. What the hell . . .?'

'You're being a coward. You fucked things up with Bruce and now you're too much of a coward to try again.'

She'd taken several steps backwards, away from him, and collided with a man taking photographs of his girlfriend. Hannah was too disorientated to apologise. Instead, she stared at her brother, not trusting herself to speak. Bruce – even then, years later, three thousand miles away, the name was like a punch in the guts. 'That's what you think of me, is it?' she said. 'That's really what you think?'

'Yes,' Tom had replied.

She'd felt a flare of pure rage. Hands shaking, she reached into her bag, detached her house keys from their leather strap and threw them at him. Caught off guard, he made a grab for them, but too late. They fell to the floor, where they settled in a perilous gap between the planks. 'Take them,' she said. 'You can have the apartment tonight. If that's what you think of me, I couldn't stand to be under the same roof as you.'

She'd expected him to soften, to move towards her and say something placatory, but instead he'd looked at her, his face hard. 'What will you do?' he said. 'Go to a bar and pick up some bloke to use for a few weeks until you realise you might actually like him?'

She'd stared back, as angry as she'd ever been in her life, then turned and started walking away, sticking her middle finger up over her shoulder. 'Fuck you,' she'd shouted, her voice eddying on the wind. 'Just . . . . fuck you.'

She'd waited for the quick footsteps behind her, the hand on her shoulder, but they hadn't come. Disciplining herself to look straight ahead, she'd marched back alone the way they'd just walked together, needing to run but thwarted by one ambling knot of tourists after another until she'd wanted to scream. Twice she'd strayed into the bike lane and almost lost an arm.

At the foot of the bridge she paused for a moment. What was she doing? Where was she going? Conscious that he might be watching and see her hesitate, she plunged across the road, crossed Broadway and headed into Tribeca. She'd walked until the cold made her face numb and her teeth started to ache, barely thinking, walking just to keep moving, with no plan or destination. She criss-crossed Tribeca, then SoHo, doubling back on herself, taking one street after another, the beat of her feet against the pavement drowning out the swirl of thoughts in her head. Finally, as the last of the daylight drained from the sky, she'd found herself in Hudson River Park, where the anger finally burned itself out.

She sat down on a bench and sank her face into her hands. It was shock, she told herself, that was all. She was shocked that Tom could talk to her like that; that he had these negative thoughts about her. She'd thought that he loved her, respected her. How wrong could she be? She'd felt a surge of defensive bitterness then. Stuff him – *stuff* him. If that was what he thought of her, then he could go to hell.

The last burst of fury kept her warm for a minute or two but then it, too, was gone and she heard the other voice, the one she'd been walking so furiously to shut out. *He's right*, it said, *and you know it. You messed up, it hurt, and you're too cowardly to put yourself on the line again.*

In her coat pocket she felt her BlackBerry buzzing for the eighth or ninth time and ignored it.

Bruce – when was the last time anyone had even said his name in her presence? It was years, three or four at least. But it had been seven years now since they'd split up. *Since you dumped him.*

Bruce was one of her brother's best friends, one of the small but tight group of mates he'd made when he started at university in London. Hannah had liked him as soon as she met him, the first time Tom had invited him and Ben and Adam up to Malvern for the weekend to go camping. She'd thought Bruce liked her, too, from the way he'd smiled at her and included her, asked what she was reading, but she hadn't stood a chance then: she was sixteen to his nineteen, years that made the difference between school and university, uniform and jeans every day, a child and an adult.

When she was at university herself, though, three years later, she'd come down to London for Tom's birthday party, a bash in the upstairs room of a pub somewhere in Brixton, and they'd talked the whole evening. At the end of the night he'd kissed her and asked for her number, and the following weekend he'd driven down to Bristol in his clapped-out Vauxhall Corsa, Maude, to see her. They'd been together for six years after that until she'd sensed that he was ready to do 'the grown-up thing', as she'd called it, her voice dripping sarcasm. 'I don't want to "settle down",' she'd shouted at him. 'I'm twenty-five, not forty. Where's the adventure? Where are the wild nights on a beach in Brazil? Where's the achievement? Where's my *life*?'

So she'd ended it and then watched as, within two years, he'd married someone much more successful than she was – apparently she was nice, too; Tom refused to say he didn't like her – and had a son. She had been on Facebook in a quiet moment at the office when she'd seen him and the baby, Arran, tagged in a mutual friend's photograph, and the pain had felt like someone had taken the paperknife off her desk and jabbed it up under her ribs.

Since then she'd been careful not to get too close to anyone. She liked men, their company, flirting, sex, but she couldn't allow herself, she thought, to get into a situation like that again. She had stuff to do – to prove. She couldn't let herself be sidelined by *biology*. Even the thought of it made her feel trapped, actually physically breathless. So instead she had fun. She met people, hung out with them for a few weeks, and then she moved on. They enjoyed it, she enjoyed it, no one got hurt. What was wrong with that?

In front of her, the Hudson glinted blackly, the lights of Hoboken glittering out of reach on the other side. She wrapped her arms across her chest, the heat she'd worked up inside her jacket dissipating fast. *Coward*, said the voice, louder now. *You think you're brave and independent, but really you're just afraid.*

In the end, so cold she couldn't feel her fingers, she'd stood up and walked slowly back to the apartment. She'd found her brother sitting on the stoop smoking the last of the packet of cigarettes he'd bought that morning. She'd climbed the steps between the glossy potted magnolias and sat down next to him, not pressing against him as she had on the bridge but three or four inches apart. A single yellow cab cruised along the street below them with its off-duty light on. After a minute or so, Tom had reached across and taken hold of her hand.

'It's still what I think,' he said.

'I know.' She'd gestured to him to give her the cigarette. She took two or three revolting puffs, felt her head spin then gave it back. 'You're right anyway,' she said. 'I am a coward.'

'That bit wasn't fair. I—'

'It was – no, it was. I'm afraid of . . . relying on anyone, being dependent. Not in control.' She'd never realised it consciously herself before, let alone said it aloud.

'Don't worry about it all so much,' he said. 'Take a risk: trust someone. Let them trust you.'

As she hurried along Shaftesbury Avenue towards Chinatown, now almost half an hour late, Hannah thought about what she was going to say, or if she was going to say anything at all. She wanted to – she needed to get this stuff out, stop it churning around in her head – and she wanted Tom's perspective on it, his calm good sense. But what she really wanted, she knew, was for him to tell her that she was overreacting and there would be a simple explanation for it all, and in her heart she knew he wouldn't do that. However much she wanted him to, Tom wouldn't lie to her; he never had.

And if she told him about Rome and Mark's phone being lost and his not being at his hotel and the missing – *taken* – money, it would all be out in the open. Real. And it could still be all right, couldn't it? There *might* still be a simple explanation – and then she would have made Tom think badly of Mark for nothing. *And,* said the voice in her head before she could stop it, *you'd have made him think he was right all along.*

'So, as you can see, I'm in a bit of a tight spot.'

Hannah picked a fragment of prawn cracker off the paper tablecloth and pressed it between her fingers until it turned into greasy dust. 'But if you've kept quiet about it so far,' she said, 'why say something now?'

'Well, that's it.' Tom dragged his hand through his hair, which was in need of a cut to prevent it from veering off into Leo Sayer territory. It was a perennial hazard: he had next to no interest in matters of the appearance and relied on the women in his life – their mother, Hannah and now Lydia – to tell him when he was getting beyond the pale. Lydia had been working away a lot recently.

'Hair,' Hannah said.

'Really? Already? I had it done . . .'

'Last year?'

He made an all-right-smart-arse face. 'No, the thing is, Paul told me yesterday that someone's

107

pointed the finger at one of the cleaning staff. She's Indian, I think, maybe Pakistani. Anyway, if it goes on she'll get fired – I don't think her English is good enough for her to mount much of a defence, frankly, and—'

'So you have to say something. And if this guy Luke took the money, if you're sure you saw him . . .'

'I'm sure. He knows I did, too. I backed out of there as fast as I could but he saw me. And – God, it's dreadful – he keeps giving me these pathetically grateful looks, as if he owes me everything.'

'Well, he kind of does, doesn't he, if you're keeping it under your hat?' Hannah pulled the last tissue-thin strip of damp paper from round the neck of her bottle of Tsingtao. Stolen money, she thought, more stolen money. *Taken* – she corrected herself.

'He's got two kids already, his wife's pregnant. If he's fired for pinching the trip money – it was three hundred pounds – what's he going to do? He'll never get another teaching job.'

Hannah looked at her brother, the two vertical lines scored between his eyebrows. 'You have to say something,' she said. 'You can't let an innocent woman take the rap.'

He sighed. 'I know. And I realise it's not much of a dilemma. I just feel shitty about it.'

'Think of it the other way round. She might have kids, too. She might be supporting her whole family.'

'If no one had suggested it was her, I would have let the thing lie. But you're right, I can't now. I'll talk to the Head on Monday.'

The waiter came to clear their dumpling plates and set their chopsticks on little china rests. With the side of his hand he swept away the curling shreds of Hannah's label.

'You'll feel better when you've done it,' she said after the waiter had disappeared.

Tom sighed. 'I doubt it.' He nodded at the empty bottle. 'Another one?'

The label gone, she went back to the remains of the prawn cracker, bisecting them with her thumb-nail until the pieces became indivisible. There was that thing, wasn't there, about how often you could fold something in half; was it the same for cutting or did that work differently? She thought about Mark's hands and how she'd used to watch them at the beginning – still did. They were always moving, always playing with something. Whenever she went out to dinner with him there'd always be some perfectly crafted little thing on the table by the time they finished. Once at the Italian place near her old apartment he'd made a miniature horse from the aluminium round the top of the wine bottle. She'd kept it and put it in her jewellery box. She'd looked at it yesterday.

'Earth to Hannah. Over. Are you reading me? Over.'

She looked up. Tom was scrutinising her, eyebrows raised. The new bottles of beer were on

109

the table; she hadn't noticed them arrive. She picked hers up and took a swig.

'Should I amuse myself for the rest of the evening?'

'Sorry.'

The waiter returned with their main courses. Hannah drew patterns in the top of the mound of rice while she waited for her skillet to stop its demonic bubbling. Tom engineered a great ball of noodles round the ends of his chopsticks and stretched his mouth almost indecently wide to accommodate it.

'Hmm,' he said, as soon as he was able to. 'I always think this place can't be as good as I remember, and it always is.' He took another giant mouthful and chewed. 'So, are you going to tell me what's going on?'

'What?'

'Something's on your mind. Is it the job-search?'

'No. I mean, yes, of course, but . . . Everything's fine, honestly. I'll find a job sooner or later. Everything's fine.'

He made a single upward nod, unconvinced, she knew, but not about to push it if she wasn't ready or willing to tell him. She pincered some beef, opened her mouth to eat it then put the chopsticks down. Across the table she saw him watch her as she took a long pull on the beer instead.

'Look,' she said. 'If I tell you something, do you promise me you won't judge?'

He frowned, dimly insulted. 'Of course. Anyway,

whatever it is, I can't think any less of you than I already do.'

'I'm being serious.'

'No, of course I won't judge you. What have you done?'

'It's not me. It's . . . It's something with Mark. It might be nothing. I'm almost certain it's nothing.'

Now Tom put down his chopsticks. 'What?'

Come on, Hannah, he's your brother. 'The thing is,' she said, 'I was expecting him to come home last night and he didn't.'

She told him the whole story, everything she'd discovered over the course of the day. He listened in silence, the vertical lines back between his eyebrows. When she told him about her savings, his eyebrows deepened momentarily into a dark V before, realising she'd noticed, he consciously straightened them again. When she'd finished, he was quiet.

'Well?' she said, the silence making her more nervous. 'What do you think?'

'It'll be something to do with the business, won't it?' he said.

She sat back in her chair, relief flooding her. 'That's what I thought. There's probably some cash-flow issue and he's using the mortgage money and his and my savings to tide them over while . . .' She trailed off, remembering the path her thoughts had taken in the office. The relief ebbed away. 'Actually,' she said, 'I don't think it's that. I think they're doing okay.' She thought of something new and lowered her voice, as if eavesdroppers from the business-software industry were seated at the tables around them, listening as if their lives depended on it. 'This is really confidential – don't ever let on to Mark I've told you – but they've been approached by one of their big rivals for a takeover, a buy-out. That wouldn't happen, surely, if the business was tanking? So they must be doing all right. They've got new clients, and I know they're being careful about spending in the recession, cutting overheads – it's the whole reason why I'm not in New York any more. Also, David thought we were in Rome, didn't he?'

'Does Mark tell him everything?'

'I don't know. Why lie to him, though, if he's involved?'

Tom grimaced slightly, acknowledging her logic.

Hannah thought about the service stations. 'And,' she said, 'what about the trips up the M1, if that is what they were? Why did Mark tell me he was in Germany if he wasn't?'

'What's this M1 thing? Where do you think he was going?'

She shrugged. 'No idea.' She put her elbows on the table and covered her face with her hands. 'Look, will you tell me if I'm being mad? I keep thinking about Mum, what she was like in the weeks before Dad left – before she drove him away, should I say? – and how I'm behaving exactly the same: sneaking about in Mark's office, reading his bank statements.' She lifted her head again and looked her brother in the eye. 'Am I nuts or do you think he's having an affair?'

Again Tom was quiet. Hannah waited. Please, she thought, lie. Just once, Tom, lie to me.

During supper she'd kept her BlackBerry in her bag, knowing that if she'd had it on the table, her eyes would have been going to it every few seconds. Under the circumstances, Tom wouldn't have minded but she hated it when people did that to her: it was so rude. Anyway, she hadn't been expecting Mark to ring again; she'd told him she might be out for dinner.

Now, though, giving her brother a final wave as the bus turned the corner, she got out her phone and saw a missed call. The number hadn't been recognised but the caller had left a message and when she listened, she heard Mark's voice.

Hi, sweetie. Just calling on the off chance of catching you before you meet up with Tom, if that's what you're doing. The fact that you're not picking up makes me think it is. Say hello from me. I'll give you a ring tomorrow. I love you.

The message had been left two and a half hours ago, just after eight thirty. She listened to it again in case she'd missed something – music, a woman laughing in the background – then deleted it. Probably he'd called then precisely because he knew he was unlikely to reach her.

She leaned her head against the window and closed her eyes. She thought about arriving home, how as she walked down Quarrendon Street from the bus stop, the house would be dark and empty. What if this was it? What if her marriage was over bar the shouting?

The idea swept away the anger and brought a wave of pure desolation in its place. Tears prickled under her eyelids and she blinked quickly, refusing to cry on the number 22 bus. She tried to distract herself, think about something else, but her mind wouldn't do it. Instead it offered a vision of a future without him, life as she currently knew it gone, no Mark, no job, no house, no plans. No love, no companionship, no more shared jokes, no warmth.

Warmth. She stopped on the word, turned it over in her mind. Yes, if he left her, that was what she'd really lose. She could rebuild the rest, find another place to live and a way to get by until she got her career back on track, but would she ever be able to replace the warmth, the colour, the sheer comfort she'd felt since she met him?

She had a sudden memory of their 'date' in Williamsburg, the night after he'd rumbled her in McNally Jackson. The warmth had already been there. He'd been waiting for her outside the venue wearing jeans and a pale cotton shirt, the sleeves rolled up to just below the elbow. As she'd rounded the corner he'd been on his BlackBerry but he'd looked up and seen her almost immediately, and a smile had spread across his face like sun across water.

All night she'd felt it. Three thousand miles from where she'd grown up, in a part of Brooklyn that she'd barely known, surrounded – with the exception of a few of her colleagues – by strangers, she'd felt at home. Every time she looked at Mark that night – while they had beers with Josh and Lily during the warm-up act, as they pressed a way to the front when Flynn's band came on, as he'd danced next to her during the encore, a decent indie cover of Lady Gaga's 'Bad Romance' – she'd felt warmth radiating off him. Later, outside, a few blocks from the club, he'd pulled her into the shadows at the side of a hipster boutique. The J train had clattered over the bridge above them on its way to Manhattan and the words *at last, at last* had gone through her head. He waited until the train was gone then put his hands round her waist and pulled her against him. When he kissed her, she'd had one thought: *I want this for the rest of my life.*

CHAPTER 8

'Come in, come in. This is a lovely surprise.' Pippa stood aside to let her in. 'Here, give me that.' She took Hannah's coat and slung it over the post at the bottom of the stairs. 'Come through. Excuse the mess.' She nudged a purple stuffed elephant towards the skirting board with the toe of her boot. 'I'm glad you rang. I'm here on my own – we've got Dan's mother for the weekend and they've taken Charlie to the Sunday Club at the cinema. They know it's the only way they stand a snowball in hell's chance of getting anything decent to eat later. Paddy's down for a nap so it's just me.'

Hannah followed the baggy seat of Pippa's jeans down the corridor with its white and green Victorian tiles. Every time she saw her, Hannah was struck anew by how tall Pippa was – five foot eleven, she said. Even in the battered UGG boots she had on now, she towered. There was a patch of something reddish on the back pocket of the jeans, pasta sauce maybe or ketchup, and both elbows of her navy jumper were worn into holes. Nonetheless, she looked good – insouciant, almost rakish.

In the kitchen Hannah took a stool at the counter while Pippa filled the coffee pot. The kitchen was about the same size as the one at Quarrendon Street and had similar double doors leading into a garden that was slightly bigger. While Hannah had managed to wrestle theirs under control, however, Pippa's was left wild. 'I'd love it to be a bit more civilised,' she'd said the first time Hannah had come round, reaching out to snap off a skinny runner from the rose that scrambled up the back of the house, 'but, you know, twenty-four hours in a day and all that.' Today a primary-coloured jumble of plastic toys collected the rain that had started to fall about an hour ago, and a ride-on tractor lay on its side, its moulded wheels gradually filling.

There was more chaos inside. Washing up was piled in the sink, and a bevy of old coffee cups had collected on the counter next to a net of sprouts. A polythene bag of muddy potatoes rested atop a pile of Sunday papers that was already devolving into a shaggy-edged nest. Next to it, perilously close to a small pool of spilled orange juice, was a handful of A4 sketches for *The Witches of Wandsworth*, the cartoon strip Pippa drew for the magazine given out free at Tube stations on Friday mornings. Her other strip, *Harrised*, adventures from the life of Emily, a woman terrorised by her three-year-old son, appeared in one of the big women's glossies. The end of the kitchen table bore evidence of potato printing – bowls of drying paint and a jam-jar of cloudy blue water – and a bowl of something mashed was browning on the tray of Paddy's high chair.

Pippa handed over a mug of coffee and nudged a carton of milk across the countertop. 'It's a good thing you rang. I said I'd stay behind and get some stuff done but I got sucked into this straight after they left and I haven't done a thing.' She tapped the cover of the thriller lying face down by the side of the chopping board. 'Have you read any of his? Don't: they're like crack. I bought this one yesterday afternoon at Nomad and I've barely spoken to anyone since. Dan had a go at me this morning for ignoring his mother.' She pulled a face. 'Do you mind if I carry on with this while we chat?' She tipped a colander of French beans on to the board and started regimenting them into lines, ready to top and tail.

'Anything I can do?'

'No, don't worry. So you were over doing a bit of shopping?'

'Just a birthday present I needed to pick up.' Here come the lies, Hannah thought. 'I quite often use Putney High Street. I like the compactness – everything close together.'

'It's good, isn't it? Much better than having to drag into town. Well, whenever you're over here, give me a ring. I'm always around at weekends.'

'Thanks, I will. Same when you're over our side of the river.'

Pippa looked up from the beans and smiled. She was the one of Mark's British friends Hannah had immediately liked the best. Pippa and Dan had been at Cambridge with him, and it was Dan Mark had called first with the news that he and Hannah were getting married. All the wives and girlfriends of his friends were nice people and they'd made her feel welcome, but Pippa was the one Hannah felt most connection with. That she didn't take herself at all seriously was a big part of it. A couple of the others – Marie, in particular – seemed to have had a sense of humour bypass in the labour ward and talked about their children with an awe usually reserved for irascible deities, apparently terrified of being struck by lightning should they so much as glance at a non-organic banana in Waitrose. Pippa had managed to remain human, despite Paddy and Charlie being only one and four.

'Booze,' she'd said frankly, when Hannah had asked her secret. 'The hardest thing about having a baby is the not drinking. I tell you, all I wanted when I was pregnant was a very large gin and tonic, and people looked at me like I was Stalin if I as much as said it. And all these toddlers who are sugar-free, gluten-free – *vegan*, for Christ's sake: the first time they have a cup of lemonade and a chocolate biscuit, their heads'll explode. Sometimes I listen to all these earnest conversations – I know they mean well, I do – but it makes me just want to . . . I don't know, drink five martinis and stand on the table smoking and flashing my knickers.'

Now, though, Hannah wondered what she was

going to say – how she could even start. In the car on the way over she'd rehearsed two or three possible opening gambits but, here in the relaxed fug of Pippa's kitchen, she couldn't see how any of them would work. Pippa was sharp: she'd be on to her straight away. And the last thing Hannah wanted was for any of this to get back to Mark. But Pippa was her best shot, and if any of his friends would know what was going on, it was Dan.

'So, what's up?' Pippa asked. 'How are things?'

'Oh, fine – good. Still haven't managed to find gainful employment, but I'm trying.'

'Bloody economy. I was talking to the *Post* about doing something for them but their budget's just been cut. Or that's what they're telling me, anyway.' She grinned. 'How's Mark? Is he away this weekend?'

'New York.' Or Rome. He could be in Paraguay for all she knew, Hannah thought. She felt a new surge of determination. She had to do it – she had to say something. 'Actually, Pip, I wondered . . . Taking the opportunity while he's not about . . . I don't know whether Dan's mentioned anything or whether Mark's said anything to you himself, but I'm a bit worried about him.'

Pippa looked up from sweeping the bean-ends into the waste disposal.

'I'm sure it's nothing and I'm overreacting, but he seems a bit . . . preoccupied.'

'Preoccupied?'

'I don't know . . . kind of stressed, I suppose. I

mean, he's working very hard, which is probably part of it, going to bed late, getting up early, burning the candle at both ends . . .' Hannah stopped, not wanting to over-egg it. 'I just wanted to make sure that's all it is, you know, that there's nothing worrying him.'

'If there was, he'd tell you, wouldn't he?'

'Normally I'd say yes but you know what he's like with that whole masculine, broad-shoulders thing. Maybe if there was something on his mind, he wouldn't tell me because he wouldn't want to worry me.'

'Hmm, yeah, I can see that. But no, he hasn't mentioned anything to us. I don't think Dan's spoken to him since you came over for dinner, actually.'

'Well, that's something. I suppose I'll just try and get him to ease up on the office hours, then.' Frustrated, Hannah took a sip of her coffee. This was hopeless, too vague. It was like trying to pick a lock with boxing gloves on. But she couldn't just come out and say it: discussing it with her brother was one thing, but telling Pippa, who would certainly tell Dan . . . Then again, no, thought Hannah. No. When she'd got home last night, she'd called the Ws again, just in case: no one with the name Mark Reilly was staying at any of them. She'd felt anger surge through her then: where the hell was he? Why hadn't he given her a contact number or any way of getting hold of him? What if she had an accident? What if the house burned down? *And what about the money?* asked the voice.

121

'Pippa, look,' she said. 'This is really awkward – I feel terrible bringing it up but . . . Mark's not supposed to be away this weekend.'

'What do you mean?' Pippa stopped, the colander poised under the tap.

Hannah thought about telling her his story about staying on for the second meeting, but then decided, why bother? It was so patently a lie. 'I was expecting him back on Friday night but he didn't show up at the airport.'

Instantly Pippa looked worried. 'Is he all right? Has something happened? Has he rung you?'

'No, he's all right. He rang me yesterday morning and he left a message last night, too. The thing is, he told me he's in New York but his colleagues all seem to think he's in Rome.'

Pippa put the colander aside, pulled out a stool and sat down. 'A mix-up?'

'That's what I thought first of all, but he told his assistant he was taking me away as a surprise. His phone's not working and he's not staying at his usual hotel. I've called all the others in the chain but he's not in any of them. If Dan were away and he'd lost his phone and he wasn't at his usual hotel, wouldn't he tell you and give you another number? What if there was an emergency and you needed to get hold of him?'

Pippa was quiet for several seconds, and the ticking of the giant wall clock above the table suddenly became audible. She laid her palms flat on the counter and looked Hannah in the eye. 'I

122

can see why you might worry,' she said, 'but don't – or try not to. There's no way Mark's messing around – he loves you. I've never seen him like this with anyone else, not remotely.'

'His ex, Laura . . .?'

'Laura? No – no way. She was all right and he tried, but his heart was never in it. Look, however dodgy all this seems when you put it together, there's going to be a simple explanation. Mark loves you – it's blindingly obvious.'

'Why lie, then? Why make up some codswallop story for his colleagues?'

'I've no idea. Maybe it's something to do with work or maybe there's just something on his mind and he needs a bit of time on his own. You know, I think that about being married sometimes. We expect it to be easy, just to be able to adjust to being part of this intense new thing, living with someone else, but it's not easy – in fact, it's bloody hard, especially now we all get married at such advanced ages.' Pippa pushed the sketches away from the pool of orange juice, apparently noticing it for the first time. 'God, you have no idea what I'd give for a bit of time alone, a couple of days' peace and quiet, walking on the beach somewhere, but I'd be missing Dan and the boys like mad every minute. It wouldn't mean I didn't love them. And Mark's so clever and he's always been so independent; he probably *needs* time alone now and again. Perhaps he hasn't told you in case it comes across the wrong way and he hurts you.'

'But—'

'Sweetheart, there's no way he's having an affair. End of story. He loves you.' She smiled. 'He's like Dan – one of the good guys.'

'I know. Yeah, I know.'

'Did he say when he'd be back?'

'Tuesday morning.'

'Talk to him then. But it'll be nothing, I promise you. Guarantee it.' Pippa stood up again and bent to get a saucepan out of the cupboard. She rinsed the beans and emptied them into it.

Watching her, Hannah felt a pang of envy. Whatever Pippa said – and she was grateful for her attempts to reassure her, she really was – it wasn't nothing. Pippa's life was going on as normal but hers, she felt, she *knew*, was about to change.

At the door, Pippa gave her a tight hug. 'You're sure you don't want to stay for lunch?'

'No, thank you. It's lovely of you to ask but I'd better get on.'

'Well, just look after yourself, okay? Try not to worry. Simple explanation – keep telling yourself that.'

'I will. Look, Pip, I've been meaning to say for ages: thanks for making me feel so welcome. It's strange, suddenly coming into a group of people who've all been friends since college. You've been so—'

'College?' Pippa looked surprised. 'Oh, we weren't at college together. Mark was three years ahead of us; he left Cambridge the summer before

124

we started. Dan met him a few years after we finished, through work. DataPro did a project for the bank.'

On Putney Bridge Hannah swerved to avoid a bus that was pulling out from the stop without indicating and almost hit a cyclist in the blind spot on her outside. The man was Lycra-covered and sinewy, his helmet a hi-tech pointed black thing that gave him an insectoid look. She wound down the window. 'I'm so sorry,' she said. 'The bus—'

'What the fuck? Why don't you look where you're fucking going?' He was older than she'd expected, fifty perhaps, and it made the language feel worse, more violent. His thin face was distorted with rage.

'I said I'm sorry. I didn't have a choice. And I didn't even touch you.'

'Stupid bitch!' He seemed to be gathering something in his mouth and for a moment she thought he was going to spit at her. Then the driver behind leaned on the horn and the cyclist's attention was distracted. She accelerated away quickly, icy air blasting through the window until she managed to get it wound up again.

Tears prickled in her eyes like they had last night, but this time, in the enclosed privacy of the car, she gave in to them. She blinked and they ran down her cheeks. Lie after lie after lie. Had Mark ever told her anything true? Why would he lie about when he met his friends? She was sure, absolutely sure, he'd told her that he and Dan and Pippa had been at Cambridge together, at the same time – she remembered a story about punting and a drunken picnic on the Backs. And if he'd lied about that, what else had he lied about? Perhaps he hadn't been to Cambridge at all, or any university. Perhaps he was just a compulsive liar, one of those people who couldn't stop themselves even when there was nothing to be gained by it. Maybe, she thought, she was about to discover that he was married to someone else and had a whole other family filed away somewhere.

Perhaps he was with them now. Whatever he was doing, wherever he was, it was a mystery to her. When she'd got in last night, she'd emailed Roisin. It had taken a while. To start with she'd written a screed, everything she'd discovered, blow by blow. Then, she'd highlighted the lot and hit delete. All these people with happy marriages – Roisin and Ant, Dan and Pippa, her brother and Lydia. She'd managed eight months, for three of which she'd lived in a different country. Tom was wrong – she was *just* like their mother. Actually, her mother had done years and years better.

In the end, her message to Ro had been a few lines. *I owe you a proper email – sorry – but in the interim I thought I'd better let you know that Mark's on the loose in NYC this weekend. He's lost his phone but he's got your number and says he might give you a call. Consider yourselves warned . . .* Roisin and her iPhone were inseparable, and her response

126

came within a minute: *Nice! Next time you talk to him, order him to* CALL US.

The rain was keeping people inside and the pavements of Quarrendon Street were empty. Hannah parked outside the house, turned the engine off and leaned her head against the steering wheel. She was exhausted; she hadn't slept at all last night. Instead, she'd lain awake next to the undisturbed sheets on Mark's side and been tormented by the stream of spiteful images that her mind had served up one after another.

Please, she'd thought, let him be in Rome: New York was *their* place. Her mind, however, had offered her picture after picture of Mark taking someone else round all their old spots. She saw him huddled at one of the tiny tables at Westville, reaching over the waxed tablecloth to take a woman's hand, his eyes never leaving her face; she imagined them having lunch at the Boathouse then walking through Central Park, bundled up in coats and hats and scarves, kicking up fallen leaves. No doubt she was beautiful, this woman, whoever she was, but in the images she stayed vague, faceless, a slim but curvaceous outline, with a soft laugh and long shiny hair.

Later, some time after three, Hannah had thought she was falling asleep – her thoughts started to wander, to leave her in peace – but at the last moment, just as she was about to tip gratefully over the edge into oblivion, she'd seen them in her bed, not here in London but in her old apartment on Waverly, Mark propped on one elbow talking, smiling, kissing this woman like he had kissed her there. At that instant the possibility of sleep disappeared completely, and she'd thrown the blankets off and stood up, heart pounding. Down in the kitchen, she'd drunk three cups of tea and surfed the net until she was glassy-eyed and the quiet hum of morning traffic started on the New King's Road.

Into the near-silence now came a trundling sound. Looking in the rear-view mirror Hannah saw the little boy from the house across the road pedalling furiously down the pavement on a tricycle, his mother running to keep up. Time to move; she couldn't sit outside in the car all day. She ran the ball of her thumb under her eyes and sniffed. As she reached for her bag on the passenger seat, however, her phone began to ring.

She pulled the bag on to her lap and scrabbled to find the phone before it stopped, almost dropping it in her hurry. On the screen was a Malvern number: her mother's. For a second or two Hannah considered not answering – she could call her back later, when she was inside and feeling a bit stronger – but then she felt guilty. To Sandy, making a phone call, even to her own children, was a big deal. She'd have made a cup of tea and put it on the little table at the end of the sofa before sitting down carefully, adjusting her glasses on the end of her nose and peering at the short list of numbers that Tom had programmed into her handset last year as if it were some arcane form of symbology.

'Hi, Mum.'

'Hannah?' Her mother sounded uncertain.

'Of course it is, you daft one – you called me. How are you?'

'Oh, fine, yes, I'm all right, darling. How are you? How's Mark?'

'Yes, we're well, both of us. Just having a quiet weekend.'

'That's good.' Her mother sounded relieved. 'I've been busy here. I went to Waitrose this morning and bumped into Mrs Greene. She asked after you both.'

'That was nice of her.' Mrs Greene had taught Hannah and Tom in kindergarten; it amazed Hannah that she remembered who they were all these years later. She'd only just retired; how many hundreds of children had she had under her care in the interim?

'And I've been making the Christmas pudding. The house smells like a distillery – the neighbours must be wondering what on earth I'm up to.'

'I hope you're trying some of it – the booze, I mean.'

'I'm not much of a rum-drinker, it's far too sickly, and I don't know anyone who drinks barley wine, do you? Where's Mark? Is he with you?'

'He's in New York, Mum. A business meeting.'

'On a Sunday?'

'No, tomorrow.' *Don't get defensive; she's not*

making a point; she doesn't know. 'He went over on Wednesday for a couple of others and then this one went in the diary at the last minute so he's stayed. He'll be back on Tuesday.'

'Good. That's good.' Again, her mother sounded relieved. Sometimes, Hannah thought, her mother seemed to interpret Mark's business travel as a sign of reluctance to be at home rather than a necessary part of running an international firm. Who knows, though? Maybe that was right.

For a mad moment, she thought about telling her mother everything, just laying it all out and throwing herself on her mercy. She wanted her support and sympathy; she wanted advice, to be told what to do. As quickly as it had come, though, the impulse was gone. It was impossible: there was no way she could reveal any of this. As soon as she let on even part of it, her mother would be proved right: she, Hannah, couldn't do it; she wasn't the sort of person who could hold down a relationship. She was too independent, too preoccupied with her career, too *selfish*. Somewhere deep in her psyche, unidentified but definitely real, something was wrong with her. Look at what had happened with Bruce; look at the disaster of the years after him. And now look at things with Mark: their marriage on the rocks in less than a year – barely more than half that.

And her mother loved Mark, absolutely loved him. Even beyond the gratitude she would have felt towards anyone who'd taken her spinster daughter off the shelf, Sandy adored him.

She'd met him for the first time at Christmas last year. Hannah had flown back from New York on the twentieth to spend a couple of days in London before going up to Malvern. Not wanting to leave all the preparation to her mother, she'd planned to take the train up a couple of days early; Mark would drive up on Christmas Eve. He, however, had got back from the office in the evening of the twenty-first and announced he'd closed DataPro early and would drive up with Hannah the next day.

If she was honest, she'd imagined his idea of helping would be to open bottles and distract them, but almost as soon as they'd arrived, he'd taken on the mantle of man about the house. While she was talking to her mother, he'd slipped outside without a word and stacked the load of logs that the log-man, finding her mother out when he came to deliver, had dumped directly in front of the garage door, blocking her car in.

The house was small – splitting the family finances had left both of their parents pretty broke – but Hannah's mother had four or five lovely pieces of furniture that had come down through her family, and a talent for finding gems in poky old junk shops. Mark had made her take him round the house and tell him the story behind everything, the details of its period and style, where it had come from. He was particularly effusive about the Georgian card table she'd inherited from her grandmother and asked Sandy if she would keep an eye out for something similar for the house in Quarrendon Street.

Afterwards he'd lit the fire, hung the mistletoe, poured Sandy a glass of wine, then perched on the fireguard and chatted to her for over an hour while Hannah cooked supper. The house had felt different, more alive, and her mother, fluttery and nervous for the first couple of hours of their being there, had become animated, even mildly flirtatious, telling self-deprecatory stories and tales of Hannah's childhood. 'He's lovely, Hannah,' she'd whispered as they carried the dishes back into the kitchen after dinner. She'd put the stack of plates on the draining board and squeezed her daughter's arm with excitement. 'Really lovely.'

And then there had been Boxing Day. After breakfast Mark had suggested a walk. Hannah had tried to convince her mother to come but she'd refused with a vigour that was quite uncharacteristic. They'd spent a few minutes trying on wellies from the collection in the hall cupboard then set off for British Camp, her mother waving to them, bright-eyed, from the step.

When they'd parked the car, they'd taken the upper footpath to the Iron Age fort at the top of the beacon, the cold air and the steepness of the climb taking Hannah's breath away. 'I blame the pudding,' she said after five or six minutes, trying to disguise the undignified heaving in her chest. 'And the mince pies. And the roast potatoes. I feel like I've put on half a stone since yesterday.'

132

'You're still gorgeous, swede-heart. I'd take on a fortful of pagans for you.'

'I think I'm only just beginning to understand the full extent of your power to charm,' she said, looking at him sidelong. 'You've got my mother under some sort of bewitchment.'

'Bewizardment.' The path flattened for a hundred yards or so and he paused to look at Herefordshire spread out in front of them, a view, Hannah always thought, that notwithstanding the occasional telephone mast and the glint of tiny cars here and there on the cotton-threads of roads across it, might not have changed in two hundred years. 'Or bewarlockment?' he said. 'Which do you reckon?'

'Whichever, it's effective.'

He'd turned to face her. 'Does it work on you?'

'What do you think?'

'I hope so.' His expression was very serious all of a sudden and she'd felt her own smile fade. 'Hannah, you know I love you, don't you?'

She'd nodded, blinking against the sun that was pouring round the outline of his head and shoulders, directly into her eyes.

'I've been thinking about this a lot – really, a lot.' He'd laughed a little, making fun of himself. 'I wondered . . . Will you marry me?'

Tom and Lydia had driven down from her parents' house in Ludlow that evening. Sandy had wanted Hannah to ring and tell him the news as soon as she'd got off the phone with her dad and Maggie

133

but she'd waited to tell Tom in person, wanting to see his face when she told him that she, the great unmarriageable, the romantic disaster area, the *coward*, was actually getting spliced.

It had started auspiciously enough. Mark had helped unload the car and referenced a line from an old *Only Fools and Horses* Christmas special that had made Tom laugh even before they'd been officially introduced inside by the fire. Wrapped in the long cashmere cardigan that Lydia – who was a far better daughter-in-law than she was an actual daughter, Hannah thought – had bought for her when the two of them had been shopping together, Sandy had hovered excitedly, unable to sit down for a minute even when Mark had handed her a glass of wine and urged her to take the chair in front of the fire.

'What's up, Mum?' Tom had said, putting his arm round her shoulders. 'It's a bit late in the season for ants in the pants, isn't it? And I can't believe you're *that* excited to see me. You saw me a fortnight ago.'

Her mother had thrown Hannah an agonised look. 'A mother's allowed to be excited about having her family all together, isn't she?'

'She is. But clearly there's something else afoot. Out with it.'

'Hannah, tell him. Quickly, before I explode.'

'Tell me what?' Tom said, looking at her.

Mark moved across the room and put his arm around Hannah's waist. She grinned at him and then at her brother, the happiness that had been bubbling through her all day threatening to spill out of control. 'We're getting married,' she said. 'Mark asked me this morning.'

Lydia gave a cry of delight and launched into a strange sort of dance with Sandy, but Hannah couldn't take her eyes off Tom's face. He did a pretty good job of covering it – the look was gone almost as soon as she'd seen it – but it had been there, unmistakable, an expression that combined shock and hurt and alarm.

'Wow,' he said. 'My God – wow. Congratulations. That's huge, Hannah.'

Hannah. It was all the confirmation she needed.

Tom had taken a swig of the beer Mark had poured him then put the glass down on the mantelpiece and come to give her a hug. 'Wow.' He'd pulled away and shaken Mark's hand. 'Well played, sir. I hope you know what you're letting yourself in for?'

Mark had laughed. 'I think so. Any advice gratefully received, though – you're the expert.'

Sandy had disappeared momentarily but reappeared now with a tray of glasses and the bottle of champagne that had lurked at the back of her china pantry for the past five years at least but had mysteriously already been chilling in the fridge when they'd returned earlier with their news. 'You asked my mother for permission,' Hannah had said, when she'd seen it, and Mark had grinned.

'I think she liked it.'

For half an hour Hannah had been trapped in front of the fire, answering excited questions from Lydia and her mother about potential venues for the reception and what kind of dress she was going to have, conscious all the time of the waves of tension radiating from her brother at the other end of the sofa, where Mark was attempting to talk to him about Cape Town, a place about which Tom, who'd taught in a school there for a year, usually proselytised at the first hint of an opportunity. In the end he'd excused himself for a cigarette and she'd waited a minute or two for appearances' sake then slipped out after him. She'd found him in the back garden, down at the end of the lawn beyond the range of the automatic light above the back door.

'So, you're pissed off with me,' she said, once her eyes had grown accustomed to the dark, making out her brother's features.

'Why would I be pissed off with you? You're getting married.'

'It seems like that might be why – for reasons I don't understand.'

The end of his cigarette glowed brightly for several seconds. She could feel him trying to keep a handle on himself but then he gave up and blurted it out. 'You didn't think maybe I should meet him first?'

'What?' Hannah had laughed. 'Not even Dad said that. Chill out, bro – no need to put yourself *in loco parentis*.'

He'd glared at her through the gloom, eyes dark in his pale face. 'That's right, make a joke out of it.'

'Well, what's the alternative, Tom? You're acting like a brat. You're pissed off with me because you haven't met my fiancé before? Well, guess what? I live in New York, it's not that easy just to meet up for a beer. It's not like you live down the road.'

'Come on, Hannah, surely you're not that stupid. You're deliberately misunderstanding me.'

'I don't think so. I'm just going on what you actually said – your words.'

He took another long drag. 'Well, what I *meant* was, how long have you known this guy?'

'*This guy?*'

'*Mark*, then – Mark. How long have you known him?'

'Five months. Almost six.'

He'd shaken his head and Hannah felt a rush of fury. If they'd been ten and twelve again, she would have kicked him.

'Don't you remember telling me,' she said, voice shaking, 'how soon you knew Lydia was The One? Or has that conveniently slipped your mind, O Great Relationship Sage? Three months I think you said it was, in case you need a reminder.'

'That was different.'

'Of course it was.'

'It was. We knew each other before. I knew friends of hers – she came with context.'

'For fuck's sake, *Mark's* got context. I've met

friends of his – Dan and Pippa – we had supper with them in London before we came up. They're decent people, clever, funny: you'd like them. Ant and Roisin – *mutual* friends – introduced us.' In the lighted window above the kitchen sink, she saw their mother appear, her anxious face peering out into the garden after them.

'Well, you know best,' Tom said.

'You know what? Actually, in this case, I do. I do know best. I love Mark and I trust him and when you get down off your high horse and stop treating me like some sort of emotional retard, you'll see that I'm right.'

'Good,' he said, and the fight had gone out of his voice. 'I'll look forward to it. I just couldn't stand the idea that you were rushing into this because of what I said to you last year.' He paused. 'About you being scared of commitment – taking a risk. I wouldn't forgive myself if . . .'

Her own anger disappeared and instead she felt a rush of love for him. 'For Christ's sake, Thomas,' she said. 'Get over yourself, will you? I can stuff things up on my own, you know. I don't need help from you.'

CHAPTER 9

As she turned the corner into Manbre Road, the eight o'clock bulletin was just starting: Assad in Syria massacring his own people; another arrest in the investigation into high-profile paedophiles. It was early enough that there were still several parking spots to be had and Hannah pulled in and cut the engine, killing the voice on the radio mid-sentence.

Out of the car, the air was so cold it felt wet against her face, and the trees and shrubs beyond the low wall that bordered the park were rigid with frost. The sky was white, not with cloud cover but a sort of evanescent haze that by mid-morning, she guessed, would pull back to reveal a day of harsh blue intensity.

The tap of her heels along the pavement reinforced her sense of purpose. She'd made scrambled eggs – the first proper thing she'd eaten since the Chinese with Tom – and had three cups of strong coffee from Mark's top-of-the-range Krups machine, and despite having been up for two hours already and having woken to find herself curled in the foetal position on the sofa with the pages of her library book crushed against her cheek, she felt rested and refreshed. Ready.

She was also buoyant with relief, at least on one front. During what she guessed was nearly nine hours' sleep – she remembered seeing the opening sequence of *Downton Abbey* before drowsily switching channels – her mind had been working over the facts, putting them in order, and she'd woken with the pure conviction – no, the knowledge – that Mark was not having an affair. He wouldn't cheat on her; she'd been crazy to think it. Pippa had been adamant, too, hadn't she? Mark loved her. He'd never been like this with anyone before, certainly not Laura. This morning Hannah chose to ignore the voice muttering that Pippa's knowledge of him was shallower than she'd been led to believe.

And he'd called her yesterday at a proper time – 3.15 in London, 10.15 in New York. When she'd finished talking to her mother, there had been a text alerting her to a new voice message. The number he'd called from hadn't registered on the phone, sometimes they didn't when he was calling from overseas, but when she'd accessed the voicemail, there he was.

Hi, sweetie, me again. Sorry to miss you – I hope you're doing something fun. I'm going to be working at the hotel most of the day but I'm about to go for a run and then I'll head out again for something to eat later on, probably. Thought about hotdogs but it's not the same without you. I'll try you again when I get back, see if I can catch you.

140

He hadn't called again but, as he'd said, he'd been working. All this – she'd been over-thinking it. The facts spoke for themselves, didn't they? What had she discovered that had anything to do with an affair? She'd found no letters, no photographs, no evidence of money spent on expensive presents, no skimpy knickers tucked into his trouser pockets. So there was confusion about where he was, but what did that mean? Even if he *was* in Rome, why did it have to be about sex? It was a major European capital: business was conducted there, too. And how did the marshalling of the money point to an affair? It didn't.

The money was the key to it, she thought as she entered the business park; if she'd been thinking clearly over the weekend that would have been obvious. She would find out what the money was for and then she'd know what she was dealing with.

She stationed herself on a bench fifteen feet from the building's main entrance, close enough to have a view of everyone coming and going without putting herself directly in eye-line. Five past eight. She opened the *Times* she'd bought before getting in the car, shook it out and pretended to read.

The denizens of Mark's building were a conscientious lot. It had been quiet when she'd arrived but within two or three minutes people were pushing their way through the revolving doors in a steady stream, coffee in hand, some already on calls or reading email on phones. At about quarter past,

David came round the corner and she quickly lifted the paper in front of her face. Today he was wearing a suit and carrying a burnished leather attaché case under his arm, and his jeans-and-plaid-shirt avatar from Saturday afternoon was hard to imagine. Just outside the doors he stopped to look at something on his phone and, in stepping out of the way of the woman behind him, he turned in Hannah's direction. Her heart leaped, but without looking up, he tapped a few keys and revolved into the building.

Most people arrived on their own but there were occasional pairs and, two or three times, small groups whom she guessed had been on the same train and walked down from Hammersmith Broadway together. A couple of people glanced in her direction, curious as to why anyone who wasn't smoking would linger outside on a morning as cold as this, but for the most part she felt invisible, safe.

By eight thirty, however, she began to think she was out of luck. DataPro had started for the day now. Surely Neesha should be here. Then Hannah remembered what Mark's PA had said on the phone, her confession that she was juggling too much. She lived across London on the other side of the river – had she said Blackheath? – and unless her husband did it, she'd have to drop Pierre at day-care, too. Hannah turned a page in the paper and feigned absorption in an op-ed about corporate tax evasion.

It was twenty to nine when she heard hurried footsteps on the steps. Neesha's face was tired and preoccupied-looking, as if she'd done the best part of a day's work already. Despite that, she was as beautifully presented as ever. Her full-length navy herringbone coat was open and revealed a black wool pencil skirt over snag-free ten-denier tights and a pair of black snakeskin heels. Her hair shone and she was wearing red lipstick that was bold enough to be a fashion statement but just subtle enough to be office-appropriate. Hannah felt a burst of jealousy, not only because, this woman was ten years younger and beautiful, but because she had a job, a career with forward momentum, a reason to get smartly dressed in the morning and *go* somewhere.

'Neesha.' Hannah stood up quickly, thrust the paper into her bag and stepped into the other woman's path. She watched as her face ran through a quick series of emotions, the initial surprise giving way first to wariness – what was Hannah doing here? Was this about what she'd said on the phone? – and then to friendly professionalism.

'Hannah – lovely to see you.' She glanced around and Hannah guessed she was looking for Mark. She drew Neesha slightly off the path, out of view from the doors.

'Sorry for accosting you like this. I wondered if I could have a quick word?'

'Of course. Is this about Saturday morning? I'm so, so sorry. I was beating myself up about it all weekend. And thank you so much again for—'

'Honestly, it's fine, forgotten about.' Hannah waved her hand, wiping the slate. For a moment, she hesitated. Asking would mean dragging Mark's personal life into the office and embarrassing him in front of a member of his staff. Was Neesha discreet? Could she be trusted not to relate this episode to all and sundry upstairs? And what would she think of Hannah? That she was mad, probably, out of control. Suddenly, though, with a burst of liberation, Hannah realised she no longer cared. She didn't care about Neesha's opinion of her; didn't care what she thought of Mark. And so what if he was embarrassed? He should have thought of that before he started lying. 'Look,' she said, 'this is really awkward, but I need to know . . . Has anything been going on lately? With Mark.'

'Going on?' Confusion flickered across Neesha's face, then indignation. She thought she was implying some kind of involvement between them, Hannah realised.

'No, God, not with you,' she said quickly. 'I mean, have you noticed anything unusual with him? Has anything changed? Has he seemed particularly stressed or . . .'

Neesha looked at her for a moment, brow furrowed, then shook her head. 'I don't think so. We've been busy, as you know. Business has really started picking up again and . . .'

'Is everything all right on that side of things? He's not involved in any sort of dispute?'

'Dispute? What do you mean?'

'There's no . . . bad blood with anyone? No trouble with payments? Or legal action?'

'No, nothing like that, and I think I'd know. Everything's fine. As I say, we're busy but that's the only cause of stress I'm aware of. Of course, I'm just his assistant, I'm not party to any of the—'

'But you answer his calls? Screen them?'

'Of course.'

'Has anyone new started calling? Anyone you don't think is ringing on DataPro business?'

Neesha stood up straighter and adjusted her bag on her shoulder. 'Mrs Reilly – Hannah – if you're worried about something, perhaps you should talk to Mark about it. I'm really not in a position to—'

'I would talk to him,' Hannah said wildly, 'if I had a telephone number I could actually reach him on.' Neesha looked startled but she carried on regardless. 'When we spoke on Saturday, you told me he'd said he was taking me to Rome. Maybe he still is and you really have got your wires crossed, but you're not the only one – David was under that impression, too. I'd like to talk to Mark, find out what's going on, but conveniently or inconveniently, depending on your point of view, he's lost his phone.'

There were two or three seconds of stunned silence that were interrupted by more quick footsteps on the path. Neesha waited until the new arrival had stepped through the doorway. 'I don't know what I can . . .'

Hannah held eye contact, not letting her look away. 'Imagine the boot's on the other foot,' she said. 'Imagine this is your husband we're talking about, that it's Steven and you're asking me. How would you feel, Neesha? How would *you* feel?'

Neesha glanced at the revolving doors as if she was thinking of making a run for it. When she looked back again, her expression had hardened. 'You shouldn't do this,' she said. 'It's not fair. You can't put me in this kind of position.'

Hannah felt a momentary sense of remorse but not enough to deflect her. 'I'm not trying to put you in any position,' she said. 'I'm asking – begging – you to help me. Please.'

'Look, I can't lose my job,' Neesha blurted. 'I can't . . . I just can't. Steven's been made redundant, he's been out of work for months. We need my salary.'

So there *was* something. Hannah's heart gave a heavy thump.

'Neesha,' she said, 'whatever you tell me stays between us. I promise – I absolutely promise. You have my word. I've said nothing about the Rome thing and I wouldn't, and whatever this is, however bad it is, I promise you Mark will never, ever know you told me.'

'If I lose my job . . .'

'You won't.' Hannah tried to sound decisive, final.

Neesha gave a short, sharp out-breath. For several seconds she said nothing and the silence of the morning rushed in around them. 'There is someone who calls,' she said at last.

Hannah felt a weight settle on her shoulders, as

146

if a lead cape had been slung round them. 'A woman?'

'Yes.'

In the space of a second, she felt her conviction crumble. She'd been wrong – she'd been deluding herself: it *was* an affair. 'How long?' she said. 'How long has it been going on?'

'Not very.' Neesha shook her head quickly, eager to play it down. 'A few weeks – a month, maximum.'

'Have you seen her? Has she been here – in the office?'

Neesha shook her head again.

'What's her name?'

'I—'

'You know, you must do. You said: you answer his telephone – you screen his calls. What's her name?'

Neesha looked really upset, as if she might actually cry, but Hannah couldn't stop. 'I'm not going to tell him,' she said. 'I've promised you.'

'All right, all right . . . Please. She's called Hermione.'

Hermione. Hannah's brain made an instant search of every woman Mark had ever mentioned, every story he'd ever told, and came up empty. 'Hermione what?'

'I—'

'Neesha.' Hannah heard the desperation in her own voice and it startled her. 'Please,' she said more gently. 'Help me.'

'Alan.'

147

'Alan? What, like the man's name?'

'Al—lane. Spelled like alley, with an "n" at the end.' Neesha looked at the doors then back at Hannah, beseeching her. 'That's all I know, I swear to you. I don't know who she is. I've got no idea. He always closes his door when he speaks to her.'

Hannah walked back to the car wide-eyed with shock, barely conscious of her feet moving. A blur of herringbone brick paving became tarmac as she came out on to Manbre Road again. Frozen shrubs in the border; a postman emptying the box on the corner, his breath white. She was trying to get the car key into the lock when reason told her to stop: there was no way she could drive like this; she'd have an accident, run someone over.

Moving as slowly as if she were underwater, she left the car and walked to the café on the corner of Fulham Palace Road. She bought a cup of coffee and carried it with unsteady hands to a table in the corner, where she hunched on the edge of a wicker armchair, her eyes fixed on a sugar bowl that shimmered and swam. The café was busy but no one came to ask if they could take her spare seat. Clearly she looked as unhinged as she felt.

She focused on the bright buckets of hothouse flowers for sale to visitors to Charing Cross Hospital across the road. Peonies, the pink-tipped buds still tightly furled, tulips in crimson and yolk yellow, delicate purple freesias. She'd been wrong; her instincts – *no, her judgement* – had been wrong.

Mark. *Mark*, who put snow-chains on her car and bought her buttery flapjacks from the delicatessen because he knew she loved them.

Hermione Alleyn. She turned the name over, testing it. Was she an old friend, someone who had always been there, lurking, waiting, or was she new? DataPro gave Mark so many opportunities to meet people – at clients' offices, in hotel bars and airport lounges. She felt sick as she imagined him on a plane, a woman arriving at the empty seat next to his, her grateful smile as he helped put her bag in the overhead locker.

Now she pieced it all together. The story about his phone was a lie, clearly, to make sure she didn't ring him. This Hermione Alleyn must have been in the bathroom or something when he'd called and left his messages. They probably were in Rome or somewhere equally romantic and perfect for long, dirty weekends. What had been up the M1? Some lovely Yorkshire boutique hotel with open fires, heavy cotton sheets and roll-top baths? And what was the money for – *her* money? A house? A flat where they could meet? She'd dismissed the idea before but now she reconsidered. This was Mark: he didn't do things by halves; he was extravagant, expansive. If he wanted a *love-nest*, Hannah thought scornfully, it wouldn't occur to him to rent one.

Was he going to leave, ask for a divorce? The idea caused a twist in her guts, then another rush of nausea that left her cold afterwards. What did it matter if he did? What difference did it make?

149

Even if he went on as if nothing had changed, she couldn't stay with him now.

But how could she leave? asked the voice in her head. She had no income and no savings. She was broke. The mug of coffee going cold on the table represented nearly a whole per cent of her net worth. She'd have to go to her brother, she realised, ask him if she could have his tiny back bedroom until she got herself straightened out. She'd have to live on her credit card, get some sort of job, any job, until she could find one in advertising. She could do it, she told herself. She'd go back to her old life and rely on herself. She'd listened to what Tom had said in New York – she'd trusted someone and let him trust her – and she'd fucked it up.

As she closed the front door, silence swallowed her. The house was always quiet – sometimes when she was here during the day she'd put on Radio 4 just for the sound of voices – but this was different. Since she'd left this morning, swinging out of the house at twenty to eight buoyed by sleep and coffee, the silence had taken on weight, and though it was noon now, the house was dark, as if daylight was struggling to penetrate the windows. The stairs climbed away into a soupy gloom, and she had the idea that the place was withdrawing from her, taking sides. She'd be leaving it soon, moving out.

She dumped her coat over the banisters and went through to the kitchen where she sat down at the table and fired up her laptop. She'd put off this moment for more than three hours, first at the café and then in Bishops Park, where she'd walked back and forth along the river path in a daze. She paused for a final few seconds, hands steepled in front of her face, then took a breath and plunged.

'Hermione Alleyn' brought up eight pages of results. She scanned the first and at the bottom saw a link to a directory enquiries site. The text below said, 'We have found 1 person in the UK with the name Hermione Alleyn.' The name was hyperlinked but when she clicked on it, she was told she'd have to register if she wanted to use the site. The same page came up when she tried the link to the address.

She went back to the list of results. The two entries at the top were for LinkedIn, but when she clicked on them, the page showed no further information. The third, though, was the site of a specialist medical journal on nephrology. Nephrology? Kidneys? Here Hermione Alleyn and Asif Akbar were listed as co-authors of an article describing a refinement to a technique in transplant surgery for patients with post-traumatic kidney failure. The link offered only a stub of the article but at the bottom she found a brief biography of the two authors. Hermione Alleyn, it said, was currently a consultant surgeon in nephrology and hepatology at the Royal London Hospital.

Was she a doctor, this woman? A surgeon? Hannah opened a new window and brought up the Royal London's site. She clicked on a button at the top titled 'Our Services' and scanned down until she found a link to the Renal Centre. Clicking that, she was invited to 'Meet The Team'. At the top of the list was Hermione Alleyn, Consultant Transplant Surgeon. There was a telephone number – a switchboard or receptionist, apparently: the same number appeared next to three or four other names – and an email address.

Was this her? There was no photograph – this woman, this obviously senior surgeon, could be sixty. Was the directory site right when it said there was only one Hermione Alleyn in the UK? Perhaps it meant there was only one Hermione Alleyn with a landline number or even a number that wasn't ex-directory. And what was there to say she was in the UK at all? Mark had met her, Hannah, overseas; he might have done the same this time, too. *This time.*

She swallowed the lump in her throat and went back to her first search. There were ten or fifteen different links to articles and papers written by the nephrologist; whoever she was, she was clearly big news in kidneys. At the bottom of the fourth page there was a link to Facebook, but when Hannah clicked it, the page was the blank one for people who took their privacy settings very seriously, all photographs and personal information reserved for friends, the profile picture just the generic outline of a female head. If the nephrologist was sixty, would she have a Facebook page? Why not? Lots of older people did, and they tended to be more careful about privacy than the daft young, who laid it all out there for teachers and employers and university tutors to peruse at their leisure. As a surgeon, too, she'd want to keep her private life private.

Hannah closed Facebook and went back to the list. More articles in various medical publications and then, on the sixth page of hits, a link referring to a nephrology conference in San Diego two years previously at which this Hermione Alleyn had given a paper. Hannah went to the page without any real expectation but when it opened, there was a small photograph of a woman stepping out from behind a lectern. She was young or youngish, not sixty but thirty-five or forty. The picture wouldn't enlarge so Hannah pulled her computer closer. Light brown hair, a little above shoulder-length, cut into a bob she'd tucked behind her ears. Hannah peered, trying to make out the woman's face, but the photograph had been taken from a distance and it was impossible to gain much of an impression beyond one of general attractiveness. She was slim and dressed in a black suit, the skirt knee-length and fitted, though even at this remove obviously not quite as well cut as Neesha's this morning. White shirt, black court shoes.

Scrolling down, however, Hannah found another photograph, this one taken from much closer range. Here Hermione Alleyn was standing next to a large, jovial-looking man in his late fifties, perhaps early sixties, with a thicket of salt-and-pepper beard and a heavy paw on her shoulder. Her face was fully visible. She had widely spaced pale eyes and a straight nose above a mouth with a full lower lip. Her ears, adorned with plain pearl studs, protruded enough to make her look a bit goofy and she was smiling in embarrassment, as if her companion or the photographer had just paid her an extravagant compliment. Glancing down, Hannah saw a caption: *Hermione Alleyn with Geoffrey Landis, Professor of Nephrology at the University of Cambridge. Landis describes Alleyn as his 'right-hand man' in his groundbreaking research project at Addenbrooke's Hospital.*

Hannah sat back in her chair and the silence flooded round her again, squeezing the oxygen from the air. Her chest felt tight; she was breathing like her brother did just before he had an asthma attack. For a minute or so she concentrated, forcing herself to exhale slowly, to stop gulping for another breath before she'd emptied her lungs of the one before; then, leaning forward, she opened a new window and typed in 'Hermione Alleyn' and 'St Botolph's', the name of Mark's college at Cambridge.

No results. Deleting Hermione's name, she typed in 'Geoffrey Landis' instead. The first link took her to a page on a college website. As well as being the university's Professor of Nephrology, she read, he was a fellow and tutor at St Botolph's. *Bingo.* It was her: it had to be. Even if she wasn't the only Hermione Alleyn in the UK, the name was unusual enough that the St Botolph's connection couldn't be a coincidence. If this man Landis taught there, wasn't it likely that Hermione had met him as a student and then later, as a high-flyer, been an obvious recruit for his 'groundbreaking research project'? And she was the right age; if not quite forty like Mark then certainly within two or three years of him, close enough for their years at college to have overlapped.

Hannah stood up abruptly, scraping the chair across the slate floor tiles. Light-headed, hands shaking, she unlocked the French windows and flung them open. In the yard she moved clear of the shadow of the house then tipped her head back and pulled in lungfuls of the bitter air. The sky overhead was the pitiless blue she'd predicted.

If they'd met at Cambridge, they'd known each other twenty years. Was Hermione an old flame, someone he'd been in love with then, now back in the picture? The idea caused Hannah a wash of despair: how could she, some woman who'd known Mark a year and a half, compete with someone who'd known him so long, who'd known his friends then and all the stories and in-jokes, who'd shared one of the formative parts of his life? She, Hannah, hadn't been to Oxbridge; she didn't know that world with all its rituals and august ancient customs, its exclusivity.

But how could she compete with someone like Hermione Alleyn at all? asked the unkind voice in her head. In her job – *when she'd even had one* – all she'd done was

155

think up inventive ways to flog things people didn't want, concocting adverts that wormed their way into their brains, forced themselves upon them like a randy mongrel when all they wanted was to read a magazine or watch TV. How could that compare with being a surgeon, performing transplants, life-saving surgery? This woman was impressive by anyone's standards.

But then, said the voice, *Mark was never going to take up with a bimbo, was he, some over-bleached, half-witted soap addict?* Mark liked bright women; Laura, she'd discovered when she pressed him, had some high-powered job in a government think-tank on defence. He liked the stimulus, the challenge. If he were in love with someone else – *If?* said the voice – or even if he were just sleeping with her, it would be because she intrigued him, made him laugh, made him think. It would be about her brain as much as her face or body though Hermoine wasn't unattractive, either, far from it. She looked clever, sharp-eyed, self-deprecating. *The kind of person you would like.*

CHAPTER 10

It was eighteen stops from Parsons Green, direct, no changes, and in the hour she'd been underground, her face composed into its neutral, big-city, don't-engage expression, Hannah had been buffeted by anger so powerful it was incredible that no one among the scores of people who'd joined the train and got off again had seemed to feel it.

A few minutes before she'd left the house, she'd called Mark's mobile. She hadn't really expected an answer, of course, but the sound of the calm but firm female voice telling her that the person she was calling was not available enraged her. The last traces of protective shock had burned away in a surge of fury so strong she'd felt dizzy, and she'd had to sit down until the pounding in her head started to subside. Then she'd stood up again and paced the kitchen, her hands shaking, itching to do violence. The milk jug had been on the draining board, and before she could stop herself, her arm had reached out and swept it to the floor. The smash had satisfied the rage for a moment but within seconds it was rising up inside her again.

She'd been duped – he'd played her. He'd lied to her and left her to sit around waiting for him like some stupid sap while he was off somewhere with *her*, Hermione Alleyn, life-saving surgeon, Cambridge graduate, key researcher, speaker at international conferences. *Success*. What was she, Hannah? A cheated-on wife, a deluded fool, an unemployed, powerless idiot. The handle of the jug lay on the floor, still attached to a circle of china. She lifted her foot and stamped on it, reducing it to powder.

Then she'd grabbed her bag and coat, slammed the door behind her and run up the street. She couldn't stay in the house – his house – with its oppressive, oxygen-sucking silence. She needed to get out, be somewhere she could *breathe*.

She'd crossed New King's Road, passed the deli and the off-licence, the hairdresser's with its tableau of swaddled, tin-foiled ladies sipping coffee and reading magazines, and taken the pavement that ran parallel to the edge of Parsons Green. A Dalmatian tore across the muddy autumn grass after a stick, and his pure, uncomplicated enjoyment as he snatched it from the air and carried it back to his mistress, tail a blur, brought sudden tears to Hannah's eyes. Biting the inside of her cheek, she'd hurried on past the pub to the Tube station.

Long as the journey had been, south-west London all the way across to the east, it had passed in what felt like minutes, the consuming rage bending time so that she looked up seemingly seconds after the doors had closed at Gloucester Road to find they were at Embankment; Mansion House; Cannon Street. The anger ebbed and flowed, and when it retreated, she felt the stab of disbelief again, the ache in her stomach that said, *Really? Mark?*

Now, as she emerged from the Underground at Whitechapel, the hospital was right in front of her. The suddenness of it took her aback. On the way across London the idea of coming here had been reinforced by her anger and the momentum of the train itself, ticking off the stations one by one, but looking at the hospital now she asked herself what the hell she was doing. What had she hoped to achieve? She'd needed to get out of the house, she told herself, before she smashed the entire place up, but that was only part of it. She could have gone anywhere. The truth was, she'd wanted to see this place, to have a picture of where this woman worked, what her life might be like.

It had been hot underground, all the train's heaters on, but here a biting wind drove the litter along the pavement and caused the awning outside the discount store two doors down to billow and flap like a loose sail. She pulled her coat tightly round her and shoved her hands in her pockets. When the traffic stopped at the pedestrian crossing, she dashed across the road.

There had been major building work going on at the hospital, that was evident: from behind the dour yellow-brick façade of the old buildings soared a new complex that seemed to belong to a different world, let alone a different age. The impression was of a three-dimensional Tetris game in which the blocks were made of highly reflective glass in varying shades of petrol blue, punctuated here and there by a tessellation in pale grey concrete. It was as if the entire thing had been snatched from the City, where it would have kept good company with the Gherkin and the Cheese Grater, and dropped down here just to highlight how tired and snaggle-toothed the rest of Whitechapel Road was, with its jumble of roof-lines and dusty shop-fronts, the bookies and Poundbuster, importers and immigration lawyers' offices, the pub on the corner painted in orange tiger-skin pattern. This was a very different London from Mark's and even from Kilburn, where Hannah had lived before she moved to New York.

The work looked almost finished now but the front of the old building was still surrounded with wooden siding. A sign on it advised that the hospital had moved and directed visitors around the corner. Hannah followed the arrows and found herself standing outside the new main entrance, sliding glass doors set into a Tetris block made of red brick, a sheer cliff of blue glass rearing overhead. The doors opened to admit a man in his sixties carrying a bouquet of ox-eye daisies wrapped in cellophane, and she stepped in after him.

She stood and looked around for a moment, getting a sense of the place, but then she was spotted by a smiling woman with a security card round her neck identifying her as a hospital volunteer. 'You look lost,' she said.

'I'm looking for the renal ward,' Hannah heard herself say.

'Ninth floor.' The woman gestured towards the lifts. 'There'll be a board when you get there to point you in the right direction.'

If the lobby was anything to go by, the new building was working at or near full capacity already. The place was thronged with people: staff, the walking wounded with their drips and plaster casts, and dozens of visitors. The lift she waited for stopped at every floor on its way down to the lobby and then every floor on its way back up to the ninth. Heart thumping, she stood pressed in at the back between a tall Indian man in surgical greens and a couple who, from the sound of their whispered conversation, were on their way to visit their daughter and new grandson in the maternity ward. A pair of women in their early twenties – student doctors, Hannah guessed – were talking about a ward round and she felt a pang of jealousy and painful inadequacy, as if she were excluded from a gang that everyone else belonged to. Hermione must have been like them fifteen years ago, at the beginning of her career.

On the ninth floor Hannah stepped out at the same time as the man in greens, who quickly disappeared through a pair of double doors to the right of the small lobby. The newness of the place was evident everywhere. The windows shone; the paintwork was

161

scuff-free. A little way down the corridor a woman operating a huge industrial floor-polisher was taking care not to hit the skirting as she manoeuvred it from side to side.

Hannah paused for just a second then followed the arrow that directed her through the double doors and down a broad corridor. She would ask. There was bound to be some sort of desk or reception area and she would ask if Hermione Alleyn was working today. If she wasn't – and really, she already knew she wasn't – then it would be confirmed.

The wards, it seemed, all branched off this central trunk of a corridor, one set of double doors after another marked by signs at ceiling height that eliminated the need for people to stop and look at the names on the walls and thus clutter up the thoroughfare. She could see the sign for the renal ward at the far end of the corridor and kept going, passing a pair of hospital porters wheeling the bed of a tiny elderly woman with an oxygen tank resting on the expanse of undisturbed sheets at her feet. The further she went, the fewer the footsteps behind her as people peeled off into the other wards.

When she reached Renal, Hannah stopped. Through the glass panel in the left-hand door she could see a little way into the ward: first what looked like a storage bay occupied by a couple of wheelchairs and an unmade bed with a plastic mattress, and beyond that the nurses' station. Behind the desk was a nurse in a short-sleeved tunic and a younger man, perhaps thirty or so, in a dark shirt. Through the other panel, the opposite side of the ward was visible: a line of single doors, private rooms or offices, she guessed, and an orderly with a cleaning cart. There was no one who looked like the woman online.

The man came out from behind the desk and Hannah stepped away from the glass. Anyone who saw her peering in like this would think she was one of those oddballs who got their kicks hanging round hospitals and doctors. For a moment she saw herself as if from the outside: what would the person she'd been on Saturday morning, only three days ago, think of this one, standing with her nose literally pressed against the glass for a view into the world of the woman who was sleeping with her husband? She experienced a burst of self-loathing so intense it was almost a taste in her mouth, and turned to go. Just as she did, however, a woman whose clipped approaching footsteps she'd been vaguely aware of came to a stop just behind her.

'Excuse me. Sorry.' She reached past to the disinfectant gel dispenser then pressed the entry button. When she was buzzed in, Hannah took some gel and followed her.

The woman went straight to the nurses' station. Hannah hung back until she'd been directed to a patient in one of the individual rooms then approached the desk herself. The nurse behind it, a woman in her fifties with grey-blonde hair pinned into a nub of a ponytail, looked at her over a pair of gold-rimmed half-moon spectacles.

'Can I help you?' she asked, in a brisk voice.

'It's just a question, actually. I wondered if Hermione Alleyn was in today?'

'Ms Alleyn?' On the desk behind her the telephone started ringing. The nurse looked at it then at a colleague, who pulled a quick apologetic expression over the shoulder of the visitor she'd been collared by. The nurse looked back at Hannah. 'May I ask why you want to know?'

'I . . .' For a moment her mind emptied. The nurse raised an eyebrow. 'I'm from the florist,' said Hannah. 'I've got a delivery for her downstairs but, well, it's big and I wanted to make sure I was in the right place and she was actually here before . . .'

The telephone stopped ringing but started again almost immediately. The nurse gave it another harried glance. 'Fine, yes. She's in today but she's in theatre at the moment. The list isn't long so I should think they'll be done shortly. If you bring the flowers up, we can keep them behind the desk here.'

'Great, thanks.' Hannah nodded and made her way to the door again. She tugged at the handle three or four times before seeing the release pad on the wall at wheelchair height. Back outside in the corridor, she walked until she was out of view from the glass panels.

Her mind was racing. What was going on? Hermione Alleyn *was* here. She was here and working in the operating theatre, which meant that wherever Mark actually was – New York, Rome,

164

Ulan Bator – she wasn't with him. Unless, Hannah thought, this was the wrong woman after all. She remembered the Cambridge connection, though, the fact that they would have been at St Botolph's at the same time – what was the likelihood Mark would know two Hermione Alleyns? No, it had to be her, this one. So what did that mean? That he was in London somewhere, holed up at her house and waiting for her to come home? No: not his style. And anyway, if he were in London, he'd be at the office, wouldn't he? There was no way he'd be here and not go to work, especially with a buy-out imminent.

Just for a minute she let herself consider the possibility that he wasn't having an affair, that Hermione had been calling him for some other reason. What? What could they be talking about? But then, if she was just an old friend from Cambridge, why had Hannah never heard of her? Why had Mark never mentioned her? And why had Neesha been so defensive? *He always closes his door when he speaks to her.*

A little further on, near the end of the corridor, there was a shallow alcove with a bench in it. Blue winter light spilled from the window behind on to the floor. Sitting there, Hannah thought, she'd be more or less out of sight of anyone approaching but she'd have a good view. She'd wait until Hermione came up from theatre and talk to her then. She wasn't going to leave here now until she found out was going on.

She walked to the bench and sat down, positioning herself at the far end so she could see clearly. The ward hadn't seemed especially busy but a steady stream of people came and went, staff and visitors, and her head snapped up at each new set of footsteps, the tap-tap of heels and the softer whisper of men's shoes, the squeak of trainers. She remembered waiting in the arrivals hall at JFK, how she used to watch the doors like a puppy waiting for its owner to come home, and was filled with disgust at herself. What a stupid bloody idiot she'd been.

Her bag vibrated against her thigh and when she got out her BlackBerry, she saw Mark's name in her inbox.

Han sweetheart, I'm so sorry we didn't manage to talk over the weekend. I'm getting some work done this morning, the meeting's at two this afternoon, and then I'm JFK-bound, coming home. Can't wait to see you – I've missed you like mad. Prepare to be squeezed to within an inch of your life . . .

She read it again, and then, incensed – *I've missed you like mad?* – she deleted it and tossed the phone back into her bag. When she looked up again, a woman in surgical greens with brown hair cut into a shoulder-length bob was coming through the double doors at the far end of the corridor, walking with energetic, economical steps that were barely audible even when she was ten feet away. She was frowning slightly, squinting against the cold light that streamed through the windows and made her

166

look even more tired, but it was the woman Hannah had seen online, no doubt about it, slightly protruding ears and all. As she approached the doors to the ward, Hannah stood up, slung her bag over her shoulder and moved quickly to intercept her. 'Excuse me? Hermione Alleyn?'

The woman stopped and the frown was replaced by an expression of polite professionalism. She gave a small smile carefully calibrated – after years of being accosted by anxious relatives, Hannah guessed – to look approachable but not too much so. She was sucking a mint that did nothing to mask the smell of cigarette smoke that hung around her.

'Yes?'

'I'm Hannah Reilly,' she said, watching the woman carefully. The neutral expression, however, remained.

'Mark's wife.'

A second passed and then a look of pure horror crossed Hermione Alleyn's face. It was fleeting but unmistakable: her eyes widened and stared but then, just as quickly, she recovered herself and smiled. 'Mark? God, how is he? Is he here?' She looked around, as if expecting to see him coming along the corridor.

Hannah felt a hot rush of anger. How dare she? How much of a moron did they think she was? 'Look,' she said. 'Don't bother with the pretence. I know something's going on.'

Another momentary flicker of panic and then

composure again. 'Going on? I don't know what . . .'

'Between you two. I know you're . . . in touch.' She paused a second, gave the innuendo room to breathe. 'I know you've been calling him at his office – his assistant told me. And I know he's been lying to me about his whereabouts.'

Hermione shook her head a little. 'I'm sorry,' she said, 'but I'm afraid you've got the wrong end of the stick somewhere. There's nothing going on between Mark and me. We were at college together in Cambridge – you know that already, I'm sure – but that's all the . . .'

'Don't,' Hannah said, her voice coming out louder than she'd expected. It echoed off the corridor's shiny surfaces and Hermione glanced around, nervous, no doubt, in case her colleagues heard. Well, stuff her, thought Hannah. Why should she lower her voice? She wasn't going to sit back and take this. 'Just don't,' she said. 'I've had enough of being lied to and patronised – it's time for the truth. Something's going on and I'm not going to leave here until I find out what it is.'

There was a click and the ward door came open. The dark head of the man in the grey shirt appeared. 'Hermione?'

'Hi, Robbie.'

'Hi.' His eyes moved quickly between them. 'I . . . Everything all right?'

'Fine.' Hermione gave a single terse nod. 'Thanks. I'll be there in a second.'

Robbie looked at Hannah appraisingly then bobbed his head back in. He stepped aside but she could see the elbow of his shirt through the glass panel. Hermione saw it as well. She stepped away from the door and put her hand on Hannah's arm, drawing her back. 'Okay, look,' she said quietly, 'you're right, we have been in touch a couple of times recently.'

Hannah felt the confirmation as a physical sensation, cold washing over her.

'No, it's not that – it's not what you think.'

'Then what is it?'

Hermione cast an anxious glance down the corridor. 'We were talking about Nick.'

'Nick?' *Nicola*, said the voice in her ear. *It's not her, it's someone else, a mutual friend, an old flame.*

Hermione, though, was looking at her as if she were stupid. 'His brother,' she said.

'His brother? What? They don't even talk. Why would you . . .?'

'Because,' Hermione said, as if it were obvious, 'he's about to get out of prison, isn't he?'

CHAPTER 11

'*What about your brother?*' she'd asked that Friday night.

Her head had been on Mark's shoulder, his skin warm and faintly damp against her cheek from the heat they'd generated in bed and the over-zealous steam heating in her old building. She'd felt a tiny tug of suction as he'd turned and dislodged her, a kiss goodbye.

'What about him?'

Happy that he was coming to Malvern for Christmas and keen to avoid making him sad by probing too deeply into his family when he'd just agreed to be thrust into the centre of hers – whom she still had the luxury of moaning about – Hannah had let the subject drop at the time, but the following morning when she'd been making scrambled eggs in her glamorous corridor of a kitchen, coffee pot balanced precariously on top of the microwave to make space for two plates side by side on the tiny patch of countertop, the White Stripes playing on WFUV with backing vocals from Mark in the shower next door, she'd thought about how his face had changed. His relaxed openness had vanished in a second, replaced by a barrier. When he'd looked at her, his eyes had been hard. *What about him?*

What had he told her about his brother before that? She'd stirred the eggs and tried to think back. She remembered the conversation very early on, the second time they'd met up deliberately in the city, when he'd told her that he'd lost both his parents when he was in his twenties, his father of complications after a stomach operation, his mother only a year later of breast cancer detected too late. They'd been at the Mulberry Street Bar then, his suggestion because she'd told him she loved *Donnie Brasco* and he couldn't believe she didn't know that scenes of it had been shot there. The temperature had been pushing a hundred all day and they'd sat at one of the high pedestal tables and drank glasses of beer that ran with condensation despite the roaring air con. 'How about siblings?' she'd asked him. 'Do you have any?'

For a moment Mark seemed to hesitate and she'd watched as he circled the dregs of his beer round the bottom of the glass.

'One. A brother. Nick.' He'd looked up, expression neutral.

'Are you close?'

A headshake. 'We're not really in touch, even.'

'Oh.' Hannah had been surprised: she'd only met Mark a handful of times but he hadn't struck her as the type to have tempestuous family relationships.

'There's no drama,' he said, 'we're just very different people.'

'Is he older or younger?'

'Younger but only a year. My mother didn't know you could get pregnant while you were breastfeeding. That was her story, anyway.' He'd grinned, the light coming back into his eyes, and reached for Hannah's empty glass. 'Same again?'

He'd returned from the bar with a snippet of gossip he'd just overheard and the conversation had taken a different tack. At that point, so soon after meeting him, she hadn't felt it was right to press him for more information than he wanted to give, but now, the end of November, they'd been together five months and he was coming for Christmas. It wasn't a flirtation any more, a short-lived fun thing; it was a real relationship. The idea sent a buzz through her: it was good but, she admitted to herself, terrifying too.

She should talk to him about his brother, she decided that morning in the kitchen, find a time over the weekend when he was relaxed and she wouldn't seem to be putting him under pressure. In the end, she'd bided her time until Sunday evening when they were wandering back along the promenade in Brooklyn Heights from a protracted lunch at Ant and Roisin's. Mark had stopped and leaned against the railings to look at the shimmering Miramax-logo view of Lower Manhattan across the river, the traffic on the Brooklyn–Queens Expressway pounding along the road tucked out of view beneath their feet. He loved this view, he'd said before, because to him it was the classic image of ambition and scale and achievement. Now he reached across and slid his hand into the back pocket of Hannah's jeans. She glanced up at him, spent a second appreciating his profile against the lights of the city behind. Remembering his sudden shutdown on Friday night she hesitated then decided she was being ridiculous. What had he said that evening in the Mulberry Street Bar? *There's no drama. We're just very different people.*

'Your brother,' she'd said, as a truck thundered beneath them, making the pavement shake. 'What's he like? What does he do?'

Mark had pulled his hand out of her pocket and shoved it into his jacket instead. He smiled, brown eyes black in the streetlight. 'Let's move,' he said, tipping his head in the direction they were going. 'It's too cold to stand around. Shall we walk back across the bridge, burn off some of that roast lamb?'

Had he even heard her? He must have – the truck hadn't been that loud. He reached for her hand and Hannah gave it to him, but she was puzzled. If he'd heard, why not answer? If there really was no drama, why this weirdness?

'What time's your breakfast meeting tomorrow?' he'd asked.

'Eight, not horrendous.' She swerved to avoid a King Charles spaniel that had slipped its leash and was haring down the promenade towards them as if fleeing a forest fire. 'Mark, look, your brother – do you find it difficult to talk about him?'

This time she knew he'd heard her. For several seconds, however, he said nothing and kept walking. She'd waited, not prepared to talk into the silence and risk provoking him or giving him the opportunity to avoid the question. She'd glanced sideways and saw that his face was shuttered again, his mouth set.

'It's not *difficult* for me to talk about him,' he'd said eventually, and his voice was calm, well modulated. 'I'd just prefer not to, okay? He lives in London, he's done a few things, work-wise. There's nothing much else to say. You have issues with your mother, I don't particularly get on with my brother; you talk about it, I choose not to. Perhaps it's a man–woman thing.'

The gender stereotype surprised Hannah, it was so unlike him, but she let it pass in the hope of staying on-topic. 'I'm sorry,' she said, 'I just . . .'

'It's okay, don't worry about it,' he'd said, and his tone had made it clear that for him, the subject was closed.

The walk home to her apartment had taken an hour and a half, and for the whole length of it she'd been aware of a distance yawning between them. They did what they usually did on a long walk, pointed out new restaurants that looked good, interesting buildings or people, but where usually the observations segued into broader conversations or sparked off new thoughts, that night they'd been like pieces of polite conversation traded by people who'd just been introduced. Back at the apartment he'd suggested watching the episode of *60 Minutes* he'd recorded while they'd been out, and then he'd brushed his teeth. After the lights had gone off, he'd shifted up behind her in bed and put his arm round her waist, but he hadn't made any further move and she was glad.

He'd been in London for the two following weekends and by the one after that, after three weeks without seeing each other, the subject of Nick had moved towards the outer edge of her radar. Then had come Christmas, and Mark's proposal, and every member of her family – her parents and Maggie, even Chessa and Rachel – had asked about his.

'If you say there's nothing odd about it, I believe you,' said Tom, when she'd told him about Nick, how she hadn't met him and didn't seem likely to at any point in the foreseeable future.

'What?' she said. 'Don't say it like that.'

'Like what? I'm saying I trust your judgement: if you say it's not odd, it's not odd.'

'But it's only my saying it's not odd that makes it not odd, that's what you're really saying.'

'Argh!' Tom clutched his head and squeezed his eyes shut as if in sudden terrible pain. 'Stop the mind-fucking – I'm a simple creature, I mean no harm.'

Nonetheless, it was patently obvious that he did think it was odd and it rankled with Hannah because privately she agreed with him. Why didn't she know anything about the only extant member of her fiancé's family other than that he was a year younger, lived in London, and it sounded like he'd had a few different jobs? Whenever she let herself think about it for longer than a minute or two at a time, she found herself starting down all kinds of lines of paranoid enquiry: was Mark ashamed of his brother for some reason? Or could he be ashamed of her, Hannah? Was that why he didn't want to introduce them? If it was late at night and she was on her own and she'd had a couple of glasses of wine, she started wondering what kind of person could be so alienated from a brother with whom he claimed just not to get on that they didn't see each other at all, even when their parents had died quite recently. Unless something actually bad had happened between them, surely they'd see each other for some sort of mutual support or just to feel connected to the memory of their family?

In the end, by the second weekend in January, the whole issue had achieved critical mass and Hannah knew she'd have to have it out with him whether he liked it or not. So on Saturday night she'd cooked a complicated pork recipe, plied him with half a bottle of Sancerre and prepared herself for the facial shutdown. Sure enough, it was almost immediate.

'Nick,' he said, glaring at her, all the easy warmth of seconds before gone from his eyes. 'Is he all you think about? You're obsessed.'

'Obsessed?' She'd pulled back from the table,

amazed. 'I've asked you about him twice before – *twice*, Mark. We're engaged, we're getting married in April – is it weird that I'm curious about your family? He'll be my brother-in-law. I'll be related to—'

'No,' he said, standing and dropping his napkin on the table. 'No, he won't. He'll be your brother-in-law in the same way that he's my brother – technically, legally, whatever. But that's it, that's all. I won't be pushed into having a relationship with him just because you've got some idea in your head. There's nothing there for you, Hannah. I don't want him in our lives and I don't want to talk about it any more. Got it?'

She'd watched in amazement as he opened the cupboard by the front door and yanked his coat out, setting off a cacophony of jangling from the empty hangers. 'Where are you going?'

'Out. I won't sit here and be cross-examined.'

'I'm not cross-examining you. All I wanted was to —'

'I told you when you asked the last time that I didn't want to talk about it. Couldn't you respect that? Couldn't you do that one thing for me? Was it really too much to ask?' He'd looked at Hannah as if he were assessing her and finding her wanting then he'd turned and gone, slamming the door behind him.

She'd sat at the table for some time, blood pounding in her ears. They'd snapped at each other once or twice before when one of them or both had been tired and stressed but nothing like this, not even close: they'd never argued; neither of them had ever stormed off. She was shocked – actually, stunned was more accurate. Mark was so self-contained, so in control, and slamming out of the apartment was so . . . teenage. She'd tried to make herself smile at the image, Mark as moody teenager, but the smile died on her lips. He was angry with her, really angry. In her head she reran the conversation, what there had been of it. All she'd said, her carefully rehearsed opening gambit, was: 'Mark, will you tell me about Nick?' That was it, all it had taken to trigger this.

Where had he gone? It was cold outside, on the radio earlier there had been talk of snow, and it was ten thirty. Well, she thought, standing and picking up the empty plates that already seemed to belong to a different era, one in which they'd been happy and she hadn't screwed it all up by prying, there was nothing she could do about it until he came back. She wasn't going to text him, grovelling, apologising for asking a simple question. If he didn't get on with his brother, why didn't he just tell her why rather than turning it into a huge issue? If she was going to marry him, she had to be able to ask questions like this. She couldn't let herself be intimidated into silence.

She'd slowly washed up the dinner things, tense with listening for the sound of his key in the door. By the time the kitchen was restored to order, though, it was half-eleven and there was no sign of him. She sat in the corner armchair, pulled her legs up under her and tried to focus on the copy of *Leaves of Grass* that she'd been attempting to get into all week. Again, the attempt was fruitless: the scarcity of punctuation meant she had to read each sentence two or three times before she could even work out which was the main verb, and when she'd done that, the words swum on the page anyway and refused to organise themselves into any thought she could understand.

She put the book down and picked up the previous week's *New York* magazine but fared no better. Where was he? Was he holed up in a bar somewhere pounding the Scotch? Was this his way of punishing her? She was exhausted but wired; all she wanted was to get into bed and disappear under the covers but she knew she wouldn't sleep until he came home or at least let her know that he wasn't going to. She checked her phone again: nothing. Anyway, she didn't want to go to bed, not really. She needed to be dressed when he came home, it seemed important. She didn't want to be in her pyjamas when he had the advantage of proper clothes.

The clock on the cable box read ten past one when she heard footsteps outside in the corridor. At the jangle of keys she sat up straight and quickly arranged herself into an attitude of casual reading, though the fact that she was still up at all made a lie of any pretence of normality.

He shut the door quietly behind him, took off

his coat and dropped it gently over the arm of the sofa. 'Hi.'

'Hi,' she replied in the same neutral tone, waiting to see what his move would be, what his mood was now.

He looked at her, his expression still neutral, then he crossed the room until he was standing a couple of feet away. He crouched in front of her and looked up into her face. 'Han, I'm sorry,' he said. 'I'm really, really sorry.'

To her shame, she was flooded with relief. As the time had stretched, the scenarios she'd envisaged had grown darker and darker: maybe it was ruined; maybe he'd decided that he couldn't live with her, that it was over, their engagement was off. By the end, she'd been battling to keep her thinking straight, to remember that she hadn't done anything wrong. Now she waited for Mark to go on.

'I'm sorry for flying off the handle like that – for being over-sensitive,' he said. 'I owe you an apology, I know, but also an explanation.'

'Look, it's okay . . .' she started but he cut her off.

'No, it isn't. It isn't. My brother and I – this is why I don't see Nick, why I hate even talking about him. It's like every time anyone mentions his name, something happens to me and I go from being a reasonable, semi-decent person to someone I don't recognise. I hate it – I hate myself for it – and yet I don't seem to be able to stop it.' His face was anguished now.

'Mark, I'm so sorry. I didn't want to upset you. I—'

'No, don't apologise; you've done nothing wrong. It's totally reasonable to ask about him. Why shouldn't you? If you marry me' – he made it sound as if she might really have changed her mind, and the idea made her chest ache – 'if you marry me, you deserve to know everything about me, even the things I'd keep hidden from you given half a chance, the stuff I'm not proud of. I only want you to see the good things, the light-hearted, fun, successful Mark, not the one who can't handle his brother and let his mother down. I let my own mother down,' he said, 'and she's dead and I can never make it right. I'll never be able to forgive myself.'

His eyes were shining now, as if he were on the verge of tears. She stood up, took his hand and pulled him gently over to the sofa before going to the kitchen and retrieving a new bottle of wine and fresh glasses. When she handed him one, he drank an inch from the top of it in a single swig. As she'd held his hand she'd sniffed surreptitiously for the smell of alcohol but there had been no trace of it and his fingers had been red and ice-cold, the bones like sticks beneath his skin. He must have been walking outside all the time he'd been gone.

'I'm going to tell you about Nick,' he said.

'Only if you want to. It can wait – it's late. We're both tired. We can talk about it tomorrow.'

'No.' He shook his head. 'I want to talk about it now. I need to explain.' He looked at her. 'Storming out like that won't be normal practice, I promise.'

'Okay. Good.'

He took another big mouthful of wine and swallowed loudly. He looked down, training his eyes on his reddened fingers as they clutched the stem of the glass. 'Nick was my mother's favourite,' he said. 'She doted on him and I think she ruined him – literally spoiled him rotten.' He blew out a quick spurt of air, as if it was funny.

Hannah said nothing and waited for him to go on.

'It's pretty easy to see why he was her favourite – I'm sure he would have been mine if I'd been her. I was awkward and self-conscious, I went through phases where I was really uncomfortable in my own skin, but he was one of those children who's just somehow golden. Do you know what I mean?'

Hannah thought of Chessa's daughter Sophia who, at seven, was already two years ahead of her peers at school and a gifted tennis player. She'd also been approached twice in London by scouts for children's modelling agencies.

'I was quite an anxious child, I think, always trying my best, worried about getting things right, but for Nick, life just seemed to roll out like a red carpet from the moment he arrived. He got everything right without trying, or that's what it looked like: he slept through the night at two months, walked at nine, made everyone laugh with his little baby faces and games. My mother's friends loved him, teachers loved him; he made friends without trying. Little girls at junior school actually wrote him love letters. I got all the childhood afflictions going: measles, mumps, whooping cough. For years I was at the doctor's all the time with terrible psoriasis but I don't remember anything ever being wrong with Nick.'

He pulled at a loose thread on his shirt cuff, avoiding her eye.

'With hindsight,' he said, 'bits of it are quite funny. There's this picture of us that encapsulates the whole thing. I'll show it to you next time we're in London. We're on the beach in Devon and I'm seven, probably, so Nick must just have turned six – he was a summer baby, as my mother never grew tired of saying, as if that in itself made him special. He's wearing these snazzy little boardshort-style trunks while I'm stuffed like a sausage into this hideous nylon Speedo-type thing which, frankly, was an affront to a man's dignity even at that age.' He smiled wryly. 'Anyway, he's wielding a gigantic ice cream, chocolate flake, the works, and if you look carefully, you can just see my cone in the bottom right-hand corner of the picture, down in the sand. I'd been stung by a wasp and dropped it.'

He smiled again trying to make a joke of it, but Hannah could hear the hurt running just beneath the surface of his voice.

'Mark . . .'

He shook his head, wanting, now he'd started, to go on, get the whole thing over with on one long breath. 'The thing is,' he said, 'none of this would have mattered, I don't think, if my mother had been different – if she'd had any self-confidence at all or even just a more positive outlook. As a child I didn't understand it – your parents are your norm, aren't they? You only know things the way they show them to you – but as an adult I've spent a lot of time thinking about it and I realise now that, for most of our childhood, she was pretty seriously depressed.'

'Really? Was she treated for it?'

'No. I tried to convince her to try treatment later on but she didn't believe in pills or therapists; thought they were self-indulgent. It's a shame. Maybe if . . .' He shrugged. 'On the surface you wouldn't have been able to tell. She was very attractive, my mother, petite and slim and always well put together even though she couldn't have had much money for clothes. She was bright, too, and funny, but she didn't see that. The truth is, I think, she went through her life believing she wasn't worth much and just waiting for people to confirm it. The only thing she was absolutely sure of was my brother, whose general rightness was so obvious that no one could dispute it. She had to be confident of Nick because it would have been blatantly mad not to. He was clever, handsome, funny, charming, you name it, and she was grateful to him because

184

it made her feel like less of a failure. He validated her.'

'What about your dad in all this? Where was he?'

'Dad.' A snort. 'My dad was not a natural father; let's just say that. We were too much for him, both of us – too loud, too boisterous, too demanding, too . . . everything. At some point around the time of that holiday, probably, give or take a year, he just checked out, told himself that as long as he was bringing home the bacon, *providing*, then he was doing his bit. He left everything else to my mother and the truth is, she wasn't up to the job either so Nick took over.'

'What do you mean?' Hannah felt herself frown.

'He's manipulative. No, that doesn't cover it – doesn't even touch the sides. He's brilliant, actually, an absolute genius at playing people to get what he wants from them. My mother was his masterstroke, though. When he was nine or ten, he realised what was going on, the power he had over her because she derived what little self-esteem she had from being the mother of this perfect being, and he started – quite consciously, you could see it – to use that.'

Hannah felt a frisson of revulsion. 'How?'

Mark gave a small shrug. 'It started innocently enough. I think one day it just dawned on him that she needed him so badly, needed his approval and general good feeling towards her so much, that it was impossible for her to say no to him – she just couldn't risk it. Once he'd realised that, it was

Pandora's Box with the lid off. When you're nine and ten, it's all about sweets and crisps and getting around your bedtime, kid stuff, but even within a few months it got more serious. He wanted things – I mean, I know children these days are supposed to be the most materialistic they've ever been, fed all these pernicious adverts on TV' – he made a face at her – 'but, frankly, my brother would have taken some beating. Scaletrix, walkie-talkies, Nintendo games, a SEGA – the demands got bigger and bigger and more expensive, and she just kept saying yes.'

'Could they afford it? You said that—'

'No, and that was a big problem, because Dad used to see all the stuff and freak out, scream at Mum, and she took it as further evidence that she was a failure, there was something fundamentally just second-rate and *wrong* with her. Then Nick would creep in and put his arms round her and tell her that everything was all right and he loved her, all the time mentally compiling his next set of demands, and the cycle repeated itself.'

'God.'

Mark shrugged again. 'By the time he was four-teen or fifteen, he was doing pretty much whatever he wanted: not turning up at school more than two or three days a week, smoking weed, having sex. My parents got home from a memorial service for a friend of theirs one afternoon and found him in their bed with Dad's boss's daughter. Actually *in flagrante*, apparently. Becca, the bloody idiot, let

186

him take Polaroids and he showed them round the whole sixth form. It very, very nearly lost my dad his job. God, Nick would have loved that – until the money dried up, anyway.' Mark rolled his eyes.

'Your poor parents.'

'At least Becca wasn't the one he got pregnant – that was the English teacher's daughter. My mother stumped up for the abortion, of course, and didn't say a word to Mr or Mrs Stevens. They kept it a secret from Dad, too. Oh, Nick did it all, every last bit of teenage miscreancy you can imagine – drugs, shoplifting. That was purely for the thrill, by the way – there was no need for him to nick anything because Mum would just give him whatever money he asked for.'

Mark took a final slug of wine and emptied the glass. When he started talking again, the hurt was back in his voice, even less successfully masked now.

'I didn't get a car when I turned seventeen,' he said, 'but a year later Nick did, a vintage Triumph Spitfire that he'd campaigned and campaigned for, and which arrived outside the house on the morning of his birthday with a big clichéd red sash that Mum had tied round the middle. He wrote it off drink-driving a month after he passed his test, but as soon as he got his licence back she bought him another one exactly the same because she knew how much he loved it.'

'How could someone behave like that? And how did your mum afford it? Two cars . . .'

'My grandmother died – Mum's mother. She didn't have a lot but she did have some equity in her house and Mum, the only child, inherited it – which meant Nick did, by proxy. By the time he graduated from university – which was something of a miracle in itself – he'd run through the lot. Mum had nothing left. The rows about that – I wasn't at home by that stage but she told me about them. It nearly ended my parents' marriage.'

Hannah reached for the cardigan that she'd taken off while she was cooking. It was half past one and the heating in the building had long gone off for the night but the cold felt like more than that, a chill in her bones. 'Frankly,' she said, 'he sounds like a total bastard.'

'He became one.'

'But what I don't understand is, why do *you* feel bad about any of this? Why do you think *you* let your mother down?'

'She asked me always to look out for him and I haven't. Didn't.'

'What do you mean, look out for him?'

'My mother was bright, as I said. She had a blind spot when it came to Nick but otherwise she was pretty on the ball. Anyway, when he and I were in our twenties, her blinkers started to come off, at least to some extent. I think she looked at him when he was twenty-three, twenty-four, living in London on money that she was giving him – she'd got a job on the tills at Debenhams so she could fund him. My God, the rows with Dad that set off. He said she was bringing the family down, humiliating him, making it look like he couldn't afford to keep his wife and had to send her out to work in a shop.' Mark blew out air. 'Can I . . .?' He pointed at the wine and Hannah poured him another glass.

'Basically, it was hell. Anyway, thank God, somewhere in the middle of that particular shit-storm, I think it began to dawn on her that she was being played. My brother's really clever, Han, cleverer than me by a long chalk, but he's lazy, totally and utterly indolent – he's not even embarrassed about it. The reason he didn't have a job was that he couldn't be bothered to get off his arse and take one – probably afraid someone would ask him to get up before eleven. Of course, he was giving Mum the whole bit about how difficult new graduates were finding it to get jobs – I can remember her standing in the kitchen one weekend repeating the statistics back at me – the state of the economy, blah, blah, blah. But finally, *finally*, she couldn't quite accept it. I think probably she couldn't get her head around the fact that no one wanted to employ her *wunderkind* so she was forced to conclude that something else was going on.'

'So what happened?'

'She asked me to give him a job at DataPro.'

'God – and did you?'

189

'Though it stuck in my craw, yes. I didn't want him working for me, obviously – for a start, I knew he *wouldn't* work and I'd only been going three years at that point, I didn't have money to pay someone who wasn't bringing anything in – but what I was really worried about was that he'd try and sabotage me.'

'Sabotage?'

'My brother doesn't like me,' Mark said, frankly. 'The antipathy's entirely mutual. He resents me, which doesn't make a lot of sense all things considered, but there it is. He looks at me and sees the straight As at A-level, Cambridge, then DataPro, and he doesn't realise that it all comes from work, nothing else. He thinks that I was just given it all, like he was given all the toys and money and abortions and cars and his rent in Borough paid for. Honestly, I think it never occurred to him that I started working like I do in a bid to get a bit of my parents' attention for a change. The exam results, Cambridge – I was like a dog with a bone, coming home with my tail wagging and dropping it at their feet in the hope of a pat on the head.'

Hannah imagined him as a teenager and felt a burst of pity that hurt her heart.

'Obviously, I'm grateful for it now because it gave me my work ethic and that's given me the life I want.' He reached across and took hold of her hand, rubbed his thumb over the backs of her fingers.

She waited a moment. 'What happened?' she said. 'Did Nick sabotage you?'

'He tried.' Mark gave a sort of half-nod. 'He was clever about it – there was always an alternative explanation for why every potential new client he went to meet decided not to go with us after all – but after a year and a half I just couldn't put up with it any more. We lost an account for the first time, it had never happened before, and when I investigated, I found out that Nick had hit on the guy's wife quite aggressively in the corridor of a restaurant while we were out for dinner. Then there was an issue with some missing money, ten thousand, and it turned out he'd "borrowed" it, which he didn't admit until after I'd given our accountant a rocket and had him resign on me. So I fired him – Nick. I had to.'

'How did he take it?'

'*He* was fine – actually, he laughed – but my mother, both my parents, were furious. I think they thought they'd finally got him sorted and here he was, back on their hands again. They asked me what kind of brother I was, to do that to him, what kind of person I was to fire one of my own family, and I just lost it, told them what I really thought of Nick and the way my mother had let him ride rough-shod over her, probably made him the person he was. They didn't talk to me for a year afterwards.'

Hannah pulled her legs up and wrapped her arms round her knees. 'But I still don't see why you feel guilty. You couldn't be expected to go on employing him if he was wrecking your business, and it sounds like your parents – definitely your dad – agreed with you about the way he'd treated your mother.'

'I think they did. That isn't what I feel bad about. I made it up with them eventually, and my father had a couple of Scotches at Christmas a couple of years after that and said that bringing up Nick had been a nightmare. It was what happened later, when my mother was dying. I told you she died after my dad?'

Hannah nodded.

'I was with her that morning. Nick got there too late. He was having an affair with a woman in Brighton and her husband was away – too good an opportunity to pass up. He didn't make it to the hospital till one, by which point Mum was gone. But she asked me that morning – she made me swear – to look after him.'

'What did she mean by that? Surely you couldn't . . .'

'Give him another chance at DataPro. He'd been drifting ever since he left, doing a bit of one thing, getting fired, trying something else, never sticking at anything . . . and I think it worried her all the time she was ill – she couldn't rest easy when Nick was still so unsettled. Things like that were important to her: she was very old-fashioned. I know it bothered her, for instance, that neither of us was married.'

'Maternal classic.'

'Anyway, I promised her. I swore. I swore to her that I would look after him. I wouldn't give him money but I'd give him a job, and she said, "Thank you, Mark," and about an hour after that, she died. I think it was the only thing I ever did that really touched her – made a difference.' His voice cracked and he bent his head. Hannah heard him give a hard swallow and put her hand out to him, but he shook his head.

'The thing is, after she died, I couldn't do it. I couldn't let him come in and stuff things up, patronise me, help himself to the bank accounts – I just couldn't do it. So the promise I made to her, I broke. I lied to my mother on her deathbed.'

The look on his face was so bleak, so full of self-hatred, that Hannah couldn't stand it. She moved across the sofa now, kneeled upright and put her arms around him, holding him so tightly she could feel his ribcage even through the layers of his shirt and jumper. She pressed her face against the side of his neck and felt his pulse beat against her lips. For two or three minutes she held on to him, saying nothing but communicating, she hoped, that she understood and pitied him and loved him. When finally she pulled away, his cheeks were wet and she kissed them.

'Where is he now?' she asked gently.

'I don't know,' he croaked, then cleared his throat. 'I'm not sure. London, I think. A couple of years ago I bumped into an old friend of my dad's and he seemed to think Nick was working for an estate agent in Highgate. But that was two years ago so . . .' He shrugged. 'I don't know.'

CHAPTER 12

It had still been light when Hannah had left the hospital but by the time the Tube rattled back above ground at Eel Brook Common the sun, such as it had been, was long gone. Though it wasn't yet five, the train had become busier and busier as it tracked its way under central London, and from Monument on, she'd been surrounded by a thicket of legs in suits, a changing cast of crotches at eye-level that swayed and lurched towards her as the carriage cornered, their owners gripping the overhead bar with one hand, texting or clutching double-folded copies of the *Standard* with the other. It was nearly Monday evening suddenly: Mark would be back in the morning.

Prison. The idea was incredible: his brother – her brother-in-law, whatever Mark said – was in prison. As she'd left the hospital, the word had been tolling in her ears: *prison, prison*. What had Nick done? Pride had stopped her from asking Hermione. She'd already humiliated herself by going there and accosting the woman in the corridor, accusing her of having an affair. Hannah felt blood rush to her face at the memory. She might just as well have

195

come out and said it: our marriage is a sham; I don't trust Mark not to sleep around, and he doesn't trust me enough to tell me about his brother. She'd played it off as though she knew all about it – *Of course! His brother, of course. Very sorry, crossed wires* – but Hermione clearly hadn't been fooled. Why would she have been? She had half a brain, didn't she?

Hannah had a momentary mental image of Hermione's face as she'd left, the lines around her wide eyes. She was very attractive, striking even, but she looked knackered, completely worn out. Actually, what she looked was worn down, as if she'd been tired for a very long time. Maybe it was smoking that had given her that pale, prematurely aged skin, the dark circles and the bony bird-like sternum visible in the vee of her green surgical tunic. Surely not, though: she was in her late thirties, forty-one or -two at most if she was Mark's direct contemporary; she wasn't old enough for the kippered smoker's look. It was stress that made people look like that, years of stress, doubtless in her case the pressure of making it to the top in the male-dominated, big-swinging-dicks world of surgery.

The train pulled in at Parsons Green and Hannah got out. A light drizzle had started to fall while she'd been underground and the paving on the platform was slick and black, the halos around the streetlights smeared against the purple sky. She joined the crush of people filing downstairs towards the barrier. What had Nick done? All the way across London she'd been asking herself the question again and again.

Had he been drink-driving again and caused criminal damage – or hit someone? Could it be drugs? She remembered the £10,000 he'd stolen from DataPro's accounts. What if he'd done that at another company, one at which he didn't have his brother to let him off without prosecution?

Everyone who'd been on the train, it seemed, was going her way and the pavement outside the station was clogged, a bottleneck forming behind a woman struggling to put up an umbrella. Hannah felt her frustration rising as she was forced to dawdle along behind a couple in matching trenchcoats who were holding hands and strolling as if it was a sunny Sunday afternoon. *Come on, come on*: she had to get home, get online.

At the White Horse, the couple turned off down Ackmar Road and the congestion started to disperse. Hannah picked up speed, her feet tapping an anxious rhythm past the girls' school and the large red-brick houses that overlooked the Green. The pavement was dark, the light from the Victorian-style streetlamps struggling to penetrate the dank November air.

Quarrendon Street was deserted, and the sound of traffic on the New King's Road faded quickly behind her. She opened the front door and the heavy silence inside rushed out to envelop her before she'd even stepped over the threshold. She slammed the door, dumped her coat on the stairs and went through to the kitchen.

Her laptop was on the table and she sat down

and pulled it towards her. Suddenly, however, her sense of urgency evaporated and a sickening dread took its place. Standing again, she went to the drawer of odds and ends and took out the half-empty packet of cigarettes that Tom had left behind the last time he came over. She lit one on the gas ring and took it out into the yard where she managed five or six drags before feeling nauseous. She tossed it into the puddle by the stone trough and heard it fizzle and go out.

Back inside, she poured a large measure of the Armagnac Mark had been given by his aerospace client in Toulouse and sat back down at the table. She brought up a new Google window then stopped again. Was information about criminal convictions available online? Was there an official record? Apart from Nick's name, she had nothing to search by. Where had he been tried? Mark had said he lived in London but who knew if that was true? And how long ago had it happened? How long had his sentence been?

Into the search bar she typed *Nick Reilly found guilty*. Links to a blog about the guilty pleasures of football and another protesting against the adoption of Sharia law in the UK, then *Business Week* talking about David Nick Reilly, president of General Motors. On the second page, there was a series of stories about people found guilty of dealing marijuana but all of them were American or Canadian; none was from the UK.

Hannah took a swig of the brandy, deleted *Nick*

and typed in *Nicholas*. She hit return and waited. This time the first hit was a story in the *Daily Mail*: **PLAYBOY 'MONSTER' FOUND GUILTY OF MANSLAUGHTER.**

CHAPTER 13

PLAYBOY 'MONSTER' FOUND GUILTY OF MANSLAUGHTER

By: Daily Mail reporter
Published: 06.02 GMT, 17 November 2002

Nicholas Reilly was yesterday convicted of the manslaughter of Patricia Hendrick, whose body was discovered at his West London home in March this year.

Hendrick, 25, known by her friends as Patty, died after a 48-hour-sex, drink-and-drugs binge during which Reilly, 28, plied her with alcohol and repeatedly injected her with cocaine.

When Hendrick experienced breathing difficulties and then fell unconscious, Reilly failed to call an ambulance. Hendrick died shortly afterwards.

A post-mortem found the cause of death to be a pulmonary embolism brought on by an impurity in the drug.

At the time of her death Hendrick's body bore the marks of rough and prolonged sexual activity, including extensive bruising, much of it intimate, and ligature marks around her wrists, ankles and neck.

Over the course of a trial whose details have often been distressing, the jury at the old Bailey heard how in the early hours of 7 March this year, Reilly and Hendrick, who at the time was dating the defendant's brother, Mark, left the nightclub in East London where they had spent the evening with him and other mutual friends. Both were already drunk and high on cocaine.

The binge continued for two days at Reilly's home in Chelsea. Reilly admitted giving the deceased large quantities of vodka and tequila and supplying her with repeated doses of amphetamines and cocaine to 'keep the party going'.

Police who attended the scene testified that the 'party' had occurred largely in the defendant's bedroom, where they discovered evidence of bondage and other sado-masochistic activity.

Though the sexual activity itself took place by mutual consent, at least initially, the defendant admitted that unbeknownst to Hendrick, he was using concealed cameras to film the encounter for later viewing. The final tape proved decisive in Reilly's conviction, showing him administering intravenous doses of cocaine to Hendrick when she was too intoxicated to give her consent.

Police arrested him at the scene after calls from a downstairs neighbour disturbed by noise. He will be sentenced on Friday.

Speaking outside the court, investigating officer Detective Inspector Michael Iveson said, 'This was a deeply disturbing case for all concerned. Though Ms Hendrick was initially a willing participant in the events that took place at Nicholas Reilly's home, there can be no question that Reilly behaved in a depraved and inhuman manner, first by administering doses of cocaine and continuing sexual activity for his own pleasure after Ms Hendrick suffered breathing difficulties and began to lose consciousness. And secondly when, aware of the illegal nature of the drug-taking and his role in supplying Ms Hendrick, and afraid of the consequences, he failed to call for medical assistance.

'This is a man who, even under the effects of sustained drinking and drug-taking, was able to calculate his own sexual gratification and freedom as worth more than the life of another human being. There can be no doubt that his callous failure to act resulted in Ms Hendrick's death. He will no doubt spend a considerable length of time behind bars and we hope that Ms Hendrick's friends and family will find some comfort in that.'

'SICK NICK' REILLY TAPED SEX ACTS AS LOVER FOUGHT FOR LIFE

By: Gazette reporter
Published 17 November 2002

Perverted Nick Reilly shot SECRET FOOTAGE of lover Patricia Hendrick as she LAY DYING.

Convicted of manslaughter yesterday at Winchester Crown Court, SICK NICK admitted to using secret cameras to film himself having ROUGH SEX with Patty, 25, as a COCAINE-related blockage in her lungs left her fighting for life.

During the course of the trial, a horrified jury was forced to watch footage of MONSTER Nick injecting a barely conscious Patty with MORE cocaine.

Even when Patty lost consciousness altogether, cowardly Nick, afraid of the consequences, failed to ring for an ambulance.

Her BODY was discovered when police came to investigate reports of a disturbance.

Before his arrest, Sick Nick, 28, was flying high, earning a SIX-FIGURE salary, enjoying several exotic foreign holidays a year and driving a brand-new PORSCHE.

Blonde Patty was well known in her circle as a PARTY GIRL who loved the company of wealthy friends, especially men. A friend who wished to remain anonymous said, 'Patty was no saint – she liked to go out, have a good time, and she liked male attention. There was always something naive about her, though, despite her wild behaviour – she was a bad judge of character. All it was going to take was for her to meet one wrong person and tragically she did.'

Early in the trial, the jury heard how the pathologist was at first confused to find DNA belonging to two different men when he examined the body. Nick's BROTHER, Mark Reilly, founder of City software success story DataPro, told jurors that HE had been dating Patty at the time of her death.

Mark Reilly told the court that he and Patty had enjoyed a TRYST in a lavatory at the club just TWENTY MINUTES before she left the venue with his brother. He returned from buying drinks for himself and Patty to find that the pair had gone.

Sitting in the public gallery yesterday, Mark Reilly wept openly as the jury delivered their verdict on his brother.

Acquaintances of Sick Nick were today reeling at news of his conviction. Liza Miller, a former classmate at his high school in Eastbourne, Sussex, said, 'I'm shocked – totally shocked. Nick had a wild streak, we all knew that, but we thought it was just fun – I never thought he could actually physically hurt someone. We were so young and stupid then, it's terrifying to think what could have happened. It could have been any of us.'

To others, the news came as less of a surprise. Martin Westing, another classmate, said, 'The blokes always knew there was something wrong there but the girls loved him. He could charm them out of the trees like birds.'

Becca George, described by others as an old flame of Reilly's, was initially reluctant to talk but told the Gazette that: 'Nick could be very persuasive. With him, everything was fun, exciting. He lived in the moment – there was no thought for the consequences.'

Speaking outside court, Patty's father, Richard, a wealthy Hertfordshire businessman, described himself and his wife as 'totally devastated. Patty was the light of our lives. We hope Reilly goes to prison for a very long time.'

Hannah tipped her head back and let the freezing drizzle fall on her cheeks and eyelids. She pulled in long breaths, willing her heart to stop beating so fast; she could feel it knocking behind her sternum as if she was going to have a heart attack. Another wave of nausea went over her, and she crossed the yard and leaned against the little wrought-iron table, bracing herself with her hands. She was hot then cold then hot again, sweating in her clothes but shivering.

She thought of the crimes she'd imagined on the Tube home – fraud, drugs, even the death by drink-driving – and she wanted to laugh: how tame of her, how *naïve*. But how could she have imagined anything like this? In one of the other tabloid pieces – she'd barely scratched the surface so far; the story had run for days, it seemed, the papers loving this tale of sex and death amongst the young and glamorous – she'd read descriptions of the look of glee on Nick's face as he'd emptied another syringe into Patty Hendrick's limp arm, then angled her body towards his hidden camera as he'd pushed her knees apart again. *Glee* – the word was sickeningly vivid. Reading it, she'd seen him as clearly as if he'd been crouching over her, Hannah, his eyes hungry, mouth wet and open, his sharp incisors just like Mark's.

Even without the references to Mark and DataPro, even though she'd never seen a picture of him before, she would have known the man in the photographs as his brother straight away. The pictures were ten years old now but looking at them she'd felt as if she were looking at a younger, better-looking version of Mark, the face a little less broad, the eyes just slightly wider-spaced, the mole on his cheek lasered away without a trace. Mark was an excellent prototype – she'd thought he was handsome from the first time she'd clapped eyes on him on the verandah in Montauk – but Nick, it was clear, was the perfected version.

And Patty had been 'dating' Mark. What did 'dating' mean in British English? Had they been in a relationship? How long had they been seeing each other? What did it matter, so far as what Nick had done? What kind of person even entertained the idea of a woman his brother was involved with or had even expressed interest in? *The kind of person who let his sixty-year-old mother work in a shop to fund his post-college lifestyle,* answered the voice at the back of her head. Who showed naked pictures of his girlfriend around school. The kind of person who could watch a woman fight for her life and not ring an ambulance.

Hannah's stomach gave a sudden heave and she dashed back across the yard and wrenched the door open. She made it to the downstairs lavatory just in time. Afterwards, empty, she closed her eyes and rested her forehead on the cold china rim of the hand basin. That poor woman, she thought, poor, lost Patty. To die like that, drugged out of your mind, filmed naked, alone with a leering, conscienceless horror of a man who'd stand by and watch you die rather than deal with the consequences of calling for help.

The papers had had several different pictures of her and, if the Internet page layouts were anything to go by, they'd printed them big. No surprise there: she was perfect for that kind of story, any kind of story, with her long straight blonde hair and wide green eyes that at first glance seemed innocent but then revealed a glint of invitation. She was slim but curvaceous, still young enough at twenty-five that the curves suggested puppy fat in the best of ways, a toothsome, almost succulent plumpness. Two of the most frequently featured photographs looked as if they'd been taken on the same night and showed her in a simple black dress with cap sleeves that she'd pulled in at the waist with a thick patent-leather belt whose studs and heavy double buckle were perfect visual shorthand for what she'd been into the weekend she died, if not ever before.

Hannah thought about the photograph Mark had described but never shown her, the one of him and his brother as boys on the beach in Devon: Nick the golden child, Mark with his wasp sting and too-tight trunks, his ice-cream cone dropped in the sand. She imagined him in the club that night, coming back from the bar carrying a drink for Patty to discover that she'd left with his brother, and she felt a rush of pity for him, an intense, bitter sadness. In seconds, however, it was gone, replaced by anger. How could he not have told her? This was so *huge*, so fundamental. Something like this must be scored into his psyche; a day couldn't pass when he didn't think about it. What kind of a wife was she to him that he'd never told her – that he'd left her to find out like this from a friend she'd never even heard of?

But then, why hadn't she found out for herself until now? How could this exist in Mark's past without her knowing? *Well, how hard,* accused the voice in her head, *did you try to find out about him when you met?* Yes, they'd met through Ant and Roisin but they themselves had only known him a few weeks by then. She had met a man in a foreign country, without any of the normal infrastructure that surrounded people: family, old friends. Mark's parents were dead, his brother estranged – she'd had none of the usual references. Teenage girls, she thought savagely, did more research into their crushes than she'd done into her husband – an hour on the Internet and she would have found all of this. She'd started once, googling him at the office one night when she was waiting for a call from LA, but after the first few links she had stopped, feeling grubby and stalkerish as she'd read pieces in the business press about his success, the big contracts DataPro had been getting then. All the talk of money had made her feel like a gold-digger, as if she was sizing him up as a catch, a potential target.

It hadn't just been that, though. As she'd finished one story and clicked on the next, she'd been ambushed by a memory from her childhood. It had been spring, March – what happened in the weeks afterwards meant she'd never forget – and she was nine years old. She'd been upstairs in her bedroom doing her homework and she'd come down for a glass of milk and, if she was lucky and the kitchen was clear, a raid of the biscuit tin. Just as she'd been about to round the kitchen door, however, she'd seen her mother.

Something she'd never been able to put her finger on – the atmosphere, a radiating tension in the air, perhaps – had stopped Hannah in her tracks and she'd stayed back, out of sight. Her mother had been putting a load of washing on, sorting it before it went in the machine, and Hannah had watched as she'd gone through her father's trouser pockets, pulling them all the way so they stuck out like cartoon ears, shaking the trousers as if she could force them to talk to her. She'd been crying, the sobs silent but strong enough to wrack the whole of her upper body.

Hannah had been physically repulsed. Why was her mother doing this? Did she want to destroy their family, to drive Dad away? Couldn't she see what she was doing? She was making his life unlivable, a nightmare. Nearly every night Hannah could hear their voices on the other side of the bedroom wall, her mother's desperate pleading that he just tell her the truth, her father's increasing frustration, his growing anger at her insistence that he was lying. Her mother was like a rat, Hannah thought as she stood at the kitchen door and watched, a rat gnawing and gnawing, eating away at their family.

Without letting her mother know she'd been seen, Hannah had run upstairs to her room, slammed the door and jammed the lock with her hairbrush. Then she'd flung herself face down on the bed and cried and cried. It was hopeless; there was no way her parents could stay together. Her dad would move out and there would be a divorce and she and Tom would be like her friend Claire from school, who lived out of a bag and felt guilty all the time for being excited about Friday nights when she finally got to see her dad.

Lying on her bed that night, Hannah had made a promise to herself: she would never creep around like that, spying on the people she was supposed to love. She would never do it. If she ever got married, she would trust her husband. Well, she'd kept her promise, hadn't she? she thought bitterly now. And look at the results.

Legs shaking, she stood up and washed her hands and face. Pink eyes stared back at her from the mirror, any benefit from the long sleep on the sofa last night wiped out. That felt like weeks ago. She dried her hands and went back to the kitchen, poured herself another half-inch of Armagnac and sat down at the table. The red light was flashing on her BlackBerry and when she went to her inbox, Mark's name was at the top again. She paused for a moment then opened it.

Just finished the meeting. Went v well, I'm sure we'll get the contract, so def worth staying. Home tonight to see my gorgeous wife – not many hours to go . . .

CHAPTER 14

Hannah lay on her back, eyes open. Their bedroom was at the back of the house and there was never any noise or light from the street, but here in the spare room an orange glow seeped around the curtains to stain the ceiling, and every few minutes, even this late, a car came cruising down the road outside, its headlights sweeping the room like a torch-beam. She couldn't go next door and sleep in their bed, though: she was too confused, too angry. This room, this bed, was neutral, no-man's-land.

She turned her head to look at the clock on the bedside table. 02.47. What was Mark doing now? He'd be on the plane, either in the air or just taking off. He might be asleep already: even if he'd adjusted to New York time in the past few days, he was one of those people who had the gift of sleeping any time, anywhere, making dead hours count. If they took a night flight together, he would arrive fresh and well rested while she, having worked her way through the films and strained to read by the overhead spotlight, always pitched up at the other end looking like the subject of some sort of clinical trial. And what would be keeping *him* awake, anyway? He had no idea she knew about any of this.

She turned over, away from the window and the demonic red glow of the clock, closed her eyes and tried again to find a comfortable position. Now her arm was the problem, uncomfortable tucked under her body, awkward held out in front. The real issue, however, was her mind, which was racing despite everything she'd done to try to switch off. She'd made up this bed with fresh sheets, watched an hour of mindless TV and had a warm bath, with her old copy of *Our Man in Havana*. She loved the book, she'd read it several times, but tonight her eyes kept sliding away from the page and none of the jokes made her smile.

Before that, though, she'd been reading all evening. She'd deleted Mark's email without responding then gone back to the computer and read article after article until her eyes ached from screen glare. Every new fact repulsed her, the words leaping out in all their tabloid horror – *death! sado-masochism! ligatures! cocaine!* – yet still she clicked on the next piece with the fervour of an addict.

In abbreviated form, the story had even reached some of the foreign newspapers. How the hell had she missed it at the time? Maybe she hadn't completely; maybe she'd seen the headlines and decided she didn't need to read the rest, all the prurient details about the playboy and the party-girl

213

and the sticky ends they'd come to. And Reilly was pretty common as surnames went; there was no reason why it would have rung a bell when she'd met Mark. But it was also possible she hadn't seen the coverage at all. When she'd been working really hard, finishing a big project, she'd sometimes gone weeks without more than a cursory glance at the papers for anything relevant to what she was working on.

Tonight she'd read coverage from broadsheets and tabloids, the websites of TV channels and news magazines, until after a while she'd thought there were no more grim details to discover. Then, just as she was about to force herself to turn off the computer, she'd found a feature-length story published in the news review section of a Sunday broadsheet the weekend after Nick's conviction. The headline was A DEATH IN CHELSEA.

The piece started with a portrait of Patty, many of the details now so familiar to Hannah that she was beginning to feel as if she'd actually known her growing up: her father's job as the chief executive of an electronics company in Hemel Hempstead; her stay-at-home mother and her brother, Seb, two years younger and identified as a future track star by the age of ten; the six-bedroomed house in a small village outside St Albans, with its swimming pool and the long paddock where Patty kept her ponies, Mischief and then Gorgeous Gus. Hannah knew about the gymkhanas and the summer sailing camps and the house in the Dordogne that Richard

214

and Lara Hendrick had bought when their daughter was twelve, and she knew about the mediocre grades that made it obvious from early on that Patty's childhood dream of becoming a vet would stay a dream.

The fact that she had been a willing sexual partner at the beginning of that nightmarish weekend had deterred the papers that trumpeted their 'family values' from the usual hagiography of the victim, but this journalist, Carole Temple, had talked to several childhood friends who described Patty's tender heart and many acts of generosity. One told the story of how she'd started visiting an elderly widow in the village and then, when she'd learned that the woman loved books but was losing her sight, had begun reading to her every Sunday afternoon.

While pretending pity, most of the other pieces had related Patty's fall from grace with relish, detailing her friendship with the 'wilder element' at her exclusive but not very academic girls' school, the slipping of her grades, her experimentation – why did they always use that word? – with alcohol and marijuana. At that point, many of the articles made it sound as if the die were irrevocably cast, as if every teenage girl who'd ever taken a drag on an inexpertly rolled spliff in the company of a few sixth-form boys from the local comprehensive had set themselves on a road to perdition whose only destination was an early demise at the hands of a Bad Man.

Temple, however, had resisted the easy picture of the good-girl-gone-bad and instead asked questions about the expectations of a young woman like Patty, well brought up and attractive if not especially bright. What part did she see for herself in a society where women like her mother, who stayed at home and raised families, were routinely dismissed as pointless non-contributors? The intrinsic value of that role, argued Temple, its respectability, had been eroded to the point of non-existence, to an extent where it was no longer acceptable for a young woman to admit that she wanted to be a full-time mother. And what had replaced that position in the eyes of young women like Patty? A culture obsessed with celebrity and appearance, where the women most venerated in the media, and some of the highest paid, were those who posed for lads' mags in G-strings, and fell drunkenly out of nightclubs. And the scorn levelled at any young woman perceived as not 'up for it' . . . So far from liberating girls like Patty, ladette culture, argued Temple, had enslaved them, turned them into walking, talking sex toys.

Hannah had assumed the piece would continue in the same feminist vein but, somewhat abruptly, the journalist had changed tack and moved on to Nick, who, in the photograph they'd used, appeared deeply tanned and laughing as he swung into the driver's seat of a silver BMW convertible, a lovely Cotswold-stone house in the background.

In his case, too, it was clear that Temple had researched deeper and harder than the other journalists; there were several details that Hannah knew only because Mark himself had told her that night in New York. The sensational piece in the *Gazette* had mentioned Eastbourne, quoted old classmates of Nick's probably contacted by phone, but Temple, it was clear, had been there.

The curtains were drawn this week in the front windows of the two-bedroomed bungalow where Nicholas Reilly spent his childhood, as if his parents, who still live in the house, want to close their eyes against the reality of the crime of which their son was this week found guilty.

Cowering under a matching sky, the small grey pebbledashed bungalow, though immaculately maintained, seems an incongruous location for a boyhood that several who know the family describe as charmed or 'golden'.

'Nick was one of those children who seemed destined for a happy life,' said a family friend who asked to remain anonymous. 'He was a beautiful baby who grew into a beautiful little boy, always laughing, always smiling. We used to say to Lizzie, his mother, that she should let him be a child model – he would have made a fortune.'

'He was bright as a button,' said Leigh Stanton, his first teacher at primary school. 'Learning came easily to him – he was a joy to teach. He read and wrote early and he was interested in everything. The only challenge was getting him to sit still – he was always restless, full of energy – and telling him off was next to impossible when he looked up at you with those big brown eyes.'

If Reilly's early childhood was charmed, however, by the time he left junior school, there were troubling signs. Though no one interviewed for this piece was willing to be quoted, a number of people hinted at Elizabeth Reilly's shyness and lack of confidence, and her emotional reliance on her younger son. Others voiced reservations about the way she lavished attention on the boy and showered him with toys and gifts that many were surprised the family could afford. His brother Mark, a year older, seems not to have been indulged to the same extent.

Perhaps his status as the spoiled younger child contributed to the wild streak that Nick started to exhibit as his teenage years began, or at least to his apparent indifference to the consequences of his actions, alluded to by many people who knew him. That sense of being untouchable – of living outside the rules or even, finally, the law – was to become one of Reilly's defining characteristics.

The first indication that something was wrong was a falling-off in his attendance record during his third year at secondary school. Truant officers soon became regular visitors to the bungalow. 'It got to the stage,' said Matt Trenton, a classmate, 'where he wasn't allowed to get the school bus any more and his dad had to drive him and walk him in through the front door, which Nick hated, obviously. It made no difference: by breaktime, he'd be gone, out the door again. He used to hang around down on the beach and drink or smoke weed. Sometimes, he said, he got the train into Brighton to play arcade games.'

At fourteen, he was excluded from school for a week for verbally abusing a teacher who had embarrassed him in front of his classmates.

There were hints, too, of darker troubles. Two long-term residents of his parents' quiet street remember tensions between Nick and Jim Thomas, an elderly neighbour, now deceased, who took issue with the teenager's habit of using his back garden as a short-cut to the street behind.

'Nick used to jump over his back fence,' one recalled. 'It scared the living daylights out of Jim, turning the light on to find Nick standing on his back patio staring in through the kitchen window. Jim had an old shed at the end of the garden, near where Nick used to come in, and several times he said he found drug paraphernalia on the bench inside. When he complained to Gordon and Elizabeth, they were very apologetic, they always were, but nothing seemed to change. Lizzie always excused his behaviour as teenage hi-jinks but it was clearly more than that.'

What passed between Nick and Jim Thomas is still the subject of local speculation but six weeks after Thomas's complaint to the Reillys, the shed on his allotment was found ablaze. Three weeks after that, Thomas's dog, a Red Setter named Molly, was found drowned on the bank of a stream that runs close to the houses. Nick had played truant from school that afternoon and had earlier been seen on the street wearing jeans soaked to the thigh.

Neighbours recall a tearful Thomas banging on the Reillys' front door but though the police were called, for reasons that remain unclear no charges were pressed. Reilly's immunity held firm.

Classmates at his senior school describe Nick Reilly as charismatic and entertaining, though they struggle to remember who his particular friends were among the other boys. Clearly, however, by the later years of school he was a major success with his female contemporaries, a fact perhaps unsurprising given his looks, reported charm, and the second-hand orange Triumph Spitfire that arrived outside the bungalow on his 17th birthday, courtesy of his mother.

If he had no particular friends among the boys, it seems also that he had no particular favourite among the girls, instead spreading his favours equally between the best-looking and most popular members of his own year and the one above. Reilly had been sexually active since the age of 13, but relationships were short-lived and casual, at least on his side. Though there is no suggestion of a causal connection, he is believed to have had a brief relationship with Emma Simpson, a lovely but emotionally fragile girl who committed suicide not long after they parted company.

Despite his poor school attendance record, Nick's natural academic ability was enough to secure him the grades for a place at university in Leeds, where he studied economics, 'at least nominally', says Rachel Jenkins, a fellow student on the course. He soon became a fixture on the city's vibrant party scene, where his use of alcohol and drugs – constants in his life for several years by that point – really took off. He graduated with a third-class degree, which many considered him lucky to get at all. Reilly was reportedly angered by the result, however, and demanded his papers be remarked. His grade remained the same.

As soon as exams were finished, he vacated his student digs in Headingley and moved south again to London. Most of his university contemporaries reduced the high costs of London living by renting houses together but Nick took a one-bedroomed flat in Borough where he lived for the next three years.

How he paid for the flat is not clear. He is known to have received financial support from his mother but not enough, it would seem, to cover life in central London. His employment record during these years was patchy at very best and included brief stints as an assistant in a high-profile PR firm, an estate agency and a record company.

He had no difficulty getting jobs – his charm made him a natural at interviews – but keeping them was another matter. The issue was his work ethic. A fellow employee at the estate agency recalled: 'He was late every day, took long lunches and called in sick three times in his first fortnight. He just didn't seem to care.'

Then, at the age of 26, Reilly started working with his brother, Mark, and seemed at last to have found something that held his interest for more than a couple of weeks.

In marked contrast to Nick, Mark Reilly had, by the age of 27, achieved tremendous success. After taking a first-class engineering degree at Cambridge, he had come to London and begun raising the capital that allowed him to start DataPro, a company that designs custom-made software for banks and brokerage firms in the City and, these days, around the world. Within three years, the company was generating an annual turnover close to £5 million.

Nick Reilly was employed as a project manager at DataPro and his job was to win new business for the firm and ensure good working relationships with clients. He seemed initially successful in the role.

He received a handsome six-figure salary, which funded the lifestyle that has already been widely reported in the press: the flat just off the King's Road in Chelsea, a new Porsche, frequent visits to top London restaurants and nightclubs, and skiing in Val d'Isère where parties at his rented chalet, fuelled by cocaine and unending streams of vodka and champagne, often lasted until noon the following day. Women – party girls, a model, two junior employees from the same fashion magazine – came and went, none of them lasting long enough to make an impression.

Nick Reilly had found his element.

In court this week Jonathan Hepperton QC, prosecuting, said: 'In Nicholas Reilly we see a man who is arrogant almost beyond belief, entirely careless of others, ultimately amoral. He is the embodiment of a sense of entitlement, a man who views life as a series of opportunities for him to take what he wants, putting his own pleasure above all other considerations, no matter what the cost to those around him.'

Those people include his brother Mark who in January this year took a rare weekend away from work and accepted Nick's invitation to join him in Val d'Isère. It was in the queue for a ski lift that Mark met Patty Hendrick, also there for a long weekend. The pair shared a lift and clearly enjoyed each other's company enough for Mark to suggest they meet for a drink that evening. Back in London, they began meeting regularly.

The relationship was not serious but there was a clear attraction between the handsome, successful Reilly and the pretty, vivacious Patty. 'They had fun together,' said Jamie Hancock, a friend of Mark's. 'Mark had been working very hard for years at DataPro and before that at Cambridge, and Patty offered him a chance to blow off steam. She might not have been his intellectual equal or his soulmate, but neither of them was looking for that. It was about fun.'

The events of the night of 7 March and the following 48 hours reflect well on none of the key players. The revelation that Mark Reilly had sex with Patty in the lavatories of the club before she left with Nick has challenged the public perception of the senior Reilly as a decent man who fell victim to his brother's remorseless sexual appetite and instead helped paint a portrait of a group of people for whom anything went.

It was an environment that suited Nicholas Reilly perfectly, a meeting point for gross consumption, his imagined entitlement to pleasure and his belief that he was immune from the consequences of his actions, literally above the law. This week the jury at the Old Bailey has surely ended that belief once and for all.

Reilly now awaits sentencing but the case continues to raise troubling questions about the world in which he lived. What kind of society have we created, people have asked this week, when young women like Patty Hendrick will willingly sleep with a pair of brothers and indulge in protracted binges of drug-taking and extreme sexual activity? When a man like Nick Reilly will let a woman die rather than stop the party? What does this case tell us about our over-privileged younger generation?

The death of Patty Hendrick is beyond doubt a tragedy for her friends and family, and a crime that is hard to fathom. For many, however, it speaks of a generation without a moral compass, one that worships at the altar of the false god of consumption – of fast cars and foreign holidays, drink and drugs, and, ultimately, of each other.

CHAPTER 15

Hannah woke to an insistent buzzing, a sound like an angry bee trapped under a glass. After several seconds' confusion she connected the noise to her BlackBerry on the bedside table, sat up and reached for it. The number on the screen was a central London one, but the phone didn't recognise it and neither did she. Curiosity got the better of her, however, and she hit the green button and croaked hello.

'Good morning. Am I speaking to Hannah Reilly?' It was an older woman's voice, with a clipped accent that evoked girls' boarding schools and crisp tennis whites.

Hannah confirmed that she was.

'Hello, my name's Jessica Landon,' the voice said more warmly. 'I'm calling from Roger Penrose's office.'

Roger Penrose – in her newly conscious state Hannah made a reduced-speed search of her mental archives. *Penrose*. The woman clearly expected her to know whom she was talking about. At last she found the index card: Roger Penrose, from Penrose Price.

Jessica Landon was talking again. 'Roger very much enjoyed meeting you on the second and asked me to apologise for the length of time it's taken us to get back to you. I'm afraid his wife hasn't been very well.'

'I'm sorry to hear that.'

'Thank you. She's feeling much better now.' A second's respectful pause. 'Anyway, as you know, we're a family company and pride ourselves on being tight-knit. Roger likes to meet the final candidates for senior roles in a social context, along with their partners. He wonders whether you and your husband are available for dinner next week?'

'Dinner?'

'It would be you and your husband, and Roger and his wife, Diane. How about next Tuesday, a week today? Would that suit? At eight o'clock?'

'Er, yes,' Hannah said. 'I think that'll be fine.'

'Lovely. I have your email address here so I'll make a reservation and be in touch again later on today with the details.'

Dinner. Hannah pictured Mark and herself sitting smiling over a stiff white tablecloth and single, interview-appropriate glasses of wine, making small-talk and pretending everything was fine, that they were an ordinary happy couple, no stolen savings or hidden killer brothers to muddy the crystalline marital waters. The idea – the fakery it would demand – was grotesque. And yet she'd have to do it. *The final candidates for senior roles*: here was a chance. If she could just get this job, a salary, she'd have options again. Choices.

She threw back the blankets, swung her feet to the carpet and went to the window. The air was cold on her bare legs; the heating was kept low in here, turned up only on the rare occasion when someone came to stay. Outside in Quarrendon Street, at least, it was a normal day, the houses across the road offering their usual inscrutable façades, the lush magazine lifestyles that went on behind them hinted at by a small Venetian chandelier visible above white slatted half-shutters, an orchid in a beautiful glazed pot in the narrow first-floor window of an *en suite* bathroom.

The tiny woman from the house opposite was just clambering down from the driver's seat of her enormous navy blue Range Rover, looking child-like as she hopped out on to the pavement. She was in yoga clothes, the hair on the back of her neck dark with sweat. Hannah glanced back at the clock on the bedside table. 9.17 – *shit*. How had it got so late? Well, she'd seen four o'clock and five, quarter past. She must have fallen asleep just after that. How much time did she have? Surely not much. If his flight had run to schedule, Mark would be home any minute: the last night flights left New York around eleven, which meant they landed at Heathrow around eleven a.m. If he'd caught an earlier one, he could even be back already, waiting downstairs. What would he think if he'd come looking and found her sleeping in here?

She walked to the door, placing her feet gingerly in case he was in the sitting room below. The brass handle made a treacherous squeak and she froze but when she listened for sounds of movement downstairs, half-expecting his voice to call up to her – *'Han? There you are. What were you doing in the spare room, you nutcase?'* – there was only the usual oppressive silence. The quilt on their bed next door was undisturbed and the bathroom was empty. On the top floor, his study door was ajar at the same angle it had been last night.

Downstairs, the dirty glass and the bottle of Armagnac, now half-empty, were still on the table. She put them away and filled the kettle. As she reached to turn off the tap, there was a sudden movement on the other side of the glass and a huge crow took off from the top of the fence, its wings black and ratty-looking against the flat grey of the sky.

What was she going to say to him? That was the question – or one of them – that had kept her brain churning through the early hours. How did you broach something like this? *'Hi, darling – good flight? Oh, while you were away, I checked my bank account, and what do you know? Someone's transferred all my money over to you. And why didn't you mention your brother was getting out of prison? Manslaughter, was it? Not to worry.'*

The water boiled and she put a new filter in the Krups machine and heaped in coffee grounds. She needed to be alert this morning, to think clearly.

As she'd lain awake, she'd thought about what Mark *had* told her about his brother. Most of it could be interpreted as the broader truth, Nick's character, his general behaviour, but even within the framework of his cover story, Mark had lied. He'd told her that Nick had missed being with their mother when she died because he was in bed with some woman when, actually, he must have been in prison. Why tell her that? Why bother coming up with such a detailed little sub-story – a married woman, Brighton?

She poured a cup of coffee and took a scalding sip. Perhaps she was over-thinking it. She'd put Mark on the spot that night in her apartment and he'd had to extemporise a complete cover story in the time he'd been out walking the freezing streets. He'd added a few details for verisimilitude; it was hardly surprising.

On the other hand, however, there was Hermione. She'd admitted that she'd spoken to him lately but, according to Neesha, there had been several calls. *There is someone who calls. A few weeks – a month. He always closes his door.* Why had they *kept* talking? What was there to say over a period of weeks? And if she and Mark were such good friends that Hermione was the person he'd turn to about this, why hadn't she, Hannah, even heard of her before?

At her laptop she brought up the site for the Royal London. She clicked through, found the number and entered it into her phone. It rang three times and then a woman's voice came on the line. 'Renal.'

'Hello. Could I speak to Doctor Alleyn, please?' Hannah remembered the form of address used by the nurse behind the desk. Yes, that was right, wasn't it? Surgeons weren't called Doctor; they became Misters and Mizzes again once they reached consultant level. 'Ms Alleyn,' she corrected herself.

'She's in theatre this morning, I'm afraid. Can I take a message?'

Hannah paused. If she left her number, would Hermione call back? No, that wouldn't be a good idea, anyway: she needed to control when they spoke. What if Hermione rang when Mark was around? How could she explain it or slope off to take the call without arousing suspicion?

'It's all right,' she said, 'I'll ring back. Do you know what time she'll be finished?'

'Sorry, I really can't say.'

'No problem. I'll try again later. Thanks.'

She hung up and put the phone back on the table. As she did, she became aware of a change in the room, a shift in the light, or perhaps she glimpsed an image in the glass of the French windows. She spun around.

'Hannah?' He laughed. 'Oh, sorry – did I startle you, darling?'

CHAPTER 16

'Who was on the phone?' Mark stepped further into the room.

'What?'

'The phone just then – who were you talking to?'

'Oh, no one.' She shook her head quickly. 'I couldn't get through. It was just a job thing – someone I said I'd call back.' She saw him glance at her outfit: the T-shirt she'd slept in, a pair of old round-the-house jeans. Her bare feet were slowly turning blue on the slate floor. He knew her pretend-you're-still-in-the-real-world, job-search rules – up and dressed by eight, act like a professional until you are one again – and making calls like this broke all of them. Mark was in jeans, too, but he was fit for the outside world, the collar of a soft long-sleeved T-shirt visible beneath a black cashmere sweater, his usual flying outfit. He still had his coat on, and just beyond the door she could see his leather weekend bag on the floor in the hallway. How long had he been standing there?

'Something interesting?' he said.

She looked at him.

'The job thing.'

231

'Oh, right. Well, I don't know yet. Possibly – maybe.'

He gave a sort of half-nod, apparently accepting what she was telling him, and moved towards her with a big smile, putting his arms out. 'Come here, you. Six days has been *far* too long.'

He was within touching distance, inches away. With a jolt of panic, she took a step backwards, colliding noisily with a chair, banging her hip. She took advantage of the confusion to slap down the lid of her laptop, hiding the Royal London's website.

When she looked up again, Mark's smile had gone. For a moment neither of them said anything and the kitchen rang with the clatter of furniture. 'I'm sorry I couldn't make it home for the weekend,' he said. 'This buy-out – there's just so much riding on it, our whole financial future, and I have to do everything I can to maximise it. I know I should have called more but I was so caught up in doing projections, and without my mobile . . .'

Hannah's whole body was shaking suddenly, the vibrations running down her arms into her hands, which felt as if they were fluttering, like leaves in a breeze. It wasn't nerves but anger, physical fury. She clenched her fists, fighting the urge to launch herself at him and thump him, beat on his chest like a drum.

'Why did you lie to me?' Her voice was shaking, too.

Wariness dropped over his face like a shutter. 'Lie? What are you talking about?'

The rage took over, staining everything crimson. 'Oh, for fuck's sake, Mark, I don't care – *I don't care*. I don't care about your bloody phone. I don't care if you call and leave messages at two o'clock in the morning. I don't care if you weren't at your hotel when you said you were – I don't give a *shit*.' She turned away, not wanting to look at him, not wanting him to see her face, which she knew was flushed and twisted with anger. A hard pulse was beating at the base of her throat. Through the door, she caught a momentary glimpse of the yard. The ragged crow was perched on the little table, head cocked to one side. It stared in at her with a single searching eye.

Behind her Mark was silent, waiting for her to speak. She turned and locked her eyes on his.

'Why didn't you tell me about your brother?'

Yes. As soon as the words left her mouth, she saw that this was what he'd been afraid of. In a second his wary expression was gone, replaced by a look of shock that he masked almost as quickly.

'What about my brother?'

Hannah felt a deep bone-tiredness. How much longer could he push it? Was he so desperate that he was prepared to keep trying even now?

'Patty Hendrick,' she said. 'What he did.'

The words seemed to cause Mark physical pain. He closed his eyes and she watched his reaction

233

travel over his face, deepening the vertical line between his eyebrows, thinning his lips. He walked to the table, pulled out a chair and sat down as if his legs would no longer hold him up. As he covered his face with his hands, the fine wool of his coat stretched between his shoulder blades and she remembered him on the beach at Montauk, the way his T-shirt had stretched across his back as he crouched by the fire. It was only seconds before he spoke, ten or fifteen perhaps, but it felt like a long, long time.

'How did you find out?' he asked between his fingers.

'Does it matter?'

'To me it does.'

'Hermione.'

'Hermione?' He turned sharply.

'I thought you were having an affair with her. I went to the hospital and accused her of it.' She saw him working backwards, or trying to: how had she even known about Hermione? Who'd told her? Hannah remembered her promise to Neesha. 'Why didn't you tell me?' she said, deflecting him.

He exhaled shortly through his nose. 'You can't imagine why?'

'I'm your wife,' she said, vibrato. 'How do you think it feels to find out that the person in the world you're supposed to be closest to, to have no secrets from, to *trust*, Mark, has been hiding something like this? It's so terrible – so *huge*.'

Another sharp out-breath. 'And you're asking why I didn't tell you?'

'Did you really think you'd be able to hide it from me for ever? For the rest of our lives?'

'I hoped,' he said, and the word hung in the air between them. 'Naive, wasn't it? But whatever I could have done to stop you finding out, I would have done it.'

'But *why*? Why not trust me? Or *don't* you trust me?'

'Of course I trust you, Hannah.' His voice was loud, the frustration only just under control. 'But have you thought about it from my point of view for a second? When should I have told you? At the start? How do you think you – anyone – would've reacted? "*Hey*," he put on a high, fake voice, "*I like you – I really like you – but your brother killed a woman? See ya.*"'

'Come on, that's not f—'

'It is. It is, and I couldn't do it – I couldn't take that risk. I really liked you, right from the first night on the beach, and if I'd told you, you would have run away as fast as your legs could carry you; we would never have had a chance.'

'How do you know I would have run away?'

'Seriously? Be honest with yourself. However tough you think you are, however independent, fair-minded, able to see the big picture, whatever – you meet a man and a few weeks in, he tells you his brother's in prison for manslaughter and it's not the *right* sort of manslaughter, either,

235

good manslaughter: he didn't cause an accident at work or hit someone in the car when he was drunk; it wasn't even diminished responsibility – he wasn't provoked, he didn't lash out. The only reason it wasn't murder was because he hadn't *aimed* to kill her. What are you going to do, really?'

Hannah said nothing.

'And then, having not told you straight away, when was the right time? I felt like I'd tricked you, let you start liking me – fall in love with me – under false pretences. I felt like I'd sold you shoddy merchandise, and every time I almost managed to get up the guts to tell you, I bottled it. God, there were so many times. But when was I supposed to do it? When we got engaged? "*I love you, please marry me – by the way, my brother killed a girl.*" Just before our wedding day? Or afterwards, when it really would look like I'd set out to trick you?' His breathing was fast and shallow.

Again Hannah said nothing, not trusting herself to speak.

'I can't tell you,' he said, 'what it's been like having to live with this – this *thing*, this boulder on my back. Ever since I met you, I've wanted to tell you, and I couldn't, and all the time I've been terrified you'd find out. It's like I've been tottering around with a jar of acid in my hands, full up to the brim, no lid, just waiting for it to slop out.'

She looked at him, assessing. 'So will you tell me now? The whole story?'

He looked back, his eyes begging her, *don't make me,* but no, she thought, however much he hated it, however hard it was, she wasn't going to move until he told her.

'All of it,' she said. 'The truth.'

He glanced at the sideboard. 'Is it too early for a drink?'

'Yes, but what does that matter?'

With a sort of half-laugh, he pushed himself up. He took off his coat and dropped it over the back of the chair then opened the sideboard and got out a tumbler. He held it towards her, eyebrows raised, but she shook her head. Appearing not to notice how much was gone, he picked up the Armagnac, poured himself an inch and carried the glass back to the table. 'Are you going to sit down?'

'No.' Unconsciously, she pressed back against the edge of the counter as he passed her.

He nodded slightly. 'So how much do you know?'

'That doesn't matter. I want to hear it from you. From the beginning.'

'The beginning.' His eyebrows twitched and he took a sip of the brandy. In the yard behind him, the crow left the little table and settled on top of the end wall, turning its back on them.

'I've told you what it was like at home,' he said, 'my mother and Nick, their *special relationship*, but maybe I was too hard on her – no, I was; I know I was. Even now, I find it really difficult not to get caught up in it all and behave like a teenager again.'

He grimaced. 'Which is another reason I hated telling you about him. I want you to think of me as, I don't know, competent, successful, in control . . . not some guy who's still in bits at the age of forty because his mother loved his brother better.'

Hannah felt a surge of frustration. 'I married you – *you*, a man, a living, breathing human. You don't think I can deal with a bit of complexity?'

'It had nothing to do with that – it was about what *I* wanted,' he admitted. Seconds passed. He looked away. 'Anyway,' he said, 'it wasn't my mother's fault – she didn't make Nick what he was. Is. He was born like it. Her softness just made her an easier target. She was like an injured sheep stuck out on the edge of the flock, waiting to be picked off.'

Another sip. He rested the glass on his knee and stared into it as if he was looking into the embers of a fire. *Come on*, she thought, *cut to the chase and tell me*, but at the same time, for a reason she couldn't identify, she was afraid.

'Hannah, look,' he said. 'I told you the truth about Nick, I did, but it wasn't . . .' He sighed in frustration. 'What I'm struggling to say is that it wasn't the whole truth.' He glanced at her then away again. 'It was worse – is worse – than that. He wasn't just badly behaved or spoiled or manipulative. Even before . . .' He paused. 'Even before Patty, it was evident there was something . . . wrong with him.'

'Wrong?' A chill crept over the back of her neck. 'What do you mean?'

'He doesn't see the world like the rest of us do. No, that's not it. He doesn't see *people*. He doesn't seem to get that they have interior worlds just as valid and real as his. He doesn't get that other people have feelings.'

She'd never heard more than his name but suddenly Hannah had a mental image of Jim Thomas, their old neighbour in Eastbourne, tears running down his face as he hammered on the Reillys' front door, a drowned dog in his arms.

'It's convenient for Nick because it means he can do exactly what he wants, behave like a monster, and he doesn't give a shit. Does he care about what happened to Patty? Honestly? No. He cares about what happened to him because of what happened to her.' Mark gave a short, bitter laugh. 'He's probably angry with her – I bet he's found a way to make it all her fault.'

Through the cotton of her old T-shirt, the edge of the marble counter was hard against Hannah's lower back, and her feet had started to ache on the cold tiles. She couldn't sit down, though: taking a seat would mean getting closer to him.

'Anyway,' said Mark, 'my parents knew. They knew something was wrong with him, seriously wrong, but he was still their son. Their response was to close ranks around him – he became this dark thing between us that we had to guard at all costs, try to protect from himself, but we also had to protect ourselves – we had to stop him from blowing up our lives. My parents' way of doing this,' he took a long in-breath, 'was to make me responsible for him.'

'What? That's ridiculous.'

'You think so? It started at school, years before they asked me to give him a job. Nick started going off the rails – he was bunking off and stealing booze from the Spar shop to take down to the beach, then turning up at home after dark half-cut or stoned out of his nut – and that was my fault.'

'How?' Again Hannah heard her scepticism.

'Because I hadn't checked at break that he was still at school, I hadn't tipped anyone off that he was missing. *You're the older brother; you have to watch out for him. You have to look after him.*' Mark's face changed, became sharp and hectoring as he imitated whoever had said it to him. His father? 'Look after *him*?' Mark snorted. 'Christ, *I* was the one who needed bloody protecting.'

He turned to look at her, seeking eye contact, and she felt another wave of trepidation. Why was she frightened? She already knew what he was going to say, didn't she?

When he spoke again, Mark's voice was quiet. 'Nick's cruel, Han – really cruel. We had this neighbour, an old guy, he was a widower, probably in his late seventies, and Nick got a kick out of tormenting him, jumping into his garden at night and creeping round outside his windows. He used to smoke weed in the guy's shed – totally needless: he always had some grovelling supplicant, male or female, to offer their bedroom for the purpose. Anyway, Jim Thomas, this neighbour, had another shed on his allotment and one night Nick doused the place in petrol and burned it down.' He shook his head, the memory clearly shocking to him even all these years later.

'How could I be responsible when stuff like that was going on?' he said. 'Stuff that was actually criminal. I was asleep in bed, for God's sake, getting ready for school in the morning like the good little swot I was. That wasn't the end of it, either. Jim went to the police, of course, and so my brother killed his dog.'

'I read about it,' she admitted.

His eyebrows lifted. 'Jesus, they really got everything, didn't they?'

'There was a lot to get, clearly.'

'Well, they wouldn't have had to look very hard, put it that way.' Mark drained his glass and pushed it away.

'This is going to sound selfish,' he said, 'but after a while, I started thinking, what about me? Who cares about me? Do I exist only to be responsible for Nick? Is that all I am, the boy with his finger in the dam, the bulwark between him and whatever disaster he's inevitably going to cause? My parents tried to put a spin on it, sell it to me as a good thing, I was the clever, sorted one, *noblesse oblige*, but it was bullshit and we all knew it. I told you before: Nick's every bit as clever as me and a lot more cunning.' He ran the back of his hand across his mouth. 'I'm just glad that when it happened, the really bad thing we'd been waiting for all those years, my parents were already gone.'

Hannah wrapped her arms around herself, feeling cold to the bone. 'Tell me about the night it happened.'

'The bit I'm really ashamed of?' He exhaled – a quick, resigned sigh. 'Hannah, all I can say in my defence is, I worked like a slave in my early twenties, at Cambridge then raising the money to start DataPro, getting it off the ground. I didn't have a life or do anything that normal people do: go to the pub or take holidays. I never had girlfriends – I never met anyone. Even the friends I'd made at university got frustrated at never seeing me and gradually faded into the woodwork.'

Hannah thought of Pippa, how she and Dan hadn't been friends with Mark at Cambridge but met him later when DataPro worked with Dan's bank. She'd just assumed they'd been there together.

'I was twenty-seven when Nick came to work for me and I was ready for a break. Not from work, DataPro was my life, but from the total focus, the non-stop application, the crazy hours. Things were going well, we'd started to make a name for ourselves, I could afford to take it just a bit easier and behave like I wasn't already fifty.

Nick came to work for me – enter the dragon – and you know what? I just thought, *fuck it*: he's here earning a great salary in the company that I created, having this luxurious lifestyle for very little effort on his part, *plus ça change*, so I'm going to have some of what he's having – some of his kind of fun. Payback time.'

Hannah looked at her husband. His face was so transformed by bitterness that for a moment she didn't recognise him.

'So, for a change,' he said, voice hard, 'I piggy-backed on Nick. I went to his parties and clubs, took his coke, messed around with the sort of girls he hung out with, bought a TVR and drove it through Chelsea late at night smashed off my face like any one of a hundred other wankers. And, I have to say, after five years of living like a monk, I loved it. Apart from some of the more extreme hangovers, it was fun. You know, actually, it was a relief: I was sick of being dedicated and responsible: *I* wanted to be wild and reckless. Why did I have to be cast in the role of boring bastard all the time? It was *my* turn.'

His hands were balled into fists on the table. Who was he talking to now, she wondered, trying to justify himself? His father? His mother? Or Nick?

'My brother was amazed when he saw that side of me. In his mind, I was a loser: a worker, an effort-maker, a drone. I loved showing him that he was wrong, that I wasn't boring – I think it encouraged me. I loved showing him that women found me attractive, too, that he wasn't the only one who could go into a club, flirt with a pretty girl and take her home. Of course,' Mark said, dryly, 'as it transpired, our style of taking girls home was somewhat different.'

He turned his head and looked at her. 'I'm sorry, Hannah, I feel like a shit telling you this. I feel like I'm disrespecting you – us, our marriage – but now we're talking about it, I want you to know everything, the whole thing. I need to get it over with once and for all. I wasn't a saint, I'd be lying if I let you think that.'

'I'm an adult. I can handle it.'

He gave a single nod. 'Okay, but it wasn't just a flash in the pan. My . . . behaviour had been going on for a couple of years by the time I met Patty. We met in France, skiing – Nick had got into the habit of renting a chalet for three or four weeks a season and I went over there now and again.'

'That was in the papers, too.'

'Of course – no stone left unturned.' He reached out and ran his fingertip around the rim of the empty glass. 'Patty was lovely, Han – sweet. That was why I liked her. Yes, she wasn't the sharpest tool in the box and we were never going to be serious but, despite the party-girl behaviour you've no doubt read about, there was something sort of . . . innocent about her.'

Remembering the photographs she'd seen, the puppy-fat curves, Hannah felt a stab of pain.

'She was a decent person,' he said, 'just young and a bit lost. But she was lovely-looking, too, and of course Nick noticed. The added bonus, as far as he was concerned, was that I was fond of her – not in love with her, not even close, but I liked her. It stuck in his craw having to do what I told him at work – he hated me having that power. A pretty girl and an opportunity to show me who was still top dog? Two birds with one stone.'

Mark reached for the bottle and poured himself another half-inch of Armagnac, most of which disappeared in the first swig. When he started talking again, his voice was harder. 'I can't stand thinking about that night,' he said. 'It was all so . . . sordid. Not just Nick, what happened to Patty, but my part in it, too.'

'Tell me,' she said calmly, but inside she was begging: *Please. Please don't let there be anything else.*

'A friend of Nick's had just bought this club in Shoreditch and so we all piled over there. We were wasted before we even arrived – we'd had cocktails first and, of course, every time you went out with Nick there were drugs. Coke, mostly, but he was into E as well and speed now and again. Patty and I had had some charlie and . . . I should have recognised the signs. Why didn't I recognise the bloody signs?'

He looked up at her as if he expected an answer. Hannah stayed silent.

'He'd been flirting with Patty from the moment she arrived at the bar, but that was nothing unusual. It was this look he gave me. We were in a stall in the toilets, doing a last couple of lines before we went on to the club, and Nick looked up at me with this look on his face. I'll never forget it – I actually dream about it sometimes. It was like . . . this sounds crazy but it was like a carnival mask, one of those ones with the exaggerated, leering features, all nose and eyes and this horrible, curling mouth showing his teeth.' Mark shuddered.

'Anyway, not long after we got to the club, Patty and I ended up having sex in the toilets – no doubt you read about that, too. It tells you everything you need to know about that night, doesn't it, that so much of it took place in toilets? I can't remember how it happened, whose idea it was, but it happened and we came back out and I went off to the bar. It took a while, there was a queue, and then I bumped into this guy who was on a team we'd done some business with a few months before-hand. By the time I got back with the drinks, Nick and Patty had disappeared and no one else could look me in the eye.' He ran his fingers backwards over his head and clenched them in his hair. 'God, I wish I still smoked.'

'We've got some – Tom left them.'

'No, I think I might actually throw up. Talking about it like this . . .' He shook his head. 'The thing is, Hannah, the whole thing, Patty's death – it was my fault.'

'What?' She heard outrage in her voice. 'No. No, Mark. *He* did it. He was the one who . . .'

'I let him. I'm the responsible one, remember? I'd known him my whole life. It wasn't just that look that should have alerted me; it had been building for a long time. It's always like that with Nick: you get a period of relative calm – *relative*,' Mark put his hands up, qualifying, 'and then he either gets bored or something in him comes to a head and then it's . . . a crisis. In the weeks before it happened, there had been plenty of signs, if only I'd bothered to pay attention. He'd been turning up later and later to work, hungover as a dog; he'd missed a key meeting with his biggest client; and then there was the evening he hit on another client's wife at a restaurant, groped her in the corridor – you know about that?'

She nodded.

'And it wasn't just work. He was taking stupid personal risks, too. He'd bought this huge bike, a Yamaha, and one night we'd all been out and he phoned me the next morning from Scotland – he'd got home at two in the morning and decided it would be fun to go to Edinburgh. He'd been smashed off his face but somehow he'd managed to get there alive – bloody miracle. Anyway, I should have known – no, I did know – that he was heading for some kind of . . . event.'

'There's still no way it's your fault.'

'But I think it is. There was this one moment that night. I stood there in the club after they'd gone and I thought about that look – *I'm going to fuck you up* – and I thought about how gullible Patty was, how keen she was to prove to him that she was fun, up for anything, and I just decided stuff them, stuff them both, they were on their own. I knew she was wrecked, I'd been with her all night – I should have rung her and made sure she was all right. Actually, I should have gone after them, but I was so angry, so furious, that I didn't. I left her to Nick's tender mercies. And look how tender they were.'

He hung his head, hiding his face. Silence rushed in around them, the deadening silence that Hannah had only ever felt in the house before when she was alone. She looked at his rounded shoulders, the curve of his back, and the word *defeated* came into her mind.

'You know,' he said, puncturing the silence, 'I *wanted* something bad to happen to Nick. I wanted him punished for all the crap I had to put up with: his shitty, cruel behaviour; his manipulation of our mother; the fact that she spoiled him, not me; because he got all the attention and the toys and the money and the cars. I wanted him to suffer for the fact that our parents seemed to think I was born to be his caretaker. I had to dance on the fucking moon if I wanted to drag their eyes away from him even for a minute. So I wanted Nick to be taught a lesson in a way he wouldn't forget.'

'Ten years in prison,' she said quietly.

'I got what I wanted, didn't I? But look at the price, Hannah. Look at the damage. Patty *died* – she died that night. Twenty-five, and they dug a hole in the ground and buried her. If I hadn't let anger and my stupid, stupid bloody *pride* stop me going after them, she'd still be alive.'

When Hannah came back, he hadn't moved. She must have been gone for seven or eight minutes, she thought, sitting on the closed lid of the downstairs loo while she tried to think, listening to the blood pounding in her ears, but Mark was exactly where she'd left him, hunched over the table, face buried in his hands. She was almost back to her position by the counter before he raised his head to look at her. On his face there was no expectation or request for forgiveness, just uncertainty, the frank acknowledgement that he had no idea how things would play out between them. It startled her that Mark could look so tentative and she felt a rush of tenderness towards him that she quickly fought down. He must have seen it because he reached for her hand. 'Han . . .'

'No,' she said. 'Don't.' She moved back behind the counter, putting it between them. 'What I want to know now,' she said, 'is where my savings fit into this.'

He closed his eyes and his shoulders seemed to drop another inch. Proud, confident Mark withering in front of her. 'I'm sorry,' he said. 'I'm so sorry. If I—'

'Don't,' she said again, putting her hand up. Until she had answers, an explanation that made total sense, she wanted nothing but the facts. 'Just tell me why.'

'I owe Nick money.'

'What?' Her eyes widened. '*You* owe *him* money?'

'A lot of money.'

That chill on the back of her neck again, as if someone had opened a window and let in the November wind. 'How much?'

'I—'

'Mark – how much?' Her voice rose and they both heard the alarm in it. 'How much?'

He looked down at his hands. 'Just under two million. One point eight.'

The floor seemed to tilt and she gripped the edge of the counter as if to stop herself falling, sliding off the comfortless slate tiles and into the vacuum suddenly yawning at her feet. 'How,' she said, 'is that possible?'

'He owns part of DataPro.'

She stared at him.

'I know,' he said, wildly. 'Do you think I don't know? I had no choice.'

'What ... Mark, it's your company. Oh, my God.' *One point eight million.* 'How? How did it happen? How could you *let* it happen?'

'I got into a mess.'

She felt her heart give a single heavy thump. 'What kind of mess?'

'In 2009, the financial crisis . . . I'd borrowed

money from the bank to finance the US office but I'd over-extended, couldn't make the repayments. We'd been doing business – quite good business – but no one was paying us. Accounts were chasing and chasing but months passed and no one paid – our cash flow was buggered. I missed some payments on the loan and the bank threatened to sue for the whole lot and I panicked. It would have hurt us so badly: I'd already had to let some programmers go, and without a full team we were struggling to get other projects finished on schedule, and—'

'And Nick?' She cut him off.

'He loaned me the money. Quarter of a million. I'd already remortgaged the house, pumped all my own money in. I was—'

'How did he *have* quarter of a million?'

'It was his half of our parents' estate. Mine was long gone, into the hungry maw. I went to see him in prison and I begged him, debased myself in front of him, basically, and he said he'd *think about it*. He kept me waiting for ten days – I nearly went off my nut. Then I got a call saying that he'd see me again – like he was the bloody Pope granting me an audience. I went up there and he said that he'd lend me the money for as long as he was in jail on condition I gave it back to him the day he got out.'

'But if he only loaned you quarter of a million, how . . .?'

'That was his other condition: he didn't want interest. I offered him eight per cent but he wouldn't take it. He wanted stock in the company or nothing. God, he loved it, Hannah, having me over a barrel – he loved the power, sitting there in his prison clothes in that stinking visiting room with all the other crims, the table covered with cigarette burns, wielding power over *me*. DataPro was *my* thing, *mine* – I'd worked so hard and there was he, dictating terms, demanding stock in it.'

'And there was really nowhere else you could go?'

'No. No bank would lend me money at that point: everyone was running scared – you remember what it was like – and our cash flow was . . . I thought I wasn't going to be able to pay the wages.' He exhaled heavily. 'I should have gone to a loan shark. Well, I suppose I did, in a way.'

'I still don't understand how you owe him so much.'

'Because we're doing well again. David's investment made a massive difference. We're debt-free, we've got business coming in and clients are paying. We had valuations done last week by two different auditors and they've both told us fifteen million. Twelve percent of fifteen mill . . . You've got to hand it to him, it was a great investment.'

'But if you're doing so well, why take my money?'

'Because I can't have Nick anywhere near the buy-out. I've got to get his name off the paperwork. The guy who owns Systema is a devout Christian, he makes huge donations to religious charities – if he hears what Nick did and finds out he's a share-holder, he won't touch us.'

'So why not just pay Nick off now?'

'We don't have the money, not in cash or assets that we can liquidate easily. And even if we did, we couldn't take out that kind of amount without raising eyebrows – Systema are going to be trawling the paperwork with a fine-toothed comb.' Hannah watched anger flare on Mark's face. 'I'm not going to let Nick screw this up for me,' he said. 'I'm not going to allow it. Everything I've ever done or tried to do, he's been there mocking or stealing my thunder, undermining me, fucking things up. But this is the end. I'll sell DataPro, I'll give him his money, then I never want to hear his name again.'

The silence poured in around them. Hannah looked over his head into the yard, where the wind was riffling the last brittle leaves of the creeper on the back wall, exposing their undersides and the bare brickwork underneath.

'If he needs one point eight million,' she said quietly, 'what good's my forty-seven thousand?'

Mark glanced at her then looked away. His face was full of shame. 'I've got some money of my own,' he said, 'about seventy thousand, and I've borrowed some more against the house. I'm going to put it together and offer it to him if he'll agree to redraw the paperwork before we have to open the books. An incentive. Otherwise, why would he do it? I wouldn't – take my name off legal documents? No way.'

'But if you explained to him about the deal, that you could pay him as soon as it all went through . . .'

'Nick doesn't care about the deal. I have to pay him one way or the other. He doesn't give a toss about things working out for me – in fact, he'd be thrilled if he managed to derail it all. The only way I can do this is to make it advantageous to him to agree. If he does the paperwork now, I give him two hundred and fifty thousand, then after-wards I'll give him two million, not one point eight.'

Two million. 'And he's said yes to this?'

'Not yet.'

'But you've told him?'

There was the sound of footsteps on the front path then the snap of the letterbox, a fall of letters on to the doormat. Mark waited until the footsteps had receded, as if he was afraid the postman would overhear. 'I'm so sorry,' he said. 'You have to believe me. I can't tell you how how shitty I feel. Because your account's annual, I thought I could put the money back when we did the deal and you'd never even need to know. The idea of you checking your balance and seeing—'

'Why didn't you just ask me for it? I would have given it to you.'

He covered his face with his hands again and after a few seconds she realised he was crying. The hard knot of feeling inside her loosened and she left the counter and came to stand behind him. He sensed her there – she saw him stiffen, expecting what? – but she reached out and put her hand on his shoulder.

'I would have had to tell you why I needed it,' he said, still facing away. 'The whole story – Patty, everything – and I couldn't.'

Her fingers tightened their grip. 'It's okay,' she said.

'I've been such a dick, Han. Such a total dick. Now I just want things to be straight between us, out in the open – no more lies.' He hesitated. 'I wasn't in New York this weekend.'

'I know.'

He started to turn but the pressure of her fingers kept him facing away from her.

'You weren't at your usual hotel. I called to talk to you and they told me you weren't there. Obviously something was going on. That's why I assumed it was an affair.'

'You really thought I would cheat on you?'

'I didn't want to believe it, part of me never did, but when you weren't at the hotel and—' She remembered her promise to Neesha and stopped herself.

Mark gave a strangled kind of laugh. 'I was trying to track down this guy who I thought would lend me the money,' he said. 'We had a meeting set up for Friday at his place in the Berkshires but he cancelled and then he kept giving me the run-around. I spent most of the weekend waiting in a B&B with no bloody mobile reception. I was going to ask him for a loan, pay Nick off and be done with it.'

'What guy?' Hannah felt a new rush of alarm. Who could you go to for that sort of money?

'It doesn't matter – I didn't even see him in the end. And now that you know, some of the pressure's off. At least I don't have to carry it around on my own any more, waiting for it all to blow up in my face.' Tentatively, he leaned back and rested his head against her stomach. After a moment, she put her other hand on his shoulder. Bending, she touched her nose to his hair.

'I've been to see Nick, too,' he said. 'More lies. I told you I was in Frankfurt but I drove up to Wakefield to talk to him.'

Suddenly Hannah felt laughter well up inside her. Wakefield – Nick was in Wakefield Prison. *Yorkshire*. She'd seen those service-station receipts from the M1 and imagined a boutique hotel, all log fires and antique roll-top baths, and really Mark had been visiting his brother in jail. It was hysterical, she thought, *hysterical* – the laughter exploded out of her, startlingly loud. Mark stood up and put his arms around her, holding her while she shook. When she stopped, as abruptly as she'd begun, Hannah looked up at him. His dark eyes were shining with tears. 'I'm so, so sorry,' he said, 'that you thought I was having an affair – that because of him I nearly fucked this up, you and me . . .'

She stood on tiptoe and pressed her cheek flat against his, feeling the scratch of his overnight stubble, smelling the sage note in his cologne. She wasn't sure who moved first but all of a sudden they were kissing, slowly to start with, then furiously. Mark's mouth was hot and tasted of Armagnac. 'I love you, Han,' he said, breaking away just long enough. 'I really love you.'

CHAPTER 17

When Hannah woke up, Mark was lying turned away from her, the shape of his shoulder outlined by the bar of daylight coming through the gap in the curtains. His breathing was deep and regular, his shoulder gently rising and falling in rhythm with it. In the distance, a church bell struck one o'clock. Gingerly, she turned on to her back. She waited a moment, making sure she hadn't disturbed him, then reached over the side of the bed and fished her T-shirt off the floor. She sat up, pulled it over her head then slid gently back down into the body-warmth.

It was ridiculous, she thought, to be uncomfortable about Mark seeing her naked. He'd seen her naked hundreds of times, and just now – an hour or so ago – they'd made love like wild things, self-consciousness cast aside along with the clothes strewn across the carpet. It had come from relief, that rush of desire, the pure relief of him telling the truth, confirming what she'd discovered, not trying to hide anything or obfuscate. And he'd volunteered what he'd said about the B&B in the

Berkshires and visiting Nick in jail, she hadn't had to ask. Now she admitted it to herself: she'd been frightened that, confronted, Mark would try and bend the story, play down or deny his part in it. But no, he'd been frank about everything: his obnoxious Chelsea-boy behaviour; the drugs; even what happened with Patty that night. He hadn't tried to varnish over it at all.

And yet now the hit of relief had passed, she was uneasy again. He was telling the truth now but the fact remained that he'd lied to her: there was no getting round it. Yes, his reasons made sense and she couldn't be sure that in his position, meeting someone she liked, being saddled with something so horrifying, she wouldn't have done the same but he'd still lied and *kept* lying so that he wouldn't have to tell her. Before all this she'd trusted him completely, as much as she trusted her parents or Tom, but it would take time to rebuild that trust again – months, years, who knew how long? And though she understood why he hadn't told her, it still hurt. She felt as if she'd been found lacking, like *she* was the one who wasn't trustworthy.

The central heating was off and the room had gone cold. She burrowed deeper into the bed, closed her eyes and let the deep exhaustion sweep over her. It would be all right, she told herself. It would take time, no question, but in the end things would be all right.

* * *

When she woke the second time, Mark was awake and watching her, his face twelve or fifteen inches away on a pillow that he'd pulled into a tight concertina between his shoulder and ear. Even in the strange half-light, she could see his anxiety.

She shifted position, breaking eye contact for a moment, and reached out to touch his shoulder. His skin was cold. 'What is it?' she asked.

He exhaled and she felt his breath on her face. 'I'm being melodramatic,' he said, 'I know I am, but . . . I've just got this really bad feeling. I'm scared I've put you in danger.'

She felt a single sharp throb in her stomach. 'What do you mean?'

He hesitated. 'The deal was I'd have Nick's money ready the day he got out of jail – all of it, the exact day. Now I'm going to him with the offer of this incentive, but not the full amount.'

'You haven't told him yet? I thought—'

'I haven't told him.'

'But when you went up there . . .'

'I was still hoping I'd find another way – that I'd be able to borrow the money I needed from this guy Manso in the States. I didn't want to tell Nick until I was absolutely sure I had to.'

Despite the warmth of the bed, Hannah was suddenly cold. 'And if the incentive's not enough – if he doesn't go for it?'

Again he hesitated. 'That's what I'm worried about.'

'Mark – please. Just tell me what you mean.'

'He'll go crazy.'

'Crazy?'

'This is why I've been so desperate to get the money, Hannah.' His voice was rising, the panic audible. 'This is why I lied about last weekend and went to the Berkshires. It's why I tried everything I could to see this guy even though I knew it might just be getting myself into a different sort of trouble.'

'What do you mean by danger?' she said slowly.

'I don't know. I—'

'Mark, say what you mean. Are you trying to tell me Nick could be violent?'

He closed his eyes as if to shut the question out. 'I think so. Yes.'

Hannah felt the word sink through the air and settle like poisonous dust around them. They lay without speaking for what felt like a long time, and she listened for sounds from outside, evidence that the real, normal world was still out there, still going on. It was early afternoon, however, and the streets were quiet.

Mark was the first to speak again. 'Han, being in prison for so long's changed him. He's . . . harder. And even without knowing about the money, he's angry with me.'

'Why?'

'For having been out living my life all these years while he's been in there rotting. He blames me.'

'But that doesn't make sense – how can he? You didn't do anything. He was the one who . . .'

'But that's it: Nick's thinking *doesn't* make sense.

261

He can't see straight because in his mind, everything's distorted, pulled into concentric circles around *him*.' Mark drew the pillow tighter under his neck. 'It sounds mad but sometimes he doesn't even seem to understand that I'm separate from him, a different person. He thinks I'm responsible – like I'm his super-ego or something and I fucked up. He's been sitting up there stewing, with all the time in the world on his hands, and he's convinced himself it was my fault.'

'I don't even understand how that's possible.'

'I brought Patty into our group, didn't I? If I hadn't started seeing her . . .'

'That's nuts.'

'But that's it – that's how he thinks. It's not . . . normal.'

Hannah turned on to her back, away from him. 'When is he getting out?'

'Thursday.'

'This Thursday?' Her voice was loud in the stillness of the room.

'Two days,' said Mark.

'It's going to be intense – I'll be doing horrible hours. David's been hard at work getting stuff ready but I haven't been able to focus at all, worrying so much about . . .' he stopped.

Hannah sat on the old church pew and watched as Mark swung around the kitchen, consulting the recipe as if it was an alchemical text, pouring splashes of port and soy sauce into one of the copper pans, adding things to the mortar, a mad scientist at work in his laboratory. He opened the oven door, releasing a cloud of steam, and lifted the roasting pan on to the counter top to baste the pork again. He'd refused even to let her peel the vegetables, and instead handed her a glass of the incredible Barolo he'd picked up on his trip out to buy the rest of the ingredients. 'You can talk to the chef,' he'd said. 'That's your job tonight.'

When the pan was back in the oven he paused for a moment. 'I've been thinking,' he said. 'Afterwards, when all this is . . . resolved, why don't we have a holiday? Somewhere lovely, hot, with nothing to do but swim and read, snorkel. I was thinking about Mauritius, or maybe the Seychelles.'

She thought about their empty bank accounts, the terrifying mortgage. 'Can we afford it?'

'Not right this minute but if all goes according to plan . . .'

Of course. If it all went to plan and Systema agreed with the valuation, he'd be able to afford almost anything. Even with Nick's twelve per cent and the twenty-five that David owned, a buy-out would make Mark very, very rich. Earlier, lying awake, she'd worked out that if DataPro was valued at fifteen million, his sixty-three per cent share was worth just less than nine and a half million pounds. Mark would be able to go on holiday for the rest of his life if he wanted.

'A proper break,' he said, tearing the plastic off a

jar of star anise. 'We need one. We've both been under too much pressure lately, you with the job-search, me with all this DataPro stuff and . . .' Again, he stopped himself. Evidently he'd made a decision not to talk about Nick tonight. 'I've been thinking we could go for three weeks, a month, really relax, perhaps somewhere for some culture first – I'd love to see more of Japan – and then on to an island in some ludicrously beautiful turquoise archipelago somewhere. What do you reckon?' He looked at her, his face flushed from the heat of the oven.

'It sounds incredible.'

'You and me, no stress, nothing to worry about, a real break.'

Thousands of miles from your brother, out of his reach.

'Then afterwards we'll come back and regroup. I'll think about what I'm going to do next, but no hurry – I don't want to rush into anything. I want to spend some proper time here, with you, and maybe that would be a good opportunity to think about . . .' He trailed off again. A week ago he'd have said it, *a baby*, but that was too much for tonight when, though neither of them would admit it, everything between them was tentative and not to be taken for granted.

'We also need to have a conversation about your car.'

'My car? Oh – no.' Hannah shook her head. 'No way.'

He smiled. 'Come on. How old is it, anyway?'

'Fifteen,' she admitted. 'But I don't need to swap it. I don't want to, either – we're friends. That's why I held on to it and kept it at Mum's all the time I was in America.'

'It doesn't make economic sense, though, does it? You'll spend more on repairs than it's actually worth. And I worry about how safe it is when you're doing those long drives up to Malvern. When the deal comes through, let me get you a new one. If you're really wedded to VWs, you could have another one, brand new. It doesn't have to be anything big – I know that's not you.'

She shook her head. 'I'm not wedded to VWs, I just like the one I have. When it bites the dust I'll get a new car but until then . . .'

'Until then I'll have a wife who goes about in an old rust bucket?' Mark rolled his eyes in cartoonish despair and went back to his cooking. She watched as he grated a piece of ginger, head bent over the little hand-held grater, the muscles in his forearms standing proud. It was always a big production when he cooked: joints of meat from the specialist butcher, unusual herbs and spices, esoteric liqueurs. Usually she loved to watch, finding his intense man-at-work concentration quite sexy, but this evening she looked at his dark head, the furrow between his eyebrows, and found herself wondering what Nick looked like now. Did they still look as much alike or had Nick's face hardened along with his character? What did it do to you, ten years in a maximum-security prison?

Are you telling me Nick could be violent?

She took a gulp of wine and looked away. The brightness of the kitchen blocked any view of the yard but the people who lived in the house behind had switched on their outside wall lights and the fine upper branches of the ornamental cherry tree stood out like veins against the sky. They must have guests, Hannah thought, with a pang at the idea of other people, noise, conviviality. There was noise here, stirring and pouring and chopping, the Dylan Mark had put on the kitchen stereo, but it patched the silence like a plaster. She would have preferred to go out, sit in a restaurant surrounded with bustle and conversation, but he'd wanted to cook, to make a visible effort for her, she knew, rather than just hand over a card.

'Where would you like to go?' he asked. 'Anywhere. You've talked about Brazil before. Perhaps we could fly to Rio and go on from there.'

'Brazil – wow.' She tried to direct her thoughts to exotic locations: he was trying so hard; the least she could do was make an effort. But could you really think about holidays when in two days' time . . .? And – she quickly turned away from that thought – there was her own job situation to consider.

'I forgot to tell you,' she said, 'Penrose Price called this morning before you got back. I'm through to the last round and they've invited us – you and me – to have dinner with the MD and his wife next week. Tuesday.'

She watched a smile spread across Mark's face. 'Seriously? That's phenomenal.' He put the knife down and came around the counter to kiss her. 'Good for you. See, I told you it was just a matter of time.'

'It's only an interview,' she said. 'And I've been here before, remember? I've had three final interviews and nothing's come of any of them.'

'This feels different, though, doesn't it, Penrose Price? And dinner: they wouldn't be doing that if there were many candidates left in the running. There'll be two or three at most.' He grinned and gave her another kiss. 'You know, they've probably already decided and just want to check me out, make sure I'm socially acceptable.' He went back to the counter, opened a pack of fresh rosemary and lifted it out on to the board. 'God, that's great news – good for you.'

'So you can do Tuesday night?'

'If there was anything else in the diary, it's cancelled.'

'Look,' she said, feeling guilty in the face of his enthusiasm, 'I feel like I should confess: I went to see Pippa at the weekend.'

'Did you? Good – you should see more of each other. I've always thought you two could be friends. How is she? We should see them together, too, have dinner again – I'll ring Dan and see if we can get a date in the diary for—'

'Mark.'

Her tone brought him up short. The knife was still, poised above the board.

'She'd never say anything, I know, but . . . When I thought you were having an affair, I went to ask her if she knew anything, whether you'd spoken to them about it. I'm sorry for doubting you – us – I just didn't know what to think. I . . . I told her you weren't at your hotel and were claiming to have lost your phone and . . .' Hannah stopped talking. Telling him about Pippa was one thing, but she didn't want him to know she'd gone to DataPro, involved Neesha. Now, though, she remembered bumping into David by the lifts. Shit: he was bound to mention it.

'What did Pippa say?'

'That there was no way you were messing around and there'd be a simple explanation for the . . . weirdness.'

'Well, there is an explanation,' he said, dryly.

'I'm sorry for embarrassing you.'

He put the knife down and rubbed his eyes, looking exhausted suddenly. 'It doesn't matter. If I hadn't put you in the position . . .'

'It does matter, and I wanted you to know. I also want to say that when I went over there, I had no idea about . . . what happened. Do they know?'

'No. I've never told them.'

'I'd always thought you were at college with them.'

'No.' He shook his head. 'We were all at St Botolph's but that's pure coincidence. They're three or four years younger than me, I'd just left when they came up. I met Dan later through work and we discovered the connection then.'

'So why did I think you'd been there together?'

'I don't know. You must have just assumed it, I suppose, because they're such good friends.' He straightened the rosemary into a neat pile and picked the knife back up. 'I don't really have any friends from before any more,' he said. 'It's like my life breaks into two parts, before and after, and I only want to be around people from after, Han. At the beginning I thought it was going to suffocate me, that I'd be crushed under the weight of the guilt, the horror of it all . . . I thought I'd never be able to live normally again. But then, thank God, time started passing and I saw a way forward – denial, essentially. Or lying to your wife and your best friends, whatever you want to call it.'

Hannah stood up and crossed the kitchen. She put her arms around him and pressed her cheek against his chest. As she listened to his heart beating through the thin fabric of his shirt, the last of her confusion and anger burned away and in their place came an overwhelming sense of his loneliness.

CHAPTER 18

What happened when someone was released from prison? Hannah tried to imagine it but all that came into her head were images from old television programmes of the seventies and eighties: a few outdated possessions handed back by a sour-faced guard, a door slamming shut to leave the free man standing lost on a stretch of desolate pavement until a car skidded round the corner to offer a lift back to the old life, one last job. But this wasn't TV and Nick wasn't a lovable rogue. What would happen to him? Would he go to a halfway house? Would he have a parole officer or, having served his whole sentence, was he now entirely free to go?

Through the floor came the faint pip of the alarm. It was set for six forty-five, as usual, but she'd been up for over an hour already. When she'd opened her eyes, she'd seen Mark asleep next to her and for a few seconds it was as if the past week had never happened and it was a morning like any other. Then, however, she'd remembered. And now it was Wednesday: Nick got out tomorrow.

Overhead, Mark's feet hit the floor. Hannah

turned away from the window and came back to the counter to fill the Krups machine. Perhaps she shouldn't have any coffee, though. She'd been agitated and unsettled since she'd woken up and it wasn't just the worry. She had the feeling that there was something at the corner of her eye, just out of focus, something that didn't make sense. It was like watching a film and knowing there was something in the plot that didn't quite add up but not being able to put a finger on it.

The fridge was empty bar a cling-filmed plate of leftover pork, just enough milk for the coffee, and four eggs. She took them out to look for the best-before date and then, at the touch of hands on her waist, nearly dropped them. She managed, thank God, not to shriek with alarm; neither of them had said anything but she knew it was essential to pretend that everything was normal.

'Old Mother Hubbard,' she said, turning inside the circle of his arms. 'The cupboard's bare. It's scrambled eggs for breakfast. If we're lucky and there's bread in the freezer, there might be toast.'

'Ideal.' He gave her a kiss then stood back to look at her, smiling. 'I've missed your morning hair.'

He went back upstairs to shower while the coffee brewed and she made the eggs, watching the sky above the skylight turn from the blue-brown of heavy light pollution through grey to a blank white. Last night when they'd turned out the lights, Mark had come over to her side of the bed and wrapped himself around her. She'd known what he was

271

trying to communicate – *don't worry, I'll take care of things; we'll be all right* – but she'd felt need in the tightness of his arms, too, a silent search for reassurance.

Over breakfast they read each other snippets of news and he talked about the issues he was going to raise at the weekly meeting with the programmers in the afternoon. She listened, nodding in the appropriate places, all the time feeling pressure building inside her. Eventually, she couldn't pretend any longer.

'Mark, when are you going to talk to Nick?'

'I don't know.' He put his coffee cup back in the saucer. 'He said he'd contact me. It's more power-play: I've been trying to reach him in Wakefield but he's refusing to talk to me.'

'Will he ring today?'

'I've no idea, Hannah – I really can't say.' There was impatience in his voice and at once Mark looked ashamed of himself. 'I'm sorry,' he said. 'I didn't sleep very well last night.' He pressed his eyelids shut then opened them wide. 'It's possible he'll call today, but if I know my brother he'll be enjoying this, keeping me stewing. Either way, by tomorrow . . .' She waited for him to go on but instead he pushed back his chair and carried his plate to the dishwasher.

They said goodbye at the front door and she watched him walk up the pavement to his car, straight-backed and broad-shouldered in his black winter coat, his leather laptop case under his arm.

The Mercedes beeped once as he unlocked it with the remote fob. His self-possession was impressive. No one who saw him, she thought, would suspect for a minute that anything in his life wasn't exactly as he'd designed it.

As his car rounded the corner, she felt the day gape open like a chasm in front of her. She went upstairs straight away and changed into her running clothes. She did three laps of the common, one more than usual, but as soon as she got back to the house, the anxiety flooded in again. She showered and dressed quickly then packed her research file into her bag. Today she needed to keep moving.

The Starbucks on the corner of Parsons Green was busy with the school drop-off crowd so she walked to Caffè Nero instead and set up shop at an empty table at the back. The file was proof in itself that she'd had too much time on her hands in the past few months, she thought. After some days away from it, she was struck by how madly detailed and over-organised it was, the sheer volume of information on successful recent campaigns collected at the front, filed alphabetically by name of the product, and then the agencies at the back. Each one had a full list of key personnel and an in-depth history including the partners' previous backgrounds, industry awards won in the past five years and the names of all the clients her exhaustive research had uncovered.

She turned to the section on Penrose Price. There were a couple of pages of notes she'd made after her first interview, and after that a chunk – forty or fifty pages – of the material that she'd gathered beforehand: print-outs of articles from *Campaign* and *Brand Republic*, a helpful potted history of the agency – not nearly as detailed as her own – and interviews with both Roger Penrose and the hotshot Lewis Marant, his hire of three years ago, who was now talked about as one of the leading lights, if not *the* leading light, of the new generation of creatives.

Hannah flicked to the full-page interview with Marant she'd found in the *Guardian*. In the photograph, he was wearing an outfit identical to the one he'd had on at her second-round interview: a faded denim shirt open at the neck, sleeves rolled to the elbow, and a pair of heavy-rimmed tortoiseshell glasses that wouldn't look out of place on a Williamsburg hipster or, more specifically, Flynn, her old assistant.

She'd read reams about him before they'd met and she hadn't expected to warm to him. His press was almost too much; the online raving about his campaign for a new smartphone bordered on fan-boy adulation. In person, however, she'd liked Marant immediately. There'd been no pretension or cooler-than-thou cultural references; instead he'd known almost as much about her work as she did about his, and he'd told her that his five-year-old son sat at the tea-table banging his knife and fork and chanting her slogan for Happy Mouth ice cream. He'd also been refreshingly frank, centring their discussion on a campaign of his that hadn't worked very well, asking what she would have done differently.

He'd left to go to another meeting and Roger Penrose had told her then that, with the new hire, he was looking for a counterpart to Marant, someone who would grow alongside him within the agency so that, after Penrose's own retirement, the two of them would head it up together. After five months of unemployment, the idea was so exciting that she'd felt almost drunk on it when she stepped out on to the pavement afterwards. She had to get this job.

Hannah pulled the file closer now and tried to read, but within a few seconds her eyes stopped seeing the words and her mind turned to Nick. With a rush of alarm she remembered what Mark had said about his brother blaming him, resenting his freedom. What if Nick attacked Mark, hurt him? She felt a wave of fear that she pushed down as quickly as she could. *Come on*, she told herself, *concentrate*, but she managed only a couple of sentences before she heard Mark's voice again. '*He's been sitting up there stewing . . . He's convinced himself it was my fault.*'

For more than an hour she struggled but in the end she conceded defeat, closed the file and shoved it back in her bag. She left the café and headed up the Fulham Road in the opposite direction to

Quarrendon Street, no real purpose in mind except putting off the moment when she went back to the empty house. Whatever she tried to do today, she knew she wouldn't be able to stop herself thinking about Nick or shake the odd nagging sense that there was something she was missing.

When Mark arrived home at seven, he looked exhausted and his eyes were small and strained from screen-work. 'Shall we go to Mao Tai for supper?' he said. 'Let's not cook tonight.'

'Have you heard from him?' she asked.

He shook his head.

The restaurant was five minutes' walk away. As they crossed the road at the corner of Parsons Green, Mark took her hand and held it tightly. They sat at the bar, ordered martinis and drank them like medicine. Mark ordered a second round and when they moved to their table he asked for the wine list. She'd never seen him drink like this on a Wednesday night. But then, she thought, it didn't feel like a Wednesday.

As they finished their starters, she glanced up and saw that the woman at the next table was looking at him; a couple of minutes later it happened again. For a moment, paranoid, Hannah thought something was wrong, but then she realised: the woman was looking at Mark because he looked so handsome. The martinis had smoothed the strain from his face and his eyes were dark and shiny in the candlelight. He'd left his tie at home and undone his collar, and in his tailor-made suit jacket he looked well made and urbane. His hands rested on the table, strong and straight-fingered, their backs dusted with hair. For a moment Hannah saw him as if she were a stranger and felt a burst of pride: he was hers. Then she remembered the description in the newspaper article of his parents' small grey pebble-dashed bungalow. Yes, it must have an incongruous place for Nick to have spent his childhood but it couldn't have suited Mark either, the boy who'd grown up to become this sophisticated man.

Halfway down her second glass of wine, after the waitress had taken away the plates from the duck, Hannah stood up to go to the loo and realised how smashed she was. Before the starters, she'd had nothing to eat since breakfast, and the alcohol was coursing through her bloodstream. She held the handrail tightly on the steep front stairs.

As she washed her hands, her body felt like a piece of machinery she was operating from the outside. She leaned towards the mirror to wipe away a smudge of mascara and saw herself up close by the light of the line of little candles along the back of the vanity unit. Wasn't candlelight supposed to be flattering? It was doing nothing for her: she looked old – old and exhausted.

Suddenly she saw it, the thing that had been nagging at her, hovering at the edge of her field of vision all day: it was Hermione's expression when Hannah had said who she was, the fleeting but unmistakable look of horror. Why would she have been horrified? If she was Mark's friend, however off the radar, why had she looked so alarmed to meet his wife?

Hannah splashed her face with cold water, angry with herself for having so much to drink: if there was ever a time she needed to have her wits about her, it was now. She dried her face and hands and made her way carefully downstairs again, gripping the banister. Back at the table, she dropped heavily into her chair. Mark reached for her hand. He'd topped up their glasses again.

'Hermione,' she said, and her voice was too loud even against the background hum. She saw him snap to attention. 'When I went to see her at the hospital, I told her who I was – your wife – and she looked scared. Why?'

Mark pulled her closer to the table. 'Han,' he said quietly, 'can we talk about this at home? Not here. I don't want to . . .'

'No, Mark, I need to know now. Tell me. Why did she look frightened? She covered it up really fast but it was in her eyes, I saw it.'

He looked at her for a moment then leaned in again, reducing the gap between them to a few inches. 'She was Nick's girlfriend.'

Through the fug of booze, it was a second or two before Hannah realised what he was telling her. 'You mean – at the time?'

He nodded.

'My God.' She put her hand over her mouth. 'I

278

thought she was a friend of yours from Cambridge. I didn't . . .'

'She is. That's how they met, through me. She liked him from day one, of course, though Nick wasn't so bothered, but after a while he realised that other people thought she was a bit of a prize – super-bright, lovely-looking – and he made a move. They'd been going out for about six months.'

'Was she there?'

'At the club? No. She was on nights at the hospital; she didn't find out till the next day when one of the girls phoned her. God, poor Herm. I'd tried to warn her but she said she could handle him. I should have tried harder. It wasn't even the first time he'd cheated on her. He'd been shagging around for weeks – another alarm bell I should have heard.'

'That look when I told her who I was – why would she be frightened? It's been ten years. Surely after all this time . . .'

Mark glanced towards the next table and lowered his voice again. 'She testified against him.'

'What? In court?' Hannah said stupidly.

'She gave evidence about Nick's . . . tastes.' Mark was speaking so quietly now that Hannah had to lean across the table to hear him. 'How he liked to restrain her, that he was into control. How, a couple of times, he'd gone too far, hurt her, and then wouldn't stop, even when she begged him. She had a really rough time in the box, his defence went to town on her, but she did it. Some of the things

279

she said . . . It was hard to listen to – literally sickening. The women on the jury – I think for them, in particular, it brought it all into focus, having someone like Hermione, who's so articulate and together, painting this picture of . . .'

Remembering how she'd confronted the woman in the corridor at work, how aggressive she'd been, Hannah was filled with remorse.

'Nick was livid – he could see how it was going down. I watched him. He had this expression on, all regretful denial, shock that anyone could say those things about him, but I know him, I knew what he was thinking.' Mark swigged his wine. 'He wouldn't forget that in a lifetime, let alone ten years. And now he's contacted her from prison, making threats.'

'What kind of threats?'

'Apparently he's told her it's payback time.'

CHAPTER 19

Lifting one end then the other, Hannah dragged the sofa away from the wall. She plugged in the vacuum cleaner, came back to the centre of the room and hit the on switch. The roar billowed up around her like a dust cloud. She'd put off the vacuuming until Mark was out of bed but already this morning she'd cleaned the whole of the ground floor, dusting and straightening, sweeping and mopping. She'd even cleaned the kitchen cabinets and the cutlery drawer, taking out the silverware and laying it on the table while she disinfected the inside of the drawer, getting right into the corners for every last bit of dust.

She'd been going since five. Even cleaning the downstairs loo was better than lying in bed desperate for sleep that wouldn't come. She'd been awake all night, her mind racing, the alcohol in her stomach swilling queasily with the fatty Chinese. Until about three Mark had been awake, too – she'd turned over several times to find him lying on his back, eyes open – but then she'd heard his breathing slow and she'd been left alone in the darkness.

Rolling back the lovely Victorian nursing chair he'd bought at a furniture auction at Christie's, she set about the rug with zeal. It was antique, too, imported from Turkey; one evening they'd sat together on the sofa and he'd told her the stories behind all its patterns and symbols. Glancing over, she saw the little silver clock on the mantelpiece: quarter past ten. Before he'd got out of bed, she'd gone online. The journey time from Wakefield to London, she'd seen, was two hours on the train, a little over four by coach. What time would they let Nick go – or was he already out? Perhaps he was already on the National Express, heading their way. She shoved the vacuum forward again, trying to drown the idea out.

Over the racket came a different sound and, looking up, she saw Mark standing on the step through from the kitchen. He was waving his arms in front of him: *cut it out*. She hit the switch and the vacuum sucked the noise back in like a bubble-gum bubble.

'Could you keep it down? I'm struggling to hear myself think in here.'

'Sorry.' She put her hands up and retied the knot in her hair. The back of her neck was damp.

'Isn't Lynda coming tomorrow morning? Leave her something to do. Go up and have a bath or have another go at getting some sleep.'

She shook her head. 'Pointless.'

'Fine, but no more hoovering.' He unplugged the vacuum and carried it back to the cupboard under the stairs. A moment or two later she heard him pull his chair up to the kitchen table again. It was for her sake that he was working at home this morning, she knew, and she appreciated it, glad not to be alone. If he thought that his being here was calming, however, he was wrong. If anything, he was making her feel more anxious. He was trying to hide it but he was as jumpy as she was. He'd snapped at her two or three times and he'd been having difficulty focusing long before she'd started vacuuming. While she'd been cleaning the glass in the internal doors, she'd seen him stand up from the table and go to the window two or three times. When he'd come back to his computer, it had been with a look of grim determination. Each time he'd lasted five minutes at most before standing up again. Usually he had no problem concentrating – she envied that about him.

She straightened the piles of magazines on the coffee table then went through into the kitchen and sat down. On the rush mat, left over from breakfast, was the teapot – always the sign of a bad morning when neither of them could face coffee – and a tumbler grainy with Alka Seltzer residue. Mark gave her a quick look over the lid of his laptop then went back to his email.

She reached for the new copy of *Campaign* that had arrived in the post. As she tore off the polythene wrapper, his phone vibrated on the table next to him, screen alight, and she gave a start, knocking the table and slopping his tea into the saucer.

'It's only David,' he said.

'Sorry. Every time it rings I think—'

Before she finished talking, he picked up the phone. 'Hi. No, fine, just a few things I wanted to get done here before coming in. Did you get the print-out?' He paused, listening. 'I'll be in after lunch. And I've got drinks tonight that might be interesting, depending on how things play out this week . . . I'll fill you in later.'

He put the phone down. Without looking up, he started typing again. Eyes barely skimming the headlines, Hannah turned a page in the magazine then another. Three seconds later the phone rang again, and she jumped again.

'Oh, for Christ's sake, Hannah.'

'I'm sorry, I'm sorry.'

He ignored her. 'Hi, Neesh, what's up?' He paused and Hannah listened to the tinny voice at the other end. 'Oh,' he said, 'I thought I'd put it in your inbox before I left. Try the pile on the cabinet in my office . . . Sometime after two, probably . . . No, I've got it – you're ringing me on it, aren't you, you nutter? I'll see you later.'

He put the phone back on the table and looked at her. 'Just calm down, will you, Hannah, for fuck's sake?'

The language startled her: she could count on two hands the times she'd ever heard Mark swear before, and he'd never sworn at her. 'I said, I'm sorry. It's just . . . I feel like I'm waiting with my neck in the guillotine.'

'Then how do you think *I* feel?' He slammed

284

down the lid of his laptop and stood up. 'I'm going upstairs.'

Now she felt bad – selfish and inconsiderate. 'No, don't, you don't need to. I'll be quiet. If I'm in the sitting room, you can—'

He shook his head, impatient with her. 'No, I've got too much to do. I'm in the middle of trying to sell my business and now I'm just sitting here, pissing my time up the wall.'

He knocked his papers into a stack, put his laptop under his arm and strode out of the room. His feet thumped an angry rhythm on the stairs.

When he came back down an hour or so later, he apologised: 'I'm wound tight as a nut.'

'It doesn't matter,' she told him. 'I can't imagine how—'

'Yes, it does.' He put his arms round her and rested his chin gently on the top of her head. 'Bloody Nick – somehow he always does this to me, puts me so on edge I end up hardly recognising myself. But look,' he pulled away again, 'I've been thinking. I've got to go into the office this afternoon and then I've got these drinks but I don't want you to sit here on your own worrying. Why don't you go into town and buy something for the interview?'

'I'm just going to wear my navy dress. It needs dry-cleaning but . . .'

'You've had that for ages and is it smart enough, really? I think you should buy an investment piece, something you'll wear for a while. You'll feel good in it next week and it's always worth spending money on something top quality.'

She hesitated. 'I don't think I can afford it.'

It was a second before he realised what she meant. 'God, sorry,' he grimaced. 'Take that credit card I got made for you – the one on my account. No, don't look at me like that – this isn't a back-door scheme to turn you into a kept woman. It's not as if you couldn't have afforded a dress if someone – *I* – hadn't taken your money, is it?' He reached into his jacket on the back of the chair and got out his wallet.

Clearly still feeling guilty, he walked her to the Tube station. As they came along the edge of the Green, he reached for her hand and held it tight like he had on the way to the restaurant the night before. 'It was Neesha who told you about Hermione, wasn't it?' he said.

Remembering her promise, she shook her head.

'It doesn't matter in the slightest. You're my wife – why wouldn't you call my assistant? I've just been trying to work it out, that's all. No one else really knows about Hermione, not that I've been in touch with lately, and Neesha just asked whether I had my phone, which means she must have had a reason for thinking I might not, which means – given that it was only you I told that fib to – you must have talked to her.'

'Yes, all right, Sherlock. I called to see if she'd heard from you when you didn't show up at the airport and I thought you'd been snaffled by some opportunistic femme fatale. I promised her I wouldn't tell you. You won't say anything, will you?'

'Of course not.' He smiled. 'I'm just flattered you both think I'm capable of such Don Juanery.'

'Don Juanism?'

He laughed. 'Or Don Juanity?'

When they reached the station he got an *Evening Standard* for her to read on the train then took off his scarf, looped it around her neck and pulled her towards him. She slid her hands around his lower back, feeling the chill silk of his coat against her skin. 'If anything happens, if I hear from him, I'll ring you straight away,' he said. 'And if you're worried – about anything at all – then ring me.' He waited at the barrier while she climbed the stairs, giving her a final wave as she disappeared from view.

The sense of comfort evaporated in minutes. She took the train to Bond Street and wandered listlessly around the huge womenswear floor at Selfridges until admitting to herself that she was never going to be able to concentrate on shopping. The interview felt a thousand miles away, like something from a different world. She left the shop and started walking, weaving her way along Oxford Street then down into Soho. She was on Charing Cross Road when it started raining, and she ducked inside Foyles and up to the café.

She couldn't stop thinking about Hermione; how

she'd stood up and faced Nick in court, testified against him. *Payback time*: no wonder she'd looked so alarmed that day. Hannah felt another wash of guilt. Perhaps she should go back to the hospital this afternoon, now, and apologise? Or would that just make it worse?

On the table in front of her, her BlackBerry started flashing and she snatched it up. She'd had it in her hand constantly this afternoon, set both to vibrate and ring at maximum volume.

Everything all right? Starting to get worried about you.

At first glance she thought it was from Mark – he'd already texted twice to check in – but looking again, she saw that the message was from her brother. She felt bad: he'd rung on Monday night when she'd been gorging herself on the news stories and again yesterday evening, but she hadn't been in touch with him since Sunday, when she'd texted to let him know about the conversation with Pippa.

Sorry, she wrote now, *poor correspondent this week. All okay. How did things go with Luke and the head-master?* She hit send and put the phone down. Seconds later, it flashed again.

Hideous. Talked to Head on Monday. Luke resigned then had meltdown in staff car park – wife had to come and get him. Feel like total bastard. How are things with Mark?

Hannah hit reply then stopped. She had to tell him something – after asking Tom's advice, she couldn't just sweep the whole thing under the carpet – and she wanted to tell him, she was desperate to. Loyalty to Mark, however, pulled her in the opposite direction. She remembered what he'd said about his life dividing into two halves, before and after, and she wanted to help him keep that distinction, at least when it came to her family. It was Nick's crime, not Mark's, but knowing about it – knowing how his girlfriend had died – would change her family's view of Mark irrevocably. They would never dream of saying anything but it would be there behind every conversation, at every family occasion, and she couldn't bear that.

Tom was different, though. He was her confidant, her best friend, and she needed to talk to him.

You did the right thing, she wrote back, *however shitty it feels. Things with Mark okay – thanks again for listening. No affair, just a long story. Pint early next week and I'll tell you?*

His response came within a minute: *Long story sounds complicated. Pint definitely in order. Monday?*

In Central London the Tube ran too deep for reception but as Hannah came up the steps at Earl's Court a new text message arrived: she'd missed a call and had voicemail. Checking, she saw Mark's number. It was a couple of minutes before seven and the platform was packed with people waiting for a Wimbledon train so she walked to the far end where it was quieter.

Message received today at 6.17 p.m., the staccato

289

female recording told her, and then, over the din of the train suddenly thundering into the station behind her, she heard his voice. *Hi, it's me. Just checking in again – hope everything's okay. I'm about to go in to drinks with this hedge-fund guy but I'm going to keep it brief so I should be home about half-eight. Let me know if you want me to pick anything up* en route.

A pause, and in the background she heard a man's voice say, *Seventeen-fifty, mate,* and a couple of seconds later, *Cheers – good of you.* The unmistakable sound of a black-cab's door slamming.

Nothing from Nick, Mark's voice again. *He's really making me sweat. Anyway, I hope you've managed to have a semi-decent afternoon and have bought something lovely – looking forward to seeing it. I'll see you in a couple of hours.* He lowered his voice and she guessed there were people nearby. *I love you.*

She managed to squeeze on to the train just as the doors were closing and was pressed into a corner by a man in an enormous orange Puffa jacket until Fulham Broadway, when half the people in the carriage streamed out on to the platform. The train came above ground and cut across the top corner of Eel Brook Common, now swallowed by darkness, the path that bisected it picked out by a line of solitary streetlamps casting their light on empty benches. When the train pulled in at Parsons Green, the clock at the top of the stairs said ten past seven. If Mark was on time, she thought, she'd have less than an hour and a half alone in the house.

The rain had stopped, or perhaps it had never reached here, but only the hardiest smokers were clustered under the heaters outside the White Horse, everyone else holed up inside in the warmth. Hannah walked quickly, pulling the collar of her coat together under her chin, wishing she had her gloves. She'd light a fire when she got home, have it really roaring by the time Mark got back. She rounded the corner on to New King's Road, passing the estate agent and the hairdresser's, raising her head again when the buildings sheltered her from the wind. Approaching the delicatessen, she turned to look at the banks of cut flowers in the buckets outside, their riot of extravagant colour against the dank November pavement. Spot-lit by an electric bulb clipped to the awning, the flower man was wrapping a huge bunch of peonies and eucalyptus for a young woman in a bright red raincoat. Another man stood behind them, looking at roses.

For a moment she thought it was Mark, home early: the height, the build, his posture, even the short dark jacket that looked like the pea coat he wore when they went walking at weekends. She must have stopped for a second or started to say something because he turned and Mark's face looked out at her from beneath a black beanie.

Almost Mark's face.

Their eyes met. He recognised her, too, or

guessed at once who she was. For a moment she was immobilised but then she turned and ran. She ran back the way she'd just come, past the estate agent's and up the road parallel to the Green, the pavement now twice as long as it had been a minute before, the streetlights further apart, the houses darker, drawn further back into their gardens. Her heart was pounding, her whole body tensed for the sound of footsteps behind her, the hand grabbing at her coat, but it didn't come and it still didn't come and at last she reached the pub, yanked the door open and plunged into the light and safety of the bar.

She threaded her way to the loos at the back, locked herself in a cubicle and leaned against the wall, breath coming in great heaves. The outer door swung open, banging back against the wall, but it was two girls having a loud conversation about their boss. When she thought she would be able to talk, Hannah dropped the lid of the loo and sat down. The hand-driers stopped and there was a snatch of noise from the bar as the girls swung out again. She held her phone with both hands to stop herself from dropping it.

Mark picked up on the third ring. 'Hannah – is everything all right?'

'He's here,' she said. 'In Parsons Green.'

'What? At the house? Christ – *fuck*.'

'No – no.' She took a shuddering breath. 'Outside the deli. I thought it was you. He looked just—'

'Where are you?' he demanded. 'Where's Nick?'

'I'm at the pub – the White Horse. I don't know where he is – I just ran. I just saw him and ran.'

'Okay, look,' he said, and she knew he was trying to think, to sound calm for her sake. 'Stay where you are. Get a drink and stay where you are. I'm leaving right now – this minute. Stay inside. Don't move until I get there.'

'You're sure he knew who you were?'

'Yes, sure. I don't know if he did before – how could he? – but when he saw my reaction . . . Who else could I have been? I was fifty yards from our house and I stopped – I honestly thought it was you. I was about to *talk* to him.'

Mark stabbed at the fire as if he hated it. His knuckles were white on the handle of the poker. 'Jesus *Christ*,' he said. 'I can't believe that he . . . But I can – of course I can. Why did I even think for a minute he would phone first? Why would he do that when he could show up here and terrify my wife instead?'

'We should call the police.'

Mark stabbed again, sending up a shower of sparks. An artery was leaping at the side of his neck. 'What could they do, Hannah? What could they actually do? Technically, Nick's done nothing. He's a free man; he's served his time. He didn't even talk to you.'

'It's harassment. Coming here, to where you live, and . . .'

'He's my brother. There's no restraining order,

293

he's not breaking any laws. And it's not like he's even trying to extort the money – he's a DataPro shareholder, there's paperwork that says I have to pay him the value of his twelve per cent on the day of his release. If anyone's on the back foot legally, it's me.'

Hannah hugged her knees tighter. She couldn't stop shaking – neither of them could. When he'd arrived at the pub, Mark had looked almost wild. She'd been sitting at a corner table, hidden from view from the door, and he'd come in and scanned the place so desperately it was as if he was expecting to find she'd been taken. When he'd put his arms round her, crushing her face into his chest, his heart had been hammering so fast she could barely differentiate the beats. It was a five-minute walk to the house, if that, but he'd kept his cab waiting at the kerb outside and he'd stood right behind her and almost pushed her into it, looking over his shoulder all the time.

'He must have been here,' she said. 'He must have come to the house. What if I'd been in? Through the glass I would have thought it was you, that you'd forgotten your keys or something.'

Mark dropped the poker on to the hearth with a clatter and stood up. He couldn't sit still – he'd been sitting then standing then sitting again every two minutes. 'I've got to warn Hermione.' His coat was slung over the arm of the sofa; he got his phone from the pocket and brought up her number, fingers fumbling on the touchscreen. With the phone pressed to his ear, he crossed to the window, pulled the curtain aside and looked out.

'Herm,' he said, 'it's Mark.' He paused and for a moment Hannah thought he'd got through. 'Look, I don't want to panic you but Nick's been here in Parsons Green this evening. I didn't see him; Hannah did, my wife – I think you've met.' Despite everything, there was a hint of humour in his tone at that. 'Call me when you get this. He's obviously come out all guns blazing so . . . Anyway, I thought I should let you know in case you wanted to organise some company for tonight or stay with someone. You're welcome to stay with us, too, obviously – give me a ring or just get in a cab and come over. We'll be here all night.' He hung up but held on to the phone, gripping it tightly.

'Does Nick know where she lives?' Hannah said.

'I don't know. She's moved since it happened – she was still junior then, she lived in residences at the hospital – but if he wants to know, he'll find out.' Mark went back to the window then turned to look at her again. 'He doesn't even need to know where she lives.'

For a moment she didn't understand.

'*You* found her, didn't you?'

He was right. All Nick had to do was go to the hospital.

Mark went out into the hall and she heard the rattle of the door handle as he checked the lock for the third time. A few seconds later, the kitchen light snapped on and she heard the clink of bottles.

When she went in, he was pouring an enormous measure of whisky. She watched as he drank half of it in a single swallow.

Hearing her, he turned. For a second or two he looked at her then he put the glass down and came towards her, arms out. The force with which he hugged her was enough to knock her off balance and by instinct she held on to him tighter to stop herself stumbling. To her surprise, he half lifted, half pushed her backwards against the wall. Her head bumped off the plaster but before the small cry had left her mouth, he was kissing her, his face crushed against hers, his tongue pushing itself between her lips. His left hand was on the wall, his forearm creating a barrier, and now she felt his right hand fumbling with the button of her jeans. 'Mark . . .' She twisted her head away, trying to free her mouth to speak, but he followed her, kissing her harder. His fingers popped the button and found the zipper. His chest was heaving, his breath hot and fast, whisky-scented.

'Mark!' She put her hands on his shoulders and pushed him away. He took a big step backwards.

For a second or two they stared at each other but then he seemed to come to himself again. The intent dropped from his face and he looked first blank then embarrassed. 'I'm sorry,' he said, touching his lip with his fingers in disbelief. 'I don't know what came over me. I—'

'It doesn't matter,' she said. 'I just couldn't – not tonight.'

'I know. I know. I'm so sorry, Han.' He swallowed hard. 'I don't want to be the kind of person who . . . God, I just feel so . . . messed up. When you rang and said you'd seen him, he was here, I was terrified. If anything happened to you – if he hurt you – I couldn't live with it.'

CHAPTER 20

The knocking tore through the house like the rattle of gunfire, *rat-tat-tat-tat*, ripping the peace of the morning wide open. Hannah jerked awake just as Mark reared up in bed next to her. They stared at each other. For a few seconds the knocking stopped, leaving a silence that rang with echoes, but then it started again, louder still. In a moment he was across the room, pulling a T-shirt over his head.

'Stay here,' he said but she was already out of bed, too, grabbing yesterday's clothes from the back of the chair, nearly falling as she caught her foot in the leg of her jeans. He took the stairs at a run but then, as he neared the bottom, she heard him slow down. When she came out on to the landing, he was standing on the bottom step, looking at the front door.

'Leave it, Mark. Don't open it.'

'No,' he said, glancing up. 'It's not . . .' The knocking started again, just as insistent. 'Okay, okay, I'm coming.' The heavy *thunk* of the deadlock, the brush of the door against the mat. Hannah gripped the banister.

'Morning, sir.' A deep male voice with a Liverpool accent. 'Mark Reilly? Detective Inspector Wells, DS Andrews. Can we come in?'

Police? Hannah let go of the banister. She went to the top of the stairs and saw them just as they looked up and saw her. The man was in his late forties, Mark's height but bulky, wearing a dark waxed jacket. With him was a woman her own age in a black trouser suit and short wool coat, her sandy-blonde hair cut in a shoulder-length bob. Mark opened the door wider and they stepped inside, the male officer standing back to let the woman go ahead of him. As Hannah came downstairs, Mark turned to look at her, his eyes full of uncertainty.

The police waited for her then indicated the sitting-room door. 'Can we?'

'Please,' said Mark.

Inside they positioned themselves in front of the mantelpiece, side by side. The air held the thick, ashy smell of the dead fire. Like every other room in the house, the sitting room was large but even so, the detective – Wells, was that what he'd said? – seemed disproportionate to it, a looming presence. 'Perhaps you'd like to sit down, sir – Mrs Reilly?'

Mark stayed standing. 'What's going on? What's happened?' His voice was loud. Hannah reached out and put her hand on his arm.

'Do you know a woman called Hermione Alleyn, sir?'

'Yes. We don't see each other much now, but yes. We were at university together, at Cambridge.'

Wells nodded slightly. 'I'm sorry to have to tell you this but she's dead. Her body was found late last night.'

Hannah's heart gave a single great thump. *Dead.* The word fell like a drumbeat, the reverberations fanning out after it, vibrating in the air.

'Dead?' She heard Mark say in disbelief. 'Do you mean . . . killed?'

'I'm afraid so, yes.'

He turned to face Hannah, giving her a wild look. 'How?'

'We won't know for sure until after the post-mortem,' said the woman officer, speaking for the first time, 'but mostly likely it was from head injuries – blunt-force trauma to the skull.'

Mark slumped on to the arm of the sofa, his hand over his mouth. His eyes were wide with horror.

'When?' Hannah asked.

'Again, we're waiting for the post-mortem to establish that more exactly but some time in the late afternoon. She left the hospital just after four.'

Mark moved his hands over his face and rocked forward. The woman gave him a moment then spoke again. 'Mr Reilly, we found Ms Alleyn's phone with her body. You left a message for her last night, at quarter to nine.'

'Yes,' he said, through his fingers. 'I rang her but I didn't get through. I wanted to tell her . . .'

'We've listened to it. You seemed to be warning her, suggesting she might not want to be alone last night. Can you tell us more about that?'

He raised his head. 'I wanted to warn her about my brother,' he said. 'Nick. He got out of prison yesterday. There was history between them – they used to go out, she testified against him at his trial, and he'd been in touch with her before he was released, threatening her. She'd been ringing me, to talk. I knew she was frightened and—'

'What was he threatening?'

'She told me he said it was "payback time".'

'Payback?'

'Nick thought it was her testimony that got him convicted. He blamed her.' Mark's hands squeezed into fists on his knees. 'Where was she? Who found her?'

'Your brother was convicted of manslaughter, Mr Reilly,' said Wells.

Manslaughter. The word hung in the air, and Hannah heard its fading echo: *slaughter, slaughter, slaughter*.

'Yes,' Mark said quietly.

'She was found in Spitalfields,' Wells said, 'about ten minutes' walk from the hospital, in the yard at the back of a pub. The landlord went out just after closing time to check the gate was padlocked. He didn't see her first off but his dog ran out ahead of him and started barking, wouldn't come away.'

Mark rocked forward again. Hannah felt the

room start to ebb and flow around her, the carpet undulating under her feet. Dead, left behind a pub with the empty barrels and the bins.

'We found a packet of cigarettes at the scene,' the woman said. 'Whether there was a struggle and he dropped them . . .'

'Your brother's fingerprints were on them,' said Wells.

Mark closed his eyes. For several seconds he was silent but then he jerked upright. 'This is my fault,' he said. He coughed, half-choked. 'I should have done something. I knew Hermione was worried, I knew about the threats and I . . .' He coughed again and swiped a hand roughly across his eyes. 'I wanted her to go away for a while, or come and stay here. I offered last night but . . .' He looked up at the female officer. 'Oh my God, her mother?'

'She's been notified.'

'Hermione was her only child,' he said, turning to Hannah. 'She's a widow – brought Herm up on her own.'

'In your message, Mr Reilly, you said Nick had been here. It was you who saw him, Mrs Reilly, is that right?' The detective turned to Hannah.

'Yes. But not here at the house – it was just up the road, at the delicatessen. He was standing outside. They have flowers – he was standing looking at them.'

'Did you talk to him?'

'No. I saw him and ran.'

'But you're sure it was him?

'Yes, sure. I've never met him before – Mark and I have only been married since April, Nick's been in prison all that time – but they – he and Mark – look so similar, I actually thought it was Mark until he turned round properly. I've seen photographs of Nick.' *Online*. 'When he saw me, it was obvious he knew who I was, too, or guessed.'

'Did he approach you? Did he try to say anything?'

Hannah shook her head. 'Like I said, I ran. I thought he'd come after me, I was terrified, but . . . I've thought about it, why he didn't, and all I can think was that he didn't want to draw attention to himself. There were other people around. One of the guys who works there was wrapping up a bouquet for a customer.'

'Why were you so terrified?' asked the female detective.

'The history – his conviction and . . .' Hannah looked at Mark.

'My brother and I have a difficult relationship,' he said, 'we always have had, and Nick's angry about his time in prison. He blames me for that as well as Hermione. But the other issue at the moment is money. I owe him money.'

'How much are we talking about?' asked Wells.

'One point eight million.'

Hannah watched the police officers exchange glances.

'Nick owns a stake in my company, twelve per cent, and we had an agreement that he'd cash out the day he got out of prison. He was emphatic about it at the time he bought the shares – on the day, the actual day, the paperwork specifies that. And he wants the money – I went to see him in Wakefield last month – but I haven't got it to give to him now. I'm in the process of selling the business, we're meeting the potential purchaser next week, and if it goes through there'll be no problem. But until then . . .'

'And your brother knows this?'

'No, that's just it. I thought he'd be in touch. I've been waiting for him to ring me and,' Mark held up his hands, 'nothing. That's why we're so jumpy, Hannah and I. He's playing games. Nick . . . it's hard to explain. Sometimes in the past I've thought it's like trying to deal with a wild animal. You can never predict what he's going to do, and when Hannah rang and said she'd seen him . . . He'd obviously come to the house but we weren't here so he decided to hang around and wait. He couldn't have planned it, bumping into her like that, but he must have loved it when he saw how frightened she was.'

'Mrs Reilly,' said the woman, 'what time was it when you saw him? Do you remember?'

'I'm not sure. No, wait.' Hannah remembered the clock at the top of the station stairs. 'I went into town yesterday afternoon – shopping – and when I got back to Parsons Green it was ten past seven. I saw the clock on the platform. It's a few minutes' walk from there to the deli, three or four.'

'So quarter past seven, give or take a minute or two?'

'Yes.'

'And tell us exactly what happened.'

'Almost nothing, that was it. I was coming along the pavement and I saw a man who looked like my husband standing by the flowers. If I'd been thinking straight, I should have known it couldn't be him – Mark was in a meeting, I'd just had a message to tell me he was going in – but the physical similarity . . . Anyway, I stopped. I think I might have started to say something, I'm not sure, but he turned round. We just looked at each other – neither of us said anything – and then I turned and ran.'

'And he made no effort to come after you?'

'Not as far as I know. I didn't hear anything – no footsteps. I just kept going until I reached the pub – the White Horse at the top of the Green.'

'Do you have any idea which way he might have headed?'

Hannah shook her head. 'All I could think about was getting away.'

DS Andrews took a notepad from her jacket pocket, leaned against the mantelpiece and made three quick lines of notes.

'Mr Reilly,' said Wells, 'when was the last time you spoke to Hermione? The last time you got through to her, I mean. Or perhaps you saw her, met up?'

'No, I haven't – hadn't . . .' Mark swallowed. 'I

hadn't seen her in person for ages – I don't even know how long. A couple of years, maybe – definitely before I met my wife.'

'We met in July last year,' Hannah said.

'But I spoke to her last week. She called me at the office. It was Tuesday, I think – yes, it must have been, Tuesday afternoon. I went to America first thing on Wednesday morning.'

The policewoman made a note in her book. 'And how was she then?'

'She was . . . anxious. Frightened.'

'Your brother had made contact with her?'

'Yes, and his release date was coming up. She was worried – she wanted to talk.' Mark's voice shook.

Wells waited a moment. 'These threats of your brother's – did she give you any details, discuss what he'd said specifically?'

'Not really. She said he'd told her he'd find her – *he'd track her down*, was what he said – and it was payback time.'

'Right.' Wells looked at his colleague, who made a final note then returned the pad to her pocket. He took out a card and gave it to Mark. 'Obviously, Mr Reilly, finding your brother is our top priority. If you hear from him, please get in touch – immediately. We'll need to speak to you again, I'm sure, but if you remember anything else before you hear from us, ring me on that number. I'm going to arrange for a watch to be kept on the house in case he comes here again. We'll have a car outside in the next hour. Is there anywhere else you think he might go? Friends, family? Anyone who might give him a bed?'

Mark thought for a moment then shook his head. 'Not that I can think of, no. Most of Nick's friends – all of them – dropped him when he was arrested. I'm not sure you'd really have called them friends, anyway – more like acolytes, hangers-on. Users – in both senses. My office, though – DataPro. I mean, I don't think he'd come up, not now, but he might try and wait for me outside.'

'Right. And where is that?'

Mark gave them the address.

'Okay,' the detective said. 'We'll have a car there, too. Just ignore it – both of them. Act like you don't know they're there – if he comes, we don't want him to cotton on. Hopefully, it'll make you feel a bit safer, too,' he nodded his head in Hannah's direction, 'but don't take any risks. If you're out, stay in busy places, don't go anywhere on your own after dark. Be careful – I don't need to tell you. And if you think of anything else, however trivial, let us know.'

'We will.' Mark got to his feet slowly, as if he'd been badly beaten. In the hallway, he opened the door and they stepped outside.

Just as they were turning to go, the policewoman stopped and looked back at Hannah. 'Mrs Reilly, in his message your husband said he thought you'd met Hermione, and yet just now he said he hadn't seen her since the two of you,' she waved her hand between them, 'had been together.'

307

'Yes,' Hannah said. 'Actually, it's embarrassing. I went to the hospital on Monday. Mark was away in America longer than I'd expected and when I spoke to his assistant she told me a woman had been calling him.' She looked at Mark apologetically. 'I was being ridiculous – I accused Hermione of having an affair with him.'

The policewoman frowned slightly. 'You didn't know she was a friend of your husband's?'

'Like he said, we'd never met.'

'Hermione and I weren't in touch often,' Mark explained. 'It was too painful. If we saw each other, the memory of Nick was always there, this . . . nightmare hanging over us. We tried to go back to how things had been before, at college, but we couldn't. We could never get away from him.'

CHAPTER 21

Mark closed the door and Hannah put her arms around him, feeling him shake. Tremors were running through his body. At the sound of approaching footsteps outside he stiffened but they continued on, pace unchanged, past the door and on towards the bottom of the street. He pressed his cheek against the top of Hannah's head, and in the parting of her hair she felt tears fall, one warm drop, then another.

'It's my fault, Han,' he said. 'I should have done something.'

'It's not your fault,' she said, fiercely. 'Stop saying that. You can't blame yourself, I won't let you. For God's sake, Nick's a killer.'

Mark said nothing and the word hung in the air. *A killer.* Yes, he was. It was no accident this time. Head injuries, blunt-force trauma to the skull – with Hermione, Nick had set out to kill.

Hannah led Mark back to the sitting room and they sat pressed together on the sofa. He made no effort to stop crying and the tears fell one after another, making dark rings on his T-shirt. 'She should have gone away,' he said. 'I told her to, I tried to make her promise me she would, but she said no, she was tied in at work, she had a conference coming up and . . .' He took a long shuddering breath.

'Mark.' Hannah put her hand on his cheek and turned his head so that he was looking at her. 'Hermione was an adult. She knew the situation and she made her own choice. You are not to blame.'

'But . . .'

'No. No. You tried to help and she took a chance and . . .' Her voice trailed off and Mark turned away from her and stared at his hands, which were clenched in his lap. The clock on the DVD player clicked from 8.13 to 8.14.

'We should leave,' said Hannah.

'Leave? What do you mean?'

'Get out of London. We should go away now – right now. That holiday you were talking about . . .'

'I can't,' he said.

'"*She was tied in at work.*"'

'I know, I know, but I just can't. The first meeting with Systema is on Tuesday and—'

'Mark.'

'No,' he said, adamant. When he turned to her, his face was set. 'No, Hannah. I've got to be here – I've got to. I've worked for seventeen years to build DataPro and I will not – *I will not* – let Nick screw it up for me. This might be the biggest deal I ever do – I am not going to let anything jeopardise it.'

'Even if you're risking your life?'

He said nothing.

'And mine?'

He closed his eyes. 'I'm sorry. You're right – of course you're right.'

'We can stay in London, I can deal with that, but just not here. I can't stand it – with him out there, knowing exactly where to find us.'

'The police car will be outside.'

'But that just makes it worse, doesn't it? I feel like we're . . . bait.'

Mark took a last look around then stepped outside and pulled the front door shut. The deadlock made a final-sounding *clunk*. Hannah watched as he closed the gate behind them and put the latch down as if it would make all the difference to the security of the house while they were gone.

They loaded the bags into his Mercedes and Hannah jumped as he slammed the boot shut. She kept her eyes down to stop herself looking for the surveillance car but as she made her way round to the passenger door, she caught a glimpse through the window of the house opposite and saw the little boy who lived there hurl a stuffed rabbit from the tray of his high chair. The sound of his gleeful laughter was just audible and she watched as his mother, the woman she'd seen in yoga kit on Tuesday, picked the rabbit up, gave it to him then laughed herself as he tossed it straight back down again. The sight caused a sudden inexplicable ache in Hannah's chest.

'Han?' Mark was watching her. She shook her head, snapping out of it.

The car's new-leather smell enveloped her as she pulled her door shut. Mark did up his seatbelt then reached for her hand. 'You're sure you're okay?'

She nodded then shrugged.

'It'll be over soon,' he said.

He started the car and pulled out. At the top of the street they turned on to New King's Road and, as they passed the delicatessen, she remembered how Nick had looked as he stood spot-lit under the awning, his face as he turned her way. She closed her eyes, as if that would block out the image.

When they reached the lights at Fulham Road and neither of them had spoken, Mark put the radio on to break the silence. While she'd been showering, he'd called and booked a room for two nights at K West in Shepherd's Bush. 'We'll see where we are after that,' he told her when she came back down, towelling her hair. 'With luck . . .'

'Is that far enough?' she said, stopping. 'Shepherd's Bush. It's only – what? Three miles away? Four?'

'Something like that. But I think you're right: the important thing is not being here, sitting targets. It's four-star so there'll be someone on reception twenty-four hours a day, people around all the time. You'll never be on your own, and when I'm out this afternoon . . .'

'You're going out?'

'I have to.'

'God, Mark . . .'

'I'll feel so much happier if I know you've got other people around.'

'But what about you?'

'There'll be a car at the office, too, remember? Anyway, you're my priority here – I want you to feel safe.' He picked up the detective's card from the counter. 'I'm going to call the police and tell them what we're doing.'

The hotel was a hyper-modern box of glass and concrete on a street otherwise lined with Victorian mansion blocks and terraced villas. It was almost as quiet as Quarrendon Street, the only real noise the muffled sound of traffic on the four-lane round-about beyond the road's dead end. Inside, the incongruity continued: the lobby was over-designed, all sleek marble surfaces, outsize lampshades and walls of backlit curtaining. Hannah hated it.

'It's like a tornado went spinning through Miami, picked up a hotel and dropped it in suburban west London,' she said, closing the door after the porter. She wandered around the room, touching the dark-wood desktop and the cold surface of the dresser, switching on one of the ugly bedside lights then switching it off again. The street was hidden from view by a great expanse of net curtain.

'Is it all right?'

'It's . . . luxurious,' she said, feeling ungrateful. 'It's just weird, that's all.'

'Like we're hiding in a nightclub?'

She looked at him and grinned. 'Exactly.'

They ate a room-service lunch before Mark went. 'I won't be late,' he said at the door. 'Do something relaxing this afternoon: watch a film or have a massage – there's a spa downstairs.'

She shook her head. She found spas uncomfortable at the best of times, and if there was ever a day when she didn't want a stranger's hands on her, this was it.

'Okay, but just . . . I need to know you're safe. Please don't go outside.'

'I won't.'

'You promise me?'

After he'd gone, she surfed the net listlessly for ten minutes then got the copy of *Our Man in Havana* out of her bag. She lay down on the bed and tried to read but it was no good: her eyes slid off the words again and the jokes still weren't funny. She closed her eyes, conscious suddenly of how exhausted she was. Sleep was like something from a different life, she thought, turning on to her side. She scarcely remembered what it was.

She was woken by the sound of a lorry reversing outside. Looking at the clock on the desk, she saw that more than an hour and a half had passed. Clearly, she hadn't moved in that time: her shoulder and hip were numb. She turned slowly on to her back and looked at the ceiling. She'd dreamed, strange scraps of stories connected by a single common thread: the knowledge that she'd forgotten something vitally important.

That sense persisted now, joining the shifting, uncomfortable feeling she'd had since the morning that something was lurking at the fringe of her field of vision again, out of view but only just, something that didn't make sense. This time, though, she didn't think it was to do with Hermione.

She closed her eyes again, hoping that by concentrating, shutting out other distractions, she could bring whatever it was into focus. Within seconds, however, a hideous parade of mental images had started up instead: Hermione running, looking back over her shoulder in terror, quick steps gaining on her, a hand reaching out of the darkness. *Blunt-force trauma*: blood and hair and fragments of bone . . . Hannah sat up, heart pounding.

If she stayed here all afternoon, she realised, locked in this room, she'd go mad. But she couldn't leave the hotel, either: she'd promised. She stalked about for a minute before she remembered the bar opposite the lobby. She could sit down there.

She found the key and let herself out into the corridor, feeling better the moment the door slammed shut behind her. At the bar she ordered a cup of coffee and carried it to a small table in the corner. When the man next to her got up to go, leaving behind a copy of the *Evening Standard*, she reached across and took it. The lead story was about house prices, on the rise again in London, but when she turned the page, she stopped. **Top Female Surgeon Murdered in Spitalfields.**

The piece took up half the page, much of the space dominated by two photographs. From the first, Hermione stared up at her. Her expression was the one Hannah had seen when she accosted her in the corridor, the polite but distant look that suggested she'd pulled herself out of a deep preoccupation to engage with the world for a moment. At the hospital Hannah had interpreted it as professionalism, a mask to help her keep her distance from needy relatives, but what she saw now was wariness and distrust.

Quickly, she read the story. There were no more details about Hermione's death – at the time the piece must have been written, the police had still been waiting for the post-mortem – but at the end there was a quote from DI Wells. 'We're extremely keen to talk to Nicholas Reilly,' he'd said, 'who, we have reason to believe, was in touch with Ms Alleyn in the weeks preceding her death. We strongly advise anyone identifying Mr Reilly not to approach him but to alert the police immediately.'

The other photograph was at least ten years old: Hannah had seen it before in the online coverage of his trial, albeit cropped differently. If she remembered correctly, the original had shown Nick on the drive of a lovely Cotswolds house, swinging down into the driver's seat of a convertible, tanned and laughing, but here the picture had been cut to provide the closest thing the paper could get to a mugshot, just his face, neck and shoulders, and in this context, next to the picture of the murdered woman who had once been his girlfriend, he looked unhinged: a handsome, dangerous madman.

Hannah picked up her BlackBerry and addressed a text to Mark.

Have you seen the Standard? *The story's on page 3 – it's big.*

She expected a reply immediately, he'd said he'd have his phone on all afternoon, but the minutes started to add up and none came. She told herself he was busy – he'd be talking to David or on a call; he'd probably gone to the loo – but ten minutes passed and then fifteen and she began to feel anxious: apart from last weekend, Mark had always responded straight away to any message she sent him, even right at the beginning when a lot of people might have played it cool and waited. *Keep calm,* she told herself, *there'll be a simple explanation,* but after twenty minutes, her nerves got the better of her and she brought up his number and called him. The phone rang and she felt herself relax a little but it kept ringing and then voicemail clicked in.

'Hi, it's me,' she said, hearing the worry in her voice. 'Will you call me when you get this?'

She rang off and sat for a moment, phone in hand. Her mind filled with images of Nick, a confrontation, Mark hurt or . . . No: she stopped herself. It would be nothing; she was overreacting. She made herself wait for five minutes then tried again. Again, though, there was no answer.

She brought up his direct line at work and dialled. This time the call was answered after two rings. 'DataPro.'

'Mark,' she said, 'thank God. It's me – I got in a bit of a stew: I was trying your mobile but . . .'

'Is that Mrs Reilly?' a voice cut in. 'This is Leo, David's assistant.'

'Oh.' Hannah was taken aback for a moment. 'Sorry, Leo – you sounded just like Mark. Could you put me through?'

'He's not actually here at the moment.'

'Has he popped out?'

'I don't think so – I haven't seen him at all today. Hang on a sec, let me check with David.' He put her on hold and Hannah got a snatch of Vivaldi before he came back on the line. 'No, sorry. David hasn't seen him either. He said he thought that he'd be in a while ago but he's not here yet.'

Hannah felt another jolt of alarm.

'Has he heard from Mark at all? This afternoon?'

'I'll ask.' Another burst of Vivaldi, jarringly upbeat. 'Mrs Reilly? No, David says he hasn't heard from him since this morning – an email.'

'Could I talk to Neesha, Leo?'

'She's not here either, I'm afraid. Hence my answering Mark's phone. I—'

318

'Could you ask her to call me when she gets back to her desk?'

'Of course,' he said 'but it won't be today. She's taken the day off. She was pretty upset yesterday so David suggested that she . . .'

'Upset? Why?'

Leo seemed to pause. 'Sorry,' he said, 'I thought you'd probably know about it. She's been put on a warning.'

'A warning?' Hannah felt herself frown.

Leo hesitated again and when he spoke, his voice was quieter. 'Apparently she messed up some figures,' he said. 'Mark told David it's happened before so . . .'

'Oh,' said Hannah. 'No, I didn't know. Look, if Mark comes in, could you ask him to call me? Straight away? It's urgent.'

As soon as she hung up, she tried Mark's mobile again. Still nothing. The lobby was hot but not hot enough to account for the sweat she could feel prickling under her arms. Where was he? From the newspaper Hermione stared up, her eyes now full of warning.

Increasingly alarmed, Hannah tried him once more then brought up Neesha's mobile number. She hesitated but anxiety overrode her misgivings and she made the call. It rang and she cleared her throat to talk but then – again – she got voicemail.

'Neesha,' she said, 'this is Hannah Reilly. I know

you're not at the office today and I'm really sorry for calling you when you're off but I wondered if you'd heard from Mark at all this afternoon. If you have, could you call me? It's pretty urgent so . . . Thanks.' She left her number and hung up.

Perhaps she should call Wells, she thought now. Maybe it would turn out to be nothing and she'd look crazy but better that than sitting here doing nothing while . . . She shook her head to stem the images that came spilling out of the dark corners of her mind. Quickly, she stood, picked up the newspaper and made her way back across the lobby towards the lifts. Mark had left the detective's card on the desk upstairs in case she needed it. He'd entered the number into his phone and now she was angry with herself for not doing the same.

'Hannah!'

Spinning round, she saw Mark standing just inside the revolving door from the street. Relief swept over her.

'What's the matter?' he said, drawing her to one side, away from a couple waiting to check in. 'Has something happened?'

The relief changed to anger. 'Why didn't you answer your bloody phone?' she demanded. 'I texted you – I've been calling and calling. I thought something had happened to you, Mark. I called DataPro – I was on my way upstairs to call the police.'

'Sorry . . . I'm sorry. I was driving.'

'Driving? For Christ's sake! Couldn't you have

pulled over? And when did you get so law-abiding? Your brother, a *murderer*, is out there and you just—'

'Shhh.' He looked around quickly.

'No, I won't. What's going on? Why are you doing this? You told me you were going to work but you haven't been there, have you? They said they hadn't seen you all day.'

'They haven't.'

To her amazement, Hannah saw that Mark was smiling. She held her hands up in disbelief. 'What the—?'

'I didn't tell you I was going to the office.'

'You did – you did! This morning.'

He shook his head. 'You assumed I was and I let you believe it because it was the easiest thing. I said there would be a police car at the office but I didn't say *I* was going there.'

Hannah shook her head. 'Forget it. I can't take any more of this. Here.' She thrust the newspaper at him.

He took it then reached for her hand. 'Come with me.' He started walking back towards the door.

'Now what? Mark . . .'

'Just come with me.' He was smiling again.

Outside, he led her twenty yards along the pavement then stopped. 'What do you think? Do you like it?'

'What are you taking about?' For several seconds she didn't understand.

'This.' He handed her a car key.

She stared at it and then, looking up, she followed his gaze to the car parked at the kerb, a navy blue Audi TT.

'It's yours,' he said.

She looked at him.

'I ordered it a while ago – the navy blue was a custom colour; it had to be painted specially – but it arrived yesterday.'

'Mark . . . I . . .'

'In a way, it's perfect timing. It's still a present but it's an apology now, too, for all this . . . the situation. I'm so sorry you've been dragged into it, Han. I can't tell you how sorry I am.'

CHAPTER 22

The bathroom door opened and Mark emerged in a cloud of steam scented with his sage cologne, a towel wrapped round his waist. The hair on his chest was matted with water.

'It's Saturday,' she said.

'I know, and I hate leaving you, I really hate it, but it's just a few more days.' He looked at *The Times* that had been delivered with the breakfast tray. Nick and Hermione were on page seven. 'I was lying awake all night thinking about it,' he said. 'If the papers are using the old photographs of him, it means they're looking at the old stories, doesn't it? David got a call from a guy at the *FT* yesterday who'd heard a rumour about the buy-out – if someone puts two and two together and Kevin Meyer at Systema hears about it, we're buggered. I've got to get this deal done before it all blows up in our faces, and the only thing I can do until Tuesday is make sure everything's ready.'

He bent to get his jeans out of his bag. 'Why don't you give your brother and Lydia a ring? I'd

323

feel better if I knew you weren't on your own. You could go over to theirs or have lunch somewhere, go to a gallery. That new Matisse show must be open now – I don't mind if you see it first.'

'I'm meant to be seeing Tom for a drink on Monday. But, yes, I'll ring him.'

'Good.' Mark pulled a jumper over his head then picked up his phone and car keys from the bedside table. 'It might be later rather than sooner this evening, maybe sevenish. Perhaps you could take me for another spin in your new wheels when I get back?'

He smiled and she smiled back, trying to look natural. 'I should think that could be arranged.'

The car. In the strange hinterland between wakefulness and sleep this morning, she'd really wondered for a moment whether she'd dreamed it. It was gorgeous, exactly what she would have chosen herself if she'd ever had that sort of money to spare, but the suddenness of it, the fact that he'd bought it without telling her, and that it had arrived now, in the middle of all this, made it feel odd and unreal. They'd driven out towards Heathrow last night so she could try it on the motorway and as she'd accelerated, feeling the power of the engine as it went from seventy to eighty, almost to ninety, without any strain at all, she'd felt as if she'd stolen it.

'Will you text me when you know where you're going to be?' he said.

As soon as the door closed after him, silence

flooded the room. She put the television on and left the bathroom door open so she could hear it while she showered. Shutting her eyes, she let the water drum on her face. In the surprise and confusion about the Audi last night it had been pushed to the back of her mind but during her now-usual early-hours vigil, it had come pressing on her again, even stronger, the nagging sensation that there was something she'd forgotten.

There was half a cup of coffee left in the breakfast pot, and when she was dressed she poured it and turned on her laptop. Opening Google, she typed in Nick and Patty's names and started going through the links one by one, looking for the story that had used the picture of Nick with the sports car. Perhaps they'd be lucky and it would be one of the pieces that hadn't mentioned DataPro directly, but either way, Mark was right: it could only be a matter of time before someone made the connection and the whole thing came out again. How much time, though, might make all the difference to whether or not he could get the deal done.

She clicked through fifteen or twenty stories before she found it and, when she did, she saw that it had been printed with the long Sunday news-review feature. Hannah was surprised by how accurately she'd remembered it: the silver car and the lovely golden-stoned house, Nick's pale cotton shirt, its sleeves rolled back to the elbow.

Her eyes flicked to the start of the text. *The*

curtains were drawn this week in the front windows of the two-bedroomed bungalow where Nicholas Reilly spent his childhood, as if his parents, who still live in the house, want to close their eyes against the reality of the crime of which their son was this week found guilty.

Who still live in the house – Hannah read it again, just in case, but she hadn't made a mistake: according to the journalist, this Carole Temple, at the time Nick stood trial and went to prison, his parents were still alive. But that couldn't be right. Since the very beginning, their second date at the Mulberry Street Bar back in New York, Mark had told her that his parents had died when he was in his mid-twenties, and when he'd told her the whole story on Tuesday – *finally*, said the voice in her head – he'd said it again: *'I'm just glad that when it happened, the really bad thing we'd been waiting for, for all those years, my parents were already gone.'*

She stood up and started pacing the small area of carpet in the centre of the room. The journalist was wrong, it was the only explanation: people didn't make mistakes about when their parents died. Mark said that his had died when he was in his mid-twenties, a year apart, and he'd been thirty when Nick had gone to prison. She tried to remember the actual years of the senior Reillys' deaths but found she couldn't. Had he ever told her? He must have. But actually, why must he? She'd never pushed him for that kind of exact fact; what was relevant was how long ago it had been, what stage of his life he'd been at, and he'd told her that. She'd let him talk about them when he wanted to, at his own pace, trusting that gradually she'd get the full picture.

She sat back down, feeling a little better. The journalist had got her wires crossed; that was all. Patty's death had happened not long after they'd died, a couple of years, maybe; perhaps Mark hadn't sold the house immediately, or perhaps another older couple had moved in and Carole Temple had mistaken them for the Reillys. That was quite likely, wasn't it? It was usually older people who lived in bungalows.

Hannah hit the back button and returned to the list of hits but as she clicked through the stories, realising now just how many had mentioned DataPro, she felt more and more uneasy. When she reached the *Gazette* piece with its SICK NICK headline and lurid capitals, she put her head in her hands.

She closed the page, shut her computer and stood up. She stacked the dirty dishes on the breakfast tray and put it outside the door. The corridor stretched away to left and right, empty. Back inside, she made the bed meticulously, plumping the pillows and smoothing the sheets until they were wrinkle-free. In the bathroom she drank a glass of water and rested her forehead against the cold glass of the mirror. Then she went back to her computer.

How did you find out when people had died? Into Google she typed 'UK death records'. The first link was to the General Register Office, the official government site. She clicked on it and skimmed down the page until she found a link promising information on birth, marriage, death and adoption records. When it opened, however, there was no access to records, just advice on registering a new death.

The National Archives advertised themselves to people looking for records of a birth, marriage or death in England or Wales. *Hatched, matched and dispatched* – Hannah heard her own mother's voice. The site was clearly designed for genealogical research but while marriage certificates could be viewed online, birth and death certificates could not. A section titled *Indexes to Birth, Marriage and Death registrations (1837 to present)* had a link to a site transcribing the Civil Register but she quickly discovered that so far, the transcription, at least for deaths, hadn't progressed beyond 1970. If Mark's parents had died when he was twenty-six or seven, say, she was looking for 1998 and 1999.

Findmypast.co.uk offered records to 2006. The search boxes on the home page asked for first and last names, the range of years in which the person might have died, the country within the UK and then the county. She filled them as far as she could, entering 'Elizabeth Reilly', 1995–2005, England and Sussex. There was a box for her year of birth, too, and Hannah tried to think. How old had Mrs Reilly been when she died? She had no idea. How old had she been when Mark had been born, then? They'd never talked about that, either. She made an estimate, working on the theory that the previous generation had had their children younger, on the whole. If she'd been twenty-six, for example, when she'd had Mark and he'd been twenty-seven when she died in 1999, she would have been born in 1946. God, if that was right, she'd died far too young – she'd only be sixty-six if she were alive now. Hannah entered 1946 with a range of five years on either side. She hit return and waited. *No results found.*

The coffee was stone cold but she took a sip and went back. Where had she gone wrong? Maybe it had been Elisabeth, not Elizabeth, though her name had been spelled with a 'z' in the news coverage. In a new window, she double-checked that Eastbourne was in Sussex then broadened the range of years in which Mrs Reilly might have died from 1990 – when Mark would have been only eighteen – to 2005. She gave the search for her year of birth a span of twenty years. *No results found.*

Going back again, she unchecked the boxes that stipulated precise matches only, allowing all variant spellings and abbreviations of the names Elizabeth and Reilly and widening the range of her possible birth year to twenty years either side of 1946. Mark had been born in 1972 so that had to cover it: if she'd been born in 1926, she'd have been forty-six when she'd had him, forty-seven when she'd had Nick the following year. If she'd been born in 1966, she would have had Mark at age six. Still nothing.

Maybe there was a problem with Elizabeth's record. Hannah cleared the boxes and instead entered Mark's father's details, as far as she knew them, double-checking with Carole Temple's feature, where people who knew the family unambiguously called him Gordon. She entered his year of birth as 1935, on the basis that he may have been older than his wife, and set the range at twenty years to either side, 1915 to 1955, making him somewhere between seventeen and fifty-seven when Mark had been born. No results.

Frustrated, Hannah cleared the boxes again and entered her own grandmother's details, leaving ten years around the date of her death, though she knew it exactly, and twenty years around her date of birth. When she hit return, Margaret Hannah Simpson, died Gloucestershire, Malvern, 1989, came up straight away. A search for her grandfather was just as quick.

She stood and walked around for a moment, pulling the curtain aside and looking down into the street. Outside one of the Victorian terraced houses, a teenage boy was soaping an old Volvo at glacial pace, and further up, a woman in jeans and a fleece was opening her front door, a nest of Waitrose carrier bags around her feet. A normal Saturday morning. Hannah dropped the curtain and came back to the table. Either there was a problem with the Reillys' records or she'd got something wrong. Maybe they hadn't died in Eastbourne; maybe Mark had brought them to hospitals in London so that he could be close to them or get them private care. She tried new searches on that basis but again, got nothing.

Into a new Google window, she typed 'UK electoral roll'. The snippet of text underneath the link to whitepages.co.uk assured her that using the electoral register was a reliable way to search for people. Her hope faded as she scanned a short introductory paragraph that told her the site used a database from 2002 but she typed Gordon Reilly's name into the boxes at the top – Gordon was probably less common a name than Elizabeth – and added 'Eastbourne'. She hit return with no great expectation but almost immediately a new page opened: '*1 Match for Gordon Reilly in Eastbourne*'. The box underneath gave an address.

Hannah frowned, went back to the search page and typed in 'Elizabeth Reilly'. This time, the site found two people with that name in Eastbourne. One of them lived at the same address as Gordon.

Heart thumping now, she went back and double-checked. Yes, the database was from 2002, when Mark had been thirty, but how well maintained was it? Could their names have been left on there by mistake? Had word failed to reach the council when they'd died? At her old flat in Kilburn, polling cards used to arrive for former residents years and years after they'd moved out: the system definitely wasn't watertight. Further on, however, she saw that the site was claiming to update its records quarterly.

The results page had three boxes giving name, address and telephone number. In the case of both Gordon and the Elizabeth who shared his address, the box for the telephone number was blank. Hannah leaned back in the chair and reached for her bag on the bed, hooking a finger through the strap and swinging it across into her lap. Finding her phone, she entered the number for Directory Enquiries. She paused briefly before making the call, checking her conscience, but discovered that every last vestige of guilt about investigating the Reillys had gone.

She gave the operator Gordon's name and address and waited. The tapping of keys and then the woman came back on the line. 'I'm sorry,' she said, 'but that number's ex-directory.'

Hannah thought. 'Does that mean,' she said, 'that there's definitely a Gordon Reilly at that address?'

'That's what the records say.'

'Could you try Elizabeth Reilly, please? Same address.'

More tapping. 'Yes, there's an Elizabeth Reilly listed but again, it's ex-directory.

'Okay, thanks.' Hannah hung up and started a text message. *Morning*, she wrote. *A favour: if Mark rings, will you tell him I'm with you but I'm in the loo or I've popped to the shops with Lydia or something, then call me?*

Within seconds, her phone started ringing. Tom's number. She hesitated, torn between the urge to pick up and tell him everything, and the sudden time pressure: it was quarter past eleven already and Eastbourne was . . . what? An hour and a half's drive from London? More, maybe. If she was going to get there and back by seven, she didn't have a lot of time to spare, and no honest conversation with Tom at this point was going to be short. She let the phone ring and got ready to go. When she came out of the bathroom, the phone had stopped ringing for the third time and there was a text instead: *What's going on?*

Perversely, she immediately felt better about dodging him: there was an obvious logic, surely, to finding out whether there actually was anything going on before she freaked her brother out. *What?* asked the snide voice in her head. *Anything other than Nick being a killer, you mean?*

She ignored it and tapped out a reply: *Nothing going on, just need a bit of space today. Full explanation coming Monday, promise.*

I don't like it. Tom's response was almost instant. *But if you swear you're telling me the truth, I'll do it. And stop ignoring my calls.*

Swear, she wrote, feeling guilty. *And I will. Thanks, bro.*

CHAPTER 23

The Underground was the quickest way to Parsons Green but it wasn't nearly quick enough. The train lingered at Earl's Court, doors wide open to the freezing platform, and Hannah was on the point of getting off and taking a taxi when she remembered that she only had six pounds in her purse. Going to the cash-point would just swallow more time. There was no guarantee that a taxi would be quicker, anyway: it was Saturday and the roads around the north of Fulham would be gridlocked, especially if Chelsea were playing at home.

She rested her head against the glass panel and tried to stay calm. Outside the hotel she'd stopped to look at the TT. It would have been much faster – it was right there in front of her, she had the key in her bag – but when it came to it, she hadn't been able to. For this, she wanted – needed – her own car.

She was standing ready at the doors as the train pulled into Parsons Green. The temperature had dropped noticeably since she'd left Shepherd's Bush and a cold wind was gusting round the elevated platform. She took the stairs at a gallop and headed out of the station, car key already in her hand. As she made her way down the side of the Green, a car slowed almost to a stop behind her and the hairs stood up on the back of her neck. Then, though, she heard it go over a speed bump and it accelerated past.

The VW was further down Quarrendon Street than she remembered. As she passed the house, she thought it looked different. They'd been gone fewer than twenty-four hours but somehow it had already taken on an empty look, the upstairs windows blankly reflecting the cold white sky, the privet of the front hedge shivering stiffly in the wind. A little way up, on the other side of the street, she'd seen a man in a non-descript blue Honda with a newspaper spread across the steering wheel: the police watch. He'd barely glanced up as she passed but she knew that he'd registered her, discounted her as not-Nick.

She ran the last twenty yards to the car, got in and slapped the lock down as if he was actually behind her. Reaching over, she took the Sat Nav out of the glove box. It had been a present from Mark but, besides the rare occasions when he was in the car, she barely used it, objecting to having orders barked at her. Today, though, it would be a godsend. Hands shaking, she entered the address from the Internet and waited for it to calculate a route. When it was finished, the estimated journey time said two hours, three minutes. *Shit.* For a moment she considered ditching the whole idea – she'd never get back to the hotel by seven; it was probably a wild goose chase, anyway – but then she heard an echo of Mark's voice: *'My parents were already gone.'*

The traffic on the roads out of town had been so heavy that twice she'd had no choice but to put the car in neutral and sit and watch as the minutes added themselves to the journey time one after another. When she saw the first signs for Eastbourne, she'd been driving for more than two and a half hours. Thirty or forty miles back, the urban outer reaches of London had given way to fields and scrubby verges covered in the dark gorse she associated with the south coast but now she could feel the influence of the sea itself. The sky was turning dark, the cloud curdling overhead, but around her, everything appeared with the particular clarity of coastal light, as if the whole landscape had been brushed with glaze. She passed through somewhere called Polegate, where the architecture – detached houses, a Harvester chain pub – had the thirties and forties look that she knew from other seaside places, Bournemouth and Poole. On her right rose gentle green hills, the tail end of the South Downs.

After another two or three miles, the houses started to huddle closer together and became more uniform. The brick-built properties on her left were still substantial, but the houses on the other

336

side of the road were smaller and less attractive. Glancing at the screen, she saw that she'd reached the outer edges of Eastbourne. Suburbia.

In two hundred yards, turn right, said the Sat Nav. She indicated and slowed, and as she made the turn, she caught sight of the street sign: Selmeston Road. *In five hundred yards*, confirmed the voice, *you have reached your destination.*

The first few houses were detached red-bricks with two storeys, but as the street climbed the hill away from the main road there were just bungalows and more bungalows. Over the tiled roofs of those at the far end swelled another hill, grass-covered and patchy with gorse, above which the sky was massing with intent, the cloud darker now and clotted with rain.

Another car had turned off the main road immediately after her and she had no choice but to drive at a reasonable speed. She glanced around, taking in as much as she could at thirty miles an hour. Proximity to the main road was clearly a status indicator. The first bungalows had an unusual semi-detached design and were built split-level into the side of the hill, but here, further on, they were squat and blank-faced, indistinguishable from countless thousands in every other retirement enclave along the south coast.

You have reached your destination.

Slowing, Hannah saw the number she'd written down painted on a floral plaque attached to a low brick wall. The car behind pipped its horn and, without indicating, she swung into a space at the kerb between a white transit van and a tired blue Ford Fiesta. The other car pipped again and roared past her up the hill.

She turned off the engine and sat back in the seat, the urgency that had propelled her from London gone all of a sudden. In the rear-view mirror she looked at the house. It was separated from the road by the width of the pavement then the low wall, inside which ran a box hedge a foot taller. The front garden was thirty feet square or thereabouts, a burgundy Vauxhall Astra occupying a small area of tarmac, the rest a straight-edged lawn of closely shorn grass edged with privets and three hydrangeas, their crisp brown dead-heads bristling. It wasn't neat so much as bleak.

The house was the same. A recessed front door separated two windows, one a bay – the sitting room, she guessed – the other smaller and cut higher in the wall: a dining room, or possibly a bedroom. Net curtains veiled both windows like cataracts. The roofs of the houses either side had skylight windows, suggesting the loft space had been converted, but as far as she could tell, the owners of this house hadn't done the same. The place was extremely neat, clearly the result of hard work, but nothing was modern or renovated or new. If you took away the Astra, she thought, you could believe you'd been teleported back to the seventies.

She rolled down the window. The other car had faded from hearing and the only sound was the blustering wind. There was no one on the pavement or in any of the front gardens, no sound of lawn mowers or DIY, no kids on bikes or skateboards shouting and clattering about. The silence was apocalyptic, as if a killer virus had swept through the place overnight. Had Mark really grown up here, in this house? And if he had, how had he survived? Malvern was hardly a hotbed of teenage excitement but compared to this place it was Times Square.

She looked at her hands on the steering wheel. What was she doing? She shouldn't be here; she shouldn't have come. This was wrong – very wrong. *Then why* have *you come?* asked the voice in her head. While she'd had the momentum of the journey she'd been able to keep the answer at bay but now she made herself face it: she was here because she no longer trusted what Mark told her. She closed her eyes as a chasm of loss opened up inside her. What good was a marriage without trust?

When she opened her eyes again, there was movement in the rear-view mirror. The door of the bungalow was open, and as she watched, a man with steel-grey hair came out and pulled it carefully shut again behind him. He was carrying a bucket that he took slowly over to the bay window and put on the ground. Gingerly, his back evidently giving him trouble, he bent over and fished out a sponge.

Hannah's heart started beating faster. He was in

his seventies, stooped and very thin: his shoulder blades were sharp through the material of his fawn anorak, and when the wind blew against his trousers, his legs looked skinny enough to snap. Even so, she could see the family likeness: he was the same height as Mark, and the shape of his shoulders and back, even his head, was the same. This man operated at a tenth of the pace but his movements had a precise quality that was utterly familiar to her. Looking at him was like seeing Mark fast-forwarded into the future

He wrung out the sponge and started soaping the window, his arm moving in slow, methodical arcs. The longer she watched him, the more sure Hannah was: this was Mark's father, and Mark had lied again – he was *still* lying, *now*, when he'd sworn he'd finally told her the truth. More than that, he'd lied to her from the very beginning, from their second date in New York, before he'd even known her at all.

The old man bent to rinse the sponge and Hannah's eyes filled with tears. If he was Mark's father – *he was*, said the voice – one of his sons was a killer and the other one, the *good* one, told people – *his own wife* – that he was dead.

The decision took two seconds. Hannah swiped her cuff across her eyes, grabbed her bag and got out of the car. The wind snatched the door from her hand and as it slammed, she saw him turn. At the bottom of the short tarmac drive she stopped.

'Mr Reilly.'

He dropped the sponge back into the bucket and pulled himself slowly up to full height, as if bracing himself. As she came round the bonnet of the Astra, he glanced up and down the street behind her. When he spoke, he kept his voice low. 'Has something happened? Have you found him?'

The last shred of Hannah's doubt evaporated.

'Your colleagues were here before,' he said. 'Only an hour ago. We told them then: we haven't heard from Nick.'

'Mr Reilly, I'm not from the police. My name's Hannah Reilly. I'm Mark's wife.'

A look of astonishment broke over his face. His eyes widened and his lips parted as if he were about to say something but no words came out. For two or three seconds he was absolutely still but then his face changed again and his expression turned hard. 'You're Mark's wife?'

'Yes.'

He glanced past her at the street again. 'Does he know you're here?'

'No.'

He considered that then gave a single nod. He looked behind him at the front door. 'Will you come inside?' he said.

Hannah hesitated a moment then nodded.

She watched as he took a key from his anorak pocket. His hand shook as he tried to get it in the lock and, after two failed attempts, he brought

341

his other hand up and used both to guide it in. He stood aside, gesturing for her to go first.

A narrow hallway with a dark patterned carpet and an atmosphere pungent with the cooking of older people: some sort of meat and gravy, over-done cabbage. Lunch – it was nearly three o'clock already. On the right were two blank closed doors with cheap metal handles: the bedrooms, or a bedroom and the bathroom. Through the open door immediately to her left, she saw an armchair with a lace-edged antimacassar. A vase of pale fabric flowers sat precisely halfway along a length of windowsill. Behind her, Mr Reilly closed the front door. 'Please,' he said. 'Go and sit down. I'll just . . .'

She went into the sitting room and a few seconds later she heard a door open at the other end of the hallway. In a cracked voice Mr Reilly said, 'Lizzie . . .'

Sitting down was the last thing Hannah wanted to do. She needed to run, kick, punch something. Mark had told her his parents were dead, for Christ's sake. Who did a thing like that? Who'd even think of it? She looked around, trying to distract herself by taking an inventory of the room: the peach floral three-piece suite, the outdated television on its wood-veneer stand, the careful coasters on the two side tables, the dark-wood coffee table where the *Radio Times* was neatly folded to the day's date. A leather spectacle case with worn corners rested on a copy of the *Eastbourne Herald*. Above the ugly brick fireplace was a print of a Scottish Highland scene, the muscular stag and his wild vista an off-note amid the utter dreary domesticity of the rest of the room. From the top of the bureau in the corner, a carriage clock ticked into the silence.

She hadn't heard it but Mr Reilly – *her father-in-law* – must have closed whichever door his wife had been behind because their voices, if they were speaking, were inaudible. The only sounds were the clock and the wind as it buffeted the front of the house. A draught stirred the bottom of the net curtain in the bay window.

After some minutes, there was movement in the corridor. Hannah turned and in the doorway behind her she saw a woman of seventy or so, her hands clasped together in front of her chest as if she were praying. Her face was heavily lined but Hannah could see that at least one thing Mark had told her was true: his mother had been beautiful. Her eyes were large and gentle, still a lovely deep blue behind her glasses, and her lips were soft and full. She was wearing pale pink lipstick – did she always wear it at home or had she just put it on? Her eyes were wet and Mr Reilly put a steadying hand on her shoulder.

'I'm sorry,' he said. 'We're pleased to meet you but it's . . . well, it's a shock for us.'

'No, I understand. For me, too – I didn't know you were . . . here.'

'This is my wife, Elizabeth. I'm Gordon.'

'Hannah,' she said to Mrs Reilly, who was

343

looking at her with unabashed curiosity, taking her in, detail by detail.

'How long have you been married?' she asked. Her voice was quiet, with a hasty, furtive quality, as if she were worried about drawing attention to herself and only dared speak quickly.

'Since April. Not long.'

'We didn't even know.'

Hannah felt ashamed, as if she were to blame, but before she could say anything, the woman shook herself, said, 'Tea,' and whisked away like the White Rabbit.

Mark's father came awkwardly into the room and gestured to the higher-backed of the armchairs. 'Please sit down. I'll put the fire on. We normally wait until the evening, the price of electricity these days, but it's cold this afternoon. We're quite exposed to the wind, here on the hill.' At the far side of the fireplace, he hitched his trousers at the knee and bent slowly. The snap of a switch and then he straightened, came round to the front and pressed the button on the outdated two-bar electric heater set into the grate. He stood back and watched, as if he'd laid a real fire and wanted to make sure it would go. 'There,' he said with satisfaction when the ends of the coils started to redden.

A fussy chintz pelmet hid the bottom of the armchair and it wasn't until she'd sat down and it lurched alarmingly that Hannah realised it was some sort of rocker.

'Sorry, I should have said. That's Elizabeth's chair – I forget it does that.'

'I shouldn't take it if it's her's. Here, let me . . .'

'No, no.' He motioned her back down. 'It's the best one – she won't be happy unless you have it.' He took a seat himself on the far end of the sofa, smoothed his trousers and looked at her. Hannah smiled at him and he smiled back, Mark at seventy. Struggling for something to say, she felt a dizzying sense of vertigo. Why had she come in? She'd found out what she'd wanted to know: they were alive. Wasn't that enough?

The clock ticked on, measuring the silence.

'Have you come from London?' he said.

'Yes, just now. The roads were terrible – the traffic, I mean.' *Traffic*? She stopped before she could say anything even more inane.

From the hallway came the rattle of china and Mrs Reilly entered with a tray that she lowered gingerly on to the copy of the *Herald*. 'Oh, I should have asked, shouldn't I?' she said, face a picture of dismay. 'Perhaps you'd prefer coffee?'

'Tea's fine – perfect. Thank you.'

She smiled gratefully. 'How do you take it?'

Mr Reilly watched his wife as she poured milk into the bottom of a cup and topped it up with a weak stream of tea from a pot in a crocheted cosy. Hannah tried to imagine Mark in this room and failed. It was a struggle to imagine his world and this one even co-existing. She remembered him in

345

Montauk, his almost animal energy as he'd jogged up the beach from the sea, the water furrowing his chest hair as he'd lowered himself down on to the sand.

The cup tottered on the saucer as his mother handed Hannah her tea. Elizabeth poured some for her husband and herself then sat next to him on the sofa, straightening her navy polyester skirt as if preparing to be interviewed or told off by the headmistress. Hannah searched for something to say but Mrs Reilly spoke first.

'How did you meet, you and Mark?' she said. 'I'm sorry – do you mind me asking?'

'No, of course not. I had a job in New York – advertising – and some friends of ours there introduced us. We hit it off and . . .'

'New York,' said Mr Reilly, as if he'd heard of it and didn't much approve.

'Last year – the summer before last. Mark was doing a big project with DataPro's New York team and . . .' The look on Gordon's face told her he hadn't known there was, or ever had been, such a thing.

'And you were married in April this year?' said Elizabeth Reilly.

'Yes. In Chelsea, at the register office.'

'Do you live in London now – with him? You're not in America any more?'

'No, I moved back a few months ago. It didn't make sense living apart once we were married.' She took a scalding sip of tea.

'That's right, isn't it? No point being married at all if you're not going to be together.' Elizabeth glanced at her husband with a look that was almost shy. 'Do you have children? No, of course you don't – what am I saying? You haven't been married long enough. Not that that matters,' she said quickly, 'being married, not these days . . .' She trailed off, embarrassed. 'Sorry.'

'Don't worry.' Hannah smiled. 'But no, we don't.'

'Would you like them?'

'I . . . Well . . .'

'Elizabeth, you shouldn't put the woman on the spot like that,' Mr Reilly cut in.

'I'm sorry,' she said, looking mortified now. 'It's just I know so little about his life these days, what he's doing, what he thinks about things . . .'

'When did you last see him?

'Ten years ago, at the trial . . .' She faltered and looked at her husband aghast, as if she'd blown a terrible secret.

'I know about Nick,' Hannah said. 'The court case. Patty Hendrick, I mean.'

'We don't talk about it,' said Mark's father, voice sharp. 'I'm sure you understand. For us, it was . . .' His voice trailed off. 'And now this other one – the doctor, Hermione.' He put his tea down, the china tinkling.

Mrs Reilly actually flinched. 'Is that why you're here?'

'No.' Hannah shook her head. 'It's nothing to do with Nick. I just—'

'Then why?' said Mr Reilly. 'Why come now?'

'Does he want to see us?' Mark's mother's eyes lit up with sudden hope. 'Is this his way of . . .?'

'No,' said Hannah as gently as she could. 'I'm sorry.'

Mrs Reilly nodded but then dipped her head and focused on her hands.

The carriage clock struck the hour, three tiny cymbal crashes.

'Mark's hurt his mother very badly, as you can see,' said his father. 'I'm not saying there aren't elements of his behaviour we understand – doesn't he think we'd like to forget, too? – but even so . . .' He looked at Elizabeth's bent white head. 'Nick was the perfect excuse,' he added.

Hannah frowned. 'I'm sorry,' she said, 'I don't understand.'

'Mark was looking for a reason to cut us off and Nick gave it to him.'

'Why would he want . . .?'

'He's ashamed of us, isn't he?'

'I—'

'Look at us. Look at how we live. Do you think he'd be proud of us? We're an embarrassment to him – the boring, ordinary, *petit bourgeois* people – he called me that once, to my face – he had to leave behind in order to create whoever he is these days, Mr Big Shot. Look at us and then look at him with his success, his money, his *lifestyle*.' Gordon's voice was full of disdain. 'You. With the greatest of respect, you seem decent but you don't fit here – advertising, New York, the way you look. I knew he didn't send you – he wouldn't want you to see us, what he came from.'

'No, I'm sure that's not . . .' Hannah started.

'It is – if you're his wife, you must know it is.'

'I don't blame him,' said Mrs Reilly quietly. 'Not for that. He's worked so hard for what he has – all his life he's worked hard. If he chooses to live in a certain—'

'You don't blame your son for scorning you?' demanded her husband with venom. 'For dismissing you from his life like an underperforming member of staff?'

'Oh, Gordon, that's not what I . . . Don't make it sound like that, please don't.'

'It's the truth, isn't it? And she's married to him; she knows what he's like. Anyway, it's not just about being ashamed, I've worked that much out. He wants to punish us, too, doesn't he?' He directed his question to Hannah.

'For what?' she said.

'For not seeing it, for not understanding about Nick. *He* did, Mark, from very early on *he* got it, but to believe that one of your own children could be capable of . . .' He looked sickened. 'I hope you never know what it's like, to have to face your neighbours, see them acting normal when you know they've been reading about your son in the papers, every sordid detail of what he did. That they all know what kind of monster you'd been . . . incubating.'

'It must have been hard for Mark, too, having Nick as a brother,' she said tentatively. 'I mean, it sounds like he felt a lot of responsibility for . . .'

Mr Reilly gave a snort. 'Responsibility? He was *never* responsible for Nick, *never*, whatever he might have told you. How could anyone be responsible for . . . *that*?' He spat the word off his tongue.

'It was my fault.' Mrs Reilly looked up from her lap. 'The way I handled them when they were growing up. When Nick was born, he was so easy. After Mark . . .'

'Easy?' Mr Reilly was outraged.

'At the beginning, Gordon – when he was younger. That's all I meant. He *was* easy,' she said, directing herself to Hannah. 'Mark was . . . different. Difficult – there, I've said it; he was difficult. Even when he was a baby, I felt like I was battling with him, like there was someone in there, an adult, looking out at me from his eyes, challenging me all the time. Judging me – that sounds ridiculous, I know, but it's what it felt like.'

'Elizabeth . . .'

She glanced at her husband, her face anxious, but she carried on. 'He was so bright – it was obvious right from the start that he was special. And then we had Nick – I got pregnant again almost straight away; they were born within a year of each other – and that's when Mark started to

350

change. I knew at the time I wasn't treating them the same but I couldn't help myself. Mark was . . . he seemed to want something from me that I couldn't give him. He stopped sleeping, he wouldn't feed, and then he started having moods, not tantrums like other children but moods – he used to disappear, go inside himself, as if he was trying to punish me. Nick was sunny, smiley, and . . . I couldn't help it, he was easier to love, he just was.'

'Elizabeth, stop,' said Mr Reilly, but she ignored him.

'Mark saw it,' she said. 'I know he did. He saw it and he felt rejected, and then he got angry, and the angrier he got, the harder it was to . . . get through to him. That was when it started – his shutting himself off from me. By the time he was five or six, he was closed, self-contained – like a bubble. He'd taken his world inside himself. He didn't need me any more, or even want me, but Nick . . .' She stood up suddenly, her movements much less of a struggle than her husband's, went to the bureau and tugged open the lowest drawer. From underneath a stack of papers she pulled out a small navy blue photograph album.

'Elizabeth, for pity's sake.'

'No, Gordon, I want to,' she said. 'I'm going to. He's still my son.'

By the fireplace there was a chintz-covered

footstool. She carried it round to the side of Hannah's chair and sat down, avoiding eye contact with her husband, who stayed on the sofa radiating anger. The album was A5-size and covered in leatherette. Inside, the polythene envelopes that held each picture were misty and crackled with age. Mrs Reilly handled them with reverence as if, were she alone, she might caress each one before turning it over.

She paged through several then lifted the book on to the arm of Hannah's chair. 'We went camping in Devon, our summer holiday. He's eight.'

The picture had been taken at the campsite and the background was dominated by a large square tent, inside the pinned-back door of which the silhouette of a man – Gordon, Hannah guessed – was visible leaning over a table. Mark sat in the foreground, just off centre, on a fold-out stool. He was wearing shorts and a T-shirt, and as they protruded towards the camera, his knees were almost comically bulbous above his skinny shins. His expression, however, was deadly serious. The photographer – his mother, presumably – had called his name and he was looking up from the book in his lap with the weariness of an elderly scholar. It wasn't tiredness, though. When Hannah looked again, she saw exactly what Elizabeth Reilly meant: he was closed off. Having no choice in the matter, he was there in person, his expression seemed to say, but the real him, the part that mattered, was somewhere else, locked up and unreachable, private.

'You see?' said Mrs Reilly. 'And look – here.' She flicked forward several pages to a picture of Mark in uniform, grey trousers and a grey V-neck sweater with a maroon stripe at the collar and cuffs, a rucksack at his feet. Another picture taken under duress: in this one, Mark's anxiety to get away was palpable. He was at an angle to the camera, his shoulder already turned, his weight on the back foot. Again his face was blank, closed, but this time there was something else, almost masked but definitely there: disdain.

'His first day at senior school,' his mother said. 'I just wanted one picture, a record, but—'

'That's enough,' snapped Mr Reilly. 'The woman hasn't come here to sit and maunder over old photographs.'

Hannah felt an urge to protect his wife, shield her from his corrosive anger. 'It's fine,' she said. 'Nice, I mean. I've only ever seen a couple of pictures of him when he was young. It's good to . . .'

'I'm amazed he has any at all. Or perhaps he likes them – maybe they're part of his creation myth: look at what he had to overcome to get to where he is today,' scoffed Mr Reilly.

Next to Hannah, Mrs Reilly gave a quiet sob.

Outside, there was a gust of wind and then a sudden sharp cracking sound as if someone had thrown a handful of gravel against the bay window.

Hail – the clouds that had been gathering all afternoon had finally reached critical mass. In seconds the room was dark.

Mark's mother closed the album and returned it to the bureau, stashing it back beneath the papers in the bottom drawer. When she turned around, she looked at Hannah, avoiding her husband's eye. 'Would you like to see his room?'

From deep in Mr Reilly's throat came a sound of disgusted resignation.

Outside in the hall, his wife gave Hannah a look that mixed gratitude with a hint of conspiracy and led her to the back of the house. Through a half-open door Hannah caught a glimpse of a small, neat kitchen with units so dated they had to be from the sixties. Outside the last door Mrs Reilly paused, her hand on the cheap handle. 'I haven't changed it,' she said. 'It's exactly how it used to be.' She lowered her voice until it was almost a whisper. 'Gordon doesn't like it, it makes him angry, but I won't let him touch it.' There was unexpected fire in her eyes as she pressed down the handle and ushered Hannah inside.

For a second or two she was confused. The room was schizophrenic. One half of it had clearly been a teenage boy's: there was a huge, obsolete black stereo with a stack of CDs; a punch-ball on a stand; and, beneath a behemoth of a television with a back about two feet deep, some sort of games console in a nest of cables. On the shelf above an ugly veneered desk, piles of GCSE Letts

Revise guides and graffiti-covered exercise books kept company with a foot-long red model Ferrari and a stack of *Loaded* magazines.

The other half of the room was immaculate and almost empty. Both sides had single beds but where the first had a duvet in a charcoal-grey cover, this one had been made up with starched white sheets. This bedside table held a lamp with a wooden base and plain cloth shade, not an Anglepoise, and where the other half had posters of Bob Marley and generously endowed women in impractical swimwear – how Mrs Reilly must love those, Hannah thought – here the walls were bare. The shelf above an identical ugly desk was empty apart from a box-file like the one Mark used for his financial papers.

'They had to share,' Mrs Reilly said. 'We've only got two bedrooms.'

'Mark's side?' Hannah indicated the cluttered half, thinking that his mother must have cleared Nick's in horror after he went to prison, but Mrs Reilly shook her head.

'No,' she said, 'this is Mark's.'

'I thought you hadn't changed it?' Hannah frowned.

Again Mrs Reilly shook her head. 'I haven't. He took his clothes and books when he went up to Cambridge, but otherwise this is how he kept it.'

'It's very . . . tidy,' Hannah said, as the word 'monastic' came into her mind. That wasn't right either, though. That implied asceticism, but the white sheets and plain lamp suggested a deliberate aesthetic, a less-is-more minimalism.

'He left this,' said Mrs Reilly. Turning, Hannah saw that she'd taken the box-file down from the shelf. 'I found it pushed right back underneath the chest of drawers just after he went to college. He wrote to me, actually, asking me to send it on to him, but I said no, he could come and collect it himself if he wanted it so badly.' She gave a small smile, embarrassed by her show of toughness but proud of it, too. 'It was a lure – I knew he wouldn't visit otherwise.' She gave a small shrug. 'It didn't work, obviously.'

'What is it?'

'Well, that's it,' said Mrs Reilly. 'When I found it hidden like that, I thought it must be something important or . . . embarrassing.' She cast a quick glance in the direction of one of the well-endowed ladies on the wall. 'But it's not. It's just pictures, pages torn out of magazines and the like.' She opened the box and lifted a slim bundle of papers out on to the desk. 'Look.' She slid it across.

On top, Hannah saw, its paper brittle now more than twenty years later, was an advert for after-shave, one of the exclusive small-batch types only for sale at Harrods or Harvey Nicks. The black-and-white picture showed a woman in a white silk dress standing barefoot on the deck of a beautiful wooden yacht. The same breeze that wrinkled the water lifted her long hair away from the smooth length of her back. A square-jawed man was emerging from the cabin with a couple of drinks and a knowing smile. The mood was romantic, cheesy, and utterly aspirational. Wear this after-shave, the picture said, and this life will be yours: the gorgeous, aloof woman; the antique yacht; sundowners on the Riviera.

Turning over, Hannah found a piece that she guessed had been torn from an interiors magazine showing an amazing glass house – laughably referred to as a summer cabin – on a island off the coast of Norway. Next was a yellowing *Sunday Times* review of a restaurant in Bruges with pictures of a spectacular dining room, and then an interview with the family who ran La Colombe d'Or hotel in St-Paul-de-Vence – with a jolt, Hannah remembered Mark talking about it only a month or so ago, saying he'd always wanted to go. There were pictures of a London townhouse not dissimilar to the one in Quarrendon Street – the kitchen in particular was very like theirs, with a slate floor and long farmhouse table – and a huge apartment in the Dakota Building with views of Central Park. Near the bottom of the pile was a run of pages with pictures of an old Jaguar XJS, and then, the final sheet, a Knight Frank advertisement, like the ones she saw in back issues of *Country Life* at the dentist, for an eight-bedroomed Tudor house in Gloucestershire, complete with walled gardens and a tennis court.

'Expensive tastes even as a teenager,' said Mrs Reilly at her shoulder. 'It's lucky he turned out to be so successful, isn't it?'

Hannah had a sudden memory of the first night on the beach at Montauk with Mark, their conversation about living in New York. 'I used to sit in my bedroom at home,' he'd said, 'devising ways I could make it happen.' There was nothing lucky about it, she thought; he'd made sure he was successful. *The boring, ordinary, petit bourgeois people he had to leave behind.*

Mrs Reilly was looking at her. To hide her face, Hannah went to the window. Like the area at the front of the house, the garden was mostly lawn, a narrow stretch of twenty-five or thirty metres extending to a flimsy panelled fence, interrupted only by a cheap wooden bird-table. The hail hammered down on a skirt of crazy paving around the house. Just beyond the fence that divided their garden from their neighbour's, she could see the pitched roof of a small garden shed.

'It must have been very hard for you,' she said, trying to sound non-committal.

'The trial?' said Mrs Reilly.

'Yes, but even before that. Mark's told me what Nick was like as a teenager, how wild he was.'

'He was a handful,' she agreed, nodding.

'It sounds like it was a little more than that.'

Mrs Reilly frowned. 'He was badly behaved when it came to girls, yes, I have to admit, and beyond a certain age, it was a struggle to get him to go to school, but otherwise . . .'

Hannah looked at the shed. 'What about Jim Thomas?' she said. 'Your old neighbour.'

'Oh, it wasn't Nick who didn't get on with Jim,' said Mrs Reilly brightly. 'That was Mark.'

Hannah felt the cold sensation on the back of her neck. 'But the fire in his shed on the allotment?' she said. 'And what happened to his dog.'

'The fire was an accident.' Mrs Reilly picked up the pile of papers and dropped them smartly back into the box-file. 'They'd been smoking in there to annoy Jim – that was bad of them, I know – and they hadn't put a cigarette out properly. We paid to replace the shed – Jim ended up better off, I should think. The old one was quite shabby and . . .'

'His dog?' Hannah pressed.

Mrs Reilly's face tightened. 'That whole thing was . . . a misunderstanding. They just found Molly. They didn't have anything to do with her drowning.'

At the door Mr Reilly gave Hannah a hard look. 'You didn't answer my question,' he said. 'Why did you come here?'

She looked him in the eye as a volley of hail hit the patterned glass behind her. She couldn't tell him the truth: it would devastate Mrs Reilly to know what Mark had said. 'Because I was curious,'

359

she said. 'You're my husband's parents and I'd never met you.'

He stared back but the answer seemed to have enough of the truth in it to satisfy him. 'He told you we were . . . estranged?'

'Estranged. Yes.'

'And the timing? I don't believe this has nothing to do with what's just happened. You've been married and living in London for months and we've never heard of you, and now Nick's out of prison, suddenly you're on our doorstep.'

'Okay,' Hannah said evenly. 'Yes, I'll admit that there's a connection. I wanted to know about Nick.' She made herself hold eye contact. 'Mark doesn't talk about his brother, won't – I found out about Patty Hendrick purely by chance. And now another woman's dead and the police are on *our* doorstep and I don't know anything about him.'

'He's a killer,' Mr Reilly told Hannah, and next to him, Elizabeth flinched. 'What more do you need to know? He's a killer and we're a killer's parents.'

Hannah slammed the car door, put her seatbelt on and programmed the GPS to 'Home'. Then she stopped. Where was she actually going to go tonight?

She rested her forehead on the top of the steering wheel. With a sudden burst of longing she thought about her life in New York – her friends, her apartment, her job – she hadn't realised it at the time,

360

of course, but everything had been so simple then. She saw her office with its huge glass desk and haphazard piles of papers and books and magazines; the view of the Empire State Building from the corridor just outside. Her assistant, Flynn, with his so-ugly-it's-got-to-be-cool wardrobe and lengthy oral reviews of whatever pop-up restaurant had opened in Greenpoint over the weekend. She'd moaned to Roisin sometimes about the weeks that passed in a blur of work but, right now, she'd give anything to be back there, strung out on coffee, pulling an all-nighter; to wake up in the apartment on Waverly and find that this whole situation – *Even Mark?* said the voice. *Your marriage?* – was just a Bobby Ewing-style alternative storyline, a nightmare.

The wind threw another stinging rash of hail against the windscreen and Hannah had a new thought. Slowly she raised her head from the wheel. If their parents weren't dead, then where the hell had Nick got a quarter of a million pounds? Mark had said it was his share of their parents' estate, money from the sale of the house, but it couldn't have been, could it? Their house was right here – they were in it.

She tried to think. Nick hadn't earned that money himself, that was for sure, not by legitimate means, anyway: the newspapers had backed Mark up on that point, talking about his inability to hold down a job and how he'd taken hand-outs from his mother to pay the rent on his flat in Borough.

361

Unless Mark had paid him a huge bonus at some point – and that seemed very unlikely – the only way Nick could have had that sort of money was if he'd been into something illegal. Hannah felt a wave of pure exhaustion: at this point, she thought, she wouldn't be surprised if she found out there was no money involved at all.

'*Oh, it wasn't Nick who didn't get on with Jim*' – she heard Mrs Reilly's bright tone and deliberately blotted it from her mind. No, not yet; she wasn't ready.

Getting out her phone, she sent Tom a text: *Can I stay with you tonight? In the car now but will explain when I see you. Really need to talk.*

She put the phone on the passenger seat where she could see it and turned on the engine. The car had grown cold while she'd been inside and her breath had fogged up the glass. The chamois-leather sponge she kept for the purpose had rolled into the footwell on the other side and she undid her seatbelt and reached for it. She was straining, her hand almost on it, when there was a sharp rap behind her. Jerking upright, she saw Elizabeth Reilly's desperate face pressed against the glass. Hannah's nerves were so jangled, she shrieked in alarm.

She rolled down the window. Mark's mother had left the house in a hurry, it seemed: she hadn't put her coat on but was holding it over her head like a shield. She pulled it forward now to protect her eyes from the hail bouncing off the car roof.

'I know you need to go,' she said, voice nearly drowned out by the radio-static noise of it, 'but I had to try . . . I shouldn't ask you, put you in a difficult position like this, but . . . can you help us? Me – it's just me. Gordon doesn't want to see him, he's too angry, but I . . . I miss my son.' She started to cry.

Over her shoulder, Hannah saw Mark's father standing on the doorstep, watching. 'Mrs Reilly,' she said, 'you're getting soaked. Why don't you get in? We can talk in here, in the dry.'

She shook her head vehemently. 'No, I can't – Gordon . . . Look, I don't care if he looks down on us,' Elizabeth said, 'Mark, I mean. Whatever Gordon says, *I* don't care. I'm sixty-eight; I haven't seen my son for ten years. I just don't want to die without seeing him again.' She looked Hannah in the eye, begging her.

Water was coursing down the gutter, bubbling into a drain somewhere underneath the car. The shoulders of her cardigan were soaked through.

'I'm not asking for a miracle,' she said. 'I know nothing's going to make it right. But if you could try – if you could ask him if he'd see me, just once. He doesn't have to come here – I can come to him, to London, anywhere. I'll find a way.'

Hannah reached through the window and touched her forearm, felt the bone even through the cardigan and the sleeve of the blouse underneath. 'I'll try,' she said. 'I can't promise anything but—'

'Thank you. Oh, thank you.' To Hannah's

surprise, Mark's mother ducked her head through the window and kissed her quickly on the cheek. 'You don't know what that means.'

'Elizabeth!' Gordon's voice over the noise of the hail. 'Come inside – you'll catch your death.'

CHAPTER 24

The food court of the service station rang with voices, mobiles, the clatter of trays and cutlery. Two babies were wailing in concert. Hands shaking, Hannah ripped open the pack of sandwiches. She hadn't wanted to stop but she hadn't eaten anything since breakfast and she was losing her ability to focus. Five or six miles back, she'd gone to overtake and nearly been ploughed off the road. She hadn't even seen the other car before she'd pulled out.

The sandwich was stale but she finished it and drank a bitter double espresso before checking her phone again. Every few minutes since Eastbourne, she'd been flicking her eyes over to the passenger seat, but the red light had refused to flash. Now, thank God, Tom had replied: *Of course you can stay. In now and will be all night.*

She tapped out a quick response and put the phone back on the table. Almost immediately, it started flashing again. *Where are you?* said the subject line.

Not her brother this time but Mark.

Her heart thumped heavily. Did he suspect

something – or know? Could his parents have contacted him? She clicked on the message and saw the rest: *Did you meet up with Tom in the end?* She sat back, breathing out. She'd forgotten to let him know what she was doing for the day; that was all. She thought for a moment then wrote a reply: *Sorry, yes, with T&L. Sara, old Malvern friend, coming for dinner – might stay if you don't mind? Haven't seen her for years.* She read it through then sent it. The lie was cowardly but so what? What was one tiny lie compared to all his huge ones? She'd send another text later to say she'd had too much wine and was going to stay the night.

She put the phone back in her bag and made her way outside. A few miles from Eastbourne, the hail had been succeeded by a heavy rain that thundered on her umbrella now as she ran back to the car. Cloud had blotted the light from the sky leaving only an angry crimson line behind the row of scrappy pines that edged the car park. The clock on the dashboard said quarter to six.

The motorway was even busier, people driving into London for Saturday night. Ahead, tail lights wove back and forth across the lanes, tens of red eyes in the dark. She stayed as far back as she could from the lorries that thundered past with their sides billowing, water spinning off their tyres in great arcs.

She'd gone ten or twelve miles when, out of the corner of her eye, she saw her phone light up. Mark, she thought, but when she reached across to the passenger seat to check, Neesha's name was on the screen. Neesha – in all the confusion about the Audi and Mark's parents, she had forgotten she'd called her.

Flashing a look in her rear-view mirror, Hannah cut across the slow lane, her rear bumper almost catching the angry muzzle of a juggernaut going much faster than she'd estimated. The driver leaned on the horn, letting loose a blast so loud it seemed to lift the car off the road. She was still doing sixty-five as she roared on to the hard shoulder, skidding on a layer of loose gravel as she braked. She answered the call just as it was about to ring out.

'Neesha.'

'Mrs Reilly.'

Even over the roar of the traffic, Hannah could hear the difference in her voice. It was thick and nasal, as if she had a heavy cold. 'Are you all right?' she said. 'You sound . . .'

'Unemployed?' Neesha said.

'What?' For a moment, Hannah didn't understand.

'He fired me.'

'Fired . . . What?'

'You promised me you wouldn't tell him.'

'I didn't,' Hannah said. 'I didn't. He . . . guessed.' Even as the word left her mouth, she realised how lame it sounded.

'Guessed?' Neesha's voice was full of scorn. 'Oh, well, that's fine then. Perfect. Thanks, anyway.

Perhaps you can tell me what we're supposed to do now, Steven and I, with a child and a mortgage and no money coming in at all. I told you . . .' her voice seemed to catch '. . . I *told* you I couldn't lose my job.'

'Neesha, I don't think it's got anything to do with that – really, I don't. Mark was fine about it – actually, he said he was flattered that you and I both thought—'

'That's bullshit,' she said. 'It might be what he told you but . . .'

'He hasn't told me anything. I didn't even know about it. Leo told me yesterday that you were on a warning – he said you'd messed up some figures. He didn't tell me you'd been . . .'

'On a warning?' Down the line came a guttural snort. 'These figures I messed up – did you ask what they were?'

'No,' Hannah admitted.

'I wrote down a telephone number wrong – I transposed two digits. I put it right in a minute, thirty seconds, all it took was a look on the Net, but Mark jumped on it like he'd caught me siphoning money from the accounts. I knew there was something going on – he was furious with me from the moment he stepped into the office. He was just waiting for an excuse.'

'Neesha,' Hannah said, 'you told me yourself that you'd been making mistakes, trying to juggle—'

'Two tiny mistakes – the other one was a spelling mistake in a letter. Nothing important, nothing

368

you'd *sack* someone for. I only said that to make you feel better – to make it seem like there really was a chance that I'd got it wrong and there wasn't actually something going on between him and that woman.'

She hadn't seen the papers, Hannah realised; she couldn't have. 'Neesha . . .' she started, but Neesha wasn't listening.

'Oh, don't even bother,' she said. 'I just thought you should know what you've done.' Before Hannah could say anything else, she had hung up. Hannah tried three times to ring her back but each time the call went straight to voicemail.

The windscreen wipers beat like a pulse as the GPS brought her back through the outskirts of south London. The roads were still busy but the pavements were almost empty, and the few people who were out hid under umbrellas or huddled in doorways. It wasn't half past seven yet but it felt late, as if the pubs and restaurants had closed already and everyone else – all the decent, sensible people – was tucked safely away at home.

She'd thought about driving to Tom's but crossing central London on a Saturday night could take hours; much quicker to leave the car in Parsons Green and get the Piccadilly line to Holloway. She imagined arriving, her relief when he opened the front door and ushered her off the street into the light and warmth. He'd take her straight to the kitchen, pour her a glass of wine and demand the whole story. The idea of telling him made her feel nauseous but she'd just have to come out and say it, there was no other way. He'd listen quietly – God, he was going to be horrified – and then he'd ask her: What are you going to do?

As she waited for the lights at the foot of Wandsworth Bridge, tears rolled down her cheeks. She was going to get a divorce. *Divorce* – the word tolled in her mind. It was so final, so – absolute. They'd fight, there would be some legal wrangling – not much: she didn't want anything except her own savings back – and then it would be over, finished, and they'd never speak to one another again. The thought caused her a pain so sharp it took her breath away. Sitting on the beach in the dark, feeding the fire with driftwood and talking as if they'd known each other for years; dancing in Williamsburg; the kiss in the alley as the J train had clattered overhead back into Manhattan – it was all gone.

But the lies . . . she knew she'd never be able to get past them. She couldn't stay with Mark now that she knew he could lie like this, lie and keep lying even when she begged for the truth, one story after another, all plausible, all perfectly woven until she picked at the one semi-loose thread and they unravelled in her hands. If she stayed, it would mean living with the possibility – the likelihood – of lies for the rest of her life.

And the things he'd lied about, too. Lying

about his brother she could understand – even forgive. In his place, meeting someone she really liked, perhaps she would have done the same in the tentative early days. *But you wouldn't have kept on lying*, argued her inner voice; *when you knew the relationship was getting serious, you would have said something, even if it meant losing him.* And his parents: he'd lied to her about them from the very beginning, before he could ever really have known their relationship would be significant.

'*The boring, ordinary*, petit bourgeois *people he had to leave behind.*' She heard his father's voice again. Was that why Mark had lied about them? Had he despised them so much? She thought of the pile of magazine clippings, the aspiration and yearning for sophistication that had risen off every hoarded page like steam. Was that why Mark kept his half of the bedroom so pared back? she wondered. Was that his way of rejecting his surroundings, refusing to own any part of that stifling bungalow with its chintzy rocking chairs and fabric flowers? He'd been designing a different sort of life for himself, hadn't he, page by magazine page?

And now Neesha. Hannah knew in her bones that Mark had fired her for talking about Hermione's calls. Why else would he have gone to such lengths to work out who'd told her? And if her for firing Neesha had been legitimate, he would have told her, Hannah, wouldn't he? He always talked to her about work – under normal circumstances, there was no way he'd fire his assistant without discussing it with her first.

She turned into Studdridge Street, only a minute from home now. *Home.* Warm light shone from the windows of almost every house, people settling in for cosy Saturday evenings of dinner and television. She thought about the walk back to the station in the rain, the hour or so she'd spend sitting soaked and cold on the Tube to Holloway. She waited for an oncoming car to pass and then made the left turn into Quarrendon Street. There was a parking spot right on the end behind a white van and she pulled in and turned off the engine. She unplugged the GPS and put it back in the glove compartment then sat for a moment in the sudden quiet. The red light was flashing on her BlackBerry again but it was just her brother, asking what time she thought she'd get there; she could answer him once she got to the station. She dropped the phone into her bag, braced herself for the rain and got out.

Tucking the handle of the umbrella between her shoulder and ear, she hitched her bag on to her shoulder and slid the key into the car door. A darting movement at ground level startled her for a second but it was just a cat, the fat tabby from across the road. Rainwater streamed along the gutter at her feet.

'Don't scream, and don't try and run.'

Hannah froze. The voice came from directly behind her, a foot away. A man's voice, quiet, in control. Mark's but not Mark's – scratchier, the accent less cultured. For a second or two the world seemed to stop. She made to turn round but a strong hand had circled the top of her arm, and it was gripping hard, keeping her facing away.

'Just do what I tell you and everything will be fine. Give me the key.'

'Get off me. Get off – you're—'

She tried to shake free of him but the hand gripped harder, fingers pressing into her flesh, sending pain shooting down her arm. She felt hot breath on her cheek, his mouth an inch from her ear. 'Shut up,' he said, his voice harder now, 'and give me the key.'

She jabbed her other arm backwards, elbow up, hoping to make contact somewhere, surprise him enough to loosen his grip just for a second, but he anticipated her and grabbed hold of her wrist. He yanked it up behind her back and she felt something tear in her shoulder. Her umbrella fell to the pavement, followed by the car key. She heard the splash as it landed in the gutter and felt a stab of despair: the plastic fob was light; the coursing rainwater would carry it away and she'd never find it in the dark.

The police – where were the police? She twisted her head but her view was blocked by the white van she'd parked behind, and the Honda she'd seen at lunchtime had been around the curve in the street, on the same side. It was hidden from sight – or she was. She opened her mouth to scream but the hand that had circled her arm was now clamped across her face, forcing her head back. She struggled but he was too powerful, and every time she tried to get free, excruciating pain tore through her shoulder. The taste of leather was in her mouth – he was wearing gloves.

He kicked her feet out from under her and pulled her sharply round. She gasped with the pain, realised her mouth was partially uncovered and screamed. The sound was shockingly loud. She felt him flinch, and hope filled her: someone would have heard it – the police, one of the neighbours. Someone would come to see what was going on. Someone would help her.

Seconds later, the hope died: they wouldn't have time. He half-pushed, half-dragged her the few steps to the van and pulled the back door open. With one neat move, he knocked her legs out from under her and shoved her forward. She fell face first, knocking the top of her head against the floor. Behind her, the van door slammed shut.

CHAPTER 25

The back of the van was windowless and, from the position she was tied in, Hannah couldn't move her head far enough to see anything further forward. When he'd pushed her inside, she'd caught a brief view of the back of the seats and the heavy wire grille that separated them from the body of the van. Now all she could see was the van's blank pressed-steel side and the patch of ceiling directly above her head, the patterns cast across it by the streetlights.

Where was he taking her?

She felt her gorge rising again and tried to swallow. If she threw up with the gag in her mouth, she'd choke. She couldn't make a noise loud enough for him to hear in the front and she'd choke on her own vomit and suffocate. *And what if he did hear her?* said the voice in her head. *Did she think Nick was going to help her?* She thought of Hermione, dead in the yard at the back of the pub, her head smashed in, blood and bone and brain.

She pushed back, trying to lift her face away from the sacking that lay piled on the van floor.

It was rough and reeked of earth and grass cuttings rotted to compost with an under-note of petrol that caught the back of her throat.

In the front section of the van, three feet away but hopelessly out of reach, she heard her phone start to ring. It rang five times then stopped as voicemail clicked in. Twenty seconds passed and then it rang again. 'Christ's sake,' he muttered, and she heard him rummaging through her bag. A couple of seconds later, the ringing stopped for a second time and she heard the long tone the phone made when it was turned off.

Her forehead was throbbing where she'd hit it. He'd pushed her inside and climbed in after her, pulling the door shut behind him. The bang to the head had stunned her for a moment but then she'd started fighting, kicking and shouting, trying to make as much noise as possible. At one point she'd managed to bite his hand and he'd sworn and snatched it away level with his shoulder. She'd thought he was going to bring it back and hit her across the face but instead he'd launched himself at her again, pushing her back down and straddling her chest, pinning her arms with his knees while he tied the cloth across her face. She'd writhed and kicked, trying to bring her legs up behind him to knee him in the small of the back, but he was too strong and in a few seconds he had forced her on to her front, pulled her hands behind her back and bound them together with something hard and sharp-edged: perhaps a plant-tie. He'd done the same with her feet.

He'd checked both sets of ties twice and, when he was satisfied, he'd crawled to the door and got out, taking her bag with him. Seconds later, she heard him get back in at the front of the van and the engine had started. He'd made a four- or five-point turn – the street was narrow with cars parked on both sides – and headed back towards Studdridge Street.

In her panic, she'd quickly lost track of where they were going – any number of streets led off Studdridge; had he turned left then or just swerved? – but now, from outside, she heard a distinctive high-pitched beeping. She knew it; she'd heard it countless times: the pedestrian crossing on Parsons Green Lane, just outside the Tube station. They'd stopped – he was waiting for the light. She thought she heard the click of buttons – was he texting? – and then there was a thunderous clatter overhead: a train on the bridge, slowing, coming into the station. She felt a burst of elation – she knew where they were – but as quickly as it came, it was gone. What good was knowing where she was? She was bound and gagged, lying helpless in the semi-darkness in a van driven by a man who'd killed a woman. Two women.

Trying to concentrate seemed to quell the panic, though, at least to some extent. It was something to focus on, a straw to clutch at. They started moving again and she pictured Parson's Green Lane, the little café, the fish-and-chip shop, the doctor's surgery. At the top, he turned left on to Fulham Road.

She traced the route in her head as he took them up Fulham Palace Road to the roundabout at Hammersmith and then – two sets of traffic lights followed by a sudden acceleration – on to the A40. The lights on the van ceiling changed, the orange streetlamp glow giving way to the strobing white of headlights passing quickly on the other side of the road. Her heart started beating faster, the panic rising again: unless he turned off soon, they were heading for the motorway. They were leaving London.

The roar of planes coming in to land at Heathrow was the last thing Hannah was sure about. After that, there was just the sound of the engine and the other traffic around them on the motorway, with an occasional rough bronchitic cough from the front. Every few minutes there was the click of a lighter and the air filled with acrid cigarette smoke. Had they stayed on the M4 or had Nick taken the London Orbital and then one of the numerous other motorways that came off it like spokes? There was no way of knowing: they could be heading anywhere. Without markers, time started to billow in and out: had it been ten minutes since she'd heard the planes or twenty?

The rain came in waves, too, sometimes drumming so hard on the windscreen that he was forced to slow down, sometimes dying away almost completely.

She took an inventory of her pain. Her head was bad – the temple she'd hit was throbbing, sending needles of pain down through her eye – but her shoulder was injured, too. Something, either muscles or a ligament, was seriously torn.

She couldn't stop thinking about her mother now. If something happened – *if he kills you*, said the voice – she'd never have a chance to say sorry. It was Mrs Reilly who'd done it, the reverence with which she'd handled that cheap photograph album, her desperate face at the car window. Despite everything, ten years of being ignored – scorned, her husband had said – she'd been prepared to beg a stranger for the smallest chance of seeing her son again.

Despite the way Hannah had behaved towards her, the brusque behaviour and constant rejection, her mother loved her, wanted to talk to her, counted down the weeks and months between Hannah's infrequent visits. Hannah remembered how she'd stood in the kitchen in Malvern as a teenager quoting *The Second Sex* – hardly her own intellectual discovery: they'd studied it for French A-level – and denouncing her mother's choices in life and she was ashamed of herself. Yes, her mother had never had a career, had never wanted one beyond bringing up her children, but couldn't she, Hannah, one of the recipients of that love and attention and sacrifice, respect that? Be grateful? Despite all the hurt she'd inflicted, she realised, she could always rely on her mother's unfailing loyalty and love. She thought of the trepidation she heard in Sandy's voice when she telephoned, her obvious fear that she'd called at the wrong time, and Hannah wanted to cry with shame. If she came through this alive, she thought, she'd go to Malvern and throw herself at her mother's feet, tell her she loved and appreciated her and was sorry.

There was the click of the indicator and they pulled out again. He was driving quickly but not quickly enough, she realised with despair, to draw the attention of the police. She could sense him, his physical presence seemed to weigh down the air, but he hadn't uttered a word to her since he'd slammed the back doors shut. The silence was worse than anything he might have said. Years ago on the news, she'd seen Stephanie Slater, the woman Michael Sams had kidnapped and kept tied up for days in a wheelie bin. She'd told the interviewer that she'd talked to him, never let him forget that she was a real person, trying to make it harder for him to kill her. But this wasn't about sex, was it, and she wasn't some poor woman pulled off the street at random.

Hannah tried to think logically. Why would Nick kill her? He'd had a reason for killing Hermione but she, Hannah, had done nothing to him. What would he hope to achieve? Then she had another thought. What if he'd finally spoken to Mark and he knew he didn't have the money? Was that it? Was this some kind of revenge attack? Or was she going to be used as a bargaining chip? Bait?

They'd been driving for a long time, maybe an hour and a half, maybe two hours, when she heard the indicator again and they began to slow down. They climbed a short slope and the burr of motorway traffic receded. A brief pause, then a green glow on the ceiling and they were moving again but more slowly, fifty miles an hour now, not eighty. She strained, listening for any clue at all as to where they were, but apart from another vehicle every minute or so and the sound of wind in the trees, there was nothing. The road had changed, too, winding one way then the other, dipping then rising. There was no glow of streetlights across the ceiling, no more traffic lights. They were out in the country.

After another ten or fifteen minutes, they slowed almost to a stop and turned off the road on to what felt like an unmade track. The van lurched in and out of potholes, jarring Hannah's hip and shoulder against the floor. Wherever he was taking her, they must be almost there.

The surface under the wheels changed again and they came on to gravel. Nick stopped the van and got out, slamming his door shut. The crunch of footsteps and then the back doors opened and she saw him silhouetted against the sky. Taking hold of her lower legs, he dragged her towards the doors and pulled her into a sitting position. He took a Stanley knife out of his pocket and she felt a flare of pure fear, but then he bent and cut the tie around her ankles with a quick upward flick. Taking hold of her by the upper arms, he pulled her to her feet. She struggled, trying to get free and head-butt him, but he tightened his grip and held her at arm's length.

'I wouldn't bother,' he said, voice neutral. 'We're miles from anywhere.'

After the fetid sacking, the cold night air smelled clean and sweet. She sucked it in through her nose, trying to flush the stink of rotting vegetation and petrol from her nostrils. Into her head came the idea that this might be the last time she ever smelled fresh air and she pushed it away, ordering herself to keep it together.

Hand between her shoulder blades, Nick pushed her around the side of the van. Cloud blotted out any moonlight but her eyes were accustomed to the dark now and she saw the front of a large, pale-stone house backed by trees. It was the house from the newspaper picture, the one where he'd been photographed with his sports car.

She stumbled as her foot caught the edge of a flagstone on the uneven path, but he caught her, yanking her backwards, sending another bolt of pain through her shoulder. One hand on the neck of her coat, he unlocked the front door and thrust her inside. Then he shut the door after himself, locked it again and pocketed the key.

Reaching out, he snapped the light on. Hannah blinked. They were in a hallway, polished stone flagging underfoot, a wide flight of stairs climbing away into darkness. There was a series of gloomy oil paintings in ornate gilt frames, and at the foot of the stairs a mounted stag's head with branched antlers. To their left and right were closed doors. The air was warm but smelled strongly of dust, as if the house had been empty for some time and the heating had only just been put back on.

In front of them, a corridor led towards the back of the house. With a sharp nudge, he directed her forward. They went round a corner, passing another pair of closed doors, and came into a room at the end. In the weak light from the window, she made out a table with chairs and then, at the other end, units: a sink, a stove.

Nick flicked the light on, pulled out a chair and pushed her into it. Going behind her, he tied her wrists to the bar across the back then came round and crouched in front of her. She aimed a kick at his face but he caught her ankle before it reached him. 'Just don't, all right? There's no need to make this any harder.'

Through the gag she made a sound she meant him to interpret as 'Fuck you'.

For the first time now, she saw Nick at close range. No wonder she'd mistaken him for Mark outside the delicatessen. As she knew from the pictures, he had no mole, and his eyes were larger and even darker than Mark's, the pupils almost indistinguishable from the irises, but the structure of their faces was the same. The only real difference, she could see now, was in their skin. Though he was forty, Mark could pass for thirty-two or three but no one would take Nick for that. He looked older by ten years, if not fifteen. His forehead and the area around his eyes were scored with lines, and other, deeper ones, the result of years of heavy smoking, radiated out from his mouth. He was wearing the pea coat she'd seen him in before, the one that had reminded her of Mark's, but his black jeans were old, faded and white at the seams, and his beanie was knitted in a cheap nylon-wool mix, completely different from the cashmere one that Mark had picked up at Barneys on a New York trip last year.

Keeping hold of her ankle, he forced it against the leg of the chair, took another garden tie out of his pocket and pulled it tight. When he'd tied her other leg, he stood up and went behind her again. She felt tugging at her hands and then, to her confusion, she realised he'd cut them free. Pain shooting through her shoulder, she brought them round in front of her and saw deep red welts around her wrists. A moment later, she felt his hands at the back of her head again and he pulled the gag out of her mouth.

She took a great gulp of air that hit the back

of her throat and made her choke. She coughed until her eyes were streaming. 'You,' she croaked as soon as she could catch a breath. 'You . . .'

Nick put his hands up, palms towards her. 'I'm sorry.'

She'd been about to scream at him but his tone pulled her up short. 'You're *sorry*?'

'Yes, I'm sorry – I'm really sorry. I wouldn't have done it like this, given the choice, but . . . Anyway, I'm not going to hurt you and I'm sorry for frightening you.'

Hannah stared at him but he seemed to be serious. 'What the hell are you doing then? You *abducted* me.'

'You were hardly going to get in the car willingly, were you?'

'But . . .'

'Getting you here is the only way of getting my brother here. He wouldn't meet me and he wouldn't answer my calls so . . .'

Hannah nearly laughed. 'He's been trying to reach you for *days*, ringing and ringing, since before you got out of prison, until—' She stopped herself from saying it. *Hermione.*

'No,' Nick said simply. 'He hasn't called me once.'

'You're lying,' she said, shaking her head. 'He told me he'd tried everything to talk to you. He came to visit you in prison. He—'

'Yes,' Nick admitted, 'he did visit me, that's true at least, but I'm pretty confident he didn't tell you why he came. Anyway,' he gave a light shrug, 'believe me when I tell you that I wouldn't have gone to this sort of trouble unless I had to. Imagine how it would look to the police as well – my third day out.'

He walked over to the part of the room with the units and she watched him open a cupboard and take out a bottle of whisky and two glasses. Bringing them to the table, he sat down opposite her. He kept his coat on but pulled off his beanie and stuffed it into his pocket. Underneath, his hair was shaved almost to the scalp. He poured an inch of Scotch into both glasses and handed her one. 'Here. I should think you need it.'

She looked at it for a second then took a swig that made her cough again.

'I've sent him a text to let him know where we are.'

She smiled. 'Then the police will be here any minute, won't they?'

Nick regarded her over the rim of his glass. 'I doubt it.'

From inside his jacket he took a cheap-looking red mobile phone that he put on the table in front of him, and a new pack of Embassy. He tore off the cellophane and pulled out the slip of silver paper inside. 'I don't know what he's told you about me,' he said, 'but from the way you ran off the other night, I'm guessing it was the full works. I want to tell you the truth.'

'I don't want to hear it.'

'Well, that's bad luck, isn't it?' he said, with a dry smile. 'Given that you're literally a captive audience.' He unscrewed the bottle again and poured himself a modest top-up. 'You need to hear the truth about what happened. To Patty – all of it.'

'I told you, I'm not interested,' she said, but there was something about the directness of the way he was looking at her that made her heart start beating very fast. *He's a psychopath*, she told herself, *an expert manipulator; this is what he does*, but his face was open and she thought of his parents, tucked away in their bungalow in Eastbourne, alive after all.

'You might be more interested,' he said, 'if I told you that Mark was there, too.'

'Yes, at the club that night. I know.'

'Not at the club – at my flat. He was there when Patty died.'

Hannah went cold. 'You're lying,' she said.

Nick shook his head. 'No.'

He put a cigarette in his mouth and flicked the lighter. When he inhaled, the tobacco crackled in the silence. 'He's told you the official version, obviously – I'm the monster who watched Patty die and didn't call an ambulance.'

'He didn't tell me.' Hannah felt a surge of relief. 'I read about it online, in the old newspaper reports. You were tried and found guilty.'

He nodded. 'I was. But the jury can only base a verdict on the evidence they've heard.'

'Oh, come on,' she said, rolling her eyes. 'Don't even try—'

'The key to a successful lie is to stay as close to the actual facts as possible. It's the first rule of deception, isn't it?'

'You tell me.'

He ignored her. 'So, a lot of it was true. I'd reached the end of my rope with Mark and I wanted to piss him off, so one night when his girlfriend was wasted, I chatted her up and took her home.' He took a pull on the cigarette, watching the end as it glowed red then faded again. 'I'll never forgive myself for what happened to Patty – I dream about her all the time. She didn't deserve that, no one would, and what I did was . . .' He shook his head. 'It got totally out of hand. We were both so messed up; we'd drunk so much and done so many lines, and . . .'

'You injected her when she was almost unconscious.'

His eyes went hard. 'Do you think I don't know that? Do you think I haven't had enough time over the past ten years to reflect on it? I'm telling you, I live with what I did every single day.' He took a long drag on the cigarette and a soft column of ash fell on the table-top. 'Mark,' he said. 'I pissed him off and he came back and fucked me up. Ten years of my life.'

'What about her life?' Hannah said. 'You let her die. You filled her with drugs, and then, when it all went wrong, you just let her die. He had nothing to do with that. He—'

'Just shut up for a minute and listen, will you?' The cigarette was down to the filter and Nick ground it out in the saucer, burning his fingertips. 'The club, my taking her home, that was Friday night – Saturday morning. On Sunday afternoon, Mark showed up at my flat. I wasn't going to let him in – he was raging, shouting and banging on the door, and I still had her there. And I was off my face, we both were – we'd been wasted for two days by that point. Mark shoved past me and came barging in. He made so much noise that Patty came to the sitting room to see what the hell was going on. She was in the doorway, naked, hardly able to stand,' Nick looked down, avoiding Hannah's eye. 'Mark grabbed her and threw her face forward across the sofa. He asked her how she liked it, having sex with both brothers.'

Hannah was seized by a sudden dread. 'Stop,' she said. 'Please, just stop now.'

He shook his head. 'You need to know.'

She closed her eyes, as if that would prevent her from hearing.

'I tried to pull him off her.'

'I don't believe you – I don't believe any of it. This is bullshit.'

'I tried to pull him off,' said Nick, talking over her, 'but he was sober and I was wrecked and I didn't stand a chance. He shoved me and I hit my head on the corner of the coffee table. I don't know how long I was out, but when I came round, he was standing over her with his trousers undone and she was face down in front of him making this wheezing noise. Her face had gone white and all blue round the mouth, and she was sweating. I said we should call an ambulance – I thought she was having a heart attack. I was crawling round the room on my hands and knees, blood running into my eye, trying to find my phone, but Mark stopped me. He said I'd go to prison for supplying and we could help her ourselves – do mouth-to-mouth, chest compressions.'

'Except you didn't.'

'I did. I tried and tried and tried but it didn't work. Jesus, when it dawned on me that she was dead . . .'

There was silence for several seconds. Hannah stared at her hands. There was a rushing in her ears, blood thumping through them far too fast, and the room eddied round her like a tide. He'd raped her – Mark had raped Patty. Her husband, the man she was married to, shared a bed with, slept with. 'And then what happened?' she said quietly.

'I said we had to call the police and he said yes but to wait a moment. He said we had to think strategically.'

'Strategically?'

'That was his word. Basically, he said, there was no way that we were going to get out of this unscathed and so we had to make the best we could of it.'

Hannah felt the contents of her stomach rise up her throat. He'd raped a woman, she'd died, and then Mark had thought about *strategy*.

'If we called the police straight away, he said, both of us would be charged – we were both there, DNA from both of us would be on her body. But things looked much worse for me. She was his girlfriend – there was a reason why his DNA would be on her, and people had seen them together at the club on Friday – it wasn't a secret they'd nipped off for a quickie. And, as he pointed out, it was my flat she'd died in.'

Nick ran his hands over his shaven head and she heard the stubble rasp. 'Mark said that if we both went to prison, we'd lose everything. DataPro would be finished, and when we got out, we'd be unemployable – no one else would give us jobs. But,' Nick looked at her, 'if one of us took the rap, the other could keep DataPro going and then, when the whole thing was over, it would still be there.'

'I don't . . .'

'He said that because DataPro was his, it made sense for him to be the one who ran it. Patty's death was an accident, it was the drugs and booze that killed her, he said, not anything that either of us had done to her, so the police couldn't charge me with anything that would carry a long sentence.'

'And you just swallowed all this?'

'I didn't *just swallow* it,' Nick said angrily. 'I'm stupid but I'm not that bloody stupid. I made a calculation. Either way, I knew I was going to be in deep shit. I mean, if you've read about it, you know all the gory details – I wasn't going to get off scot-free whatever happened. I gave her the drugs; she was in my house; there were . . . marks on her: I was going to jail. Mark told me that if I kept quiet about him ever being at my place that afternoon, he would pay me a dividend from DataPro when I got out.'

'How much?' she said, though she already knew.

'Two million.'

Hannah closed her eyes for a moment. 'You don't own any shares at all, do you?' she said.

'What are you talking about?'

'He told me that you owned twelve per cent of the company; that you invested your share of your parents' estate – quarter of a million.'

'Estate? Our parents aren't dead.'

'I know that now,' she said. 'But I didn't until today. Mark told me that you'd invested your inheritance and the two million was to buy you out.'

Nick expelled a short burst of air. 'I wish.' He opened the pack of cigarettes again and took out another. He lit it and took a deep drag, holding the smoke in his lungs. 'What would you have done, in my shoes?' he said. 'I was going to jail anyway, and if I did it this way, there'd be money waiting when I got out, enough to keep me going for the rest of my life even if no one gave me a job ever again. I told myself that serving the sentence would be my job: I'd put the time in and then I'd get paid. It made sense.'

'It would if you thought you were only going down for a couple of years,' she said.

He tipped his head. 'I didn't think they'd charge me with manslaughter.'

'Why didn't you say something, when they did?'

'I never thought I'd get ten years. My lawyer said it would be three or four – Patty was a grown-up, she'd known what she was doing. With time off for good behaviour, and parole . . . So I went along with it. Only to be shafted by Mark yet again.'

'You mean . . .'

'He's not paying me.' Nick stared at her. 'Whatever reason he gave you for coming to Wakefield, he lied. He came to tell me I could have two hundred and fifty thousand – an eighth of what we'd agreed – take it or leave it.'

Her savings and his own and the new mortgage.

'And if you left it?'

'If I didn't accept the "new terms", as he called them, he said he'd make sure I was back in prison before my feet touched the ground. All my life,' Nick said, 'he's been trying to take what's mine. However much he's got, it's not enough – he's not happy unless I've got nothing. The day he came to visit me – the second time – he even walked off with my bloody cigarettes.'

Hannah went cold again. 'Did he tell you how he was going to have you put back in prison?'

'He mentioned Hermione – I think it was the only thing he could think of. In court she said some stuff about our sex life that was a bit . . .'

'You hadn't been in touch with her? You didn't threaten her?'

'What?'

'Nick, Hermione's dead.'

He stared at her and the cigarette dropped from between his fingers. If there'd been any doubt left in Hannah's mind, one look at him now would have put paid to it.

'Dead?' he said, and his voice had gone faint. 'Are you . . .? You're telling me the truth, aren't you?'

'She was attacked near the hospital, on her way home – battered to death. She died of head injuries.'

'When?'

'Thursday afternoon – late afternoon. Nick, they found a pack of cigarettes with your fingerprints on at the scene.'

He made a terrible sound in his throat as if he were bringing up some deep, integral part of himself, but Hannah barely registered it. Mark had killed Hermione – *Mark*. He'd planned it – set out to do it in cold blood. Her mind went scrambling back over everything he'd told her, everything that had happened. She remembered that evening – she'd seen Nick outside the delicatessen and Mark had come tearing back across London to find her. Where had he been? He'd left that message on Hermione's phone at quarter to nine; he'd stood in their sitting room and left a message for a woman he knew was dead – he'd made a *joke*: '*Hannah . . . my wife – I think you've met.*' Now she remembered his weird, nervous energy, his white knuckles on the poker as he'd jabbed at the fire. Oh, God – he'd kissed her; he'd pushed her against the wall and tried to have sex with her. And the next day, when the police had come, the way he'd trembled . . . She'd taken it for shock, grief, but he must have thought they'd come for him. Hannah retched and retched again. He'd killed a woman – not just a woman: a friend. He'd come home from beating a woman to death and tried to have sex with her.

Nick reached across the table and took hold of her hand. He held it tightly and she looked at their fingers, hers pale, his stained at the tips with nicotine. 'He told me you'd threatened him, too,' she said. 'He said you were violent.'

'Judging by the way you ran the other night, it worked.'

'What do you mean?'

'He didn't want you to talk to me, did he? So he scared the living daylights out of you, made sure you'd run a mile the moment you saw me.'

Hannah remembered how urgently Mark had

bundled her into the cab outside the pub that night, how he'd made her promise to stay inside the hotel, how he'd gripped her hand when they'd walked to dinner at Mao Tai. The conversation that night – he'd told her Nick had been threatening Hermione, that that was why she'd looked so terrified in the corridor at the hospital, but it was *him* she'd been scared of. He was the killer.

She closed her eyes again as if she could shut it out, unsee it. She'd loved him, she'd trusted him, and all the time, he'd been working away at a filigree of lies so carefully made it took her breath away.

For a long time they sat in silence. Nick smoked one cigarette after another, slowly filling the saucer with butts, but he didn't touch the whisky again. Every few seconds, his eyes went to the cheap red mobile, and after a while he began picking it up, pressing buttons to light up the screen, checking, then checking again.

Hannah watched their silhouettes in the glass of the window behind him, the back of his head, her own white face. The cuts around her wrists throbbed and she was grateful: the pain was something to focus on, an anchor in reality. Otherwise, she was floating. She examined her feelings with a sort of detachment. She should have been afraid, she should have been wild with panic, but instead she felt a strange sense of calm. Perhaps it was a protective thing, she thought. Perhaps this was too much for a person to take in at once and her mind had gone into some sort of fugue state. Perhaps, when this was over, she'd have no mental record of any of it.

In an odd way, too, she felt better – clean. For days and days she'd been sifting through his lies, feeling dirtier and dirtier as she dug down through the layers. Now, finally, she could hold it in her hand and lift it up into the light: the hard kernel of truth he had worked so hard to hide.

'All this because you hate each other,' she said, breaking the silence.

'No,' said Nick, looking up from the phone. 'Because Mark hates me. He's hated me from the day I was born.' He picked the bit of silver cigarette paper from the table and turned it between his fingers. 'He hated me because my mother loved me. That was my crime back then, when we were babies: I loved my mother and she loved me. Mark couldn't stand it.'

'When did you realise? How old were you?'

'I can't remember a time when I didn't know,' he said. 'It was a fact of my life, there from the beginning, like having parents and getting bigger and knowing you'd go to school one day. My brother hating me, constantly looking for ways to hurt me.'

Hannah thought of gentle Elizabeth Reilly, and her guilt. 'Do you think your mother *was* biased?' she said.

He rubbed his hand over his head. 'I don't know

– by the time I was old enough to have any sense of that, it had been going on for years. But even as a small child I remember thinking it was weird, how Mark acted towards her. I used to think about it when I was inside, how fucking terrible it was. He wanted her love so badly, he craved it, but he only wanted it if it was exclusive. There were times I thought he might kill me to get it. Even when we were kids – small kids – I used to think that.'

Yesterday, Hannah thought, she would have laughed at the idea.

'I used to be careful on railway platforms,' Nick said, 'that sort of thing. It sounds ridiculous but I could see it – I could imagine a day when he'd spot the opportunity and take it. You know, the push on the empty platform, no one there to see.'

'That's . . . horrific.'

He shrugged. 'It's the story of our lives, Mark's quest to hurt me. If not actually to kill me, then to fuck me up.' He pressed the phone to light the screen: nothing. 'As you've probably realised,' he said, 'Mark's a master planner. He runs rings round me, he always has – I'm stupid and impulsive, I screw things up, but he . . . he's like a spider. He makes a web, a big intricate thing, then he sits on it and waits, legs on all the different threads, waiting for a change in the tension, the sign that his prey's been snared.'

Hannah wrapped her arms around herself.

'He's a genius at it, actually. The long game.

398

That's why he never pushed me under the 2.10 from Brighton – it would have been over too quickly. More fun for him to see how he could screw me up over years and years. It was him who got me into drugs – he knew my personality, how easy I find it to get hooked. He could do it: smoke a bit of weed, take some E, get hold of the good stuff and make sure I was getting really into it, then stop. Meanwhile, there was I with a brand-new habit. You could count the number of times he did coke on your fingers, probably, but I . . . Well, it really messed me up. It wasn't just . . . what happened. Before that, for years, I was hopeless. I lost job after job, barely scraped through my degree – there were days I just couldn't get out of bed. And it wrecked me financially, of course – swallowed every penny I managed to earn.'

'What about Jim Thomas?' Hannah said. 'Your neighbour.'

Nick looked at her. 'Jim?'

'What happened to his dog, the one that drowned? The papers said you did it but your mother told me it was a misunderstanding.'

'No misunderstanding. Mark drowned Molly. He hated Jim, absolutely hated him – Jim was wise to him and he knew it.'

'Your mother says you – the two of you – found her drowned.'

'No, I found her drowned. I'd been with this girl after school and I was coming home the back way near the stream. Mark had put her in a bag with stones – when I came along he was cutting her out of it. I waded in but . . .'

'Then why did people think you did it?'

'Because I was the one with the wild reputation – the girls, the drugs, bunking off school.'

Hannah frowned. 'Why didn't you say something?'

'Because he told me that if I did, he'd grass me up for selling weed at school, which I *was* doing. You see? This was what he was so good at – he knew everything, calculated everything. And everything could be tied back in to something else. The spider's web.'

Hannah pointed at his cigarettes. 'Can I?'

He pushed them across the table with his lighter. 'He used to make out that I was some sort of wild animal – stupid, uncivilised. A brute.' He took the packet back and got one out for himself. 'Of course, the irony is, I am a brute now – ten years in prison brutalised me.' He lit the cigarette, pulled smoke into his lungs and let it out in a long thin stream. 'It was . . . if I imagined hell, I'd imagine prison. Wakefield's where they keep the sex offenders, the rapists. It wasn't Ford, with Jeffrey Archer knocking out a novel and a load of dodgy MPs playing ping-pong. No one warns you about the noise – all day, all night, the banging and knocking and shouting and singing, metal doors slamming, buzzers. I shared cells with people who were illiterate, disturbed. Ten years without privacy, counting the hours until you could go to bed and say you'd done another day. Not that there was sleep, even then. There was this one time . . .'

He stopped and she saw his whole body stiffen. Echoing through the house came the sound of the doorbell.

CHAPTER 26

Hannah worked her fingers between the tie and the leg of her jeans and pulled as hard as she could. The plastic cut her, sending a line of pain through the pads of her fingers, but it didn't give at all. She tightened her grip. It wouldn't break but if she could stretch it enough, maybe she could get her foot through. Clenching her jaw, she tried again, leaning back in the chair, pulling with as much of her body weight as she could. *Come on, come on – please*. Nothing. It wouldn't budge.

He was leaning on the doorbell now and it rang through the house like an alarm, shrill and constant. 'All right, all right,' Nick shouted, and then, seconds later, she heard Mark's voice.

'If you've touched her, you fucking little *germ* . . .'

'You'll do what?' Nick said. 'Set me up for murder? Have me thrown in jail?'

'Where is she?'

The sound of quick footsteps down the hallway. Hannah yanked at the tie again, almost tipping herself forward out of the chair, tears of frustration in her eyes. She tried standing again but the

402

ties were too tight: she couldn't straighten her legs.

'Hannah.'

Mark stood framed in the doorway, the mouth of the corridor dark behind him. She was seized by terror. He was wearing jeans and his black jumper, the outfit she'd watched him put on in the hotel room that morning, but it was as if she'd never seen him before. Who was he, this stranger? *This rapist. This killer.* She saw him look at the ties round her ankles and then at her hand, and when she followed his glance, she saw that her palm was covered in blood.

'What's he done to you? Has he hurt you? He's hurt you.' He came towards her, arms out, but she twisted her body away from him, hands out, shielding herself.

'No. Don't touch me.'

'Han . . .' He reached out but she shoved his arm away, recoiling from the contact.

'I said, don't touch me.'

She flailed, trying to keep him off, but he grabbed her head and held her face between his hands, forcing her to look at him. At first she resisted but then she stopped struggling and stared back.

'I know,' she told him. 'Patty, Hermione – I know everything.'

His hands dropped. Slowly, without breaking eye contact, he stepped away from her. His body seemed to sag momentarily, as if she'd knocked the wind out of him. Transfixed, she watched his expression change from shock to regret and then, too quickly, to a kind of resigned acceptance that sent a chill through her. He looked at her with detachment for a second or two, and then, as if coming to himself again, he spun around. Nick was standing near the door, watching them.

'What have you done?' Mark said.

'She needed to know.'

Mark shook his head as if he was actually pained. 'You're mad.' He turned to Hannah. 'See, I told you – he's insane, crazy.'

'I don't think so,' she said.

'Will you kill her, too,' Nick asked, 'now that she knows? It would be a shame – you actually love her, don't you? The first time in your life you've ever cared about anyone other than yourself. Except for Mum, obviously.'

Without warning, Mark launched himself across the room. He swung, aiming for Nick's face, but Nick anticipated him, took a step sideways, then drove his fist into Mark's stomach. Mark doubled over and Nick grabbed his collar, pulled him back and then hurled him against the wall. A dull thud – the wall was plasterboard, soft.

'I hope you did better than that inside, pretty boy.'

Nick made a sound, half-groan, half-roar, and threw himself at Mark. He brought his knee up, aiming for his brother's groin, but he missed and Nick caught hold of him by the hair, pulled his head down and dragged him across the room, feet scuffing against the flagstones. He threw Mark against the wall by the door and there was the crack of skull on stone. Mark started to slump but Nick's hands went round his throat and pinned him against the wall. 'You killed Hermione.'

'You're mad.' Mark laughed as much as the hand round his throat allowed. 'You've always been mad. Headcase,' he said to Hannah, 'that was what they called him at school.'

Nick took hold of the collar of his jumper and bounced his head off the stone three times, each blow harder than the one before. 'Admit it: you . . .' *Crack!* '. . . Killed . . .' *Crack!* '. . . Hermione.' *Crack!*

When he raised his eyes, it was a second or two before Mark could focus. 'All right,' he said. 'Yes.'

She'd known, she'd already known, but it still hit Hannah like a fist in the stomach.

'You . . . It was you who threatened her,' said Hannah. 'It was you.'

'I didn't – I didn't have to. She was scared of me, anyway. Because she knew,' he said.

'Knew what?'

'That I was there. That afternoon.'

Nick stared at him. 'How?'

'Let go of me – I can't breathe. I can't breathe.'

Nick bounced him backwards a final time then let him go. Mark staggered. When he'd steadied himself, he ran a tentative hand around his neck. Hannah saw the gleam of blood in the hair above his left ear.

'She saw me leaving your place,' he said, voice

hoarse. 'She'd heard about you leaving the club with Patty and she'd come to finish things with you. We bumped into each other on the street.'

'Bullshit,' said Nick. 'If she knew then, why didn't she go to the police?'

'Because I sorted it out, you fuckwit. Like I've always had to sort everything out.'

'How?'

'I asked her what Geoffrey Landis and her employers at the hospital would think if they knew about the drugs she'd sold us over the years, all those dodgy prescriptions. What she'd do if she couldn't be a doctor any more.'

'You . . .'

'I had to. All my life you've fucked things up for me. You're a worthless piece of shit.' He moved his hand to his pocket and then, before Hannah could even shout a warning, Nick gave a horrible cry and doubled over. Mark pushed, driving the knife further in, then twisted his hand and pulled it out. Nick grabbed for it but missed and Mark jabbed it in again, higher this time. Nick staggered backwards. Looking down, he saw the two roses of blood blooming across the lower part of his T-shirt. 'What . . .?'

Mark lunged forward and grabbed him by the neck of his coat. He drew his arm back and Hannah saw the knife, a long, mean razor of a thing. 'When are you going to learn?' he said, shoving it forward again. 'You should know! You should know not to try to screw with me.'

Nick leaned forward and for a split second Hannah thought he was falling. Then, though, he reared back again, looked Mark in the eye, and head-butted him in the face. Mark gave a cry of pain as blood poured from his nose and Nick grabbed him by the collar and spun him sideways into the table, sending chairs flying.

The knife lay on the floor. Hannah saw Nick look at it and then at her. Hand pressed to his stomach, he stooped, picked it up and came towards her, holding it out. He bent at her feet, and with two quick strokes cut the plastic ties.

'Get out of here!'

Light-headed, holding on to the arms of the chair, she stood. Mark was on his feet again, too, holding his wrist under his nose, blotting the blood with his cuff. With a shout, he lurched across the kitchen and fell on Nick, bringing him to the ground. Nick fought but the wounds were already making him weaker and Mark quickly pinned him to the floor and smashed his face into the tiles.

'Run, Hannah,' Nick said, voice thick with blood. He brought his knee up and smashed it into the small of Mark's back, making him grunt with pain. 'Go.'

Mark swiped at her, grabbing the leg of her jeans, but she pulled free of him and ran. Down the corridor and back to the front door, their grunts and cries loud even there. It was a fight to the death: one of them was going to kill the other.

The door was unlocked, Nick had unlocked it

for Mark, and she yanked it open and lurched out on to the path. In the dim light, the white van seemed almost to glow. She ran to it and pulled the driver's door open. Without much hope, she checked the ignition but of course Nick hadn't left the key. She went to the back door in case he'd left it there by mistake when he'd pulled her out, but it wasn't there, either. He must have it – it must be in his pocket.

Mark's Mercedes was parked at the mouth of the drive, facing out, ready to go. With a glance back at the house, she ran to it. She tried the door but it was locked.

She felt a burst of panic that she quickly suppressed: there was no time; she had to concentrate, think clearly. *Come on, Hannah.*

Her phone: it was in her bag. She ran back across the drive and climbed into the van's front seat. At first she thought the bag was gone but then she saw that it had fallen forward into the footwell. She snatched it up and scrabbled through it, cursing the clutter of old receipts and tissues. *Come on, come on.* Glancing through the windscreen she saw the front of the house, the door gaping blackly open. What was happening? Who was winning?

At last she found the phone. She pressed the button to unlock it but nothing happened. For a moment, she panicked again – it had run out of battery; it was useless – but then she remembered: Nick had turned it off. Almost laughing with relief, she turned it on and dialled 999, fingers fumbling.

Nothing. She tried again: still nothing. Looking at the screen, she saw the signal icon: there was no reception. They were too far out in the country.

With a cry of despair, she threw the phone down on the seat. It bounced and fell into the gap by the handbrake. Almost in tears, she stuck her hand down and groped for it, getting her fingers on it but then feeling it slip farther away.

In the doorway of the house now, a man appeared, visible only in outline. She froze. Which one – Nick or Mark? Who had won?

'Hannah.' The shout seemed to fill the whole sky.

Mark.

He stepped free from the shadow of the house and started down the path towards the van. For a moment she was immobilised by fear but then she yanked the passenger door open and got out. Her feet sounded deafening on the gravel.

'Hannah!' He came after her and she heard herself give a cry of alarm. 'Hannah, get back here.'

A wall ran from the side of the house, and in the dim light, she made out a wooden gate partly hidden by overhanging foliage. Shoving it open, she found herself in some kind of formal garden, raised beds divided by paths paved with stone. Mark was ten feet behind her, she could hear him breathing, and without thinking about where she was going, she plunged down the central path.

'Hannah!'

At the back of the garden there was a long brick

wall and what looked like a greenhouse. Next to it was another gate. She headed straight for it, trying to find the quickest route through beds full of fruit canes and the moon faces of leeks gone to seed, but Mark saw where she was going and climbed over one of the beds to cut her off. He snatched at her coat, just missing, and she screamed. 'Get off me!'

He jumped down right behind her but then he skidded, almost falling over, and she took her chance and ran again. In her terror, she seemed to find a new gear and she reached the gate and managed to slam it before he could get through. Ahead of her now, she saw, twenty or so feet away, was a deep ditch, an old ha-ha, and then fields, just fields, and here and there a stand of trees and then – *thank God, thank God* – she saw a handful of lights, tiny, like jewels, a mile away, maybe more, but lights.

The gate slammed shut again.

Into the ditch and then up the other side, legs burning, Mark thundering down after her, ten feet behind. She tripped, put her hands out to stop herself, felt thistles. Across the first field, her ankles turning over again and again as her feet found rabbit holes and stray briars, a half-buried lump of stone. Overhead, the sky was smothered in cloud and gave hardly any light. Her heart was thumping, her breath coming in great jagged gasps. He would kill her – if he caught her, he'd kill her. *Run.*

The next field was ploughed into furrows a foot

high, each one a mini-breaker of solid mud. She started hobbling across it, heading towards the lights, tripping on huge clumps of clay, struggling to keep her balance.

Then, without warning, she caught the tip of her boot. She sprawled, hitting her head on the crest of a furrow, cutting her palms on stones. As soon as she landed, she started to get back up but before she could do it, a hand grabbed the material of her coat. He pulled her up, threw her down on her back and straddled her.

She fought, hitting him, scratching his face, trying to get her knees up behind him like Nick had, but he was too strong. He caught her wrists and forced them down on either side of her head. She wrenched her upper body sideways, turned her head and bit his forearm.

'You . . .' He lifted her by her collar and thumped her head backwards against the ground. The pain was stunning; it spread in waves across her skull, and for a moment she lay still. Above her, his face was lost in the darkness; she could only make out his eyes by the shine across them.

'Nick was right, Hannah,' he said, breathing hard through his mouth. 'I do love you.'

'Oh, God, you're mad.' She struggled again, trying to get her hands free, but he just held her down harder, pressing her wrists further into the mud.

'Stop it. Stop fighting and listen to me.'

'You're a murderer – you killed Hermione, Mark.

411

She's dead. Do you even know what you've done? Do you know what that means? You're a killer.'

'How can you say that?' he said, and to her amazement, he sounded hurt – actually wounded. 'This was for you.'

'What?' Her voice was full of horror. 'No.'

'It was all for you.'

'No, Mark. No. This had nothing to do with me.'

'It had *everything* to do with you. Do you have any idea how hard I've been working to try and keep this all under control, to try and save our marriage?'

'Save our marriage?' She was incredulous.

'The stories, the explanations – layer after layer and nothing seemed to satisfy you. You just wouldn't stop digging – it was like you were trying to destroy us.' He seemed to choke and she heard blood bubble in his nose. Was he crying?

She tried to move but he pressed his weight down again, pinning her firmly.

'You're the first woman I've ever loved, Hannah. Do you know what *that* means? Before you, everyone I'd ever met was with me for one of two reasons: as a way of getting to *him* or for my money. But when I met you – I can't *give* you my money. You don't want it.' He laughed, as if the whole thing were delightful. 'You won't use my cards, I know you feel weird about the Audi – and I love it. It's wonderful – you're with me because you want me. *Me.*'

'Mark, please – let me go.'

'No, I need you to listen, Hannah – I'm trying to explain. You're different. You're everything I ever wanted – remember I told you that, on our wedding day? I could have had a lot of different women – once you've got money, it's amazing how attractive you are suddenly – but you're not like that. What I'm trying to say is that you've got class. It's in everything you do – the way you dress, how you look. Your books and music and films. Even your running – I know you hate it but you do it because you've got backbone. That's class.'

'Mark . . .'

'Hannah, I love you and I want to be with you for the rest of my life. We can keep a lid on all this, Nick, until the deal's done – we'll find a way. I'll sell the company and then we'll leave London, go wherever you want. We can forget this ever happened – put it behind us and . . .'

'What? Mark, you *killed* someone.'

'Only because I *had* to – to stop you finding out.' His voice rose in frustration at her refusal to understand. 'I didn't *want* to but I had no choice. Nick was going to ruin everything – it was all going to come out, I was terrified of losing you. I had to try to—'

'Is he dead?'

'I think so. Yes.' Mark said it calmly, matter-of-fact. 'See? He's gone and you know everything now. We can start again with a clean slate. We'll go somewhere and make a fresh start. We can make this work; I know we can. Tell me we're going to be fine.' He tightened his grip on her wrists. 'Say it.'

'I . . .'

'Say it.'

'I can't – I can't. You've killed people – we can never go back.'

He gave a cry of pure anguish. 'You . . .' He looked at her for a second, eyes shining in the dark, and then he let go of her wrists and grabbed hold of her coat by the neck. He pulled her towards him and now, at this angle, she could see his eyes, rage-filled and terrible.

He lifted her higher, jerking her upwards, then thrust her back against the ground. Her head hit something hard in the earth – a rock. The burst of excruciating pain was still resonating through her brain as he dragged her head up and smashed it back down again. He was going to kill her, too. She was going to die here, in the pitch dark, in the middle of a vast, empty field miles from anywhere. She thought momentarily of Tom at home in London waiting for her and she thought her heart would burst.

Up again and down. Her vision was starting to chequer – she was going to black out. With her right hand, she scrabbled around, searching. Down went her head again and for a moment, everything turned black. Then her fingers found what they were searching for: a stone the size of her hand, cold, sharp on one side. Through the fear and panic came one clear thought: *This is it.*

She gripped the stone, lifted her arm and then, screwing every ounce of her terror and panic and horror together, she smashed it into his temple. For a second Mark seemed merely stunned. Then he gave a single grunt and slumped on top of her.

CHAPTER 27

The temperature hadn't risen above freezing for ten days but overhead the sky was a blue better fitted for July than the last week of January. There had been a lot of foot traffic here over the weekend, evidently, and the snow was long gone from the path, but up on the steepest parts of the hill and in the lee of the trees, virgin drifts of it remained. Down to their right, untouched by the farmers, the patchwork fields of Herefordshire were white.

Claiming the need for a head start, Sandy and Lydia had gone on first while Hannah and Tom bought the ticket for the car park. Hannah looked up now and saw them a hundred yards or so up ahead, Lydia willowy in her black jeans and borrowed parka, Sandy six inches shorter and bundled up as if for a polar expedition. The sound of their laughter reached back through the stillness of the air.

Tom put his arm through hers as they negotiated a steep section in the path and came up on to a small plateau that gave a clear view of the grassed-over skeleton of the iron-age fort.

I'd take on a fortful of pagans for you, swede-heart.
Mark's voice, as clear as if he was standing beside
her.

'All right?' Tom was looking at her.

'Yes.'

'Sure?'

'Of course.' She smiled and took a square of the
chocolate that he was proffering. He put the rest
of the bar into his pocket again and turned to look
back the way they'd come. His cheeks were already
ruddy from the cold.

'Is this where he proposed to you? Up here?'

'Yes.'

'Is this meant to be an exorcism?'

'Of sorts.'

'Is it working?'

She shook her head. 'I hear him all the time,
wherever I am. I always will, I think.' She started
walking again and Tom caught her up and gave
her back his arm. 'I killed someone,' she said. 'The
idea of it – another human being is dead because
of me.'

'A human being who killed two other human
beings – maybe three – and was about to kill you.'

'I know. But still.'

They walked on. The Malverns lay ahead of
them, the peaks of the line of hills like vertebrae
in the spine of an ancient beast that had curled
up and fallen asleep underneath the earth. Every
night of the two months since it happened Hannah
had lain awake and replayed it scene by scene: the

417

confrontation in the kitchen, the chase through the garden out into the pitch-dark fields. The weight of the stone in her hand and the sickening crunch when she'd smashed it against Mark's temple.

He'd died instantaneously, they'd told her after the autopsy, but she'd known that from the way he'd fallen. Dead weight. It had taken almost all the strength she'd had left to roll him off her, she'd barely had enough energy to stand afterwards, but somehow, slowly, she'd started moving again, stumbling towards the handful of lights, falling many times, her legs weak, her head throbbing with pain. Twice she'd stopped and thrown up, her stomach heaving over and over again though it had been empty except for the half-inch of whisky Nick had given her. Eventually, six huge fields later – she still had no idea how much later in real terms – she'd reached the lights and discovered that they belonged to a pub on the fringe of a village. Bloody, covered in mud, she'd staggered inside.

With the help of the landlord and one of the regulars who'd done gardening work there, the police had managed to identify the house. Despite what Mark had said, Nick hadn't been dead when they found him, but one of his twelve knife wounds had caught an artery and he'd died of blood loss in the back of the ambulance carrying him to hospital in Swindon. She'd cried when they told her, hysterical tears that took ten minutes to bring under control. It had been three weeks before she'd been able to cry a single tear for Mark.

'The new flat will help.'

'What?'

'Having your own place again,' Tom said. 'Being freed from our back bedroom.'

She smiled. 'I like your back bedroom. But, yes, it's the right thing.'

Two weeks ago she'd woken late. Tom and Lydia had left for work and the house was quiet. She'd gone downstairs, feet bare, and filled the kettle for coffee. Standing at the window, watching a robin fly back and forth from the bird table that Lydia had given Tom for Christmas, the deadening fog that had filled her head had cleared for a moment and she'd known that it was time to get moving again, to break the spell of the horror and get on with her life. She'd made the coffee and sat down with her computer to look at flats to rent.

She'd seen seven or eight before she'd found the one she'd taken, a one-bedroomed place on the third floor of a Victorian red-brick mansion block a few minutes' walk from Russell Square. As soon as she'd walked in, she'd been able to see herself living there. It was a little bit shabby, she'd have to hide the carpet in the hallway with rugs, but the landlord had given her permission to paint, the kitchen was newly renovated and there was a nook under the window in the sitting room that would be perfect for a desk.

More than ever, what she craved now was work.

She hadn't got the job at Penrose Price; Roger Penrose, despite his cutting-edge advertising campaigns, had proved to be old-fashioned about the idea of hiring someone embroiled in a case that had been splashed across the national papers for a week. He'd written her a letter full of compliments in which he also communicated that they'd hired a candidate with substantial experience of working with clients similar to their own. When she'd looked up the announcement in *Campaign*, she saw that the job had gone to someone who'd interned for her before she went to New York.

There was hope, however. Ten days ago, Leon, her old boss, had emailed to say that he was in London on a flying visit. Over drinks at his hotel in Charlotte Street, he'd asked her for ideas for two major new pitches. If he won the business, he said, he'd like her to work on them with him, in what capacity they could discuss later. 'As head of the London office?' she'd said, raising an eyebrow, and though he'd rolled his eyes, he hadn't said no.

In the meantime, her mother had lent her money to keep her going. Eventually – at least in theory – she would be rich: everything Mark had owned, he'd willed to her. She didn't want any of it. She'd decided that, when the time came, she would give it all to his parents, though she suspected that Mark's father's pride would stop him from touching it, too.

Up ahead, Sandy slipped on the path, nearly

pulling Lydia down with her. Hannah laughed, and when she stopped, she saw that Tom had been watching her.

'I'm glad you and Mum are getting on better,' he said.

She shrugged. 'It was Mark's mother, how much she loved him despite everything. It just made me realise how harsh I was to mine. We had a chat.'

Tom nodded. 'She told me.' He took the chocolate from his pocket and snapped off two more squares. They'd walked twenty yards or so before he spoke again. 'Look,' he said, 'I want to tell you something.'

'What?'

'Mum made me promise I never would, but now I think you should know.'

'What, Tom?'

'Their break-up, the divorce – you've always blamed it on her, her paranoia, but she was right. Dad *was* having an affair.'

Hannah stopped walking. 'No, that can't be . . .'

'He met Maggie before he and Mum split up.'

'Then why the hell didn't she say something? Jesus – all those years. And I was so furious with her . . .'

'She knew how much you loved him and she didn't want to damage that. She let you go on believing she was the bad guy so that you wouldn't be angry with him and let it damage your relationship.'

Hannah looked at her mother and felt a lump

come into her throat. She'd got everything wrong – everything. Suddenly, though, on top of the beacon under the cold blue bowl of the sky, the realisation felt liberating. From now on, surely, she could only do better.